THE HIDDEN RIVER

A MURDER IN THE EVERGLADES

MARK THIELMAN

Copyright © 2025 by Mark Thielman.

All rights reserved.

No part of this book may be reproduced in any form or by any electronic or mechanical means, including information storage and retrieval systems, without written permission from the author, except for the use of brief quotations in a book review.

Severn River Publishing
www.SevernRiverBooks.com

This is a work of fiction. Names, characters, businesses, places, events and incidents are either the products of the author's imagination or used in a fictitious manner. Any resemblance to actual persons, living or dead, or actual events is purely coincidental.

ISBN: 978-1-64875-651-1 (Paperback)

ALSO BY MARK THIELMAN

The Johnson and Nance Mysteries

The Devil's Kitchen: A Murder in Yellowstone

The Hidden River: A Murder in the Everglades

The Firefall: A Murder in Yosemite

To find out more about Mark Thielman and his books, visit

severnriverbooks.com

To Jack and Sam
You complete our story.

1

April 8th

The humidity arrived early. The air felt heavy, like a shroud. Heka had thrown off the blanket and alternately kicked on and off the sheet. The ceiling fan over his head squeaked once with each revolution. The noise reminded him of the call of a baby alligator. It shouldn't bother him, but it did.

The Everglades didn't have four seasons. Here, there were only two—wet and dry. The dry season was winding down. Soon, the rain would begin. Tonight, however, remained calm. Only the humidity foretold the coming storms.

Heka reached behind him. Above the low headboard, the wall felt cool and damp. Moisture collected on the masonry. The Pine Island bungalow the National Park Service had provided him had been built to survive hurricanes. Its profile stood low-slung and solid, with concrete block walls and impact-resistant glass on the windows and doors. The bungalow was like a fortress, constructed to withstand the wind and the rain. The walls, however, held the humidity. Heka always allowed extra time for his paint to dry.

When he got home from the club, he'd spent some time thinking about his painting, mapping its progress in his mind. He'd jotted down ideas. The sticky notes littered his table. Heka knew where he'd go when he held the brush. With his eyes closed, he could visualize the completed work in his head.

His desk lamp illuminated his art in progress; the bulb's warmth, he hoped, also sped the drying. Heka knew it drew the mosquitoes. He heard them outside the screened porch, probing the mesh, searching for chinks. Their high-pitched drone drowned out by the regular alligator squeak of the ceiling fan.

He had spotted the old hardwood while poking along the Ingraham Highway. Heka had been to the hammock countless times. Today, he'd finally recognized what he'd been looking for. The mahogany was older than the United States. This tree knew the Calusa, the natives who had lived on this land before the Seminoles and the Miccosukee. This tree had looked down on so much tragedy and pain. The old mahogany had seen fire, storms, and environmental degradation. It had watched the Seminole Wars and the Civil War. It had stood witness to slavery and pollution and misguided dreams of draining this land to plant crops, houses, and highways. It had heard rumors of a jetport to be built in the Everglades with supersonic aircraft landing nearby. Antiballistic missiles had defended it. The stories that old mahogany could tell. If only someone would take the time to listen.

He turned and looked at the pictures on his bookcase. With the lone bulb of the desk lamp, the bookcase stood in the shadows. Heka saw only the black silhouettes of the frames. He knew the pictures; he didn't need the light. Generations, forward and back, looked at him lying in bed and silently asked if he'd found the place. He shifted his gaze and considered the outline of the painting on the wall. Peering through the darkness, he studied the old picture. Did it show his long-sought goal? Was this his personal Eden? Heka had waded through this shallow river of the Everglades, searching so many of the small islands, battling sawgrass and sinkholes, watchful for snakes and alligators. Might the hammock he'd been searching for have been right there at the side of the road this entire time, he wondered. Heka thought again about the old tree. Had it ever shared its life with a mate?

He heard again the whine of the mosquitoes. They'd get their chance, Heka knew. He'd be outside. In the cloister of the hammock, no breeze would blow the insects away. He didn't care. Heka had applied for the artist's residency for one reason, to have the time and the access to search. The prestige and the publicity proved invaluable. He'd seen the demand for his art increase, and, as a result, the price had spiked. He'd surpassed where he'd formerly been. The old dealers were calling him again; the ones who'd lost his telephone number a few years ago suddenly found it. But he didn't need the money. His eyes swept the living and work spaces of the tiny bungalow. Every material thing he wanted, he had here. But he may have finally found the spot for which he'd searched. That was the stuff of dreams.

Dreams. His mind paused at the word. There would be no sleep dreams tonight. He checked the digital clock on the nightstand. He wouldn't sleep. He'd lie there until the alarm gave him permission to rise. He thought about the sinewy nature of time. Moments seemed to stretch, like when he waited for the clock. Others, such as when he got lost in his painting, would disappear. A day would be over before he noticed. He'd find himself standing in paint-spattered clothing, realizing he'd forgotten to eat.

Heka mentally ticked through his plans for the morning. Before sunrise, he and his camera would go to the borrow pit across from the Coe Visitor Center during the golden hour. A small pond stood just behind his house. Heka liked to walk over there with his morning coffee and greet the birds. This morning, however, he would head to the pond off the main road. He hoped Jerry would be there, the roseate spoonbill that sometimes fed at that pond. Jerry reminded him of a boxer he'd once known, the round nose a testament to every time the man failed to keep his guard up. The pink wings—Jerry always had been a bleeder. Heka wanted the spoonbill in a painting. He had first seen Jerry two mornings previous. Heka should have stopped and photographed him then, but Heka had an appointment in Homestead. He had missed the opportunity. Heka hoped the bird would return to feed in the same spot. Other borrow pits stood closer to the bungalow, but Heka wanted him where he'd first spied Jerry. Heka knew where he'd stand to keep the cattails out of the photograph. He thought about the painting that might follow if Jerry cooperated. Heka envisioned a memorial piece about people who got lost when a man got too busy, too important, or too drunk to take the time to hang onto his friends.

After searching for Jerry, he'd drive back into the park. The visitor use assistant at the entrance station would wave him through. They knew his old beater, with the salt rust and worn-out muffler. He'd pass the royal palms, those graceful trees with curved trunks that stretch one hundred feet skyward and were hard as rocks. He'd heard those stately trees were really something before Hurricane Andrew ripped through here and devastated the ancient foliage. Heka would drive by the overlooks of golden sawgrass. He'd stop at the hammock. He had no other plans for the day. Heka would take his time to see if Old Man Mahogany had once known a mate. The tree would tell him where to look.

A slight breeze passed through the screen. Heka threw back the sheet again to feel the air against his legs. Outside, the clack of slash pine boughs and the rustle of the saw palmettos replaced the mosquito whine.

He heard a crunching in the dry grass. The sounds were too heavy for a deer or a rabbit. Which of his neighbors, he wondered, had gotten out of bed this time of night. Many of the Everglades employees who worked in and around the southern entrance to the park had homes here. The Park Service rented them to house their workers. The park also had RV hookups for those seasonal employees who didn't have bungalows. Heka again heard the crunch of the dry grass. He looked at the clock and shook his head. It wasn't time for a shift to start. Some poor soul had been called out in the dead of night; likely broken plumbing had the maintenance guys scrambling to repair the infrastructure before the visitors arrived. Maybe an alligator had wandered into someone's campsite and had tourists who wanted to get close to nature, but not too close, in an uproar.

He thought about getting out of bed. Heka rarely heard his neighbors. When the Park Service had set up the Creative Artist in Residence in the Everglades program, they'd purposely given the artist housing apart from the rest of the community of employees in the Pine Island area. The artists who rotated in and out of the bungalow during the fellowships had the privacy to create. The solitude of the natural surroundings stimulated inspiration. That was how the program had been designed. That was also why there wasn't a phone jack in the walls or a television antenna on the gently sloping roof of the cream-colored bungalow. Of course, only an artist Heka's age remembered the need for television antennas or telephones attached to cords. Only fossils like him recalled such things. It was like being surprised that the Everglades had no phone booths.

He had a cell phone, of course. He wasn't that crazy or eccentric an artist. He flew on airplanes, drove a car, and used an ATM and a laptop computer. Heka kept the cell phone in a drawer. The coverage was spotty in the vast expanse of the Everglades. He always carried a compass when he hiked off the main road.

The dry grass crinkled. The noise sounded closer to Heka's house. Someone else couldn't sleep either. Heka considered commiserating with them. He might brew coffee and invite them inside before they rushed off to solve whatever crisis had inspired the late-night call. He didn't have the door locked. This was different from Miami, where he had his last studio. The community of park workers looked out for one another.

Coffee wouldn't hurt. Heka knew he wasn't going back to sleep anyway.

The screen door slid along its track. Heka sat up in bed and scratched at the salt-and-pepper stubble of his bald cut. Whoever was out must have seen the desk lamp and thought he was still working. He heard the glass door close.

"Just close the screen. It pisses off the mosquitoes when they can't get in," Heka called to the porch. "Give me a quick minute; I'll make coffee." He stood up and reached for the paint-spattered khakis hanging over the back of the chair. The armchair by the bed had a companion on the porch. Early in his fellowship, he'd dragged one beside the bed. He'd covered the cushions in plastic trash bags. If he had any wet paint on his pants at night, they wouldn't spot the upholstery.

Sitting on the side of the bed, he wiggled his first leg into the pants. "That you, Drake? Don't be messing with me." A masked man appeared in front of him. Heka thought he recognized the eyes. Heka had never expected to see them in his house and never in the middle of the night. Heka stood, but with one foot halfway down his pant leg, he stumbled and fell back onto the bed.

The man grabbed his arms and spun him around, pressing his knee against his back. Heka tried to yell but found his face forced against the mattress. He kicked wildly, the half-empty pant leg flapping. His attacker twisted his wrist. Heka felt the pain shoot up through his arm. He didn't panic. In the lean days, he'd lived and worked in a studio in a lousy part of Miami. He had guns pointed at him, been robbed for the small amount of money he carried, and been threatened by other addicts. Experience kept him calm. He knew enough to go with this. Heka had been through worse. The man would take what he wanted and leave. Mostly, he felt glad that the dude had twisted the arm he didn't use to paint.

Heka willed himself to relax. He remembered his guided meditations and slowed his breathing. "Take whatever you think I got. I ain't gonna fight you."

The man grabbed him and spun him into the chair. The plastic trash bag rustled when he landed.

The man pulled both arms behind Heka's back, dropping a zip tie over his wrists. Heka heard the quick whine of the strap being tightened. It sounded like a mosquito. The rigid, flat plastic felt a little like sawgrass. The edge bit into his wrists. "Take it easy. I said I ain't gonna fight you."

"Grab the computer," the man said.

Heka became aware of a second man standing behind the first. He watched the man snap the lid on the laptop closed and yank the power cord free from the wall. "That old thing? That's what you hit this lick for? You can find better computers at the Goodwill."

The man at the table pulled a laptop, identical to Heka's, from a pillowcase. He plugged the replacement into the wall. Heka watched as his computer disappeared into the pillowcase. For the first time, he felt real fear.

The first man pressed his body against Heka's and opened a bottle. He pinched Heka's nose. The old artist opened his mouth to breathe. When he did, the man shoved a Hennessy bottle between his lips. Heka swallowed. He felt the burn of brandy streaming down his throat. He gagged, coughing and sputtering. His eyes watered. He lurched forward, his face pushing back against his attacker. A thin stream of mucous connected the two men. The man pushed Heka's head away. The glass banged against his teeth as his attacker wrenched the bottle from Heka's mouth. The brandy poured, wetting his shirt. Along with the liquor, Heka tasted blood. He coughed. Blood, saliva, and alcohol dribbled down his T-shirt.

The attacker swiped his arm hard across Heka's face. He slapped duct tape over his mouth. The gray tape stretched from ear to ear. His mouth was sealed. Heka felt the panic rise within him. No junkie ever behaved like this. He thrashed about, throwing his shoulders, trying to buck the man sitting on him.

"Get his other arm," the man said to his accomplice.

Heka felt two pairs of gloved hands grab him. One man held each arm. They pulled him out of the chair and across the room toward the small table that served as the dining area and desk. Heka got his feet under him and thrust himself upward. The second attacker lost his grip. Heka drove himself into the man still gripping his arm. They crashed into the wall. The painting tumbled to the floor. The man grunted. Heka felt his grip loosen. He spun and broke free. Heka ran for the screened porch. He could crash through the wire netting and be outside. Someone might hear him.

Heka's unfastened pants slid down his legs. He tripped and stumbled, falling hard into the glass door. Heka straightened up, momentarily stunned. He stepped back, leaving blood on the glass. Before he could recover, both men grabbed him. The original attacker slammed a fist into his kidney. Heka grunted and collapsed. The men dragged him back to the table. They dropped him to his knees. His original attacker stepped on his calf and grabbed his bound wrists. Heka twisted, but he had no leverage.

The man lifted his arms. Heka felt the pain in his shoulders. The edge of the table pressed hard against his chest. He felt himself pushed lower. His eyes focused on his Corelle plate sitting on the table. The colored squares of the sticky notes surrounded it. Even with everything swirling around him, the confusion and the panic, he recognized the white powder the plate held. An artist couldn't live in Miami in the 1980s and not know cocaine.

Heka stiffened his neck and fought the men pushing him downward. The attacker grabbed the back of his head, squeezed his scalp, and drove his head downward.

"Just stick the goddamn plate in his face," the man said.

Like some modern slapstick comedy, the other man grabbed the plate and mashed it into his nose. The cocaine prickled his nostrils. Heka twisted his head, sweeping the drug off the plate. It stuck to his shirt and dusted the floor.

After what felt like hours, the two men pulled him back from the table. They hoisted him to his feet and dragged him toward the glass door. Heka saw his reflection in the glass. White powder surrounded his nose. Blood stained his chin.

"Get the door. I got this asshole," the first man said.

Wordlessly, the second man released his grip and threw back the sliding door.

Heka begged to know what they wanted. Through the tape, the indecipherable words came out as grunts. If they understood his pleas, the men ignored him.

They half carried, half hauled him out the back door and across the wild vegetation. They moved largely in a single file line. The first man pulled him from the front while the second man clutched his wrists and drove Heka from the back. A bungalow in Everglades National Park had no yard. His feet banged against the rocks and scraped on the fronds of saw palmettos.

Heka dripped sweat. Despite the pain and fear, the breeze cooled his body. He felt almost chilled. The two men towed him to the edge of the small pond behind his bungalow. They stopped. Strangely, he felt his body relax. He'd seen this pond many times, studied the water, stained oxblood by the decomposing leaves fallen from the surrounding trees.

Before Miami, before the spell of art had seized him, before the alcohol and the drugs had dragged him through hell, before everything that had dominated his last decades, Hezekiah had grown up on a farm in South Florida. He had lived near the water and learned to swim in the river. He'd been a strong swimmer in his youth. He didn't fear anything that might be lurking there. The snakes and the alligators would want no piece of him. He understood them.

His plan emerged through the shrouding fog in his brain. When they threw him in the water, he'd kick his way to safety. Heka knew he could never match the stamina he'd possessed when his body had been lean and hard. But he also knew that the drug years, the wasted years, had taught him how to endure. He felt the tension leave him. No matter how long they stood on the shore, he knew he'd be safe once they threw him in the water.

The man punched him again, and Heka's body buckled. His knees banged hard against the limestone shoreline. His attacker squeezed his scalp and snapped his head back. Heka stared skyward, his face looking into the vaguely familiar eyes of his attacker.

The man reached down and grabbed the duct tape. He ripped it free.

Heka's face burned. Fresh pain shot across his cheeks and mouth. His throat clotted with phlegm, Heka tried to gasp out a plea. He had barely uttered a sound when the man pushed his head into the water. Heka fought to press upward, but the hand squeezing his scalp kept him locked, with his face beneath the surface. The man's body weight sat on his back, his knees pressing on either side of Heka's spine. He tried to kick his legs and then tried to buck. Nothing removed the weight.

Heka tried not to breathe. The need for oxygen overwhelmed him. Water rushed into his mouth. Reflexively, Heka swallowed. A coughing fit followed. He retched. Air bubbles and water churned around him. His blurred vision narrowed. The crushing weight remained. After a time, the struggling ceased.

The man remained on his back until he felt confident that Heka no longer breathed. Then he got to his feet. Stooping, he cut the zip tie from Heka's wrists. He looked around. He saw no lights. Nothing suggested that anyone had heard the disturbance.

Not even the roseate spoonbill had been there to see.

2

April 7th
(One day earlier)

"I thought there'd be jungle," Alison Nance said.

"You're disappointed you didn't hear monkey sounds or toucans?" Clarence Johnson asked.

"I don't know. I just thought there'd be something more." Nance turned her head and looked out the window of her tiny office. The sunlight drew a line across her face, shadowing her left side.

"They had a panther-crossing sign just before we pulled into the parking lot."

"I'm used to seeing megafauna every day. Not road signs," she said.

"I'll requisition a parrot on my next DI-105. I'll sneak it in with a stapler and copy paper. No one will notice."

Silently, Nance kept her eyes focused on the world outside.

"It's the Everglades, not the Amazon." Clarence set a cardboard box down on her desk.

She spun suddenly and faced him, her intense brown eyes locked onto his. "I know what it is. I've got the orders that stuck me here." Nance turned her head back to the window.

Her five-feet-nine-inch athletic frame blocked the view from where Clarence stood. He stepped around the desk and followed her eyes outside. Clarence saw the edge of a small round lake. Behind it, a sawgrass prairie stretched out, the long blades waving in the morning breeze. Nance squinted slightly; the morning sun illuminated her face, highlighting her auburn hair. After a moment, Clarence spoke. "I thought you'd be happy that the assignment changed. You got seriously angry when the Park Service assigned you to Atlanta."

Nance pulled her toned arms close to her body and turned her palms outward. "Forget it. I'm just tired. It's a long drive to the Everglades from Yellowstone."

Clarence shrugged. "Can't drive much farther and still stay in the country. You should try it in an RV sometime." He chose not to pursue the unanswered questions.

"Did you find an RV hookup?"

"They found me a place in the employee housing compound. We're probably neighbors."

Nance shook her head. "My day just gets better and better." She paused for a moment. "Where's Tripod?"

"She's resting in the RV. The little girl is kinda tired. I let her drive the second half of the trip."

"You know your dog only has one front leg?"

Clarence nodded. "That's why we came in the RV. It has an automatic transmission. I hate seeing her let go of the wheel when she needs to shift gears in the Ferrari."

Nance smiled, seemingly despite herself.

"But I'm tired too. Even when I wasn't driving, I couldn't sleep. I had to make all the radio station decisions."

"You probably forced Tripod to listen to jazz and blues for the entire trip."

"My dog appreciates the great American art form."

"I'd be willing to bet Tripod dreams of hearing country music."

"Beg to differ," Clarence said. "You ever heard of Howlin' Wolf? American blues artist and canine kindred spirit."

Nance's smile looked genuine. "That dog is the best part of you."

"The same could be said for most people." Clarence pointed to the box. "Start unpacking this one, and I'll grab the other one from your SUV."

"You know you don't have to do this."

"It's no trouble. Your SUV is right outside."

"I mean any of it. You don't have to be here."

Clarence nodded. "Yes, I do. The Park Service assigned me to work here. We can't split up the team."

Nance grunted and turned back to the window. "I can take care of myself." Reaching into her pocket, she pulled out her phone and read a text. She tapped quickly and returned it to her pocket.

"Let your dad know you made it?"

Nance made a noncommittal noise. Her eyes returned to looking outside.

Clarence studied the back of her head. When she didn't turn back or speak, he left. Clarence stayed outside for a few minutes. She clearly needed some time alone. After the Yellowstone case, the local press made him a hero. "Park Intern Solves Murder," the media had reported. The stories made him sound like an eighteen-year-old kid, not a medically retired homicide detective from Fort Worth. Nobody corrected the reporters to say that Clarence was a seasonal ranger and not an intern. If the National Park Service administrators were mad at the political firestorm that had been stirred up, they decided not to take it out on a temporary employee who barely made expenses. The service had elevated his role in the case. Clarence had been lionized in the press releases. By the end of one article, he seemed like someone who should wear a cape rather than a campaign hat. Wyoming's congresswoman had her picture taken with him. She'd shaken his hand and noted how proud she was to have him serving in the national park community. When the service had reassigned Alison Nance, the investigator leading the Yellowstone case, Clarence had asked to come along. The Park Service could hardly refuse, at least not as long as Congress authorized the budget.

He returned to the office, carrying the final two boxes. Nance sat at her desk. She'd opened the first box and had her head down, studying the contents. Slowly, Nance pulled items from the box and put them away. She stuck a Yellowstone tourist magnet to the drawer of the metal desk. As he watched, she removed a small lodgepole pine branch. The lodgepole was the pine associated with Yellowstone. She held the branch in her hand, turning it over, looking at both sides. Nance brought it to her pert nose and inhaled. She carefully placed it in the bottom desk drawer. Nance glanced back at the drawer and smiled. She looked up and saw him. Blushing slightly, she quickly closed the drawer.

"There's an auto parts store in Homestead. I can get you a three-pack. They've also got daiquiri scented if you get tired of pine." Clarence placed one box on her desk and carried the other over to a small bookcase in the corner.

"I'll never get tired of pine." She removed a coffee cup from the box and set it on the corner of the desk. "You were gone awhile."

"I let Tripod out. I needed to explain about the sawgrass. She needs to know it's got sharp edges."

"You don't think the name gives it away?"

"Plant names can be tricky. Take rose. You'd think they'd be a warm pink color. That's rose. But Texas has yellow roses. You can't judge a plant by its name."

Her face looked skeptical. "And you explained all this to Tripod?"

"No. I just told her that it's a good thing she's not a boy dog. An accident while urinating could be devastating. A boy without a leg is a novelty. A boy without a penis could be..."

"Not single-minded? Not obsessed?"

"My dog is a sensitive soul."

Nance nodded again. "Your female dog is a sensitive soul. Your male dog would be a loudmouthed braggadocio, a literal press hound."

Clarence felt the sting of that last shot. He didn't respond.

She turned back to her desk. If Nance felt badly about the jab, he couldn't see. Neither of them spoke. After a minute, she broke the silence. "What's your dog doing now? Instead of jeopardizing private parts in the sawgrass."

"She heard this place has alligators. When I left, she was on the laptop researching."

"Learning anything?"

"Hard to say. Tripod was having trouble with the research."

"Latin name for *alligator* too long?"

Clarence shook his head. "She's good with that. But she's trying to paste her research into a new document. With only one small paw, it's hard to hold down both the Control and C keys."

"You're so full of it," Nance said, shaking her head.

"I have my uses." As Clarence spoke, he opened the box he'd set on the bookcase. Clarence removed a coffeemaker. He unscrewed the lid from a bottle of water and carefully filled the reservoir. Clarence thumbed between the two packages of beans before settling on the Colombian medium roast. He ground the beans and then, using his particular spoon, measured coffee into the basket.

"It's java, not pharmaceuticals."

"Then you don't understand one of the purposes of good coffee." He picked up her mug and examined it, made a face, and then emptied the water bottle on a paper towel. He began wiping out the inside of her cup.

"That's seasoning."

He held the cup for her to see inside. "That's disgusting."

Nance glanced at the mug, shrugged, and said nothing.

They remained quiet. She unpacked while Clarence looked out the window. In the hall outside, he could hear phones ringing and keyboards clattering, the sounds of park administration. In the room, the sputtering of the coffeemaker provided the only noise.

Clarence poured coffee into two mugs. He glanced at her mug again before surrendering it. "I did my best, but it's a little like asking da Vinci to paint the *Mona Lisa* with a dirty brush."

"Pretty high opinion of yourself."

"Taste it and see."

Nance sipped the coffee and nodded.

"Now imagine how it might taste in a clean cup."

She smiled. "Like a big mug of steaming Folgers when you're just back from the barn on a snowy morning."

"Folgers, I'm hurt." Clarence pushed his lower lip forward in a pout.

Nance tasted the coffee again. "Really, it's good. But don't call a press conference."

This time, Clarence's frown was genuine.

"I'm sorry, that was cheap."

Clarence looked away for a moment. Then he turned and faced her. "I'm sorry you're not looking out your window at the Rockies. I'm sincerely sorry you didn't get the credit you deserved for the Ocone case. Finally, I'm sorry the Park Service sent you across the country and away from your home. But you work for the Investigative Services Branch. There are only thirty-five of y'all to cover all the national parks. You'd had Yellowstone to yourself, but you had to know someday things might change."

"I'm burning weeds in Tuzigoot."

Clarence's face pinched in puzzlement.

"Still things to learn, intern. It's a Park Service expression for when you're banished to the middle of nowhere to do something pointless."

"Community Relations, Midnight Shift was what we called it at the police department."

Nance nodded. "I've been sent to other places. I've conducted investigations at monuments you've probably never heard of. But I always thought I'd get to go back home."

"Chain of command is a bitch. We go where we're sent."

"Unless you're special and get to choose."

Clarence set down his mug and rested his hands on the desk. He leaned forward. "I didn't ask for all the attention, just like you didn't ask to come to the Everglades. But when the Park Service gave me the option to come down here, I took it. I've never been to the Everglades. I'm scratching it off my bucket list. Don't combine our two situations."

Nance met his stare. Clarence normally found her brown eyes attractive, but in this encounter, they were hard. For a long moment, both refused to blink. Then, her gaze shifted. "Don't let your coffee grow cold."

Clarence smiled, grateful she'd ended it before one of them, likely he, said something stupid. "Microwaved coffee is a sin against man and nature."

She picked up her mug and looked out the window. She stared for nearly a minute. Then, she exhaled, her breath fogging the tempered glass. "At least it's not Atlanta."

"What have you got against Georgia?" Clarence asked. The Park Service had its headquarters for the southeast region in Atlanta. From there, she'd expected to be deployed to locations where the local Visitor and Resource Protection rangers needed additional investigative support. Before she could get packed, Nance's orders changed, sending her straight to Everglades National Park.

"I don't hate Georgia. It's cities I don't like. Atlanta, New Orleans, San Francisco, take your pick."

"Any reason in particular? You don't look like the hermit type."

Her face darkened for a moment. "Big cities make me wiggly."

"On the Ocone case, you didn't complain when we drove to Bozeman."

She grunted a laugh. "I think you've proved my point."

Clarence felt a twinge in his leg. He'd been shot while working as a Fort Worth cop. The free time following his medical retirement from the department led to him taking a seasonal job with the National Park Service. He pointed to the office chair alongside her desk. "May I borrow that?"

Nance nodded.

He dragged the chair around to the far side of the desk, then pulled a piece of paper from the small printer in the office. Resting his boot atop the paper, Clarence leaned forward, stretching his injured leg.

"Still hurts?"

"Too much time sitting behind the wheel without the chance to move around. Things start to tighten up. A couple of days walking around the park, getting to know the place, and I'll be fine." He bent lower, reaching his fingers out to clasp the toe of his boot. He held the pose. Clarence straightened and rolled his neck in a circle. "I used to do stretches to stay in shape. Now they're necessary to make sure I can always walk." He picked up the paper and folded it in half before handing it to Nance. "Do you mind?"

She tossed it into her trash can. Clarence, meanwhile, settled into the chair.

"Here's how I see it," he said. "I know how to investigate cases in the city. I know when to be a good guy and when to be an ass. If a fight breaks out, I can hold my own. When I was a cop in Fort Worth, I understood the city's politics. I knew who was trying to screw me and what I needed to do to prevent it. But here in the Park Service, I got no clue about who the players are. And as for some of this backcountry investigation, I need a bit of a refresher."

"You did all right in Yellowstone."

"Who are we kidding? When I arrived, if you said bear scat, I thought you were talking about some naked jazz singing."

Nance laughed. "Look around. Does this look like bear country?"

"Did I mention the panther-crossing sign just outside the front gate?"

"And I tell you, it's there for the tourists."

"My point, Investigator Nance, is that in the Park Service, you're the expert. I'm just a seasonal interpretive ranger. You're in charge. My job is to support."

Nance smiled. "Your job is to support." She raised the mug to her lips. "And to make coffee."

"You're the boss. However I can assist the dedicated professionals of the NPS."

She reached out her cup. The two mugs touched in a toast.

"Am I interrupting?" a voice from the doorway asked. "You're just who I needed to see."

Clarence and Nance turned. A thin man with dark hair, thick eyebrows, and a sharply cleft chin looked at them. More accurately, Clarence thought, he looked at Nance. Men's eyes always went her way first. Even in jeans and a loose shirt, her lithe body commanded attention. The gaze quickly shifted to Clarence. Although he had yet to continue speaking, the visitor's jaws seemed in constant motion as he chewed hard on a piece of gum. Both Clarence and Nance recognized him as the man in charge of Everglades National Park.

They quickly stood. "Superintendent Ramirez, we didn't hear you come up," Nance said.

He waved away any apology. The superintendent's gum cracked when he spoke. "You've had a long drive down to the bottom of Florida. I wish I could give you some time to settle in and relax after crossing the country. Unfortunately, I've got to put you straight to work."

"I'm at your service, sir. Whatever you need," she said.

"You clearly misunderstand, Special Agent Nance. I need him," Ramirez said, pointing at Clarence.

3

April 1851

William and the other runaway slaves noisily splashed their way south, struggling against the mud, water, and the endless field of sharp-bladed grass of the Florida Everglades. When he heard the steady thud of a tool striking wood, William signaled for the others to stop and be silent. Quietly, he crept forward. Behind a sabal palm, William spied on the Indian crafting a canoe. William slid his hand down the walking stick he had relied upon while walking in the slough. If necessary, he could throw it like a spear. His other hand hovered just above the hilt of the knife he carried strapped to his waist. As always, the bugs swarmed around him, biting his exposed flesh. When William decided he could no longer stand the pain, that he had to slap at these cursed stinging mosquitoes and biting flies, the Indian laughed and waved him out from his hiding space. The man kept waving when William stepped out of the water and onto the small island. His gestures continued until Myrna, William's wife; Samuel, his son; and Josiah and Eli, the other two men who had fled the plantation with them, had all appeared.

William gestured to the man. The native did not respond. The Miccosukee wore a full shirt and deerskin leggings. Around his neck, a leather thong was strung with polished shells. He crowned his head with a red turban.

The loose-limbed native moved gracefully. Although William had spent years lifting bales and outweighed the man by thirty pounds, he knew that if the two struggled, it would be a battle between a bear and a panther.

The Indian laid down his tools and walked over to Myrna. She stiffened but did not move. The man looked down at Samuel. The boy's eyes widened in fear, and he sought refuge behind his mother's skirt. When they had started walking this morning, Myrna had hiked the garment up, enabling her to move more quickly through the water. She stood now, her bare legs dripping on the small island. Myrna leaned on her walking stick. She had struggled through the wetland with a bulbous clay pot the size of a water bucket strapped to her back and Samuel at her side. The native knelt and looked at Samuel through her legs. Samuel squeezed against her thigh, trying desperately to hide himself. Myrna unbound her skirt, and the end dropped like a blanket. Samuel's face became entangled in the cloth. The Indian laughed at the boy's efforts.

It was clear to William that the man had seen slaves before. He showed no surprise that a party of darker-skinned people had descended upon his work site.

Gesturing for them to follow, he set off across the small island. At the water's edge, he pantomimed for Myrna and Samuel to get into his canoe. He poled the craft through the shallow swamp as the other men followed. The exhausting efforts to stay with the boat showed William how slowly they progressed through this water-filled prairie. At the rate they traveled, it seemed only a matter of time until a slave hunter found them. Most of the hunters, he knew, searched north. Everyone whispered stories of the underground railroad for spiriting escaped slaves to freedom. Slaves, plantation owners, and the men paid to find runaways all heard the tales. A few slave catchers, however, would likely turn and look to the south.

The native poled the canoe to another small island. The boat scraped against the earth and stopped. The man waded into the water and held the boat steady. Myrna and Samuel stepped onto dry ground. The three men pulled themselves from the water and crawled onto shore. Josiah and Eli dropped to the dirt, breathing heavily.

William bent at the waist, gasping for air. He kept his head up and his eyes watchful. Ahead of him was a series of wall-less huts mounted on stilts. They had raised floors and sloping thatched roofs. In front of the huts, a gar cooked on a spit over red coals.

The Indian saw him looking. "Chickee," he said and pointed at one of the shelters.

"Chickee," William repeated.

The man nodded and walked past the huts. He disappeared into the trees behind the clearing.

William looked around. Again, he lowered his grip on the staff, hoping to use it as a throwing weapon in the event of an attack. If a band of natives charged, his knife would be inadequate. Quietly, he moved to where Josiah and Eli lay. He tried to signal his concerns to them without scaring Myrna or Samuel.

Josiah sniffed the air. "I could eat that whole damn fish."

"What are we gonna do if'n they attack us, William?" Eli asked. "We gonna fight off the whole tribe? I say, just let them kill us if that's what they aim to do. It'll most likely happen anyway, and this way, I ain't gonna have to slap one more mosquito."

William turned away in disgust. They'd come so far and endured so much hardship. He would listen to no talk about abandoning his dream of freedom.

Before he could berate Eli, the native reappeared from the trees. Behind him trailed a man, darker than William but, like the native, dressed in deerskin pants and a loose shirt. His hair had been plaited into small gray braids. This man stopped at the clearing and surveyed them. He looked first at Josiah and Eli, then his eyes swept across the island to Myrna and Samuel.

The other four fugitives clustered around William.

The man approached. William forced his arms to remain relaxed and not hover near the knife. The man stopped; his gaze dropped to William's feet and slowly crawled up his body.

William felt like he was being appraised in a Charleston slave market. He fought back his growing anger. He kept his eyes locked on the man's face, seeking to discern his true intentions. The man looked older than

William, possibly old enough to be his father. He still appeared sturdy and able to work a full day. His eyes showed no emotion. No joy at seeing another black face or anger at the intrusion.

He met William's gaze. "Y'all look a little like somethin' the dog carried up." Then, he smiled. "Welcome to the Kahayatle. That means 'bright shining place.' That's what the Indians call this mess you've been wading around in." His gaze roamed across the group. "And you can call me Old Johnny." He grunted a laugh. "'Cause you ain't never gonna learn to pronounce the name they've given me. Come along."

Old Johnny turned and led them into the trees along a narrow path.

"Where we going?" William asked.

"I'm taking you to my chickee."

"You live here?"

"I live near here," Old Johnny said. "I live just outside the village. These are the Miccosukee people, the Otter clan, and we have an arrangement. I help them out when they need help, sometimes with planting and building, once in a while with fighting. And they forget I'm here whenever slave hunters nose around this area. Where you running from?"

"A plantation near Edgefield, South Carolina." As William spoke, he glanced down. Battle scars marked Johnny's forearms.

"And where exactly are you running to?"

"There's stories around the plantation of an island not too far off the coast where slavery ain't allowed. Where all men might live free."

"And you really think this place exists?" Old Johnny asked.

"The Bible says that Moses had to cross the water to find his promised land," William said.

"You read this yourself?"

William shook his head. "No, but that's what I've been told."

Old Johnny grunted. "How come you didn't run north?"

"Why didn't you?"

They emerged from the path into a small clearing. In front stood a chickee constructed like the others. The group stopped. Old Johnny made a slow walk around the structure. "This here's my house." He looked at William. "I 'scaped from a plantation in Georgia. Like you, I figured Florida coast is closer to Georgia than Ohio."

"But here you are."

Old Johnny scratched at the earth with his moccasin. He shot a quick glance at Myrna and Samuel. He pointed at the chickee. "Boy, you ever seen a house like that?"

Samuel shook his head.

"Well, you remember what it looks like. Roof keeps the rain out. No walls keeps it cool." Old Johnny turned back to William. "Here I am. These Indians found me wandering in the Kahayatle. They took care of me. As long as I don't spoil it by trying to lay down with their women, here I'll be. I wouldn't be freer no place else." He surveyed the group. "Don't be getting no ideas. One runaway slave is a help. Six runaways is a threat. Y'all are going to need to be moving along. The place you're looking for is in the islands called the Bahamas. The place is Red Bay on Andros Island. Some Seminoles made their home there." He waved his arms at the trees. "They is the other people who live in Kahayatle. The Seminoles and the Miccosukee, they gets along mostly. But don't you worry none." Old Johnny laughed. "They'll see right quickly that you ain't Miccosukee."

William walked to the trees and collected a piece of palm frond lying on the ground. With a charcoal stick from Old Johnny's fire, he sketched out the chickee. He handed the drawing to Samuel. "So you don't forget."

Old Johnny looked at the picture and smiled. "Pretty good."

"Red Bay on Andros Island," William repeated, memorizing the name.

Old Johnny's face grew serious. "The story goes that the Seminoles had been hunted by the army, shot, and starved almost to death. Then Chief Billy Bowleg had a dream about a safe island to the south. He loaded up his people into seven dugout canoes and paddled across the Atlantic Ocean until they found it. Chief Billy and his people founded Red Bay on the west beach facing the ocean. That way, they could see their brothers and sisters coming to join them."

William turned and faced east. He closed his eyes and pictured this Red Bay. "And slaves are welcome?"

"Ain't no slaves in Red Bay. Everybody free."

William smiled. He looked around. The faces on the rest of his small party lit up, too.

"And you don't have to paddle no canoe over there. I've heard that them

Bahama people bring their boats to shore. Sometimes, they salvage wrecks, and sometimes, they pick up runaways. Whatever they find that might be valuable. Course, they don't work for free. You got anything you can pay them with?"

William looked to Myrna and then to Josiah and Eli. "We'll figure out something."

"You got bad news and good news." Old Johnny looked toward the sky. "The wet season may be starting a little early this year. That's why there's water in the grass. The bad news is you going to get wet, and the water brings out the bugs."

William looked down at Myrna's soaked skirt.

"But it rains on slave hunters too. They get less excited about hunting in the rain. And you don't have to dig no holes to find something to drink." Old Johnny turned and took a step toward the thatched hut. "Gonna be a bit crowded in my chickee." He stopped and turned back. "Don't be in no rush to get to the coast. That's where the slave hunters tend to be. Them Bahama boats used to go to the same place to pick up runaways, but the government got sneaky. They put up a lighthouse there to scare them boats off." He swatted in the air. "I hear them slavers is thick as mosquitoes down there. So you had best go down the middle of this old Kahayatle until you are below that old lighthouse, then you go fast and hard until you run into the ocean. Then you best pray a boat finds you before them slave hunters."

"And how will we know when we are below that lighthouse?"

Old Johnny looked up at the sky. He frowned. "The Bible says that old Moses, when he came to the Red Sea, held out his staff, and the sea split apart." Johnny fixed his eyes on William's walking stick. "I reckon you'll have to try that."

4

April 7th

Superintendent Ramirez chomped down hard on the gum. For a moment, the cracking of his gum became the only sound in the room.

Clarence saw the mix of anger and shame on Nance's face.

Ramirez looked at Clarence. "Have you heard about the CARE program?"

Clarence shook his head.

"I'm not surprised. You just got here. CARE is the Creative Artist in Residence in the Everglades. We bring artists from different disciplines into the park. They stay for up to six months. They live alongside the rest of the employees at Pine Island." He waved his arm generally toward the housing facility where Clarence had parked his RV. "You've probably seen it. We give them one of the small places. It's set apart from the rest. We know artists need solitude to get all their creative juices going." He paused and smiled. "Or maybe we do it because we know they're smoking weed, and we don't want to have to enforce the drug laws." He paused again.

Neither Clarence nor Nance smiled.

"Regardless, the program brings positive attention to the park. It also attracts donor dollars. It's an inexpensive program with a big return in terms of money and positive public relations."

Clarence nodded. "What's this got to do with me?"

"I'm getting to that," Ramirez answered, his voice sharper than it had been earlier. He chomped on the gum. "A big local donor has sponsored a seminar on the art of Florida. We're mostly focusing in and around the Everglades. Your bio says you've got a background in art."

"I majored in art history in college."

Ramirez's eyes appraised him. "Must have been the biggest student in class."

"One of our tackles took some of the classes with me. That guy was bigger."

"Know anything about the art of the South?"

"I took a class on American art history. We spent some time on the region, but that was about fifteen years ago."

"I want you to be a part of the seminar. Call yourself the Park Service liaison. The public information officer has been working with the planning committee. But the PIO has got too much on her plate right now." If Ramirez had been listening to his limited background, Clarence couldn't tell.

"Sounds fun, how long do I have?"

Ramirez reached into his back pocket. He pulled out a brochure and unfolded it before handing it to Clarence. "The seminar starts tomorrow."

"Tomorrow?" Clarence looked at the brochure. The date on the front confirmed what the superintendent said. "Just what am I going to do, hand out pamphlets?"

The gum cracked. "The current artist in residence is a painter named Hezekiah Freeman. You heard of him?"

Clarence and Nance shook their heads.

"Apparently, he was pretty famous a decade or so ago. Then he got into booze and drugs and dropped out of sight. He cleaned himself up and started making art again. He paints waving sawgrass and royal palms, stuff like that. His landscapes are pretty, although I find them a bit depressing." He paused as if waiting for some comment on his artistic criticism.

"I guess I'll find out," Clarence said.

"Mr. Freeman lives in Miami. He is a bit of an authority on the art of this region. The man draws a good crowd to hear him talk about his work and tie it to the historic art community. I'm told he gives a good lecture when he can stay sober."

"And you want me to babysit him until after he gives his talk?"

Again, the gum cracked. "I prefer to say that you are the Park Service liaison to our featured speaker. But you can call it what you wish so long as he shows up sober and on time. I also want you to have some remarks prepared. Something to say about the region's art just in case he sneaks something by you."

"And you want this backup lecture ready by tomorrow?"

Ramirez nodded. "Get the groom to the wedding on time, and we won't need a stand-in."

"What makes you think that he's relapsed?"

"He missed a final planning meeting yesterday. He called the PIO in the afternoon. He said he'd gotten caught up doing fieldwork and didn't notice the time. She said his voice sounded off."

"Did she describe 'off'?" Nance asked.

Ramirez glared at her before returning his attention to Clarence. "Fieldwork sounds like code for 'I'm drinking again.'"

"Or it could mean fieldwork like the man said." Clarence thought about the times he'd been studying game film and lost track of time. The same thing happened when he worked for the department. He'd get caught up in a case and forget that time existed.

"I suppose it could," Ramirez said, although his voice suggested that he didn't believe it. "If so, I just need you to be his alarm clock tomorrow. Get him to the opening session. You can handle this?" Ramirez gave Clarence his best professional stare.

In his time, Clarence had been eyeballed by coaches and the police department command staff. He felt he could evaluate the icy stare of leadership. He gave Ramirez credit. Despite the gum, the man could bring his A game regarding a silent display of authority.

Clarence nodded. "Roger that, sir."

Ramirez smiled; the eyes softened. "I knew they'd sent me one person I could count on."

Clarence felt Nance stiffen beside him.

"The PIO has arranged for Mr. Freeman to pick you up in about an hour," Ramirez continued. "He'll show the new guy around the park. Give you his perspective. Like I said, Freeman used to be a big-time artist. You'll probably enjoy it."

"You've got a guy who you think drinks too much taking me for a drive in the swamp?"

"Everglades staff don't call this a swamp. Swamps are stagnant. This is a river of grass, to quote Marjory Stoneman Douglas."

"To quote me, I think you're missing my point."

Ramirez's stare returned. "I understand your point perfectly, Seasonal Ranger Johnson. And if you do your job as directed, we won't have a problem. Now go meet the man. If there is an issue, relay your concerns to the public information officer." His head snapped to face Nance. "I've heard a great deal about you, Special Agent Nance." Ramirez's face pursed. He looked as if he'd just bitten into a lemon.

"Since you've read my file, you know I spent years as a homicide detective," Clarence said, interrupting the silence. "I've known a lot of investigators. Nance is one of the finest officers I've ever worked with. She was praised for her handling of the Ocone case."

The slight cock of Ramirez's head suggested that he had heard things differently. "I appreciate your loyalty to a...coworker, Johnson. I'll have to decide for myself." He shifted his gaze back to Nance. "We've got a poaching problem here in the Everglades. We're the largest subtropical wilderness in the United States. Our park boundaries protect important habitat for more rare and endangered plants and animals than you can count."

"Yes, sir," Nance said through gritted teeth. "I've read the website."

"You may not have read that people want what we've got, and they'll go to some lengths to take it. They want our softshell turtles to sell in Asian markets. Every time Louisiana has a hurricane, someone wants our alligator eggs. And we haven't begun to talk about the plants. We are a bazaar for black marketeers. Catch them. We need some high-profile arrests to signal that we're serious about enforcement. You can't eliminate poaching, but send them someplace else to do their stealing. Bring me some heads, Special Agent. That's your assignment."

Nance nodded. "Can you recommend someone who can help me get the lay of the land, sir?"

Ramirez shook his head. "The staff here is swamped." He laughed at his own joke. "That's why I called Atlanta and asked for someone from ISB to be deployed here. The Visitor and Resource Protection rangers are busy. You'll have to make do on your own."

"But, sir," Nance said. "In my Yellowstone experience, we had two kinds of poachers. Opportunistic ones, usually hunters who stumble across the game and fail to resist the temptation, and we have professionals who know the backcountry. If you want me to compete with those outlaws, I will need some support."

Ramirez's gum cracked. "You are the support. That's why the Region Two director pawned you off to me." The gum cracked again. "You're Investigative Services. I'm sure you'll investigate."

5

April 1851

William poled the half-carved canoe through the sawgrass. The Miccosukee had allowed them to stay for two nights. They had fed the runaway slaves. William smiled as he remembered lying on the floor of Old Johnny's chickee, his belly feeling full for the first time since they'd run from the plantation.

The slaves had little to use as trade goods. William had given away his knife. The group had insisted on keeping Eli's. Myrna had three pairs of colored beads made by the plantation's chief potter. He had given them to her when she'd married William. The beads represented love, affection, and loyalty, the potter said. Stealing from the master might have gotten him whipped. The slave had accepted the risk and pressed them into her hand. He wished her happiness. The beads' red, green, and blue colors shined more brightly than any dishes in the master's dining room. They were among Myrna's few possessions in the world. William knew that it grieved her to part with them. But to secure their freedom, she surrendered them without a tear.

The Miccosukee had not demanded Myrna's pot. She carried it strapped to her back, holding the food the natives had given them for the journey, dried meat and flour. The flour, Old Johnny said, came from a coontie plant. He warned Myrna not to gather her own. "It's poison if you don't prepare it right," he said.

Eli and Josiah floated along in the other dugout the Miccosukee had given them. An old boat, the canoe leaked and had to be bailed periodically. The natives were probably happy to be rid of it. Still, the boats allowed them to travel far more quickly now, as they no longer had to slog through the water and mud.

Standing atop the dugout canoe allowed William to peer over the top of the sawgrass. Ahead of him, as far as he could see, an endless plain rolled out in front of him. At the horizon, the blue sky met the yellow-green grass. Only the occasional bump of a tree cluster interrupted the view. William wondered if it would ever end. He kept his fears to himself. Myrna did not speak either. When their eyes met, however, he knew she asked the same silent question.

He poled the boat along a jagged course, seeking his way through the clumps of grass. The dugout glided through the open water. They dragged the boats when they could not find the water route. The twists and turns made the navigation challenging. William kept his eye on the sun. In the morning, he held it with his left hand; in the afternoon, he clutched it with his right.

He navigated by the sun when he could see it. The clouds, at times, blanketed the sky. Then the rain came as if someone above was pouring buckets down on them. The runaway slaves pressed forward, drenched. When the water vanished, the men were forced to drag the canoes through the slimy thick muck. They sometimes sank in to their knees, and the sharp blades nicked their skin as they slogged. Engulfed by the thick grass, they could not feel the breeze. Only the scorching sun remained. Both the rain and the dryness brought misery in equal shares.

Eli swiped at a cloud of mosquitoes that encircled him. "I don't know what's the worst. When we snuck through Georgia, the hunters were out with packs of dogs. If they'd found us, them dogs woulda taken a bunch of blood all at once. But at least you can fight 'em." He paused and swiped again. "They is like a cloud. These devils all take a little bit of blood. And there ain't nothing we can do about it."

When no water path showed, Myrna led the way, waving her staff to scare back any snakes they might come across. Samuel walked between his mother and father. When the mud became too deep, they placed the boy atop the canoe, only increasing the weight. Every time they paused, the runaways bent over, exhausted by the labors.

Besides the snakes, the rain, and the unforgiving sun, the bugs attacked them relentlessly. Horseflies feasted on the blood drawn from the innumerable scratches they received making their way through the sawgrass. The no-see-ums would buzz their ears, making it impossible to sleep. In the front of the boat, Samuel began to cry.

"Make him quiet," Eli demanded. "If the slave hunters hear him, they can find us."

William knew that if a fugitive hunter tracked them, the grooved paths they carved, dragging canoes through the sawgrass, would be easy to follow. He also understood, however, that Eli was right. They needed to be quiet. The two men had been tolerant of the slower pace necessitated by bringing along a child. They were sleep-deprived and scared, just as he and Myrna were. Eli and Josiah could see over the top of the sawgrass. They had glimpsed the endless prairie. William did not complain about Eli chastising his son.

Instead, he looked to Myrna and silently implored her to do something.

The woman reached into the water. She grabbed a handful of the golden-brown muck that seemed to float everywhere. The Everglades moss, they called it, for they had no other word, soaked up the water. She formed a small round wet ball and dabbed at Samuel's wounds, blowing on his cuts, and humming a quiet song. The boy calmed down.

"You think any of these mosquitoes have a shovel?" William asked Samuel.

The boy frowned at the question and then shook his head.

"When we find the tree island, before you go to sleep tonight, we'll slather you in mud. You'll be covered in mud so thick that any mosquito that wants to bite you is gonna have to carry along his own shovel."

Samuel smiled and then began to laugh. The sound lit up William's heart. He poled the canoe harder, determined to push forward.

They made camp that night on a raised bump of land, one of countless small rises they'd seen that day. The sawgrass waved around them. Sometimes they saw light. They'd hide behind logs and pray that the slave hunters hadn't found them. Sometimes, when the canoes came close, they recognized the language they'd heard at the Miccosukee village. Old Johnny had said the men sometimes hunted frogs at night. No one ever stopped at the island where they camped. Still, no one relaxed until the lights and sounds of the canoes disappeared.

When it was safe, Myrna made a small fire and boiled a stew in the pot she carried. She fried the meat the Miccosukee had given them. Myrna scraped the bottom of the pot to loosen all the crackling. Then she added water and a swamp cabbage. Old Johnny had told her how to find them. The five made simple bowls from palm leaves and drank their soup. No one spoke.

In the night, the sounds surrounded them. Owls screeched. Alligators bellowed. Everybody jumped, startled at some point by a noise in the darkness. The scariest moments, however, came when the noises stopped.

An eerie silence fell over the tree island. Then, a sharp grunt broke the silence. Samuel jumped, dropping his palm.

Myrna brushed off the leaf. She wiped the leaf inside the pot, scouring the inside and collecting the last drops of soup. Myrna handed the palm to Samuel. "Lick that off."

"What'd that noise sound like to you?" William asked.

The boy ran his tongue across the leaf's surface. He smacked his lips. Taking a breath, Samuel pursed his lips and imitated the grunt. "It sounded like the master's pigs."

William reached out a hand and caught the boy's wrist. He pulled Samuel close to him and looked into his eyes.

The boy's eyes widened in fear.

William's voice remained low but firm. "Don't say *master*. You ain't got no master. You are gonna grow up as a free man."

The boy nodded.

"If you respect a man, you call him *sir*. But no man is gonna be your master. Not while your mama and I got breath in our bodies, you hear?"

Samuel nodded again.

William took a deep breath and stared into the darkness without saying a word. Another grunt punctuated the night. "Hear that sound like a pig?"

The boy nodded.

"Old Johnny calls that a pig frog. He says they got frogs out here that sound like different animals. He says another one makes a noise like a cricket."

Samuel's face showed his concentration as he listened.

"They probably got some frogs out here that sound like horses and dogs." William looked at the boy. "If you listen hard, you think you might hear a dog frog?"

The boy laughed. For a moment, everyone forgot about their deteriorating clothing, the bugs, and all the other miseries.

"Daddy," Samuel asked, "how much farther do we have to go?"

"As far as we have to."

6

April 7th

Tripod slowly worked her way around the RV's exterior, mapping the property. Clarence loosely held the dog's leash. Four other mobile homes were parked near his. Farther out, a cluster of low-slung, cream-colored houses stood. From the far edge of the Pine Island housing unit, Clarence watched a red Dodge Charger rumbling in his direction.

The brakes squealed as the car stopped alongside him. The car coughed. Its black racing stripes looked faded and peeled. Inside, the driver cranked down the window. An older African American man, with closely cropped hair and grizzled whiskers, leaned out his head. "I s'pose you're my babysitter?"

Clarence stood six feet, four inches tall. He had broad shoulders, narrow hips, and biceps that most men envied. His thighs, once thick, had slimmed since his injury. Since he felt himself being appraised, he considered striking a pose and flexing. Instead, he asked, "Are you Hezekiah Freeman?"

"People call me Heka. My granddaughter couldn't pronounce Hezekiah." The man gestured to the other side of the car. "Get in. Bring the dog."

Clarence scooped up Tripod and carried her around to the passenger side. When he pulled on the handle, nothing happened.

"You got to lift up a little bit," Heka said.

Clarence yanked on the handle. With a groan, the door opened. A 35 mm camera lay on the passenger seat, and a sketch pad rested on the floorboard. Clarence moved the camera onto the pad and sat down, twisting his feet to avoid stepping on the sketchbook.

"We ain't going too far," Heka said, pointing the car back to the Ingraham Highway.

"I'm Clarence Johnson."

Heka nodded. "They tell me you're an art scholar."

Clarence shook his head. "I majored in art history in college."

"Why'd you do something like that?"

"The money."

Heka grunted.

"Coach told me to. The classes fit with the football practice schedule. And do you know the ratio of female to male students in the art history program?"

"Now you're being honest," Heka said. "What did you play?"

"Tight end."

"Any good?"

"Got drafted by the National Park Service."

Heka reached over and grabbed Clarence's bicep. "Still got your football arms. How tall are you?"

"Too tall to be screwing my legs around all this stuff on the floorboards. How far is not too far?"

Heka grunted and stared through the windshield.

"I was listed at six four."

The driver nodded. "We ain't going far. What do you call your dog? Easel?"

"Tripod."

Heka nodded and asked no more questions. He paused briefly at the entrance to Everglades National Park. The woman working the booth smiled and waved. Heka waved back and drove through the checkpoint. He looked over at Clarence. "I bought this car back when I had more money than sense. The two of us tore through the streets of Miami. Police man once pulled me over for speeding. He looked at me, looked at my car. He said, 'You know that's gonna cost you a hundred dollars.' I looked at him. Then I reached into my shirt pocket, I did, and I pulled out two Benjamins. 'Good thing I got a couple of these,' I told him, "cause I'm coming back this way in about an hour.'" Heka shook his head. "More money than sense."

He drove to the intersection of a road leading to the Royal Palm Visitor Center. Heka pointed ahead. "Keep exploring this road. Nine miles up ahead, there's a nearly invisible trail on your right. Leads to one of my favorite spots." He gazed down the highway and nodded. "Treasure all up and down this way if a man knows where to look." Heka drove into the parking lot. An oversized green roof shaded three small white buildings and a red patio. Behind the center, Clarence saw a lake. "Hand me my camera," Heka said and got out of the car. Clarence followed. Tripod promptly settled on the passenger seat and slept.

The old man walked along the paved trail that skirted the buildings. Around them, tourists milled. While a few conversed in English, many spoke German.

Heka paused at a small wooden bridge. He waved out at the watery landscape. "I'm told you just arrived. This is a good place to start looking at the Everglades. Most days, a fellow can see an old bull alligator sunning himself near here. That's all most of these people want. Take a picture of a gator and get on down to South Beach." Suddenly, he stopped talking. Heka knelt and raised his camera. Twisting the lens, he snapped off pictures. "See that," he said without turning from the eyepiece, "that's a purple gallinule, the peacock of the Everglades. Them big yellow feet let it walk on the spatterdock, searching for a meal. Looks like it's walking on water." He refocused his camera. "The spatterdock gets them yellow blooms. If you can get the gallinule standing next to the flower..." Heka stopped talking and focused his attention on the camera. "Gotcha," he said and pushed himself to his feet. He leaned and rubbed his right knee. "Can't do that as easily."

Clarence nodded understanding.

"Gallinule is a pretty bird. Saw a spoonbill this morning. Beautiful shade of pink. Didn't have my camera with me." Heka's eyes dropped down.

"Look down at the water." He paused for a moment and watched Clarence. Heka bent again and, picking up a twig, dropped it into the water. He grunted as he stood. Heka pointed. "It ain't standing still. All the time, moving slowly from north to south. Not in a hurry but heading toward Florida Bay. People call this place a swamp. That's not what it is. This is a river that starts at Lake Okeechobee and drains south. Or it did, till people rerouted it with drainage canals and elevated roads. A hidden and mysterious river full of secrets." He paused and surveyed the landscape. "The Everglades you're looking at is just a small piece of what it used to be. Look out at the sawgrass, and then picture it stretching out endlessly. You got to understand what this was if you're going to pretend to talk about the art."

Clarence raised his head and gazed across the water. "I've seen your recent work, mostly on the internet. Radically different from your early paintings."

"More money than sense." Heka turned and walked back toward the car. Clarence started to follow, but a quick pain shot up through his leg, and he limped for a step before finding his stride. If Heka noticed, he said nothing. Instead, he pointed toward a clump of trees. "That's the Gumbo Limbo Trail. Takes you into a hammock. You need to walk both trails if you're gonna learn something about this place. The hammock is shadier, but the bugs will eat you. Keep an eye out for Liguus snails. They're big as a hand and cling to the trees. Poachers steal them to make jewelry or ornaments or some such." Heka chatted all the way to the parking lot. When he opened the car door, Tripod sat up and thumped her tail. Heka looked at the dog. "Let's get you back to the house, Easel. I'll get you some water."

Back at his bungalow, Heka opened the unlocked door and walked inside. Clarence paused; his eyes surveyed the interior. A screened porch covered the back wall of the small house. The sparsely furnished interior had a table with two chairs. The table held a laptop computer. Above the table hung a painting, the varnish cracked with age. It showed a dusky scene of an Everglades panorama. An island rose from the sawgrass. Clarence mentally corrected himself and called the island a hammock. Two great trees dominated the hammock; both trunks were marked with crimson teardrops. An easel with the beginnings of a painting stood in the far corner of the room. Although incomplete, this painting varied greatly from the Hezekiah Freeman works Clarence had seen on the internet. No waving sawgrass or palmettos. The top half remained blank. On the bottom, Heka had painted a solid block of golden brown, black lines and swirls showing through. Although he painted the canvas horizontal rather than vertical, the current work in progress looked more like Mark Rothko than Hezekiah Freeman. Clarence turned away from the easel. The room's lone bed was bordered by a nightstand and an armchair. The partial wall that separated the bedroom from the kitchen held a bookcase filled with framed pictures and books. Clarence automatically stepped closer to read the titles.

"Sit down," Heka said before he could get there. He cocked his head toward the table. Heka pointed to the island scene hanging on the wall. "You noticed my painting. Only thing I wanted from my daddy's estate. Connects me to my past." Heka turned and looked in the kitchen. Tripod's head bent low, lapping water from a bowl Heka had placed on the floor. "Easel there was thirsty. How about you? Drink coffee?"

Clarence nodded.

Heka moved the laptop to the bedside table. He punched one of the keys. Blues music from a scratchy old recording began to play from a speaker on the bookcase. The smell of brewing coffee began to fill the house.

Clarence thought he might be in heaven.

"How does an art historian pay the bills?" Heka asked.

"I used to be a cop."

Heka frowned. "Policing in America has its roots in slave hunting. Since the start of the eighteenth century, slave patrols existed for one purpose, to catch and return runaway slaves. Their job was to keep the Negro in his place. Things only got worse with the Fugitive Slave Act of 1850." Heka leaned across the small table. "What do you think about being established by law as a civil rights violator?"

Behind the two men, the sounds of the blues mixed with gurgling coffee.

Before Clarence could answer, Heka got up from the table. He returned a moment later with his finger through the handles of two mugs of steaming coffee. Heka carried a pint of milk in the other hand. He set one mug and the milk down beside Clarence. Then he returned to his chair. "I didn't figure you liked it black."

Clarence's expression remained unchanged. He picked up the mug and tasted the coffee. He nodded and set the mug back on the table. "I only violated the civil rights of those who needed it."

Heka looked at him, studying Clarence's eyes. The frown still marked his face. Then Heka smiled. "I've known a few police in my day." He stretched out the word *police*, emphasizing the P and making the O long. "Some join because they want to be bullies. The police badge justifies them pushing people around. I've met a few who understand that they gotta try to do good. I like a man who won't be pushed or intimidated. Tells me which of the two you were."

Clarence accepted the compliment without comment. He took another sip of the coffee and leaned toward the speaker. "And if somebody didn't put Lead Belly in jail, he might never have had something to sing about."

Heka looked at the speaker and then went back to Clarence. He stood. "Put your cup in the sink. Leave the dog." He walked out the door of the bungalow. Clarence trailed behind, curious about where they might be going.

Heka wrenched open the door to the Charger and settled in behind the steering wheel. "I was hoping to go celebrate tonight. I figured my encounter with some white cop would come along at the end of the night, not the beginning." He put the car in gear and drove back to the main road.

The road out of the national park passed a string of plant nurseries. A billboard advertised an alligator farm. Another offered both live bait and apparel. The utility poles were square and concrete. Clarence assumed that made them better able to withstand a hurricane. He looked ahead out the windshield. One of them ought to.

Heka turned in his seat and faced Clarence. He had one hand on the steering wheel, except when he got animated. "I'm celebrating tonight," he repeated. "I think I've finally found what I was looking for." He pointed both index fingers toward Clarence. "Have you ever had a moment when you feel like your past becomes your present?"

Clarence shook his head. He really had no idea what that meant. He tried to listen, but mostly, he wanted to grab the steering wheel. Fortunately, the road ran straight, and the Charger maintained a true line despite the rattles and creaks.

"There weren't much in Homestead when Prohibition came along. So they built a club out here for the white folk to drink their liquor. Too much trouble for the revenuers to come this far." He paused and put a finger on the steering wheel. "Of course, if you were rich enough, you could ignore Prohibition entirely." Heka paused briefly at a stop sign. The road naturally bent north. Heka turned south.

With the turn complete, Heka's hands again became visual aids. "When drinking got legal again, white folks quit coming to the club. Too far away. So the poor folk got it. We turned it into a blues joint. Poor folk understand the blues."

He stopped outside a weathered building with peeling white paint. It had a false front behind a second-story porch to look like a business. A man stood on the porch, leaning on the railing and smoking. The red shingles on the overhanging roof highlighted the faded white paint. Behind the façade, a pitched roof had been covered with tin. The back entrance had a ramp and a sign advertising "Bar" and "Pool." The place, apparently, needed no name.

The place looked uncrowded. Heka parked in front. "No band," he said and opened the door.

When Clarence got out, he smelled marijuana. He felt Heka's eyes watching him. "I wouldn't trust a blues club that didn't have weed."

Heka smiled. He opened the trunk. After depositing his camera and sketch pad, he led Clarence inside. He waved to the bartender and took a table near the empty stage. Music came from a Rock-Ola jukebox in the corner opposite the bar. Clarence looked around. The crowd, although sparse, appeared diverse.

"When the music got good, the whites started returning," Heka said. "The owner didn't discriminate. I think he figured that with more people, the bartender, the customer, and the musician weren't just trading the same dollar."

The bartender appeared alongside the table. He had large, round eyes, a shaved head, and a beard. Heka stood. The two men clasped hands. The bartender's thick arms surrounded Heka in a hug. The artist patted the man on the back, and they separated. The younger man eyed Clarence with a hint of suspicion.

"This man is going to be helping me with my speech tomorrow," Heka said. "Bring me my usual and a glass of your special for him."

The bartender nodded. "Coming up, Mr. Heka." He turned and walked away.

"Big fella," Clarence said.

"Kemo's even bigger when he holds the Louisville Slugger he keeps behind the bar."

The clack of pool balls drew Clarence's attention to the back of the bar. Two men circled the pool table. The bar walls were plastered with handbills and photographs of musicians who'd played in the club over the years. "If these walls could talk," he said.

"They have the right to remain silent." Heka nodded. "Probably best that way."

The bartender returned carrying a beer stein filled with ice and brown soda. A maraschino cherry floated on top. "Cherry Coke, just like you like it, Mr. Heka." He set another beer stein and a shot glass alongside Clarence. "And the house special for you."

"Thank you, my brother," Heka said.

Clarence looked at the alcohol.

"Can't know the blues without some pain," Heka said.

Clarence tossed back the shot and chased it with the beer. He set the mug down and exhaled, smelling the alcohol on his breath. He pointed at Heka's drink.

"I've had enough pain." Heka raised his glass. "And I am Sir Percival on a quest."

"A scholar."

"Got to know the world to paint it. My grail is two spots of red against a field of brown. My Coke is a symbol of the quest." He took a drink and did not elaborate.

Clarence didn't press. Instead, his eyes settled on the ebony guitar resting on the small stage.

Heka followed his eyes. "You like the guitar?"

Clarence nodded. "A Gibson ES-355. Looks like B.B. King's Lucille. Pretty expensive to be left unattended."

"You try to carry it out while Kemo is working, watch what happens. You play?"

"Me, a narcotics cop, and a couple of guys from patrol had a band in Fort Worth."

Heka waited.

"I played lead. The narc had vocals and harmonica. The two uniforms had bass and drums."

"What was your name?"

"The Police," Clarence said and paused. "Then we heard that name was taken. So we changed it to Back the Blues."

Heka laughed. He pointed at the guitar. "Why don't you climb on stage and take her for a test drive?"

Clarence shook his head. "Nah, I'm rusty."

Before he could protest further, Heka turned in his chair. "Kemo, shut off that ratty old jukebox. My friend here wants to try out that Little Lucy."

The bartender looked at Heka, then shifted his gaze. Clarence made a slight shake of his head. The man ignored him and unplugged the jukebox. The sudden absence of music brought the crowd to silence. Clarence heard a low grumbling.

"Better play something, Mr. Lawman," Heka said. "If not, you might have to deal with a riot."

Clarence took a quick swallow of his beer. "You better give a damn good lecture to make this worth it." He pushed back from the table and climbed onto the stage.

"Come on, babysitter, show us something," Heka shouted, then he leaned and rested on the back two legs of his chair.

Clarence ran his hand along the top of the amplifier. He wouldn't show it to Heka, but his gut tingled. He could feel the electricity of playing this guitar on a vintage Fender tube amp. Clarence plugged the guitar's cable into the jack and turned on the amplifier. He slipped the guitar strap over his head. The bluesman who owned this guitar was shorter than Clarence. While the old Fender warmed, Clarence adjusted the strap.

"Quit stalling, babysitter."

"You asked, I'm answering, but I'm doing it on my schedule," Clarence said.

Kemo handed Heka a fresh glass and collected the empty. The old artist, again, leaned back further in his chair. Clarence saw a steady stream of folks come by to talk to Heka. He seemed to know everyone in this old bar.

The amp made a popping noise, followed by a series of clicks. The Fender was ready to go. Clarence swallowed. He'd rather be back in the RV, playing with just Tripod in the audience. But Clarence had accepted the challenge. He ignored his nerves. Like catching the ball on a Saturday in a stadium, he needed to block out the distractions and focus on the job.

Clarence fingered the strings and adjusted the tuning pegs until his ear told him he had the right sound. He ran his hand up and down the neck, feeling the frets and introducing himself to the instrument. Every guitar had its eccentricities. Cops developed relationships with a particular duty weapon and guitarists with their instruments. In theory, every one manufactured by the same company should be identical. Every practitioner disagreed with the theory.

Heka peppered him with insults. "Were you the band's guitarist or the manager?"

The old man stopped talking when Clarence began his cover of Stevie Ray Vaughan's "Life by the Drop."

"Let me hear it," one of the patrons yelled.

Clarence cranked the volume and smoothly transitioned into a Gregg Allman tune. He saw that the players had quit the pool game and were listening to him. Somewhere in the middle of the tune, Kemo turned on the spotlights shining on the stage. Clarence felt himself sweat. He closed his eyes and was transported to a life he thought he'd left behind.

Clarence tore through his final chord and let the last note hang. He shook the guitar's neck, wringing the last bit of sound. The crowd hollered and clapped. He looked at Heka.

"Not bad, babysitter. But you know black folk play the blues, too."

Clarence nodded. When the applause died down, he launched into "Hoochie Coochie Man." People stood and began to dance. Heka smiled and bobbed his head in time with the blues standard. Then he turned and started waving to someone in the back of the club. He beckoned them forward. Sweat clouded Clarence's vision. He saw shapes move aside, allowing someone to pass through to the front. He wiped his forearm across his brow, succeeding only in trading perspiration. He laid down a lick and, again, held the final note.

A pair of dancers helped a woman climb onto the stage. She handed him a bar towel.

Clarence nodded thanks and wiped his face.

She pressed a beer stein into his hand. "Kemo said you earned this."

Clarence pressed the glass against his forehead, feeling the condensation. He took a quick drink and mopped his forehead again.

"My name's Mae. I'm supposed to sing."

Clarence looked at the woman. She appeared to be in her early twenties. She wore torn, baggy jeans and a tight blouse held up with spaghetti straps that crossed her back. Mae had almond-shaped eyes and a flawless complexion. Her coloring reminded Clarence of the golden-brown sawgrass he'd seen earlier. She wore earrings made from green sea glass. Her hair hung down in long braids. "What can you sing?"

"If you can play it, I'll sing it," Mae said. Then she turned and began adjusting the microphone stand.

A woman had never fronted Back the Blues. Clarence searched his memory. He launched into the opening bars of Etta James's "I'd Rather Go Blind." Mae listened for a minute, nodded, and turned to face the audience. She wrapped both hands around the microphone and began to sing.

Clarence nearly stopped playing when he heard her voice. It came out deep and sultry. Her smoky vocals belied her age. The crowd stopped talking. Mae let go of the microphone with one hand and began beating time, swaying her hips to meet her palm. No one looked at Clarence. All eyes, including his, were focused on the singer.

The crowd erupted when the song finished. Mae turned to him and smiled. Clarence felt another surge of electricity. He played the intro chords to a Bonnie Raitt song. Mae turned and faced the crowd. Clarence took a step back. Mae owned the stage.

When the song ended, he returned to Muddy Waters. After the first chords, Mae turned, dipped her shoulder, and looked at him. Her eyes narrowed, and her lower lip pressed forward into a pout. Clarence tried to read the expression. He realized what song he'd struck up as she began growling the opening lyrics to "I Just Want to Make Love to You."

With the lights baking his face, no one could see Clarence blush.

When the song finished, Clarence unstrapped the guitar. He felt sweat-soaked and exhausted. Mae put her arm around him. He could feel the heat from her body. The crowd stomped and cheered.

Mae looked at Clarence. "You a nasty man." Then she dropped her arm and hopped from the stage.

He cradled the guitar back on its stand and returned to the table.

"You can come back anytime, Clarence," Heka said.

Clarence drank some warm beer and wiped the glass across his forehead. He felt the bar towel until he found a dry patch and pressed it against his face.

"Heka, your boy can be Mae's sideman anytime he's in town," a voice said.

Clarence lowered the towel. Possibly the ugliest man he'd ever seen stood next to Hezekiah. His eyes didn't seem to be in line with one another. Hair grew at random spots on his head and face. The teeth he had were stained brown. The man's eyes followed Mae as she crossed the room.

"What gets you out on a school night, Joe Bob?" Heka asked.

"Huh, I'm just spending my poaching money," the man said.

His open mouth again exposed the man's teeth. Clarence promised himself he'd floss when he got home.

"I guess if you're out raping the land, at least you ain't making money as a racist," Heka said.

"Don't let the Confederate flag at Southern Nursery fool you. That's just marketing. You can come by anytime. I'll let you pick any field you want," Joe Bob said.

"Get the fuck away from my table, you old bigot."

Joe Bob appeared unfazed. He faced Clarence. Despite himself, Clarence wanted to push back from the table, increasing his distance from the man.

"The blues are the roots. Other music is the fruits. Willie Dixon said that. Music and plants, two of the many things I know." He smiled, giving Clarence another look at his teeth. "I know you could find a better class of folk to associate with." Joe Bob turned from the table. "See you, Hezekiah."

"Not if I see you first."

"Charming," Clarence said after Joe Bob had left.

"But what he lacks in social grace, he makes up for in looks," Heka said. "You about ready to go? One of us has to sound smart tomorrow."

When they stood from the table, Clarence paused and stretched his leg. Heka said nothing.

On the drive back to the Everglades, Heka talked animatedly about the region's art. He rarely touched the steering wheel. Like a trained horse, the Charger seemed to know its way back to the barn.

"How about John James Audubon? He came down here to draw pictures of his birds. You know how he made them look so lifelike? Shot 'em. These days, that old slaver has his name on the stationery of a conservation society." Heka jabbed at the air with his finger.

He rattled off a list of artists' names. Clarence wished he'd had his phone out to take notes.

"Did I tell you I was writing my memoir," Heka said. "I'm calling it *Three Times a Slave*." He held up a finger. "Like most black folk, my ancestors was brought here as slaves." He raised his second finger. "Them drugs chained me up."

"What's the third time?" Clarence asked.

"How come you ain't still a cop?" Heka asked.

"Retired."

Heka turned completely in his seat and studied him. "What are you, thirty-five?"

"A little north of that."

"Pretty young, man."

"Medically retired."

"Hope the other guy looks worse."

"Became a lawyer."

"At least he feels worse." Heka turned back to glance at the road before returning to Clarence. "You don't look raggedy-ass enough to play the blues, with your short sandy hair and your muscles. Good thing you got your broken nose, or they might not let you in a decent blues place. Your tires have got to lose some tread."

"These tires have skidded a few times, believe me."

"Then how'd you stay so pretty?"

"White don't crack."

Heka's laugh made his hands shake. The steering, Clarence noticed, was loose enough that the motion didn't change the alignment of the wheels on the road.

"I'll try to find an eye patch and a heroin addiction before the next gig," Clarence said before dropping his eyes to his driver's belly. "Or maybe I'll just swallow a bowling ball."

This time, when Heka laughed, the car rocked to the left and right. "When you been down as many times as I have, you learn to enjoy the ups."

They rode quietly in the dark.

"What am I doing here?" Clarence asked, breaking the silence. "You can talk about art in your sleep. You could do this better by yourself. Tread or no tread, I'm a spare tire."

Heka grunted a laugh. "The CARE people and the park folks get the heebie-jeebies every time I open my mouth. They don't know what might come out. Truth be told, I'm never quite sure myself." He laughed again. "They call me eccentric. That's the polite euphemism when they think I'm listening. Your job is to listen. If you hear me starting to piss the rich people off, you just talk louder and drown me out."

Clarence nodded. "I can do loud." His ears still rang from the evening on stage.

"And I may not show up." Heka pointed at the approaching Everglades. "There're riches to be had out there. And I'm close to finding them."

7

April 1851

"When we get to the coast, we'll have to take turns hiding and watching for a boat," William said.

"How we gonna make it to da coast?" Eli said. His eyes looked tired and yellow.

"We got to make it. Ain't no way we're returning to the plantation."

"We're gonna die out here, wandering around all this swamp," Eli said.

William glanced at Samuel. The boy, fortunately, looked to be asleep. He turned sharply on Eli. "You hush. There'll be no talk about dying. In a few days, we gonna get to the coast. I reckon we about as far south as we need to be. Old Johnny said we got to get to the cay."

"That old man fillin' your head with stories he don't know nothing about," Josiah said. "We should have gone north."

"And crossed all those states crawling with slave patrols and we running around without permits. We'd be back working the cotton fields already," William said.

"Once we get to this place below the lighthouse, how we gonna get across the water?" Eli asked.

"We'll find a boat. We got to believe. A little bit longer, and we'll be bathing in Red Bay. This will be just a story to tell our grandchildren."

"We can't pay for no boat," Myrna said.

William's eyes pleaded for her to trust him. "We'll figure out something."

Eli grunted and turned away. Myrna bent over the pot she'd been carrying and stirred the soup.

"Are we ever gonna be able to eat something besides this fish soup?" Eli asked. Josiah nodded in agreement.

The escaped slaves had made their camp between a pair of great mahogany trees on a piece of land that rose above the water. They had pulled their canoes up onto the shore. Myrna had built a small fire on which the evening meal boiled. They all showed the strain of the journey. Stress and little food stripped everyone of their weight. The clothes they wore were shredded to tatters. Although they covered themselves with mud, the bugs feasted on them relentlessly. The mosquitoes and flies were the only well-fed members of the party.

Despite the misery, the great expanse of water sometimes surprised William. Myrna said the water was as clear as the glass in the plantation house. William had to believe her. He'd never looked through those plantation windows. The water surrounding their island held fish, small ones and large ones. Long-legged birds prowled the water searching for food as earnestly as William and the other runaways.

The water was clear, except on the islands like the one they camped on tonight. Sometimes they'd find a rocky pond in the middle of these tree islands. The water in these holes wouldn't flow. The fallen leaves from the trees stained the water brown, as brown as the chestnuts they gathered back at the plantation. The water looked nearly as dark as Josiah. They'd seen alligators floating in the dark water. Myrna wouldn't go near the ponds.

When they reached an island, Eli and Josiah collapsed most nights, exhausted from the day's labors battling the muck of the dry season. Before he rested, however, William always walked around the campsite. He searched for an escape route in case of trouble. The path he sought offered the quickest and easiest route away from the camp. He always tried to find a hiding place for his family. Usually, he'd find dense vegetation and pull back the vines to form a cave. The islands were uniformly flat and never offered rock outcroppings. The holes in the limestone floor held water and the threat of alligators.

The islands had grown more plentiful as they had traveled south. The small mounds emerged from the choking sawgrass with their thick tree cover. When they had escaped the plantation, they'd traveled through the woods of South Carolina, hiding from slave hunters. William had seen deep woods, but he had never encountered entangled plants like he saw on these tiny islands.

William watched the birds as well as the sky and the endless horizon. He'd seen pure white wading birds as well as some colored gray-blue. He had watched black birds fly by, some with white stripes marking their wings. They were heading somewhere else, just like the runaways.

The endless sea of sawgrass surrounded their tiny island. William had lain on his belly at the water's edge. He kept his hands motionless in the water. Occasionally, a fish would swim lazily above his fingers, and William could flip it onto the bank. This day he'd been particularly successful and happily carried a pile of fish and three big frogs to the cookfire. They supplied the meat for Myrna's soup. The runaways had finished the food Old Johnny had given them five days earlier.

Lone pines, looking like single fence posts reaching for the sky, stood around the island. The fugitives had learned that the pines grew when they could remain permanently out of the water. They and the hardwoods, like the mahogany, marked high spots in the water.

The mangroves, on the other hand, the stumpy red trees they were beginning to see, could grow in the water. Their roots stretched out from the trunks. They grabbed the earth and held the trees in place.

Samuel woke up and began scratching at the bites that covered his body. When Myrna grabbed his wrists to stop him from clawing his flesh, he began to cry.

"Don't let that boy cry," Eli said. His eyes glowed with fury, and his hand hovered over the knife.

Myrna moved quickly, placing herself between the two of them. "He's a child, Eli."

"Won't matter if his whimpering brings a pack of hunters down on us."

William edged closer to Eli and softly touched Eli's wrist. "He won't cry. Just sit yourself down. Food will be ready directly."

Eli looked at him. William nodded and patted his wrist softly. "Won't be no trouble." Eli turned away. He walked between the two great trees and sank to the ground.

Samuel's bottom lip quivered as he fought the urge to cry. William sat on the ground next to him. He pointed out over the water. "See that tree with the fingers poking down into the water?"

The boy's small hand wiped his nose and eyes. He squinted at the water before nodding.

"That little tree is called a red mangrove. Old Johnny told me that they got a tree by the ocean that he called a black mangrove. He told me what to look for and how to find it. Old Johnny said that the smoke keeps the bugs away when you burn the black mangrove." He looked at Samuel. "You be strong until I can find you some black mangrove."

The boy's eyes searched his face, and then he nodded. "Can Mama sing me something?"

"Ain't nobody can be singing. We got to be quiet as mice so we don't get caught. You listen to the pig frogs singing when the sun goes down." He picked up a piece of shed tree bark and a thin stick from the fire. William blew out the fire and began drawing on the bark. "Instead of singing, we'll make some quiet pictures instead."

When William saw that Samuel had fallen back to sleep, he laid the bark and stick down next to Samuel. William moved to Myrna's side. "You know we got a little money hidden away. We'll have something for the boatman when we get to the ocean."

William tried to look at her, to pump a little faith into her scratched and bleeding body. Every time he tried to meet her eyes, she turned away.

"What's your pot say?" William asked.

Myrna didn't answer.

"Carved into the clay, what's your pot say?"

"You know ain't neither one of us learned to read," Myrna said.

"I also know you remember what it says. Tell me."

Myrna turned to William. She closed her eyes. "What I carry. What I hold. Worth more than pots of gold."

When she finished reciting, William nodded. "That pot. It holds our food and our water. It's been holding our freedom. Worth more than a fortune." He kept his voice low to not risk waking Samuel. "In the mornings when we see the sun come up, do you ever look at it?" He knew that she didn't see what he did. Her mornings were occupied keeping Samuel settled so that the shallow dugout they rode did not tip. "The sun comes up, and on the clear days, it glows bright gold. The light shines on the sawgrass and turns every bit of the ground gold. It is impossible to tell when the ground stops and the sky starts. We're poling our boat into a sheet of gold. A place where the streets are paved with riches, what's that place called?"

Myrna looked out to the night's horizon. "Heaven," she whispered.

"That's what I saw this morning. Heaven. Where the streets are paved with gold. And that's where we're going. And we're gonna be there soon. My soul tells me."

Myrna shook her head. "Them two trees we sleeping under. They both have an evil eye looking down on us. This is a bad place, William."

"We'll be leaving first thing in the morning. We're almost to the ocean, Myrna."

"I see them two eyes looking at me. We in a place with two evil eyes. They got red blood dripping down." Myrna began shivering with fright.

William's hands had been rubbed raw, poling the canoe through the Everglades day after day. His rough skin stroked her arm. "You are the most beautiful woman I've ever met. Don't let them fears spoil your prettiness. That red ain't nothing to be scared of. It's just plants growing on the crook of those limbs. Nothing to be scared of. We'll be gone in the morning."

Myrna shook her head. "I won't be sleeping tonight. Not with those eyes watching us."

"Sleep on the other side of the tree. The eyes are looking this way."

"They not that kind of eye, William. You can't hide from an evil eye like that if it's looking for you. This is a bad place. I can feel it."

8

April 8th

When Clarence came through the door of the admin building in the predawn, he saw only one light on in the offices. He wasn't surprised.

Nance looked up from her desk when he tapped on the doorframe. She had a detailed map of the Everglades open. A stack of printed reports lay alongside. Her laptop was on, and the screensaver showed a picture of Old Faithful with a bison in the foreground and Geyser Hill behind. Nance glanced at her phone, smiled, then nodded a greeting before returning to her work. "I'm locating recent poaching episodes, both plants and animals," she said, anticipating the question.

"Remember Liguus snails. Apparently, there are snail rustlers out there."

She looked at him; her face showed skepticism.

Clarence lifted his hands in surrender. "That's just what a witness reported."

Her eyes shifted to the paper cup he carried. "You bought coffee?"

Clarence set the cup down on her desk. "Went a different direction this morning. There's a fruit stand near here. I'm told it's been around since the Jurassic period. I got you a mango-and-guava milkshake."

She eyed the cup. "Kinda early for a malt."

"Call it a smoothie. That makes it breakfast." Clarence checked the time. "Come on, we've got to go."

"Where?"

"You said you needed to get a feel for the park."

"I've found somebody to show me around. He'll be here around eight o'clock."

"We'll be back by then. C'mon." Clarence turned and walked out of the office.

After a moment, Nance grabbed her drink and followed.

She wore nylon trail pants and a long-sleeved wicking T-shirt with the sleeves pushed up to her elbows. Nance carried a baseball cap. One advantage of the Investigative Services Branch: they wore plain clothes. Clarence, by contrast, had on crisp khakis and his uniform shirt.

He drove into the park and stayed on the main road. Clarence looked over at Nance. Her lips encircled the straw. Her cheeks sunk, and her rich brown eyes bulged slightly. She pulled the straw from her drink and ate a piece of mango skewered on the bottom. She faced him. "What's the mystery?"

"Be patient. Eat your breakfast."

A few miles further, he turned into a parking lot and stopped. A barred owl sat on the branch of a spindly cypress tree and watched them. Clarence pointed out the bird as they walked to a boardwalk that began just past the parking area. Nance stopped, drew her phone, and snapped a photo. She followed Clarence out onto the boardwalk. Ahead of them stood a series of steps leading to a covered observation deck. He stopped before they arrived. "This is the Pahayokee Overlook. That's the Seminole word for 'River of Grass,' or the Everglades. Heka says it's the best place in the park for a sunrise." He stopped in the middle of the boardwalk and pointed east. "Look that way." Clarence leaned against the railing. After a moment, Nance joined him. They stood quietly; neither one spoke. The breeze rattled the sawgrass. Occasionally, her straw squeaked against the plastic lid.

The gilded morning pushed its way into the Everglades. The sky lit up with a range of yellow colors, gold at the locus of the sunrise, tangerine at the periphery, and brown hues where the sunlight was masked by clouds. The small irregular pools separating the sawgrass reflected the morning's light, giving the water a flaxen glow.

Clarence looked at the landscape. "That would inspire poets." He turned to Nance.

She fixed her gaze on the scene and studied it. Then she turned to Clarence. When she wanted, Nance had the warmest brown eyes. When he worked homicide for the Fort Worth Police Department, he'd have loved to have her working alongside him. Men would confess to those eyes. Her eyes looked at him. This wasn't one of those times.

"Once on the ranch, I got kicked by a horse. After a couple of days, the bruise turned about these colors."

Clarence shook his head and returned to the truck.

No one spoke on the ride back to the admin building. Clarence pulled into the parking lot and stopped. "See you later."

"Come inside. I'll make some coffee."

"I've got to work. First day of the CARE seminar."

"Remember yesterday, you said I was in charge."

"So, is this an order?"

"Does it need to be?"

Clarence frowned but turned off the ignition.

He stood, his back pressed against her doorframe while the coffee brewed.

Nance sat in the desk chair. "I need to apologize. The sunrise was nice. I'm sorry I was a bitch. I'm just tired."

Clarence's shoulders relaxed. "I'm a little bleary-eyed myself this morning. Stayed up too late reading the books Heka gave me about art around the Everglades."

"How'd the introduction go?"

Clarence shrugged. "He called me a jack-booted racist."

"I'm surprised you didn't punch him."

"He said it in a nice way."

She nodded.

"By the end of the night, I'd won him over with my wit and charm. We're besties."

"The man must have a high pain threshold."

Clarence pointed at the reports. "Tell me what you've learned about poaching."

"No geographic pattern. Poachers go where there is something to steal." She poured coffee and handed him a cup. "Orchids, especially around Big Cypress. Saw palmetto berries everywhere."

"And Liguus snails?"

"I haven't mapped them yet."

Clarence leaned over the map. When he set his cup down, he accidentally bumped into her computer. The geyser disappeared and was replaced by Nance's résumé. He looked at it for a moment.

She quickly minimized the screen. "I'll start a search for snail poachers if that will make you happy."

"What's the résumé for?"

"You never know. I'll grab softshell turtles."

"Seriously, what's the résumé for?"

"Montana Fish, Wildlife and Parks has openings."

Clarence stood stunned. "You want to quit to go check fishing licenses?"

"I'm not saying I'm quitting. I just looked." Nance straightened up in her chair. "And game wardens do more than license checks." She waved at the papers across her desk. "Poaching patrol, I'm doing game warden work already. At least in Montana, I'd know my way around."

"You'll learn your way. We've only just arrived."

She leaned forward and rested her head in her hands. "You know it's not just that. They want me to find some cartel or maybe a rich dentist collector to bust so that the US Attorney and the Park Service can make an example. I'll likely grab some low-wage guy desperately trying to feed his family. Then they'll drop the hammer on that guy."

Before Clarence could answer, Nance continued. "The Park Service is like every other organization. You heard the supe. The file says I did a commendable job or showed exemplary initiative in the Yellowstone murder. The superintendents tell one another that I cowboyed the investigation and am not a team player. The Washington Support Office and the Visitor and Resource Protection honchos spread the same stories."

"The shit sandwich is a triple-decker club," he said.

"They'll find ways to sideline me until I can't stand it. That's how they take their revenge." She crumpled up a blank sheet of paper and slammed it into the trash can. "Or they'll give me some impossible task, like finding a poacher in two thousand square miles without any knowledge of the landscape. Then they can punish me for a job-related failure."

"If you quit, they win."

"Maybe I don't care if they win. Maybe I just want to get out before they grind me down into a miserable human being who drinks too much."

Clarence looked at the laptop and then back to her. "Fishing licenses?"

Nance smiled. "I'd probably also teach boating safety."

"Well, then, feel free to put me down as a reference." He paused. "Are you going to do it?"

"Still trying to decide."

"What about in the meantime?"

Nance looked at her reports. "I'm going to catch a plant poacher. I'm calling it Operation Nero Wolfe."

"Don't get it."

She smiled at her small victory. "The fictional detective, Nero Wolfe, loved orchids. I'm going after an orchid poacher." Her phone buzzed. Nance glanced down and smiled. "My Everglades guide is here." She passed by Clarence and hurried down the hall.

Clarence settled into the office's spare chair. He heard her walking back down the hall, talking excitedly. She came through the door. "I think you've met my Everglades expert."

Tom LaFleur walked through the door.

The man looked thinner than when Clarence had seen him in Yellowstone. His cheeks appeared sunken. He still, however, had his shoulder-length golden hair.

"Thor, back from Asgard," Clarence said, holding out his hand.

LaFleur grabbed and shook it. "And you're back from wherever assholes come from."

Clarence looked at LaFleur and then at Nance. "He's your Everglades expert?"

"'Expert' is too strong," LaFleur said. "But I've got a light-duty assignment in Miami while I'm rehabbing." He looked to his left and right and then spoke in a stage whisper. "I'll let you in on a secret. Drugs come in through Miami. The DEA has an office here." He took another look around the room before returning to his normal voice. "I come out to the Everglades to ride my bike several times a week."

"So if we're looking for a poacher in spandex."

"I also have done some hiking. I've been kayaking around Nine Mile Pond, Flamingo, and Cape Sable. I get a little bored, you understand." LaFleur glanced at Clarence's leg.

Clarence couldn't argue with the boredom that comes with rehab.

"When Alison texted and said she was getting stonewalled by management, I offered to help. How could I pass up a chance to do a little interagency team building." He stepped in Nance's direction but kept his eyes on Clarence.

"You're a peach, LaFleur. Your cooperation will get your name on a DEA plaque somewhere."

"Already got that. The DEA scratches your name on brass and mounts you on a plaque when you get injured in the line of duty. Get killed, they name a building after you."

Clarence knew he couldn't punch him, but that didn't mean he didn't feel the temptation.

LaFleur turned to Alison. "Cartels have been dropping stuff in the Everglades for decades. You should hear the old heads tell stories about the cocaine traffickers in the eighties. The local office still gets copied on reports about nighttime activity. We've got a decent database from the agencies outside the park. I've asked one of our data analysts to process the reports for anything recent that might look like poaching. When she sends me the spreadsheet, I'll forward it to you." He turned back to Clarence and smiled his perfect smile before shaking his blond hair. "Getting your name on a plaque buys you a few favors."

"Then I'll have something to show them," Nance said. "Watch them try to put me on the bench."

"They don't know who they're messing with," Clarence said.

"I bet we end up with some minimum-wager guy who needs bail money for his brother-in-law," Nance said.

"The same guys who dream about finding some trafficker's lost money," LaFleur added.

"Or pirate treasure, Ponce de León's gold, or some hidden Confederate booty." Clarence could play this game.

"Desperate people with a long-shot dream," Nance said.

"They're gonna make a YouTube special out of the hunt, sell it for big money," LaFleur added.

"Granddad told them that the treasure is beneath the mangrove." Clarence stretched out his fingers, mimicking mangrove roots.

Everyone laughed. Clarence felt the tension in the room evaporating.

"We'll have a clue tomorrow. That's when my analyst thinks she'll be finished with the first pass through the reports."

"In the meantime, Tom has promised to show me mountains," Nance said.

Clarence felt the tension shoot back into the room with a nearly audible pop. "I thought you said you'd studied the maps?"

"I did, but he's bet me drinks that he can show me the mountains."

"A bet is a bet," LaFleur said. "You should come with us?"

"I'd love to, Tom, thanks. Your invitation means a lot." Although he'd hated this entire conversation, Clarence did enjoy LaFleur's facial reaction. "Seriously, I've got to work this morning."

"He's leading a seminar on art in the Everglades," Nance said.

"A serious step up from handing out brochures at the front entrance," LaFleur said.

"I'm doing that at the seminar too. If I give away twenty, Park Service will let me speak." Clarence felt the telephone in his pocket buzz.

"Sitting in a classroom listening to you talk sounds like a lot of fun. And I would love to help you meet your quota of handouts." LaFleur glanced over at Alison before returning to Clarence. "But we're crime fighters, not art lovers. We've got to get out in the field and start apprehending bad guys." He turned again to Alison.

She looked back at LaFleur and smiled.

"And I'm not really a guy for sitting," LaFleur added. "I need activity. I'm the kind of guy who likes to touch and feel."

Clarence looked at Nance. He tried to gauge the smile. Did he see sincerity or awkwardness? Clarence wasn't sure. There was only one thing about which he was certain.

He really wanted to punch a rehabbing DEA agent.

9

April 1851

Inspired by Old Johnny's story about the black mangrove, the small band of escaped slaves gathered sticks from the variety of plants and trees they found. They burned bits of the cord-like vine wrapped around trees like a noose. They collected leaves, hoping the thick smoke might discourage the bugs.

Some of the trees, they learned, would not readily surrender to the fire. Some had thorny limbs. The spines made it nearly impossible to collect and carry the limbs. When William saw the branches, he called Eli and Josiah to him.

"Lay a line of them sharp sticks around our camp. If the slave hunters come, let's pray they wear moccasins."

After a moment, William's idea became clear to them. Both men smiled at the thought.

"Be sure to leave us two holes to escape," William said as they set the boundary.

The party had slathered themselves in the oils from the fish William had caught. Unlike the mud they had used, the oil did not crack and fall off their bodies. The group remained protected against the biting insects. The fugitives quickly settled down, their bellies fed, their bodies unbitten, and their muscles exhausted by another day's labors. Before he fell asleep, William looked around the group. He felt hopeful. The disagreements from earlier seemed resolved. He had convinced them that they had nearly crossed through the valley of the shadow of death. Soon, they'd be hearing the lap of the ocean waves. Everyone had taken heart. The journey's end felt imminent.

Steady breathing surrounded him. Everyone slept. Although the fire had died down, a faint haze of smoke still hung over the campsite. Around them, the Everglades beasts croaked, clicked, and bellowed. Fireflies flittered about in the air. The noises no longer scared them. They no longer felt strange, he thought. Everyone, including Samuel, had grown accustomed to the wild sounds. William still had his heart set on living as a free man in Red Bay. Still, sitting there on the island unmolested by bugs, beasts, or man, he understood why Old Johnny had made the choice he had.

William lay down next to Myrna. She smelled of fish and wood smoke. He quickly dropped into the most restful sleep he'd known in days.

William awakened suddenly. He didn't move, not wanting to disturb Myrna or Samuel. He heard a noise. William could see no sign of morning. They remained in the clutch of night. He listened but heard nothing. He settled back and closed his eyes.

Then he realized that the beasts had gone quiet.

William rose, fought back his fear, and listened. He had heard this happen before. Occasionally, it seemed that the whole Everglades held its breath. Every animal grew silent. The landscape offered an eerie silence. Then, the noise returned, signaled by something William could not discern. The frogs, owls, and alligators, all the beasts that crawled off Noah's ark, settled in the Everglades and resumed their conversations. William sat in the darkness and waited for the sounds to return.

"They's around here. I smells 'em," a voice in the darkness said.

"Shush," another man commanded.

The voices came from the sawgrass some distance from the tree island. William slid quietly to the campfire and threw dirt on the embers, hoping to hide any glow or scent. He crawled back to Myrna and covered her mouth with his hand. Her eyes shot open in surprise. William pulled her face close and pressed a finger to his lips. She nodded understanding. He withdrew his hand and pointed out into the darkness. She turned her head, concentrating. Myrna squinted her eyes and pressed her lips tightly together. Even in the darkness, William could sense her fear.

Quietly, he crawled over to Eli and Josiah and awakened them. He pointed out onto the grassy plain. He could hear the occasional thump. Each man recognized the noise. A pole struck the side of a shallow-bottomed boat. A small light cast a narrow beam across the water. It could only be a lantern.

"Maybe they is frog hunters," Josiah whispered. "They out for a night hunt."

William shook his head. He knew whom these men were hunting. William motioned for them to stay low and to remain quiet. Then he crawled back to Myrna. She had awakened Samuel.

"Don't let that boy make a peep," Eli whispered.

The child's eyes were wide with fear, but he remained quiet.

William squeezed Myrna's hand and prayed that his family would remain silent and be protected. He felt his heart pounding in his chest. His arms felt clammy. Sweat formed on his forehead. It ran down his face, mixing with the fish oil. The slippery substance made his eyes sting. He needed to see, but he feared wiping his face. The movement might draw attention. He blinked, hoping to clear his eyes.

"There ain't nothing here," a voice from the darkness said. The voice was deep and rumbled across the water.

"I told you I smelled woodsmoke," the other voice said. His tone squeaked. He sounded excited.

"I'm tired," the first man said. "Let's go to camp."

The light at the front of the boat seemed to bend back from where it had come.

William didn't relax. He held his fingers beneath Myrna's and Samuel's noses. William mapped out the escape route they were to follow. His hands gestured, reminding them of the thorny barrier they had erected around the camp's perimeter. When his wife and son nodded understanding, he crawled to Josiah and Eli and repeated the instructions.

"I see something on the hammock," the squeaking voice said.

"You see trees," the deep voice answered.

"At the edge of the water."

"The big shape?"

"That's it."

William heard a deep laugh. "Sleeping alligator. You go wake it up. I'll wait here. Let's go. I want to eat and go to sleep."

"That ain't no alligator. Paddle closer, I'll show you."

"If I take you over there and you look, are you gonna quit whining and let us go eat our victuals?"

"Fair enough," the high voice said.

William watched the lantern swing side to side as the small boat pulled closer to the edge of their island encampment.

"Lookie there. I told you it weren't no alligator," squeaking voice said.

"You're right, it's a log. A tree fell in the water, and you found it."

The light floated outside of view as the deep-voiced man poled the canoe around the edge of the tree island.

William strained to listen for any sound of movement. He willed himself to look into the darkness. Myrna's face showed the strain of fear. He grasped her hand and squeezed it. Every muscle in her body felt taut. He knew she was prepared to grab Samuel and race to the island's heart, hoping to avoid capture. Eli and Josiah were similarly poised to flee.

William heard nothing. The light had disappeared. How long should they wait before they could begin to breathe again? Everyone looked to him for the signal to relax. He looked up at the cloudless night sky and started to pinpoint stars. He kept his ears sharply focused. When he'd counted as high as he could go, if he hadn't heard anything, William would give the all-clear sign. He picked the brightest star to begin. *One, two, three...*

A heavy boot stomped on the thorny branch, snapping it in two. The metal shield of a lantern was thrown open, illuminating the campsite.

"Gotcha, you curs," the tinny voice shouted in the night.

Eli and Josiah scattered, crashing through the thick underbrush.

William heard them tripping and falling, entangled in strangler vines. He heard a splash as someone jumped into one of the island's ponds. He didn't have time to worry about the two men.

Scooping up Samuel, he led Myrna quietly along the trail he had planned earlier. Bushes rustled and sticks cracked as they struggled through the vegetation, but their sounds were drowned by the shouts of the hunters in pursuit of Eli and Josiah.

William and his family could only flee so far. The tiny island offered few ways to go. To step down into the sawgrass risked becoming trapped by the muck. He wouldn't be able to aid Myrna and carry Samuel. They had to hide out on the island.

The hunters' lights waved wildly in the black night. William heard a club hitting flesh followed by Eli's scream of pain.

He pushed Myrna and Samuel into the cave he'd crafted, a limestone cove covered with brush. William quietly pulled the vegetation back as best he could to conceal the entrance. In the dark, the fugitive slave hunters would not have been able to count bodies. They'd have no idea how many escapees were on the island.

The deep, rumbling voice yelled in victory. William knew that Josiah, too, had been captured.

William trusted Josiah and Eli not to reveal their presence. He regretted that the other men had been captured, but he could do nothing to assist his companions. His family became his sole concern.

Beside him in the dark hole, he could feel Myrna and Samuel shaking.

The bushes would hide them in the darkness. William hoped the men would leave before light. He could hear the mournful cries of Josiah and Eli back at the camp. William wrapped a calloused hand around Myrna's and gently squeezed it. He clutched his son with the other hand.

William heard twigs snapping beneath a pair of boots. The footsteps made a squishing noise when they walked across the peat of fallen leaves. A lantern light swung back and forth, casting irregular beams through the gnarled vegetation. The squishing drew closer. No one inside the cave breathed.

As his lungs felt ready to burst, William heard a liquid stream hitting their hiding place's leaves and branches. The fluid spread across the front.

William gulped fresh breath through his mouth and felt an inkling of hope. No man would empty his bladder where he intended to reach his arm.

"Can you smell that over your own fish stink?" the tinny voice asked. "I've poured coal oil on this here bush. You curs might best come out. I don't know how many of you runaways is in there. I ain't about to come in to look. I'll set this whole island on fire. You can either bring your asses out or burn like you're in hell."

The voice had been directed at the plant cave where they'd hidden. There was, William knew, no chance for escape. Myrna knew it, too. She began crying in the darkness. William fought the tears. He didn't want Samuel to know how much fear his father felt.

"We're coming," he said. William squeezed Myrna's hand one last time and began scooting himself out of the hiding place.

As he began to emerge, the man grabbed his arm. His hand slipped free. "Goddamn, you're an oily bastard." Then, the man stepped back and pointed a pistol at William. "Just stay on the ground." He tossed a looped rope to William. No explanation was required. As slaves, they'd been bound this way before.

William slipped the loop over his head. The man pulled the loop taut. He repeated the process when Myrna emerged.

The man held the light and led them back to the camp. He clutched the rope in his other hand. Samuel remained unbound. He clung tightly to his mother.

"I found some more," the tinny-voiced man said as they entered the camp. The other man looked up and smiled. He sat on the ground facing Josiah and Eli. They too had been bound. Escape was impossible. Josiah and Eli had their heads down, staring at the earth. The deep-voiced man had rebuilt their fire. It blazed brightly. They had no reason to hide.

Myrna's eyes drifted upward to the red plants in the high limbs. In the campfire light, they showed only as dark shadows. She began to cry.

William looked at Samuel. The boy's eyes were on their captor. A scar ran down the man's left cheek.

"He's looking at your ugly face," the deep-voiced man said and laughed.

The squeaky-voiced man looked at Samuel. Then, he moved alongside the boy.

William moved to protect his child, but the choking rope stopped him.

The man pressed his face against Samuel's. "You looking at this?" Samuel turned away, but the man grabbed his chin and pulled his head back. "You know how I got this scar?"

Samuel's bottom lip quivered. After a moment, he made the slightest shake of his head.

"I got it wrestling an alligator." He reached into his pouch and produced a large hollow tooth hanging from a leather cord. "Made this charger for my musket after I kilt him."

The deep-voiced man's laughter split the night. "Why you practicing your lies on this boy, Paul? He don't care if you got cut trying to bed George's wife."

"Being with her was like wrestling an alligator."

"Don't matter none," the deep-voiced man said. His eyes roamed over the group of frightened runaway slaves. "The only thing we got to talk about is what exactly are we going to do next?"

10

April 8th

The text message from the park superintendent was short. *CALL NOW.*

Since Clarence already stood in the administration building, walking to the office seemed more efficient. Superintendent Ramirez glanced up when Clarence knocked on the door. He had a phone pressed against his ear. Ramirez stood facing a bay window that looked across a pond. Egrets fished in front of him. The supe had a postcard view of the Everglades. Nothing in Ramirez's expression suggested that he liked what he saw.

Ramirez stabbed his phone. "Hezekiah isn't answering his phone. Where the fuck is he?"

"Has someone gone to his house? Heka's not really a phone guy."

Ramirez put his palms down on the desk and leaned across it, closing the distance to Clarence. "You had one job—to get one old man to the seminar."

"You didn't tell me that it was a sleepover."

The superintendent slapped the desktop. "This park is tax funded. But if we had to rely on those dollars alone, every roof would leak. We couldn't do routine maintenance. Our staff shortages would worsen. Most of the programming wouldn't exist. We depend on volunteers and grants to stretch our dollars." He turned and looked out the window. "This seminar isn't just about art. Some of our biggest, most influential donors wanted it. And Freeman is one of our stars. If we don't deliver the goods for our donors, they will go elsewhere. You should understand that. They told me that you were the smart one."

"I frequently disappointed my mother, too."

"You had one job," Ramirez repeated.

"You gave me two jobs. In your words, I was to liaise with Hezekiah Freeman and prepare some remarks. I left the man sober and in his bungalow late last night. Then I went home and started reading. I needed to get a backup presentation ready."

"I hope you wrote a good speech, because it looks like you screwed the pooch on that first job."

The chief ranger entered the office. He had a round face and wore a moustache and goatee. His sideburns were flecked with gray. The name badge said Zamora. Clarence imagined on a better day, the man might look jolly.

"Tell me something good, Zammy," Ramirez said.

The park's top law enforcement officer shook his head. "My guys just radioed. They entered Freeman's house. The door was unsecured. No sign of him." The chief ranger paused.

"What else?" Ramirez asked.

"They said it smelled like a liquor store in there."

After Clarence had been dismissed, he made the short walk from the admin building to the Coe Visitor Center. Volunteers sat at tables in the lobby around the displays of the Everglades plants and animals. A banner outside the theater entrance announced, "Art in the Everglades." In smaller print, the sign said, "Sponsored by the Carroll Foundation."

The building had a small gallery alongside the theater. Art by former CARE artists adorned the walls. A pair of easels showcased paintings by Hezekiah Freeman. Clarence paused, captivated by the first. Heka had painted a sawgrass landscape at sunrise. The grass ran to the horizon, interrupted by a smattering of lone trees and the occasional bunch of cattails. Clarence had seen this view when he'd taken Nance out to Pahayokee. He'd also seen this painting on the internet.

Clarence found the difference between the digital image and the actual painting striking. Although the scene looked golden, he felt an indescribable darkness as he looked at the actual painting. Heka had somehow taken sunrise, the typical metaphor for hope and optimism, and stood it on its head. A despair came through the image that Clarence couldn't express in words. The dissonance between what he saw and what he felt was profound. Clarence knew he'd invite himself down to Heka's house another night to discuss how he'd achieved the effect with him.

The gloom in the second painting could not be overlooked. Osceola, the Seminole leader, surveyed the Everglades landscape. The unobstructed river of sawgrass, dotted with small islands of trees, appeared pristine. Yet again, Clarence could not escape the bleak feeling.

Depressed. Hell of a way to prepare to be the fill-in speaker.

Clarence tried to identify the source of sadness. As a modern viewer, he knew what Osceola could not even imagine—that the Everglades would be drained and shrunk to support agriculture and the development of cities. Clarence also knew Osceola had been captured after being tricked into attending a peace conference. The army's deceit had made headlines. Perhaps Clarence's own knowledge of the betrayal influenced his viewing. He didn't think so. It seemed to Clarence that even someone who didn't know the stories would sense the gloom in the paintings.

He hoped Heka would reveal his technique. Clarence also wanted to ask the man why he seemed to be switching styles. He thought about the abstract painting in the bungalow. Why would Heka change his process when the painter could achieve such masterful effects as these? The artist may have needed a new challenge. He thought about the many permutations Picasso had gone through. Clarence wanted to explore the artist's mind.

His phone rang. He quickly answered, hoping Heka had wandered home. "Hello."

"Hey, it's me. Checking to see how the seminar is going," Nance said.

"To hell. Heka's wandered off. You're officially no longer the biggest failure among the new guys."

"Sorry." Nance's voice sounded genuinely pained. "I know where they're hiring game wardens."

"I've been chewed out worse. This hardly registered. But it looks like I'll have a speaking part today. How is the orientation tour?"

She laughed. "I've seen the mountains. Did you know that the limestone beneath the Pine Rockland can rise to an elevation of eight feet?"

"Did you bring snowshoes?"

Nance chuckled again. "And we drove through Rock Reef Pass, elevation three feet."

"We went through there this morning."

She paused. "Oh, I didn't notice."

Clarence heard LaFleur in the background. "Tell him about the missiles."

"During the Cold War, the government built a secret missile base in the Everglades. We're going there next."

"But did he show you a barred owl?"

"You're the only one who's done that. And the owl was cute."

"No, the bird was the only one. And I am cute."

"Why did you have to go and spoil it by being an ass?"

"Job stress. I've got to give a speech."

"Need any help?"

"You kids just enjoy the field trip. I've got this. Tell LaFleur I want to see pictures of his missile." Clarence regretted the words as soon as they came out.

"Talk later," Nance said and hung up the phone.

Great, say something stupid, Clarence said to himself. The perfect way to prepare for a speech. He shoved the phone into his pocket and walked into the theater.

Except for the front row, most of the seats in the theater had been filled. Superintendent Ramirez stood onstage, speaking with an older woman wearing a well-tailored suit. Her hair looked the color of burnished silver and had been curled under just before touching the clavicle. The style looked timeless, seemingly at home in the Coliseum of Rome or the antebellum South. Without needing a name tag, Clarence knew her last name was Carroll. Everything about her said old Florida money.

Alongside her stood three men. Clarence could see two of them in profile. He judged them to be brothers. Although one more closely favored the mother, they shared similar features and coloring. The third man had his back to Clarence. Since Florida was football country, he judged this man to have been in the secondary. Clarence wondered how they'd have matched up.

Ramirez waved for him to join them.

"This is Clarence Jensen," he said.

"Johnson."

"He will be filling in until Hezekiah recovers."

"Cut the shit, Rico. We all know Hezekiah is sleeping off a binge. When he staggers out of whatever Homestead motel he's fallen asleep in, I hope he calls. One of your people can pick him up," the woman said. She turned to Clarence. A warm smile burst from her face, and she extended her hand. "Mr. Johnson, my name is Kathryne Carroll. I am very pleased to make your acquaintance. On behalf of the Carroll Foundation, I'd like to thank you so very much for filling in on such short notice."

Clarence noted that the gentle lilt of an accent appeared when she had downshifted from Ice Princess to Southern belle.

"I'm happy to help, ma'am."

"Please, call me Kathryne."

"I'm happy to help, Kathryne. But I'll be a pale substitute for Hezekiah Freeman."

The football player snorted a laugh. "He said pale substitute, get it?"

Kathryne Carroll frowned. "I'd like you to meet my sons. This is US Congressman Michael Carroll."

Clarence stuck out his hand. "It's a pleasure to meet you, sir."

"Everyone but my mother calls me Mike," the congressman said as he grabbed Clarence's outstretched hand.

Clarence noted that the congressman had a grip to match his square jawline.

Kathryne pivoted slightly. "And this is my son Matt."

"I look after the family business while my little brother saves the world," Matt said as they shook. Taller and broader than the congressman, he too had a firm grip. Perhaps Kathryne had taken them both to handshake class as schoolboys.

Kathryne's voice regained its earlier edge. "And this is Mr. Sucrito. He works for National Sugar."

"John Sucrito." The man thrust out his hand. He wore a Rolex wristwatch and a pinkie ring with a diamond. The ostentatious display of wealth stood out against the understated clothing of the Carrolls. New money versus old, Clarence assumed. "I didn't mean anything rude if Freeman is a friend of yours. It's just that he's black," Sucrito said.

"We got it," Clarence said before returning to the congressman. "I hope you're not missing a vote on park funding to be here."

"We'll keep the money coming. But I had to be back. Mother called. And a boy doesn't say no to his mother." He looked at her.

Kathryne smiled. "He'll be the next senator, you know. Then you'll never have to worry about the Everglades getting its budget."

"She forgets that the general election isn't until November."

The group laughed politely.

"My son will win," Kathryne said. "But in the meantime, I've arranged some help in case Hezekiah stays on his bender."

"He'll show," Clarence said. "I was with him last night. He wasn't drinking."

"Well, let us hope he's just delayed," she said.

"Probably stuck in traffic," Sucrito said.

No one laughed.

Superintendent Ramirez glanced at his phone. "We should start." He turned to Clarence. "We'll hold off announcing Hezekiah's absence until the last minute in case he shows. Be ready."

Clarence nodded.

Mike kissed Kathryne on the cheek. She, joined by Matt and John Sucrito, took a seat in the front row.

Ramirez walked to the middle of the stage. He introduced himself and welcomed everyone to the seminar. He mentioned the generosity of the Carroll Foundation three times in his remarks. Clarence glanced at Kathryne. Her face retained the slight beatific smile. Clarence had seen the smile on the paintings of angels. It never wavered. She was, he assumed, accustomed to fawning.

"And although the National Park Service stands outside of the political arena, let me introduce a longtime friend of the Everglades. A man who hopes to take that support to the United States Senate." Here, Ramirez paused and winked. The crowd tittered. No one doubted how he would be voting. "Ladies and gentlemen, Mr. Michael Carroll."

Representative Carroll walked onstage to hearty applause from the audience. He waved to the group and thanked the superintendent before accepting the microphone. Like his brother, he showed perfect teeth, a healthy tan, and a body that demonstrated proof of good genes and a staff of personal trainers. Clarence hoped the family would tip well at the factory where they stamped out politicians. This guy had received the deluxe package.

"I'm not here today as a candidate for office but as a proud son. A son proud of his mother." Here, he paused for the inevitable applause. "And a proud son of the state of Florida." He waited again. "My family has lived in this area for generations. And our respect for this land and its inhabitants remains as strong as ever. That's why my campaign adopted the slogan, 'Old Florida, New Ideas.'"

The crowd applauded again.

The congressman began wrapping up his remarks. Clarence looked at the Carrolls. Mom's smile had moved from beatific to full wattage. Matt, meanwhile, checked messages on his phone. In his peripheral vision, Clarence saw a few late arrivals streaming into the auditorium. They might be able to find seats when he started talking.

Superintendent Ramirez glanced at the theater door before turning to him. "I'd like to introduce a special guest, Clarence Johnson of the National Park Service."

Applause greeted him as Clarence walked to center stage. Everyone here was a fan of the national parks. He thanked the superintendent before turning to the audience. "I have some bad news. Hezekiah Freeman, the resident CARE artist, cannot be here this afternoon. He's ill. But we hope he'll recover quickly and be with us tomorrow."

The audience groaned.

"Although I can't replace him, I've been asked to talk a little bit about art in and around the Everglades." A few people got up and exited. Apparently, hearing Clarence wasn't worth fighting Miami rush hour.

Clarence smiled at those who remained. "Let's begin at the beginning. The Spanish explorer, Ponce de León, stepped foot on what we now call Florida at St. Augustine in the year 1512. A rival French expedition came to north Florida in the 1560s. That expedition brought the first artist to work in Florida. Jacques Le Moyne de Morgues. Le Moyne began drawing native Floridians, the Timucua. To give context, that was around the time when Michelangelo's design for the dome of St. Peter's in Rome began construction. Titian and Brueghel the Elder also worked around this time."

A few more people moved toward the exit.

"But to call Le Moyne the first artist is to do an injustice."

One man stopped at the door and looked back.

"The Calusa people inhabited the area around us. Wooden masks, tablets, and carved shells have been recovered and have been scientifically dated from the eighth to the sixteenth century. Again, for context, they were creating representational art while European art was still in its infancy. Although to be fair, the Book of Kells was produced during this early period."

The man sat down.

Clarence continued to talk, bringing the audience forward. "But we must view art in a regional context. Some voices, like the Calusa, are underrepresented because they didn't get to write the history. Others, as we know, were enslaved. That doesn't mean that slaves didn't have artists. Dave Drake, an artist from Edgefield, South Carolina, was the region's most famous. Many know him as Dave the Potter.

"Why do we know Dave? Because Dave was literate at a time when it was illegal for a slave to read. And he risked his life by marking some of his pottery with verses or his signature. These acts of protest in the name of civil rights have made Dave Drake's pottery extremely valuable, setting records at auction for American pottery."

Clarence skimmed through a few more names, including John James Audubon and the Highwaymen, a group of African American artists who often sold their work along the highway beginning in the 1940s. He paused and surveyed the crowd. "A thousand years in an hour. Someone needs a break. Come back in ten minutes."

Some in the audience laughed. Most applauded briefly before filing out of the theater.

Clarence leaned against the podium and closed his eyes. He had six hundred seconds to figure out what he might say next.

"You need some help, Nasty Man?"

He opened his eyes. Mae stood before him, her smile as blindingly white as he remembered from the stage. Today, she wore drawstring khaki pants and a blue blazer over a brown T-shirt. Across the shirt was written, "You can't have a heart without ART." Mae's paint-spattered canvas shoes squeaked on the floor of the theater. Her eyes, he noted, looked bigger than they did last night, and her pupils dilated.

Mae watched his eyes. "Nasty Man." She delivered her spoken words higher than her singing register.

"I'm just thinking," he said. "You can't have a heart without 'he,' either. You think anybody makes a pro-male line of T-shirts like that?"

"I think you'd be better off thinking about what you'll say next. You gonna talk to these folks about the future? You already covered the whole past."

John Sucrito joined the group. His eyes roamed Mae's front, centering on her chest. "It's always good to see you, Mae." His tongue touched his top lip.

"Love to catch up, John. But Mr. Johnson and I have to talk." As she spoke, she crossed her arms over her chest.

"I won't bother you, then. Just wanted to check out an old friend." Sucrito turned and walked back to his seat.

"Went to high school with him," Mae said.

"You go to school with Matt or Mike?"

She shook her head. "Too old. And they're private schoolers, anyway."

"What are you doing here?"

Mae ran her fingers through her braids. She still had green paint on her right knuckles. "I'm a painter. I hear there's talk about art going on." She paused and smiled. "Dame Carroll called. She told me to get over here. You don't say no to Dame Carroll." She smiled again. "I grabbed my jacket and hauled ass."

"What do you think I should do?" he asked.

"Let me talk for a bit." Mae giggled at his discomfort.

"I see you two have met." Kathryne Carroll walked up to them with Matt in her wake. She leaned forward and air-kissed Mae's right cheek. "Thank you for coming, dear."

Clarence saw that Mae, too, got the beatific smile.

"What do you want me to do?" Mae asked.

Kathryne waved her arm out over the seats, which were slowly refilling. "Talk to them about local art. Mr. Johnson has adequately covered the history of the region. But I wanted this event to draw attention to what occurred locally."

Mae nodded. She walked outside the theater. When Mae returned, she had knotted the tails of the button-down across her stomach. Mae held one of Heka's paintings by the picture wire in her right hand. She dragged the easel with her left hand. Under her arm, she carried something wrapped in a trash bag. Alongside the stage, Clarence helped her erect the easel. Mae turned to face the crowd. Clarence watched her transform into the singer he'd seen on stage. "I know many of y'all came here to listen to Hezekiah Freeman talk about art."

The audience nodded.

"Well, as you've heard, he's sick and can't be here."

The crowd acknowledged this fact with a low grumble.

"But I'm Mae Jefferson, and I'm his goddaughter. I've known the man my entire life. And since he's not here to give you his bullshit, let's talk about him."

Her energy and profanity brought the room to life. The crowd whooped and applauded.

Mae worked the small room like a cabaret, walking back and forth across the stage. "When you look at this painting, what do you see?"

"Sawgrass, Everglades, sunlight," came back from the audience.

Mae acknowledged each comment. "Let's ask our expert. Clarence Johnson, what do you see when you look at this painting?"

Clarence looked briefly at the scene. He found that his earlier feelings had not altered. "The natural setting should bring me joy. But the piece saddens me for reasons I cannot put my finger on."

Mae's eyes roamed the crowd, and her voice dropped to a stage whisper. "Why ever would this man, a Park Service employee, feel sad gazing upon the Everglades?" She pointed to a man in the audience. "Do you see any alligators?"

He shook his head.

She pivoted to a woman in the back. "What about a Burmese python? The snakes that are eating everything. Do you see any of those?"

"No," the woman shouted.

Mae stood beside the painting. "There is nothing gloomy about this picture. Yet, Mr. Johnson says it depresses him. Who else feels the way Ranger Johnson does?"

About half the room raised their hands.

"I agree the picture is sad. And we need to figure out why. Let's look first at Hezekiah. Like most black folk in this country, he grew up knowing he has slave roots. He is acutely aware that his earliest elders did not choose their path in this society. Their lot, occasionally, brings him down, makes him feel the weight of the past. You don't have to be black to understand. I imagine Jews, when they think about the Holocaust, feel the same way."

Heads nodded in agreement.

"Heka has talent. He moved to Miami and made good money as an artist. Then, he squandered that money, becoming a prisoner of alcohol and drugs. He felt himself falling into a life where he lost his agency. Where he lost the ability to choose his path in society." Mae interlocked her hands. "Maybe he saw the link between his life and that of his ancestors, I don't know." She paused and looked out over the audience. "What I do know is that one day, his heart stopped. The drugs and the lifestyle killed him for a time. But God wasn't finished with Hezekiah Freeman. Like Lazarus, he raised him up. And when my godfather awoke from the dead, Hezekiah was a changed man. He didn't need drugs. He didn't fear death. Hezekiah

Freeman emerged from that moment with a calling. He began painting for those who didn't have a voice—for the environment and the downtrodden. For everything and everyone who could not speak for themselves, Hezekiah Freeman paints. He has a pulpit, and it is his art. He likes to call it his brush with death."

"Brush with death," Clarence repeated to himself and made a quick note.

"Now we know that the Comprehensive Everglades Restoration Plan is supposed to fix the problems here in our slow-moving river. But we also know that big agricultural companies, particularly sugar producers, want to get water, too. Of course, real estate developers want their share. Have y'all ever seen what a golf course looks like if you don't water it? And the Everglades are left with what's left over. Too little water and too much pollution. Heka was afraid for the Everglades, and he gave them a voice with his art. He made the picture depressing and wasn't scared of who he might make angry. He'd been dead. He didn't have to be afraid."

Like a sultry lounge singer, she had the audience leaning forward in their chairs, wanting more.

"I don't care if you can draw or not. I want everyone to go outside. Pick someplace in the Everglades and sketch or paint a scene. If you see joy, then paint joy. If you see sadness, draw depression. You don't have to agree with Hezekiah." She put her hands on her hips. "'Cause that old man didn't show up to argue with you."

Everyone laughed.

Mae pulled Heka's picture down. Carefully, she leaned it against the wall, still facing the audience. Then she pulled a canvas from the trash bag and placed it on the easel. "This is one of my paintings. I've got the landscape, same as Heka. Can y'all see the 'glades in decline'?"

Heads nodded.

"This ain't church. Let me hear you."

A chorus of agreement came from the room.

Mae nodded and waved her hand near a tree in the upper corner of the painting. A menacing creature gripped the branches "While Heka went subtle, hinting at sadness, I'm in your face. Anybody recognize this?" She paused and waited.

The crowd murmured. No one offered an opinion.

"Heka was a Miami guy," Mae said. "I grew up in Homestead, surrounded by the native folktales of the Miccosukee. This is the stikini—the man owl—some might call it a vampire. The stikini grows more powerful the more evil it brings to the world. What are the sources of evil in this swampy world we call the Everglades?" She paused and let the audience compare the two paintings. "Think about the threats to nature and in nature. When we reconvene tomorrow, we'll talk about what you saw. And we'll consider in more technical detail how the artist achieved the desired effect in the case of this painting." Mae pointed again to Heka's picture of the sawgrass. "Now get out there," she ordered.

People immediately stood and began filing out of the room.

Clarence stood alongside her. "You know how to work a room on stage."

She smiled and giggled. The voice had returned to the higher pitch.

John Sucrito strode toward them. "You didn't have to join the chorus who want to blame the sugar farmers for everything wrong with Florida."

Mae crossed her arms over her chest again and pushed out her chin. "I said what Hezekiah believes." She looked at Clarence and then locked eyes with Sucrito. "If I'd have given them my full opinion, you'd have really hated it."

"My farm helped sponsor this seminar. Remember that."

"The farm you manage," Mae said. "You own as much of it as I do." She smiled as Sucrito stomped away. She pivoted back to Clarence.

The woman knew how to handle herself. "Mae Jefferson," Clarence said. "We didn't get formally introduced last night."

"Now you know me. And my godfather. And you met my daddy."

Clarence thought for a moment. Then his eyes widened. "Joe Bob Jefferson."

Mae nodded.

"He's…"

"A white guy. It happens."

Clarence had almost said that Joe Bob was the ugliest man he'd ever met. He was amazed that he could father a daughter with anyone who looked like Mae. He decided to exercise his right to remain silent.

"Daddy always says everybody is the same color with the lights off."

"Your father is..." Clarence struggled to find a good descriptor.

"I know what my daddy is."

Neither of them spoke.

"What should we do now?" Mae asked, breaking the silence.

"Do you want to get something to eat? We can discuss tomorrow's program. We need a backup plan in case Heka stays gone."

"I'd love to get food." Mae smiled and moved slightly closer.

"I'll drive. You shouldn't be behind the wheel."

Mae pushed her lower lip out in a pout. "It was just a gummy. No big deal."

"Big enough."

Nance entered the auditorium and came straight to Clarence. Superintendent Ramirez followed. He had his head down and looked shaken.

"You're back sooner than I thought..." Clarence stopped talking when he saw the expression on her face.

Nance turned to Mae. "You're the fill-in speaker. Johnson will have to meet you tomorrow. I need him."

"But we were going to get food," Mae said, her words delivered in a singsong voice.

"Mae shouldn't be driving," Clarence said.

Nance turned to Ramirez. "Can you get someone to give this woman a ride? She sounds wasted." Nance grabbed Clarence's arm. "You. With me, now." Her tone allowed for no argument as she pulled him out of the theater.

"What's the emergency?" Clarence asked.

"They found Hezekiah Freeman. He's dead."

11

April 1851

William felt like he was staring into the pit of hell.

The roaring fire threw eerie shadows across the earth as the mousy-voiced man led them back into the encampment. Everyone he knew had been tied to the ground. Myrna's pot had been knocked over and lay on its side. The deep-voiced man's skin reflected orange in the light of the flames.

The mousy-voiced man yanked on the rope coiled around his neck and Myrna's. He pulled them forward. He kicked William hard just below the knee. The leg buckled, and William collapsed to the ground. The man turned to Myrna and drew back his leg. "Sit," he said. She, too, dropped to the ground.

He encircled the rope around the big tree that Myrna said had cried blood. He pulled it tight. Myrna choked.

"Don't kill them," the deep-voiced man said, "they's valuable." He patted the two canvas packs he'd carried from their canoe. "Sit down, Paul."

"Just don't want none of our property running off." Paul, the squeaky-voiced man, took shorter pieces of rope and tied their hands, first William's and then Myrna's. He walked a slow circle, checking the bindings on Eli and Josiah. He took a long piece of rope, coiled it in his hand, and tossed it across the overhanging branch of a gumbo limbo tree. The man grabbed both ends of the rope and pulled it back and forth. The rope whined as it scraped across the bark. "See this rope?" the man said in his squeaking tone. "If'n anybody tries to get loose, I'm gonna hang the boy right here. You're gonna watch him kick, listen to him gasp his last." His eyes moved from William to Myrna. "Don't think I won't."

William saw Myrna push her bound body closer to Samuel.

"Just don't make no trouble, and everything will be fine," the squeaking voice said, settling on the ground next to the other man. He let out a long, contented sigh and then farted.

"Comfortable?" the deep-voiced man asked.

"Yep, I am, Jeb," Paul said. "Our work is done. We caught what we was looking for. I'm just gonna sit back, relax, and think about spending my money. How about you, Jeb? I reckon you're feeling pretty settled yourself."

Jeb shook his head. "Paul, we still got to get all this back out of this swamp." He jerked his head toward the fugitive slaves.

Paul dug around in his rucksack. He drew out a slab of smoked beef, sliced off two pieces with his knife, and handed one to Jeb. Then, Paul produced a whiskey bottle. "That is tomorrow's problem." He waggled the bottle in front of Jeb's face. "I've been saving this. But I think tonight calls for a celebration. How about you?"

Jeb smiled.

Paul unstoppered the bottle and took a long pull. Then, he handed the whiskey to Jeb. They passed the bottle back and forth for a time without either man speaking.

Paul exhaled. "It ain't right."

Jeb turned and blinked twice. "What ain't right?"

Paul waved the bottle at the captured slaves. "This. Us. Ain't none of it right. We out here, getting all ate up by bugs, risking our lives to capture these curs in this godforsaken swamp."

"This place ain't all that bad."

"There ain't no place worse on earth," Paul said, waving the bottle around in a circle. "That's why only them Indians who don't know no better live here."

"I sometimes think a man could make a nice life out here if a body was willing to work." Jeb gazed past the fire out into the darkness surrounding him.

"Work, that's just what I'm talking about," Paul said. "We do all the work, and what happens? We bring them back. Mr. Foley collects the bounty, and we get paid shit."

The other man shifted his focus and stared into the fire. "I'll tell you what I tell my boy. That's just the way of the world."

"Why?"

"It just is. Think about the railroads. Men get blown up and run over, killed every day to lay them tracks. Then, the railroad comes along and makes some men richer than Midas. Do you think that man beating the rocks with a hammer sees that money? Same with us."

"It ain't no sense," Paul said. He drained the whiskey and dropped the empty bottle on the ground. "Makes no sense."

Jeb laughed. "When you get to be king, I want you to remember to make them things right."

"Damn right I will."

Jeb laughed again.

"Are you laughing at me?" Paul turned to Jeb, his eyes yellow in the firelight.

"The idea of you being king." Jeb chuckled again.

"Don't laugh at me."

"But it's funny."

"Don't laugh at me," Paul shouted. He threw his body at the other man and began to punch. Jeb pushed him back hard. Paul rolled across the ground, his back landing on the red embers. He cried in pain and jumped to his feet. Drawing his knife, he dived back onto Jeb, stabbing wildly. Jeb made short guttural laughs. Paul stabbed with fury. He pulled back and held up his knife, the blade dripping with blood. "Who says I can't be king?"

William heard short gasps from the deep-voiced man before one long final exhale. Beside him, he heard Myrna crying.

Paul turned on them. "Tell that cur to shut up." He pointed the knife at William. Myrna gasped. William heard her take a deep breath and hold it, trying desperately to make no sound.

Paul paced in front of the fire. "Can't kill no white man." He knelt and wiped his blade on Jeb's pant leg. "I didn't mean nothing," he said to the dead man. "But I told you not to laugh at me." He stood and paced again. "Can't kill no white man." He stopped moving. "I got to get rid of the body."

Paul grabbed Jeb's shirt collar and began to slowly drag him across the ground. After a few feet, he stopped and sat down, exhausted. He looked at the man. "Why'd you have to go and laugh at me? Can't kill no white man." Paul sat quietly. Then he stood and looked at William. He pointed the knife. "You're gonna help me carry him." Paul walked to the gumbo limbo limb. He quickly tied a loop in one end of the rope and strode to where Samuel sat, huddled against his mother. The slave hunter jerked him away. "No," Myrna cried and reached out her bound hands as he pulled the boy away from her. He dragged Samuel to the gumbo limbo and dropped the noose over the boy's neck. "Grab ahold of the rope."

Samuel clutched the noose.

The slave hunter hoisted him off the ground. Samuel's feet kicked in the air. Raspy sounds of choking came from his throat.

"Please," William begged. Myrna wailed.

"Y'all shut up and listen," Paul shouted to be heard over their pleas. "I don't know how long him holding the rope will keep the boy from choking, so we best hurry." He looked at William, the yellow eyes full of menace. "I'm going to take the rope off you so you can help me carry this body to that pond back there. One of those gators will have old Jeb for dinner, and no one will know what happened here." He paused and pointed behind him. Samuel gasped for air. "You might use that opportunity to fight me. But I reckon with your hands tied, even if you win, the boy will be dead before you can wrestle me down and get back here. So I expect no trouble, you hear?"

William nodded.

Holding the knifepoint against William's back, the slave hunter loosened the rope around his neck. William raced to Jeb's feet and lifted the man's legs.

Paul followed behind him. "You sure can hurry when you want to." He picked up the dead man by his shirt. Together, they carried him through the trees to the edge of a shallow pond.

Jeb's body splashed when he hit the water. He lay partially submerged.

"Don't matter," Paul said, "gators will find him soon enough."

"We got to get my boy," William said.

The yellow eyes flared. "Don't tell me what to do. I'm the king on this island." The man turned and strolled back to the encampment.

Even in the weak light of the fire, William could see that Samuel's color was ashen, the gasps weaker. His bound hands encircled Samuel's hips. William lifted the boy up, taking the pressure off his neck. He could hear Samuel's breathing ease. A few moments later, Paul appeared out of the trees. He untied the rope and lowered Samuel. "Had to piss."

William carried the boy to Myrna and gently laid him down. The breath, although still raspy, slowly eased. He stroked the boy's hair. Then William sat heavily on the ground. He said nothing as Paul looped the rope back over his neck and, again, tied him to the tree.

"You coulda set us free," Eli hissed.

William ignored him.

Paul dropped to the ground. He stared into the fire, frowning.

"You trying to reckon how you gonna be able to do all this?" William asked.

"I didn't say that you could speak." Paul raised his fist.

William ignored the implied threat. Although the man might hit him, he'd been beaten before and would be again. He knew the slave hunter wouldn't seriously injure him. The slave hunter needed William to walk out of the Everglades. "Five slaves, one a woman and another a boy. They can't walk through the muck. How can one man get them all back to this Mr. Foley?"

"I'll do it. I'll do it," Paul screamed into the night. "You just watch me. I'll do it."

"If'n you didn't have that woman and the boy, you could move faster through the muck and water."

"We all going back," Myrna said. "Samuel and me ain't gonna separate from you."

"If'n you didn't have them slowing you down, wouldn't things be easier?" William asked again, ignoring his wife.

Paul looked at him. "You think maybe I should kill 'em. That's what you want?"

"I think you should let them go," William said. "That way, they won't be no rope around your neck dragging you down."

"We ain't leaving you, William," Myrna said.

"Hush," William commanded. "I'm talking to this man here."

Beads of sweat dotted Paul's brow. He dragged a hand across his forehead. The slave hunter stood and took a step to find his balance. "I ain't just letting no slaves go."

"How much you gonna get for bringing us back?"

The man spit on the ground. "I ain't gonna get shit." The man jumped up and stomped around the fire. "Why you talking like this, anyway? You know when you get back to the plantation, they likely to cut off a couple of your toes. That way you can stand to work but can't run away no more."

Myrna began crying.

"I want my boy to live as a free man. If it takes all the toes, I'll give 'em." William paused, then he pointed at Myrna and Samuel. "What if you could make some money for these two? Collect the bounty on three field hands and let the mother and child go. You'd have money in your pocket, and your boss would still be happy."

"Where would you get money?"

"We need that for the boat," Myrna said.

"Won't be no boat if we go to the plantation." William looked at Paul. "If I could find some silver, some real money, would you do it?"

Paul licked his lips. Then he drew his knife. "Maybe I just take your money. What are you gonna do about it?"

William shook his head. "I can't stop you. But we'll tell your Mr. Foley that you killed Jeb. Murdered his man in cold blood. What do you s'pose Mr. Foley or Jeb's family will do when they hear that?"

Paul frowned. William could see the thoughts of Jeb's family taking revenge playing out in his mind. Paul's eyes ran over the group.

"You can't kill us to keep us quiet. Then you get nothing." William kept his voice calm. He saw the slave hunter looking at him, silently asking him what to do. Despite the ropes around his neck and hands, William felt a surge of power. He'd never before spoken to a white man like he talked to

Paul. William cocked his head to Eli and Josiah. "These men know I'd buy freedom for all of us if'n I had the money. But I don't. I got enough for the woman and the boy. What do you say?"

"What do we do?"

"First thing we do is wait until morning. Myrna can't leave at night. You'll get your money, and she'll be on her way."

The slave hunter frowned. William thought he might need to demonstrate that he was in charge. Paul opened his mouth and then closed it again. "I'm a light sleeper," he said. "Anybody tries anything, I hang the boy." He sat back down and promptly fell asleep. His snores, William discovered, proved deeper than his voice.

"There's got to be another way," Myrna whispered.

"Go to sleep, woman. You got a hard journey ahead of you tomorrow." William sat back and stared into the darkness.

He was still sitting when the sun crawled over the horizon. William nudged Samuel awake and called the boy over to him. "You leaving this morning. Promise me you'll help your mama."

The sleepy boy nodded.

"You see the sun, Samuel?"

Another nod.

"In the morning, it rises in the east. That's the way you want to travel. In the morning, you find the sun. Then, pick a landmark on the horizon, a tree. Something you can see from a distance. You help your mama steer the boat that way. Stay quiet and hidden when you get to the ocean until you see a boat."

"Any boat?"

William shook his head. "Your mama will know what to look for. She'll tell you the right boat." He paused and blinked several times. "And when you get to Red Bay, you remember everything. I need you to tell me all about it when I see you again."

"Soon?"

William, again, shook his head. "Gonna be a long time coming. But you never forget I love you."

Samuel bent over and hugged his father. William patted him gently with his bound hands.

"Shit, my head." Paul's complaining interrupted them.

The slave hunter dragged himself upright and rubbed his face. He swished his mouth with water and spat it out. Bloodshot, unfocused eyes looked at William.

"You still want to make some money?" William asked.

Paul looked at Myrna and then to Samuel. Finally, he nodded.

William pointed his chin toward the pack of the dead man. "First, you go through Jeb's pack. You take out anything he's carrying that you ain't already got. The stuff you don't need, Myrna and Samuel get to keep. I am gonna give you the money. They take one of the canoes and paddle away. When they is out of sight, I'll not make no trouble on the trip back to the plantation."

"Let me see the money."

"No," Myrna said.

"It's the only thing to do," William said. "I got to get to my canoe."

"I ain't letting you go."

"Keep the rope around my neck, but I've got to get to the canoe."

The man studied William's face. He drew his knife and approached. "You do one thing I don't like, and I'll gut you like a fish." He pointed the knife toward the fire. "You seen me kill a man. You know I will."

William nodded, his face serene.

Paul tightened the ropes. Grabbing one end of the leash, he followed William to the hammock's edge. "I carved myself a hidey-hole in this here dugout." He reached inside. Paul, he saw, pointed the knife and clutched tightly at the rope, preparing for trickery. Moving slowly, William straightened up and showed him a handful of small, flat, round pieces of silver.

Paul's eyes widened. "Them's not coins."

"But they all silver."

"Where'd you get them?"

"Sometimes a spoon maybe gets lost in the house. Myrna finds it. I melted them in the pottery furnace. These coins is easier to carry."

"How'd you hide them?"

William looked down and said nothing.

"You carried them back there?" Paul's face took on a look of disgust.

"That's why I made them round. Didn't want no edges."

"Well, I ain't taking them till they is washed." Paul led William back to the encampment. The slave hunter pointed his knife at Myrna's pot. "Scrub them in that."

William stooped and uprighted the cooking pot. The remains of soup sloshed in the bottom. He dropped the coins inside. They rattled together as William cleaned them. He pulled out his hands and shook the silver in the air to dry. He opened his palms and showed Paul the money. "They's clean."

"Lay them on the ground." Paul pointed with the knife to a rock. William complied, stacking the silver pieces. Paul shifted the blade tip, pointing William back to his spot on the ground. The runaway slave retook his place. Paul quickly secured him to the tree. The slave hunter scooped up the silver. He held the pile in his hand and weighed it. Paul poured the pieces from his right hand to his left.

"They's not quite thirty," William said.

Paul did not appear to catch the reference. He grunted a laugh and dropped the coins into his pocket. Paul turned to Jeb's pack and dumped the contents on the ground. He tossed aside the man's clothes. He reached for the dead man's knife.

"Let Myrna keep that," William said.

"I ain't letting her have no knife to stick in my back."

"You got a knife. She and the boy is gonna need it. She won't hurt you, I promise." William turned and looked at his wife. "Will you."

"No, I won't," she answered after a long moment.

Paul dropped the knife. Instead, he collected a small hand axe and a mirror. The slave hunter jumped in the air. When he landed, the silver in his pocket jingled. Paul smiled.

"You gonna get caught if you show up with that money, you know," William said.

The slave hunter's eyes narrowed.

"You show up with a pocket full of silver and start showing it around, someone is going to get suspicious that you either robbed Jeb or sold off a couple of captured slaves. How you gonna explain all that money?"

Paul frowned.

"Can you find this hammock again?"

"I'm a tracker, ain't I?"

"If you can find this island again, put that money in Myrna's pot. Hide the pot in one of those holes in the rock. Cover it with branches, but remember where you put it. Come get the money at a different time. Get it when people have stopped associating you with that man's death or this slave hunting."

Paul stood in the early morning light, frowning as he thought. Then, he nodded and smiled. He collected the pot and walked off into the woods.

Myrna watched her pot disappear into the trees. Tears ran down her face.

"You don't need that old thing. In a couple of days, you'll be at Red Bay. They'll have all the pots you need."

Paul returned empty-handed. He walked to Myrna and drew his knife. He sliced through the ropes that bound her.

She rushed to William and hugged him.

"Get out of here before I change my mind," Paul said. He kept his knife drawn and never looked away from her.

William pushed her away. "Go along. For the boy. I'll see you again in a golden city."

Myrna backed away from him slowly. Then she swallowed and took a deep, ragged breath. Myrna turned and looked at Paul, her eyes full of hate. She moved quickly, gathering up Jeb's spare shirt and the knife. She slipped the shirt over her arms and looked for a place to tuck away the knife.

"Samuel can carry it. He's the man now," William said.

Myrna handed the blade to her son. Samuel stretched to his full height when he accepted it. Taking his hand, Myrna led him to Jeb's canoe. She paused, spat, and moved to the partial dugout that had carried them this far.

William watched them float through the golden sawgrass of morning until they disappeared from sight. He smiled. Myrna had left safely, and Samuel would, William prayed, grow up to be a free man.

12

April 8th

They drove the short distance to a small pond near the employee residential area. Clarence kept quiet; he didn't pepper Nance with questions. She would tell him when she knew something.

As if on cue, Nance began speaking. "We were nearly back to park headquarters when I got the call. The wife of one of the maintenance guys found him. She is a bird-watcher. She's got a usual spot near the Royal Palm Visitor Center she likes to go to in the morning. Stopped by this pond when she got home." Nance thumbed through her phone. "Apparently, she's hoping to see a black rail. Cross it off her life list."

"She didn't see the bird," Clarence said.

She shook her head. "Found Hezekiah…"

"Heka. He liked people to call him Heka. The name his granddaughter gave him."

"She found Heka Freeman lying facedown at the water's edge. She turned him over. The woman said she felt for a pulse, but there was no bringing him back. A protection ranger has her writing a statement at the admin building."

"Where's the body?"

"Emergency services would be picking him up. They'll take him to the medical examiner for Miami-Dade County. They won't touch the scene until we get there. I've asked Tom to make sure they hold in place."

"LaFleur. Have we got a drug angle?"

Nance shook her head as she parked. "Not that I know of. But he was available and had a badge. I needed personnel, and he agreed to help."

"Get another dinner out of it?"

Nance climbed out of the SUV, retrieved a camera from the back, and walked to the ambulance. Clarence followed. "I've been reassigned," she said. "Homicide takes precedence. No longer on poacher patrol."

"The tree snails are grieving."

"I saw one," she said.

"One what?"

"A tree snail. Tom showed me the Gumbo Limbo Trail. You step off the path from bright sunshine into shade. It looks like jungle. The temperature dropped, and the humidity climbed. They say it was even more amazing before Hurricane Andrew. Still, I thought I'd stepped into a Tarzan movie set."

Clarence tapped his fists against his chest.

"Gumbo limbo trees have red bark that peels off regularly. The locals jokingly call them the tourist tree." She held her arm horizontally to the ground. "I passed under a limb hanging over the trail. I turned and looked up. A big white snail with a black belt running down the whole body."

"I hope you didn't steal it."

Nance shook her head. "I named him Karate and left him stuck to the tree branch."

Clarence stopped and narrowed his eyes. "The black belt."

He nodded and resumed walking.

"You can't corner the market on bad jokes." Nance exhaled. "It was a good morning."

"I'm sure Heka is sorry he spoiled it."

At the ambulance, LaFleur nodded to Clarence. The paramedic thrust an e-cigarette into his pocket.

"I appreciate you protecting my scene, Agent LaFleur," Nance said.

"Freed the ranger up to take the reporting party's statement," he said.

The three of them made their way through the trees to the pond. Clarence kept his head down, careful to avoid stepping on anything that might prove to be evidence. The group stopped well short of the body. At the edge of the water, Heka lay covered by a sheet. Clarence's eyes swept the area around the body. Beside him, he felt Nance doing the same. He noted the trampled grass and divots in the dirt.

"What's changed?" Nance asked LaFleur.

"The witness who found the body turned him over to try and save the guy. When the responding ranger arrived, he verified the man was dead." LaFleur pointed to footprints. "He said those were his. He radioed in the cavalry and sat on the body until I relieved him. The ranger drove the woman over to take her statement. They know each other. She wanted to have a familiar face. Pretty shaken up."

Nance nodded. "Anything else?"

LaFleur shook his head. "Nobody has come to watch. We've been quiet. I've kept my eye on that pond. Don't know what's swimming in there, and I didn't want some alligator taking your body away. When the ambulance arrived, they gave me a sheet to cover the body."

Clarence knelt and appraised the crime scene from a different angle. Then he stood and looked back toward Heka's bungalow. He heard the rustle of grass and felt Nance beside him. Clarence liked knowing she was there even if the reason was a murder. "Pretty secluded, even though it's not that far. Can't see any of the houses from here," Clarence said.

"Makes it a good place for that bird."

"The black rail?"

"Why would he walk down here in the middle of the night?"

"Who said he came voluntarily?" As he spoke, Clarence pulled out his cell phone and snapped photographs in all directions. He quickly sketched the pond and surrounding area using a small pad he carried in his breast pocket.

Nance, meanwhile, leveled her camera and began shooting pictures of the same area.

"Probably miss PPT about now," Clarence said. PPT had been Nance's nickname for the Yellowstone ranger who often doubled as her crime scene officer.

"I miss everybody." She turned and photographed the pond and the body.

When Clarence felt satisfied that he'd observed everything he might from a distance, he turned to Nance. She looked at him and nodded. Clarence instinctively shoved his hands into his pockets. Although, here, in the middle of the outdoors, the likelihood he'd further contaminate the crime scene was small, he didn't want to accidentally touch something. As she walked, Nance snapped on a pair of latex gloves.

She turned suddenly. "You're going to have to stay back, Tom. Essential personnel only."

LaFleur frowned. He looked at Clarence.

Nance saw the glance. "He's my…"

"I'm her intern," Clarence said and shrugged. "Excellent learning opportunity."

She shook her head. "I really don't have time for this. Wait here," she said to LaFleur and resumed walking toward Heka's body. The path to the water's edge proved surprisingly rough. Although flat, small lumps of white limestone popped up at irregular intervals, making the route clumsy.

Clarence picked his way, scanning the dry ground. "If the rains had started earlier, we might have gotten better footprints."

"Or we might be standing here soaked, with no hope of recovering any trace evidence." Nance lifted her head and looked out at the stained water. "When we were at the ponds, the most surprising thing was the clarity of the water. It's even more crystal than Yellowstone. You could see the fish and the plants. So much lies below the surface."

"Much below the surface," Clarence repeated. "That's always the way."

Nance turned and looked at him. She seemed to expect him to expound further.

"If there's any evidence to be had in that pond, we'll just have to solve the case without it. I'm not diving."

"Afraid of an alligator?" she asked.

"Very."

"Maybe you're not just some dumb jock, after all." Nance turned her attention back to the body. Slowly, she lifted the sheet.

Heka lay on his back, sightless eyes staring at the blue sky above. His mouth sat partially open, baring teeth stained with age. The arms had drawn up in a pugilistic pose. The legs lay crossed, with the right overlaying the left. Dried mud clung to his toes. Heka's unfastened pants rode low, exposing boxers. The investigators studied the body in silence. Then Nance stood and focused her camera. Clarence backed away and continued his examination from a distance.

She moved to his side and pointed her camera. "Looks ready to fight."

"But look at the hands. No defensive wounds. If Heka fought, there would be marks."

Nance nodded and leaned down to capture an image of his right and left hands. She pointed to a small abrasion on the underside of his left wrist. She stood. "Can you smell that?"

Clarence shook his head. "Nothing besides the alcohol."

"Don't be an ass."

"It's part of my masculine charm."

"You really need to read better relationship books," Nance said as she moved to view the body from a different angle.

Clarence pointed to white granules clinging to Heka's shirt.

Nance zoomed in with her lens. She lowered the camera. "Cocaine?"

"That's what it looks like."

"We've got an expert." She waved LaFleur into the crime scene. Nance pointed at the shirt. "What do you think?"

LaFleur stooped and looked. He nodded. "Cocaine."

"I thought you guys always touched it to your tongue and tasted it before making such a bold declaration," Clarence said.

"Only when trying to get the purity assessed to the fourth decimal." LaFleur sniffed. "Seems like somebody had a party."

Clarence wanted to disagree. He'd left the man perfectly sober. But he couldn't deny the evidence in front of his eyes and nose.

The three studied the scene until everyone felt satisfied that nothing more would be gleaned. Nance signaled the ambulance driver to collect the body. She scratched her finger across his laptop, signing his required electronic forms. Clarence helped the man load Heka's body into a body bag and transport him to the ambulance. Pallbearer seemed the last thing he might do for the man. Clarence wished he'd had the chance to know him better.

When the body had been loaded, he rejoined Nance. She had moved to Heka's bungalow. Before entering, he slipped paper shoe protectors over his boots. He stepped into the kitchen and promptly stopped.

"See something?" Nance asked.

He pointed at the floor. "Tripod's water bowl. Heka didn't want my dog to be thirsty."

"If you don't want to be here—" she began.

"I'm not leaving," Clarence said, the anger apparent.

She nodded. "Then be useful. You were the last known person inside. What's different?"

Clarence made a slow turn around the small kitchen. The coffee cups from their last meeting sat upside down on the drying rack. Clarence pushed down the memory. That was for another time. "Nothing here." He moved around the small divider wall. "Bed was made. Didn't smell like a liquor bottle." He pointed at the Hennessy bottle. "That wasn't on the floor. Or that." He pointed at the plate near the table with the remains of cocaine. He stepped over to the picture lying on the floor. "This hung on the wall." He pointed at the nail.

"What about these?" LaFleur asked, pointing at the sticky notes.

Clarence looked at the small colored squares. "We sat at this table. If they'd been there, I'd have noticed."

"Look a little bit like dope notes," LaFleur said.

"Numbers on a sticky, just numbers."

LaFleur nodded. "Like I said."

Clarence pointed at the sliding glass door. "Pretty certain I would have noticed the dried blood. That's new."

Nance photographed the blood. "Anything look missing?"

Clarence made another slow turn around the room. He looked at the computer and then shook his head. "Best as I can tell." He stopped. "Do you see the man's camera?"

Three sets of eyes toured the room.

LaFleur took three quick steps to the bookcase and bent down. "Found it." He held up a small rectangular Canon camera with no lens attached. "Looks kinda gimmicky."

"That's not the one Heka used." He looked around the room again but didn't see anything else. He shifted and looked at Nance. "Theft?"

"But left the computer? I don't think so." She looked around the room a final time. "Not much here to suggest there was any sort of struggle."

"Just the blood, the painting, and the bed," Clarence said.

LaFleur pointed at the brandy bottle. "Consistent with a stumbling drunk."

"Not the man I was with. Wouldn't happen." Clarence gave a disapproving sigh. "No way."

"And you hung with the man for a few hours. Hardly enough time for a psychological profile."

Clarence knew he should listen to LaFleur. He owed the man more than he could ever repay. But he didn't want to.

"We'll learn more when I get back from the medical examiner's office," Nance said.

"When we get back from the autopsy," Clarence corrected.

"They can't cancel the artistic seminar. I think the park is going to need you here."

"They'll have to figure out something. Because I'm coming with you."

13

April 1851

Myrna poled the dugout canoe away from William and the hammock. Tears ran down her face. Samuel wondered what she would have done if she had seen his dad watching them disappear. She had not looked back. Instead, she put her energy into driving the boat forward.

Samuel remembered his father's instructions. Every morning, he did as William had told him. He made note of the spot on the horizon where the sun rose. Samuel identified a landmark to guide them in that direction. They drove the boat toward the place where the sea met the land, where they might find a bigger boat to take them to freedom.

Two days into their journey, his mother refused to go further. She sat at their campsite and stared at the small cooking fire. Rocking back and forth, she hummed her strange song. Samuel moved, drawing up close to her face, but she appeared to look without seeing. The light he usually saw in her eyes had grown dark. She lay down in the dirt, her face pointed toward the sky. "Toward heaven," she said.

From the trees, a native appeared. Samuel had not heard or seen him before the man suddenly stood before them. He looked at Myrna and then at Samuel. "She's sick," Samuel said. "I don't know what's wrong with her."

The man turned and disappeared.

Samuel told himself that he'd been dreaming. He turned back to his mama. "We got to go. Them Bahamas is waiting for us."

"You go, child," Myrna said, looking into the blue sky. "I'll wait here for your daddy."

Before Samuel could speak, the branches parted. The man reappeared. A woman trailed behind him. She walked to Myrna, knelt, and hoisted his mama's head onto her thigh. Slowly, the woman poured water from a cup into Myrna's mouth. Liquid ran down the side of her face and dribbled on the ground. The woman stopped. Myrna swallowed. The woman poured more.

"Where you go?" the man asked Samuel.

Samuel tried to explain their journey. He told the man about William's instructions to follow the sun. "We're going to Bahamas."

The man looked across the top of the boy's head, then over at Myrna. The woman attending to her had guided her to a seated position. The man pointed to himself. "Seminole," he said. He waved his arm in a circle. "My home." He jabbed his index finger at Samuel. "Bahama, your home?"

Samuel nodded. "My mama and daddy say it will be. There, we can live free."

"Free," the man repeated and nodded. He stood and disappeared back into the trees. When he returned, he brought a blanket and some food. The woman made a pallet. Myrna lay down and promptly fell asleep. While his mother slept, Samuel learned that the man had been named for the tribe's great leader, Osceola.

The woman prepared a meal. The aroma of food tantalized Samuel and seemed to rouse Myrna. Her eyes opened. Samuel could see a bit of life returning to his mother. He saw the light behind her eyes again. Samuel helped his mother off the blanket, and the four of them ate.

After they had finished, Osceola stood. He rolled up the blanket and pointed to the east. "Come."

Samuel and Myrna followed. The woman remained behind, cleaning up the camp.

Osceola led them into the trees. They traveled along a twisting path, walking along bits of high ground Osceola spotted. As they traveled, insects swirled around them. Osceola focused on their foot path. He found a skinny trail and guided them through a long stand of mangroves. They stood at the edge of the water. Osceola pointed to a strip of land a short distance away, almost connected by the mangrove forest. "Cay," he said. He gestured with his arm out from the land strip. "Ocean."

Traversing the mangroves proved as taxing as any part of their journey. They quickly became entangled in the roots. Inky-black water collected at the base of the trees. Samuel could not see where he stepped. His feet sank in the muck. He feared the snakes. Sometimes, Osceola picked him up and set him down in a shallower pool. When they finally reached the limestone marking the edge of the cay, Myrna and Samuel collapsed on the rock, exhausted.

Osceola handed Samuel the blanket and a small pouch of food. A cloud of mosquitoes hovered around Osceola. He did not appear to notice. The native made the arm gesture, reaching over the cay. "Ocean," he repeated. "Free." Then he turned and began recrossing the mangrove sound separating the island from the mainland.

"Thank you," Samuel called to Osceola. As he had previously, the native disappeared into the trees.

Samuel clasped his mother's hand. "Come on, Mama."

Myrna sat still for a moment. Then she nodded and drew a deep breath. Squeezing his hand, she stood. Together, they crossed the island.

The pair found a stretch of beach, the shoreline littered with crates. A stand of trees, thick with vegetation, offered ready cover. Here, they settled. Myrna pointed at the beach. "The sand, it's like the sugar in the plantation house." She ordered Samuel to remain hidden while she walked across the beach to one of the crates. Myrna pulled it open and, reaching inside, grabbed a bottle. Her eyes studied it before dropping the bottle on the sand. She began walking to the next crate when, suddenly, Samuel saw her stop. Her eyes widened. Then she raced over the sand to their hiding spot.

She crashed into the vegetation. "A boat. Hide!"

"But we need a boat to get to Bahamas," Samuel said.

"Bahama boat or slave hunter, we don't know. Hide."

They both ducked low. Samuel felt his mother quaking beside him.

A small shallow-drafted boat sailed almost up onto the shore. A man at the front threw an anchor over the side and then jumped into the water, quickly followed by a second man. Both wore knee breeches, loose-fitting tan shirts, and wide-brimmed straw hats. Both men were far darker-skinned than either Samuel or Myrna.

One man laughed and quickly began gathering the crates. "We be lucky today."

The other man, taller and broader than his companion, said nothing. His eyes traced the line of footprints Myrna had left in the sand. His gaze stopped at the copse where they hid. Samuel felt the man staring at him. "Come out. We won't hurt you."

The first man stopped loading the boat. "Who you talking to?"

The taller man pointed to the trees. "I don't want to come get you. It only slow down da work."

Myrna hung her head. Then she took Samuel's hand and led him out of the trees.

The men said nothing as they approached. Samuel watched the taller man look at him. Then he shifted his gaze to look at Myrna. His head moved from her sand-encrusted feet to her face. He smiled. "You runaways?"

When Myrna didn't answer, Samuel nodded.

"And you looking to go to da Bahamas?"

Again, Samuel nodded.

"You got money to pay?" the other man asked.

Myrna's face frowned.

"No money, no boat," the man said and resumed loading a crate.

"Just a minute," the taller man said.

The man holding the crate looked at his companion. "You know the rules."

"I'm the captain. I decide the rules." The taller man turned back to Samuel. He pointed at a crate. "Who found dis box?"

Samuel looked at the crate Myrna had pried open. He pointed to his mother. "She opened that one."

The captain shifted his gaze to Myrna. He smiled again. "And did you take out da wine?"

"Yes." She delivered her answer in a weak and halting voice.

The captain's smile broadened. He turned to his shipmate. "First captain to find a wreck's cargo is in charge of da distribution. You know the rules."

The man loading the boat stopped. "She no captain."

"She found da cargo. She opened da crate." The captain faced Myrna. "My name is Erris Rolle, and I captain dis boat. If we take you and da boy to Nassau, we get the wrecking. Agreed?"

"Agreed," Samuel said when Myrna failed to answer promptly.

Samuel sat at the front of the boat, his mother a lump alongside him. Myrna repeatedly hummed the tune she had begun earlier. They had to remain here, pressed against the lone mast of the dinghy. The captain and his mate had loaded the boat to the gunwales with casks and boxes they recovered from the ship that had run aground. The only room left for the passengers was a plank of wood nailed to the front. Depending on the direction of the wind, the lone sail occasionally offered shade. At other times, the pair huddled under the Seminole blanket to hide from the unrelenting sun. Captain Rolle had tried talking to Myrna, but she had returned to that quiet place where she had gone before the Seminoles arrived. Captain Rolle promptly switched and began conversing with Samuel. He filled the boy's head with nautical terms as he identified the parts of the dinghy. Then, his bare feet gripping the gunwale, the captain walked to the back.

Samuel closed his eyes and concentrated. The word "stern" came to his mind. The captain sat alongside the mate. The captain had his arm loosely wrapped around the tiller. The two men shared a laugh. They were in high spirits. The boat bobbed easily on the gentle waves of the calm sea. "A perfect day," Captain Rolle said. "Da boat be full. Da seas be calm, and we be headin' home."

The mate nodded in agreement.

The lilting sound of the captain's words fascinated Samuel.

His dinghy, Rolle had explained, was a wrecker. It sailed the coast of Florida and along the cays, searching for ships that failed to navigate the shallow waters and coral reefs. The captain had pointed to the northeast. "Da prevailin' winds come from dere," he said, with an accent Samuel had never heard. "And dey push dese boats into our pocket. We sells what we finds in Nassau. Da trip almost over."

Bits of spray off the bow dotted Samuel's face. He blinked the salty water away. It tasted like tears.

They sailed throughout the night. He heard the gentle breathing of his mother beside him. Samuel, however, could not sleep. For the first time in his life, nothing obstructed his view of the night sky. He had never seen so many stars. Again, Captain Rolle walked effortlessly along the thin gunwale to stand beside Samuel. He pointed out stars and told Samuel how he used them to navigate toward his home. "I am constant as da northern star of whose true-fixed and resting quality, there be no fellow in da firmament."

Samuel looked at him.

"Da William Shakespeare wrote dat," Captain Rolle said before returning to the tiller.

With the morning light, a harbor appeared before them. Captain Rolle guided the small dinghy among the larger ocean vessels moored there. "Nassau," he called to the front of the boat. Around them, sailors bustled, preparing the other ships. Samuel felt his stomach tingling with excitement. Even Myrna seemed to be caught up in the energy. Her eyes sparkled, and she looked all around. Samuel's eyes roamed the seawall. Everywhere he looked, he saw black men and women. None of them had overseers. None of them wore chains. He heard laughter coming across the water. Everyone looked to be free. Some even wore fine clothes and appeared to be wealthy. The sight seemed unimaginable. He picked up the lid from a broken crate and drew with the charcoal-covered stick he carried. He channeled his excitement into sketching the ships and activity.

"Who taught you da perspective?" Captain Rolle asked. Once past the big ships, he had surrendered the tiller to the mate, who guided them toward a wharf. He had moved forward and stood alongside Samuel.

"Perspective, what's that?" Samuel asked.

Rolle pointed at the sketch. "Da closer da boats, da bigger you made dem. You made da picture look like it got depth."

Samuel looked at the nearing harbor. Then he gazed down at his picture. He wasn't sure what Captain Rolle asked him. "I drew what I saw."

The captain looked at the scene. "Not many boys can see dis." The captain's eyes fixed on a man holding papers. Rolle pointed. "Dat man work for da government. He come to catalog the wrecking. He likely ask you your name."

Samuel looked at the man growing taller as they neared the wharf. "My name is Samuel Freeman."

14

April 8th

The wrought iron gates out front swung slowly open. Clarence drove his Suburban past the brick gateposts and down the tree-lined avenue. His headlights illuminated the Spanish moss hanging from the limbs. He passed the fountain and stopped in front of the Carrolls' portico.

Matt Carroll met him at the base of the house's front steps.

"Nice place," Clarence said.

"Just our cottage in the woods."

"I'm surprised you can find space to turn around."

Matt smiled. "You think this is small, you should see the place on the water. There isn't room in that place to change your mind."

"Want me to move my ride behind a bush? It looks like a pimple on a supermodel."

Matt's smile broadened. "Don't let the façade fool you. In our souls, the Carrolls are pickup people. Mother loves to have the chauffeur drive her around in one while she throws coins to the peasants."

Clarence grinned. He liked this guy.

Matt turned and led him across the driveway. They passed a Corvette convertible. The license plate read *SGR DDY*. Clarence guessed at the owner. The pair went up the stairs and through the front door. Matt deposited him in the formal dining room, nodded to his mother, and departed. The group had settled around the table. Silver candlesticks and serving pieces were replaced by open laptops. John Sucrito had a seat to Kathryne's left. The congressman was not present. Mae entered last. Her eyes looked red and puffy.

Kathryne stopped whispering with Superintendent Ramirez. She stood and walked to Mae, wrapping her in her arms and hugging her. "I am sorry for your loss. If you don't want to be here, we can manage."

Mae shook her head. "This is where I need to be." She sat. Instead of a laptop, she pulled out her phone. A box of tissue sat on the table next to her elbow.

Kathryne returned to the table's head. "We're here to figure out what we'll do. I do not believe we should cancel the conference. Does anyone disagree?"

Clarence saw her eyes circle the room. No one dared oppose them.

"We are agreed. Next, we need a plan for the two remaining days. Who has Mr. Freeman's lesson outline?" Again, she scanned the room. When no one spoke up, she looked at Superintendent Ramirez. Her eyes showed disappointment. "I would have hoped that someone had thought to retrieve it."

Ramirez cleared his throat. "I assume it's at Hezekiah's house, probably on his laptop."

"Then send someone to get it."

He again cleared his throat. "The investigation continues. His bungalow is off-limits."

"I was told he relapsed, fell, and drowned. Poor soul." Kathryne looked at Mae. "I'm sorry, dear."

"That's my understanding, but law enforcement must be satisfied." Ramirez's cold eyes turned to Clarence.

"Drowning is surprisingly difficult to resolve. We should know more after the autopsy tomorrow morning. I plan to be there."

At the word "autopsy," Mae buried her face in her hands. Her shoulders shook. No one spoke. Ramirez pressed a tissue to her fingers.

Clarence's cell phone interrupted the silence. He grabbed it from his pocket. "It's the lead investigator." He stood and walked out of the dining room. He stepped into a sitting area. "Hey."

"The chief ranger cleared you to go to see the ME tomorrow. We leave early. Don't stay out too late."

"I'm with the supe. We're trying to determine how we'll run a seminar without the star. I'll be home when they let me go."

"Still leaving early." Nance disconnected.

Clarence dropped the phone back into his pocket. Audubon lithographs hung on the walls. He leaned forward and studied the drawing of a roseate spoonbill. He looked up when he heard footsteps on the oak floor.

Matt stood in the doorway, holding a tumbler. "They break you already?"

"I had a phone call." Clarence gestured to the art. "Got distracted."

"You know how Audubon made them look so lifelike?"

"He shot them first," Clarence said.

Matt grunted. "Ironic." He stepped inside. "You're looking at the family museum." He pointed to a wall of old photographs in heavy, ornate frames. "The family tree. Generations of Carrolls who have added to the family fortune and the luster of the family name."

Clarence paused before a photo of both boys in football uniforms. Michael gripped the ball and smiled. Matt crouched in a three-point stance to his right. His expression projected ferociousness.

Matt shook his head and made a low whistle. "We were one badass pair." He formed two fists, one slightly in front of the other. "Quarterback keep, I'd pull. Flatten anyone in front." His hands moved in sync, demonstrating the movement. He paused the motion and pointed to another photograph.

Clarence studied the picture. "These days, they might call that block a chop."

Matt adopted a posh British accent. "The Carrolls don't clip or chop. That's simply not cricket, old man." He shrugged.

The last photo showed Michael Carroll on the steps of the United States Capitol. He had his jacket unbuttoned and a hand in his pocket. His gaze looked off into the future.

"How'd the family get its start?"

Matt gently tapped a sepia-tinted picture of an elderly man in a chair. Clarence studied it. The man had a shock of white hair and a serious expression. The picture showed itself to be slightly overexposed, the cheek looked bright, not uncommon for the cameras of the era, when much of photography consisted of guesswork.

"We like to say that although he came from a line of proud Southerners, he did not embrace the Confederacy with the enthusiasm of many of his neighbors." Matt looked at the picture. "He had ambition, foresight, and a deep sense of personal integrity. Consequently, he had money when it was a buyer's market for land." Matt paused. "Of course, maybe we've just been fortunate."

"Can't be all luck."

Matt raised his index finger. "Don't discount luck." He pointed to another picture.

Clarence could see the family resembling Matt.

"Uncle here. He knew that Florida could be America's sugar bowl if only we could squeeze out the water. Cuba had a stranglehold on the market, but he started planting. Then, Castro comes along, and the US embargoes Cuban sugar. I'd love to tell you that my family played chess while everyone else played checkers, but…" The man stopped and sipped his drink.

Clarence smiled. He liked that Matt Carroll didn't assume it was foreordained that his family would become wealthy. In Clarence's experience, chance often determined how a person fared in life. For instance, whether they or the car next to them got jacked proved pure luck.

Matt tapped the original picture. "He started the family fortune. Successive generations have expanded our interests. We've diversified. We still are. My brother handles the good works these days, and I look after local businesses." He sipped again. "I shouldn't keep you. Mike runs the country, I run the business, but the grande dame runs us both. If she finds out I held you up, she'll ground me."

Clarence smiled again. He liked Matt's easy, self-deprecating manner. Clarence returned to the dining room and slid into his chair.

"I was about to send Mr. Sucrito to find you. Is everything all right?"

"Sorry, I bumped into Matt. He was showing me around."

Kathryne frowned. "Well...in your absence, Mae has courageously agreed to handle tomorrow's talks. She'll help everyone evaluate their art from today."

"And I've got an old talk from a lecture I gave to the community college a few months back. It covers much of what you discussed today but in more detail. We'll cover the Highwaymen, Audubon, and Dave Drake." She turned to the group. "That's Dave the Potter who Ranger Johnson referred to in his remarks."

The rest of the table nodded.

"But if you're free the next day, I could use your help."

"Ranger Johnson will be at your service," Superintendent Ramirez said.

"Chief Ranger Zamora assigned me to assist Investigator Nance," Clarence said.

"It's a good thing I'm the chief ranger's boss. That way, we know where we stand."

"And Mae," Kathryne said. "Mr. Sucrito will assist you with any details in the ranger's absence." If Kathryne saw Mae's shudder, she ignored it. "He can't talk art, but he is very good at getting things done." Kathryne looked around the room. "If there is nothing else, I think we should adjourn. We all have busy days tomorrow, and everyone needs to rest. Mr. Sucrito, if you will show them out." Kathryne stood and left the room.

The moment the door closed, Ramirez turned on Clarence. "A drowning is complicated, nonsense. I want you to wrap this up quickly." He stood and looked at Mae. "The family and the park need this resolved." Ramirez snapped his laptop closed and left.

John Sucrito smiled. He handed Mae a business card, his fingers brushing the outside of her hand. "You heard the lady. I'm here to help you. If you need me, call me. Day or night." He smiled again.

After he left, Mae shuddered again. She looked at Clarence. "You hungry? I'd kill for some nachos." She paused and giggled. "Sorry, I guess that was poor taste."

"Are you stoned, Mae?"

"My godfather just died. Of course I had an edible. No biggie."

"Let me drop you off. And then we should both get some sleep. Like Kathryne said, we've both got a busy day tomorrow."

Mae grabbed his shirt and tugged. Clarence took a step closer to her. He could feel the heat radiating off Mae's body. "I'll go home tonight. But we're having dinner tomorrow." She traced a finger around his shirt button. "We've got things to talk about. Like the lecture. And how we're going to pull it off."

"Pull what off?"

"That depends on how dinner goes."

After Clarence left Mae, he drove over to the farm that Sucrito managed. There was a light on in the house. Clarence parked alongside a blue Ford F-350 pickup. The Corvette got the space beneath the carport.

The house's front door opened, and Sucrito stepped out into the night. He had a semiautomatic handgun against his left hip. "Whoever you are, I saw you on my cameras. You better have a reason to be here."

Clarence stopped walking. "It's me, Ranger Johnson." He saw Sucrito relax.

"You could get yourself shot prowling around. Come inside." John Sucrito turned around, leaving the door ajar.

Clarence looked at the truck with only a bit of envy, climbed the two porch stairs, and went inside.

"Like the truck? Work for the Carroll family. They buy them by the fleet. Let the property managers use them. Get a great deal when you buy in bulk." He opened the refrigerator. "Rich folk always get great deals. Want a beer?"

"No, thanks," Clarence said. "I'll just be a minute." He looked around. Clarence mentally described the style and furnishings as Expensive Testosterone. The open ceiling showed roughhewn exposed beams. A fireplace built from river stones dominated one wall. Sucrito had heavy leather furniture and a high-end video gaming system. Twin televisions were mounted on the wall, one for gaming and the other for watching. A deer head hung on the wall and faced the televisions. He had silver-plated rifles displayed in a gun case. A laptop lay open on the breakfast table as well as the kitchen island. The display for a multicamera security system was mounted near the door. Bookshelves framed the televisions. Clarence didn't see any books. Instead, the shelves held sports memorabilia.

Sucrito returned the handgun to a drawer. His left hand retrieved an open beer. He gestured with the beer toward the footballs lining the shelves. "I played safety for Florida State. They said I was going to be on the watch list for the Thorpe Award."

"What happened?"

Sucrito slapped his knee. "I went right. It went left." He took a long drink. "What can I do you for?"

"Mae's going through a tough time. Give her a little space until she gets on the other side of this."

Sucrito set down the beer can. "Sounds like someone is afraid of a little competition." He cracked his knuckles.

"You can make it sound any way you want. She needs some air to breathe right now."

Sucrito drained the beer can and then crushed it. "And if I think that maybe she needs something else to help her feel better?"

"Then I think she'll squash you like that can. You and the deer enjoy your video games."

15

April 9th

Nance arrived at his door at 7:00 a.m. Clarence stood outside the RV. The two waited in the early light, watching while Tripod conducted her early morning patrol. Clarence handed Nance a travel mug. He carried a small paper sack.

Clarence picked up his dog and settled her inside. "Guard the house. Don't know how long I'll be gone."

Nance watched the two. "You can bring her along."

"Would you mind?"

"Cool day, the back seat shouldn't get too hot. She'll give me somebody interesting to talk to." She opened the door and climbed into the SUV.

Clarence settled Tripod on the back seat. "Good choice. She's a better navigator than I am."

"I know where I'm going."

The dog sniffed the seat belt holders and pressed her nose against the window. After briefly exploring, she settled down and went to sleep. Clarence opened the sack. "Egg-and-cheese burrito?"

Nance nodded. Holding the steering wheel with one hand, she wrapped her other hand around her breakfast. As the aroma filled the compartment, Tripod sat up on her seat.

"Here's yours," Clarence said, laying a folded paper plate laden with scrambled eggs on the back seat. "Don't spill."

"You fixed a plate for the dog."

In the gray light, Clarence nodded.

"So I got played into inviting her?"

Clarence nodded again. "Shamelessly."

Behind them, Tripod lapped at the plate.

She steered them onto the Ronald Reagan Turnpike. As they neared Miami, the banter they had traded trickled off. Nance's responses became shorter. She grunted yes or no if she answered at all. Her jaw stiffened. Clarence could see Nance's knuckles whitening as her grip tightened on the steering wheel.

The traffic slowed. "Damn, all these people."

"No movement. That's why it's called rush hour."

She blew out a breath. "I just hate cities."

Her phone called out directions, telling her to take the next exit.

Clarence pointed through the windshield. "ME's office is downtown."

"We're early. I wanted to make an extra stop. Won't take long."

Clarence reached back and scratched Tripod. Then he settled back and tried to enjoy the ride. The turn for Key Biscayne surprised him. But the causeway running over the ocean and the line of cruise ships moored in the bay grabbed his interest. Fort Worth, Texas, got little cruise traffic.

Palm trees and resorts lined the route along the key. They crossed the length of the narrow key and, at the far end, entered Bill Baggs Cape Florida State Park. She parked. A classic lighthouse stood tall behind them.

"This will just take a minute," Nance said without explanation.

He followed her along the brick, palm-tree-lined path to the white-washed lighthouse topped with a jet-black lantern room and roof. Nance momentarily paused and gazed at the lighthouse, then walked through a gap in the fence onto the beach. She stood still, staring out at the rolling waves of the Atlantic. The beach was uncrowded. A few walkers meandered up and down near the water's edge. The waves lapped the shore, making a peaceful noise.

As he watched, Nance untied her boots and pulled off her socks. She rolled up her pant legs and walked through the white crystalline sand. She jogged a few steps and stopped. Then Nance tousled her bobbed hair with her fingers and tossed her head.

Clarence didn't know what ritual he witnessed, but it felt private. He turned away and read the visitor information signs. They described the lighthouse. He also learned that Cape Florida had been a place where escaped slaves sought boats to take them to the Bahamas. The sign called this route to freedom the Saltwater Railroad. He'd never heard of it before.

"We should get going," Nance said. She held her shoes and socks. They walked to the SUV. She leaned against the car door and brushed her feet before sliding back into her boots. Nance started the SUV, saying nothing.

The traffic slowed as they neared the causeway from Key Biscayne back to Miami. A car sharply cut over in front of them. Nance braked, then pounded on the steering wheel. "Damn cars. There ought to be a law allowing me to shoot some people."

"I can drive. I used to have a license. I don't think they took it away after my felony," Clarence said.

She smiled and brushed away the suggestion. "I'm fine." She paused. "Maybe shooting would be a bit extreme."

Clarence nodded but said nothing to interrupt.

Traffic eased, and the vehicle began climbing the causeway. "There was this guy." She paused and chewed on her lower lip. "Mr. Stephens. He had this store, Montana Outfitters. He made this catalog for outdoorsy clothing. Wanted to have a big mail-order business. He brought me and some of my high school girlfriends to this spot for a swimwear photo shoot." Nance looked over at him. "It wasn't as creepy as it sounds. Our moms came along as chaperones. Think Lands' End or L.L. Bean, only more Western."

"One-piece bathing suits with buckskin fringe."

"Something like that. Mr. Stephens hired a professional photographer. We did hair flips and posed by the lighthouse. I had longer hair then. Mom was proud. And I got paid for hanging out at the beach. It was the best week of my life." She turned and looked out through the windshield. "I just wanted to see if it looked like I remembered."

"And did it?"

She nodded.

"What happened?"

Nance looked at Clarence. "The store failed. The internet made it too easy to buy clothes online."

"What about you?"

"I came away convinced I'd be a famous model and actress. And why not? I had four pages of a local catalog with me in a bathing suit. Why wouldn't Paris want me?"

"What stopped you?"

"Carried that dream for a while in college. Then I woke up. Being tall was fine, but my build was too athletic for the style of the times."

Clarence thought about what he should say.

"Mom got sick around the same time I fell out of love with the idea," Nance said before he could decide. Then, she turned and looked straight ahead. Nance drove in silence to the Miami-Dade Medical Examiner's Office.

She parked in the shade. They cracked the windows to allow the air to circulate. Nance poured water into a cup and set it on the floorboard. Having taken care of Tripod, the pair headed inside.

A woman in a crisp lab coat introduced herself as Dr. Hsu. She led them down a tiled hallway to an elevator. "Have you been to an autopsy?"

Clarence nodded. Nance said nothing.

The examination room was located on the basement level of the medical examiner's office. Heka lay upon a stainless steel exam table. An assistant stood alongside with a camera.

"We begin with an external inspection," Dr. Hsu said. She dictated into a microphone as she described her observations to the two detectives. "A small defect in the inside of the upper lip." The doctor paused at Hezekiah's right cheek. She collected a magnifying glass and studied the area. "Grains of white powder, visually consistent with cocaine, identified along the zygomatic bone." Dr. Hsu turned to the detectives and pointed to her own face. "You'll see it along the cheek."

They leaned in and nodded.

"Some bits of residue on the cheek also. Sticky to the touch. Adhesive, maybe?" Dr. Hsu looked at the investigators. "Any evidence that your deceased was a huffer?"

"We've got no evidence of that," Nance said.

"We'll try to process the sample." Dr. Hsu made a note. "At intake, the staff noted that his clothes smelled like alcohol. They've bagged them to check for trace evidence, including cocaine." She turned back to the body and continued working her way down. "Minor linear abrasions to the left and right wrists." As he had with the lips, the assistant photographed the described areas. The doctor noted the absence of injuries to the fingers and knuckles.

When she had finished with the front, they turned Hezekiah's body over and examined his back. "No obvious injuries," Dr. Hsu said. "But then, bruising is often difficult to see on an external examination of a person with a dark complexion. We'll have a better idea following the internal examination."

Clarence glanced at Nance. Some investigators had difficulty witnessing an autopsy. Whatever had upset her earlier seemed to have resolved. She sat unflinching as the doctor made a Y incision across the chest and opened the body.

"I do find evidence of water in the lungs, consistent with death by drowning."

She made a series of cuts with a scalpel to examine the fatty tissue beneath the skin. Dr. Hsu looked up at the detectives upon completion. "Some subcutaneous bruising at the small of the back. No significant injuries."

Using syringes, she collected a series of fluid samples. "We'll have to await toxicology before we can issue a report," the doctor said. "Right now, I'd have to call the cause of death inconclusive. I have an elderly male who appears to have ingested a variety of intoxicants. No significant injuries indicative of force. Passing out in a pool or pond can't be excluded. We can't rule out accident."

Clarence dipped his head and exhaled. "What about the evidence of a struggle?"

Dr. Hsu looked surprised.

"There was an impression in the mud near his foot as if a toe had been pressed down hard into the mud, and his house has evidence that may be consistent with a struggle," Nance said.

"A single impression?"

She nodded.

"Won't change my opinion," Hsu said.

"I was with him the night he died. The man didn't drink anything."

Dr. Hsu squinched her face. "When did you leave?"

"About midnight."

She nodded. "We'll have to wait for the toxicology."

"And how long will that take?" Nance asked.

"The lab has a backlog." The doctor shrugged. "Miami-Dade has many pending cases. You're in line."

"Could I get a blood sample?"

The doctor furrowed her brow. "Souvenir?"

"I know a guy who might be able to get it looked at and give me something, unofficial, of course." She pointed at the body. "He was a bit of a celebrity. It's somewhat high-profile for the Park Service."

The doctor collected a syringe and drew blood. She packed it in a container with a cold pack. "A bit irregular." She handed over the lab sample. "Might cause an issue if our results prove inconsistent."

"I'll worry about that later."

"I've seen his work." The doctor pointed at Hezekiah. "They carry his art in some of the galleries I visit. His work changed over the years."

"We were supposed to talk about that later this week," Clarence said.

"He grew more somber. There's a depth to his art that wasn't in his early paintings. More below the surface." The doctor looked at Hezekiah's body. "Happens to lots of us as we get older." The doctor dropped her latex gloves into the trash and walked toward the elevator.

Nance and Johnson followed her to the door. Clarence stuck out his hand. "I didn't know the man well, barely at all. But I think Hezekiah would be pleased to know that an admirer performed his autopsy."

Nance and Clarence walked back to the SUV. Before she started the vehicle, she looked at him. "Do you think that's true?"

"What?"

"That Hezekiah would like an admirer to perform the autopsy."

Clarence checked on his dog. After a brief bounce of activity, Tripod had settled back onto the seat, prepared for the trip home. He looked at Nance. "I do. A body is never more vulnerable than during an autopsy. If you're going to expose yourself, it's good to know that you've got a friend in the room."

She nodded and started the SUV. "Thanks."

"For what?"

"Just thanks." She put the car in gear.

The traffic heading away from Miami proved light. Nance's mood brightened the further they got from the city center. "How will we solve this case?"

"The same way you solve any of them. Keep picking at loose threads until you find one that unravels everything."

"That assumes there is a case." Nance exited onto the Ronald Reagan Turnpike and accelerated.

"You saw the crime scene."

She steered around an old pickup with a Florida Marlins bumper sticker. Her speed increased. "Not everyone agrees it was that clear-cut."

"The dissenters are wrong," Clarence said.

"Doc doesn't seem convinced it was homicide."

"She didn't see the man." Clarence frowned. "And what's the deal with the blood sample?"

"LaFleur can get it tested faster. The DEA has labs, and they owe him favors."

"What's that gonna cost? Another dinner? Got to be careful around three dates. He might want you to move in."

"You never know."

Clarence turned away and looked at the passing cars outside his passenger window, wishing he hadn't asked.

16

April 9th

At the RV, Clarence set Tripod on the ground. The dog bounded to the bushes.

"Hey," Nance said.

Clarence turned.

"Earlier, about LaFleur. Bad joke. Sorry."

"We're adults. What you do is up to you."

Nance gazed in the direction they'd come. "Miami, the autopsy, the beach. It stirred up stuff. I was a bitch. Shouldn't take it out on you. LaFleur and I, we're friends. He's a good guy."

"You don't have to explain. LaFleur saved my ass."

She checked her phone. "Tom is meeting me in about an hour. Says he has news. You should be there."

Clarence nodded. "I'd like to go back to Heka's place and have another look around."

Nance shook her head. "You can't go there without an escort. You're not commissioned."

"So escort me."

"I've got to call Zamora. Tell him that the ME is leaning toward an inconclusive ruling. That'll fire him up."

"And I'm supposed to tell you the supe wants you to wrap this case up. He finds it inconvenient with park operations."

Nance nodded. "Hezekiah found it inconvenient too. I can deal with the brass."

"Won't survive long if you can't face the heat from everyone who wants the case resolved yesterday."

"Don't go to the crime scene without an escort."

Clarence nodded solemnly. "I wouldn't dream of it."

"Do I need to keep my eye on you?"

"Only if your Hunk-of-the-Month calendar hasn't arrived." Clarence flexed his biceps.

"You do have the diploma to prove you graduated from junior high, don't you?" With a final shake of her head, Nance put the SUV in gear.

Clarence waved and watched her drive away. He moved his dog back into the RV, grabbed his laptop, and walked to Heka's bungalow. Sometimes it's better to ask for forgiveness than permission.

Along the way, he thought about Nance. Should he act more boldly, he wondered. Clarence remembered the day he got shot. Clarence had been decisive. He'd taken charge. For that, he'd gotten wounded and lay bleeding on the sidewalk. Later, a security guard hit his head and sustained a massive brain injury. A civilian he'd never met had died because of Clarence's decisions. He paused. Clarence knew what the therapist had said. The criminal made the choices. He had merely done his job. The slogan sounded good, and some days he believed it, almost. Bold had cost him his career and his girlfriend. In Yellowstone, bold had nearly gotten Tom LaFleur killed. Bold can fuck things up. Maybe he should just let this situation take its natural course. If she ended up with LaFleur, at least he was a good and honorable man.

Clarence arrived at Heka's front door. He shook his head to clear it. The artist deserved his best, not some distracted fool thinking about the wrong decisions in his personal life. He took a deep breath and walked inside.

The first thing he noticed was the quiet. Clarence had been here twice. Once with Heka, the room filled with blues music and conversation. The second time, Nance and LaFleur had been searching for clues to the artist's killer. The place felt empty.

He took down the odd-looking camera and studied it. Clarence stepped outside and pointed it at the landscape. The line of pinelands stretched in front of him. Above, lazy clouds floated. He snapped a series of pictures. He popped the memory card from the camera and slid it into his computer.

Clarence grabbed a sharp breath when the pictures appeared. He looked like he'd transported the Everglades to Mars. Everything was shown in shades of red and pink. He captured fabulous detail but messed up the colors. He dropped the card back into the camera and pointed it at random objects around the house.

When Clarence reinserted the card into his computer, the otherworldly images reappeared. He realized what he was looking at. The camera captured images in infrared, a wavelength below the visible spectrum. Clarence had read about conservators and art historians using infrared to see beneath the surface layer of a painting. The tool helped researchers to see things without destroying the art. Articles reported finding the artist's signature and painted-over figures. Details from earlier drafts had been found. The infrared camera helped art scholars study an artist's process in a painting's creation.

Clarence returned the memory card to the camera. He pointed it at the old painting, the one Heka had liked. Clarence took a series of shots, some straight on and others at differing angles. When he slid the memory card into his computer, nothing showed. He needed to adjust his computer to accommodate the nonvisible spectrum. He snapped a pair of pictures of the painting on the easel with the block of golden brown. Clarence checked the time. He'd research the process of shooting with infrared on the internet, but after the meeting. He dropped the camera at his house and hurried to the admin building.

When Clarence arrived at Nance's office, LaFleur had already taken the lone visitor chair. Clarence leaned against the wall. Tom should take the chair; he'd been the more recently shot. LaFleur flipped open his pad. "I'll be quick. My analyst can't make sense out of the dope notes. And the computer is blank."

"At least your analyst got to listen to some decent music," Clarence said.

LaFleur looked at him and shook his head. "I said nothing on the computer. I mean, no files, just the basic setup."

"I listened to his blues mix at his house."

"Internet radio?" Nance suggested.

"You got a browser history? Did he have a music app?"

LaFleur flipped the pages of his notes. "They didn't give me a report yet. Transcribing takes time. But they said nothing but a standard image on the computer."

"Something's wrong," Clarence said. "I heard it."

"Maybe the analyst didn't report music," Nance said. "Double-check with them, Tom."

LaFleur nodded. "But it still doesn't change the fact that you got no evidence he didn't just pass out in the pond."

"I was with the man. He didn't drink."

"Were you with him all night?"

"No, but when we got home, the night was over. He went to bed. I'd bet on it."

"Got home," Nance said. "Where did you go?"

"To a blues club."

LaFleur laughed. "You were at a bar, and you say he didn't drink."

"He had a Coke with a cherry. I saw the bartender bring it."

"And a bartender never poured a little something into a cola for you? Were you ever underage?"

Clarence knew how it sounded, but he also knew what he knew. "I'll go interview the bartender."

"We'll interview the bartender," Nance said.

"And I'll get the blood tested." LaFleur held up the box. He spoke in a calm voice. "Facts are facts. We got nothing in the house."

"Just blood on the glass and a painting on the floor," Clarence said.

"The cocaine dish shows he was acting clumsy."

"Or that he was in a struggle."

"With no meaningful injuries on his body," LaFleur said, his tone rising. Nance had obviously briefed him.

"Hands could have been tied. He's got an abrasion on the wrists."

"Or he wore a watch too tight. Or, hell, I don't know, you tell me that he felt strongly about his slave ancestors. Maybe he chained himself up for the experience. I know you're a big art guy, but that doesn't mean artists don't do stupid things sometimes."

"And I know you're a big drug guy, but that doesn't mean everyone is a doper," Clarence said.

"Just the guys with a drug history."

"That was a decade ago. Heka had walked away from that life."

"How do you know? Because he said so?"

Clarence chopped his hand into his open palm. "What about the adhesive on his face? Somebody taped his mouth."

"Or he put a sticky note on his face, or he was sloppy with honey. Nobody knows what made the cocaine stick to his face." LaFleur paused. "But we know he had cocaine."

"Look at your so-called dope notes. The handwriting looks ordered, sloppy but coherent. No sign to indicate that the man had been drunk or stoned." He chopped his palm again. "And his computer was tampered with."

"Forensics said it was clean."

The hand chopped, harder this time. "That isn't Heka's computer."

"All right, everybody calm down." Nance's voice allowed for no disagreement. "We're proceeding with the investigation, at least until we have something definitive on the fluids. Tom, tomorrow, please take the blood to the lab. Promise the lab tech the drinks are on me." She turned to Clarence. "We'll talk to the bartender."

"I've got to show up at the seminar, or the supe will have my ass."

She nodded. "Talk fast. When you're done, I'll have the car running in the parking lot."

"That's it," Clarence said, chopping his hand again.

"What?"

"Heka's camera. Has anybody looked in the trunk of his car?"

Nance shook her head.

"He put it there before we went inside the club. With everything going on, I completely forgot."

Nance looked around the room. "Let's go see."

Clarence hurried outside. LaFleur quickened his pace. Clarence walked as quickly as his wounded leg would move. He beat LaFleur to Nance's SUV by a step. He climbed into the front passenger seat. LaFleur hesitated a moment and then slid into the back behind the driver. Clarence faced his side window, hiding his victory smile from Nance.

At Heka's bungalow, he grabbed the keys and popped the trunk. The lid rose. Clarence stepped back. A 35 mm camera case lay in the trunk bed. Clarence looked at Nance. "Ready to open Door Number One?"

She nodded.

He unzipped the case and removed the camera. "I knew it was there all the time. Just waiting to see if you intrepid investigators would think of searching the trunk."

"If you give me the memory card, I'll get you great prints. With our UC operations, we've got the equipment," Tom said.

"Undercover," Nance said to Clarence.

"Thanks for woman-splaining. Fort Worth PD has a narcotics division."

"I need them in the morning," Nance said, ignoring Clarence.

LaFleur pocketed the disk. "I was coming back anyway. Planned to bring my bike and ride or jump in the middle of a criminal investigation. Rehab and light duty get boring."

For all their differences, LaFleur's sentiment was something Clarence well understood.

"Do you have PPT's number?" Clarence asked after LaFleur had left.

"Sure," Nance said, drawing her cell phone.

"I've got a photography question and need an expert."

She punched the call and speaker buttons and handed him the phone. PPT had been the best photographer among the rangers at Yellowstone. She had frequently assisted as the crime scene officer for Nance's cases.

"Is this the ex–best investigator in Yellowstone?" the voice on the other end of the phone asked.

"It absolutely is," Clarence said.

Silence followed. PPT clearly wasn't expecting a male voice.

"It's Clarence Johnson," Nance said.

"The old football player with the gimpy dog?"

"I'm not old, and she's not gimpy. We both remain stunning examples of our species."

"And still modest. What do you want?"

"Know anything about infrared photography?"

"Do it all the time up here. IR is fantastic on a snowy day." PPT talked him through adjusting his computer to improve the image quality. "It won't look like they were taken by a Martian."

"It's like you were looking over my shoulder," Clarence said, handing the phone to Nance, who continued talking with her old friend and former colleague. He waved goodbye and hurried back to his RV. Tripod thumped her tail when he entered. "We'll catch up later, girl." He filled her food bowl, adding extra to compensate for his time away. He grabbed Heka's IR camera and the laptop. He drove to the visitor's center and entered the CARE gallery.

Heka's pictures had been returned and were on display. A black ribbon hung from the two frames. Clarence walked around both paintings, snapping a series of IR photographs. He processed the picture like he would a crime scene, trying to record everything. Clarence worked until he was satisfied that he'd captured the paintings' secrets, if any were to be had.

He sat down on the floor of the CARE gallery; his leg mildly protested. Clarence fired up the laptop and inserted the memory card. He made the adjustments PPT had outlined. He opened the file. Clarence began with the old picture, the one knocked from Heka's wall. The man had cherished it. What, Clarence wanted to know, were its mysteries.

A small circle had been painted over. Clarence couldn't deny the sense of disappointment. His police officer senses had told him that he was on to something. The IR photography laid bare initials he'd not noticed earlier. Clarence saw that the painting had been done by S.F., likely an earlier Freeman. At least the mystery of why Heka held onto the dark and gloomy scene had been solved.

Clarence looked at the gallery painting of the sawgrass and cattails, the Pahayokee landscape at sunrise. He shifted his focus to his computer and studied the photographs of the painting. Clarence inhaled and held his breath. His eyes widened. What he saw astounded him. He reached for his phone and quickly punched in Mae's number.

"I thought you'd ghosted me," Mae said.

"Are you stoned?"

"No, Nasty Man. I stayed straight just for you. We had plans for nachos."

"I'm at the gallery. Can you meet me? I know what we'll talk about tomorrow."

When Mae arrived, she brought beer and a bag of tortilla chips. The bag had been opened. "I got hungry," she said. Mae then lifted up the six-pack by an empty ring. "And then I got thirsty." She sat cross-legged on the floor and crunched on a tortilla chip. "What are we doing? Because the nearest restaurants are in Homestead."

"I think you'll find this worth skipping a meal." Clarence pointed at the waving sawgrass painting. "When you look at this painting, what do you see?" Clarence parroted Mae's words from day one of the seminar.

She rolled her head. "You know I'm the one who asked that question." She bit into another chip, scattering crumbs on the gallery floor.

"But you never answered."

Mae lowered the tortilla chip and focused on the painting. Clarence watched as her world narrowed. The art commanded her full attention.

"Like you, I see sadness. I sense loss...for reasons I can't quite describe."

Clarence spun the laptop around so that Mae could see the screen. "I think I can explain it." He stabbed the Enter key, bringing the screen to life.

Mae's eyes dropped to the computer screen. Then, they snapped back to the painting. She repeated the back-and-forth several times. She looked at Clarence.

He smiled and nodded, then showed her the IR camera. "Heka had this camera in his house. It takes infrared pictures. When I photographed his paintings, I found all of this. He has a world beneath the surface."

Mae pulled the laptop away from him and leaned, intently studying the photograph. She crawled on her hands and knees to the painting, sat back on her haunches, and pressed her face close to Heka's art. She rocked back and forth. Clarence found himself distracted from the art, her movements lissome and primal. Mae's head slowly moved along the length of the artwork. She sat back. Her chest rose and fell with excitement. "It's amazing. He has an underdrawing unlike anything I've ever seen. The roots of these cattails crawl across the bottom of the art. They strangled an alligator. They're wrapped around the neck of a white fisherman and a Miccosukee. The cattails are killing everything in their path. And then he covered it over with paint." Mae paused. "Well, almost. You can see the occasional black swirl, but it appears to be part of the sawgrass." She waved Clarence over to her. "Look close." She drew his face alongside hers.

He blinked to clear his eyes. "From this distance, you can see some of that detail."

Mae sat back again. "But it's subliminal. You really perceive it more than see it."

"At least I understand why I felt gloom when I looked at the sunrise."

"And it's been here all this time." Mae frowned. "I should have seen it."

"Heka didn't want you to see it. That's why it's in the underpaint. He only wanted you to sense it. And you did."

"But why the cattails?" Mae reached for her beer.

Clarence shook his head. "I don't know. We've got till the morning to make up a story."

Interpreting the second painting proved easier. The artwork showed the Seminole leader, Osceola, gazing over the Everglades. With the IR photos, they saw in the underdrawing a businessman in a suit handing out money. Another man looked away from the transaction. Bulldozers massed in the distance. "This one is pretty clear. Someone is selling out the Everglades. The underdrawing is full of corruption."

"Look there." Mae pointed at Osceola. "Heka first painted a tear. Then he covered it over. His pain remains out of view." Mae turned back to the original painting. She stared at it and then turned to face Clarence. Her eyes glistened. She sniffled. "God, I wish that old man was here. Now that I see all this, I want him to explain it. Not just the symbols but the technique. It's remarkable."

"It truly is," Clarence said.

"And you found it. Thank you."

"Hope it was worth missing nachos."

Mae wrapped her arm around Clarence and pulled him to her. She reached up and kissed him. She tasted of salt. Her soft lips parted, and her tongue touched his.

Clarence reached around, placing his hand against the small of her back. He drew her closer to him. Clarence could feel her heat along the length of his body. He stepped back.

"We should go someplace besides the gallery," Mae said and then giggled. "Though I think Heka might like the idea. He was all about living life."

"I think I need to go home...alone. We have a busy day tomorrow."

Mae laid her index finger on his shoulder. She traced a gentle, meandering line down his shirt to his thigh. He shuddered.

"Not every part of you thinks me leaving is a good idea."

Clarence closed his eyes. He opened them and nodded. "I know. But a little of me thinks so." He took a step backward. "I'll see you tomorrow, Mae."

Mae frowned. She picked up her bag of chips. Before she left, Mae turned. "If you change your mind and get any bold ideas, text me. I'll be at my place alone." Pinching the chip bag, she formed her fingers into a heart shape and pressed it against her chest. She crunched a tortilla chip as she disappeared.

Bold, he thought. There was that word again.

17

April 1863

Captain Rolle lived in a small wood-framed house near the Nassau harbor. He had hired Myrna to be his housekeeper and cook. She and Samuel slept in a small room off the kitchen. In time, she moved to Captain Rolle's bedroom.

    An Anglican priest at Christ Church Cathedral began giving Samuel art lessons. Father Fredrich had studied painting before he took his holy orders. Samuel walked to the cathedral. He passed Parliament Square and the heart of official Nassau. Ships packed the harbor. Wreckers like Captain Rolle's had to find their way among the great ships built to cross the Atlantic. When Samuel had time, he paused to watch the harbor at work. The port bustled with activity. Since the American Civil War started, Nassau's port traffic had boomed. The Union forces blockaded southern ports, trying to starve the Confederacy into submission. The Confederate forces countered with blockade runners. Fast, shallow-drafted ships from the southern states arrived at Nassau. Workers transferred their cargo, bales of cotton, to the heavy British vessels for transport to the cloth factories of England. The harbor laborers filled the holds of the blockade runners with everything the South needed to import. Samuel watched the working men load cannons on board. Some boats got packed with crates of guns or medicine. Others, the workers packed with luxury goods. The boats slipped out of the Nassau harbor bound for the Confederate states. They followed the route that Captain Rolle took when he went wrecking. The arriving blockade runners followed nearly the same line they had followed when Samuel and his mother came to Nassau years earlier.

One day, shortly after settling in Nassau, Captain Rolle took the boy to the rectory of Christ Church. Father Fredrich had laughed excitedly when Samuel first met him. Captain Rolle explained that the boy intuitively understood perspective. "He shows remarkable talent," the priest had said as he watched the boy draw. "We may have our own John Constable or perhaps Joshua Reynolds." Samuel smiled. Although he did not recognize the names, the priest's tone made them sound complimentary. The boy had found it thrilling to be bent over a clean sheet of paper, working with something better than his charcoal stick and bark.

The priest led the boy through lessons on drawing. Then, he began teaching him the techniques of painting. Together, they painted portraits, the priest guiding him through the steps necessary to create an image of the person's face. Lifelike, he said, but not too realistic. "You can make a tidy living as a portraitist," the priest said. "Flatter your customers. Make them look as they see themselves, not as they actually look." He paused. "Unless they don't pay. Then make them as ugly as the debauched sinners they are."

Father Fredrich led him along the quay to the heart of the harbor. There, they would set up the easel and paint the scene. Samuel learned to paint fast. The Bahamian sun would dry the paint almost before it left his brush. The boy looked at the scene and captured the image in his mind. Then, he would focus his attention on the canvas and paint furiously. He applied the color with long brush strokes followed by quick dabs for accent and detail. "The jewels," Father Fredrich called them. After working outside, Samuel carried his art back to the rectory. There, he could complete his painting at a more leisurely pace. Father Fredrich taught him how to pair colors for dramatic effects. Samuel practiced shading to add fullness and depth. The priest filled his head with knowledge about painting. Samuel also learned to read and to master figures. He could feel himself becoming a new person.

But Samuel never completely forgot his old self. At the end of one lesson, he asked Father Fredrich about the blockade runners. All the harbor workers were the children or grandchildren of former slaves. Why, Samuel wondered, did these men help fill the holds of ships with cannons when those guns would be used in a war to help keep slaves in chains?

The priest gazed out the window of the rectory. His eyes took on a faraway look. Samuel recognized the face of the priest thinking deeply. Father Fredrich turned away from the glass. "The harbor workers must feed their families. Men do not always get to choose the work they do. When you become a renowned painter, you may be solicited to paint the portrait of men whose wealth was earned by means you do not abide. We will pray that the Union successfully prosecutes this war and that those who seek your services are not slavers. But they may express their cruelty in other ways. And you will have to choose. To go without food, perhaps, or to do their bidding." Father Fredrich turned back to the window. "Each man has good and evil within him. Which of the two controls his life may be decided by his needs and ability to resist temptation."

Myrna made sure that Samuel never forgot where he came from. She told him the old stories, including the day the two men captured them and how William bought their freedom with his own. "Beneath them wicked mahoganies, them trees crying blood over the evil they shaded."

Once, after he'd been practicing, he painted her portrait. Samuel painted the picture as he remembered her face when he was young. When he showed her, she quietly studied it for a long time. Then she returned the portrait to him, tears running down her face. "That's how I looked when I was with your daddy. Thinking too hard about those days brings my heart a pain I can't bear." Then she told him again about the tree island where the mahoganies cried blood.

Some days Samuel walked to the water and just sat. He watched the waves curl. Each presented a slightly different image. The way the rolling water swirled and the minute differences in color commanded his attention. Sometimes, Samuel thought he could see inside the wave and spot something hidden, something only he could see. And then the wave fell in on itself, and whatever was there disappeared.

Samuel attended Christ Church on Sunday, April 5th, to pray. The day was Easter, and he could hear church bells from across Nassau. Samuel felt obliged to attend. His appearance at worship prodded by not only his gratitude to Father Fredrich but also his concerns about Myrna's declining health. She had been sweeping Captain Rolle's floor when a seizure struck her. Samuel had found her lying on the floor. He had carried her to the bed and raced for the doctor. That had been three days before. Since then, she had only occasionally been conscious. When she was, she often talked to William. Once, she had introduced him to her son, Samuel Freeman. She had posed William's questions to Samuel. He had answered the apparition.

After church, he hurried back to the doctor's house. His mother's health worsened. As he walked, he collided with a man dashing in the opposite direction. The man grabbed his arm. "Have you heard? The American President Lincoln declared that all the slaves are free."

Samuel felt his heart race at the news.

"I hears that he said it back in January, but you know how news is sometimes. We only get boats from the Confederates, and they don't want no one to know, so they took their time spreading it."

"What happens if Mr. Lincoln and the Union don't win the war?"

The man frowned. "Then I guess it doesn't matter much what President Lincoln says." The man stepped around Samuel and continued on his way. Samuel hurried ahead to the doctor's house. The physician had a round face and obsidian-colored skin. He gave Samuel a small glass vial. "This is a tincture of morphine. It will help with your mama's pain."

"Will this heal her?" Samuel asked.

The doctor bowed his head and slowly shook it. "She's in the Lord's hands."

Samuel raced through the streets back to Captain Rolle's house. Entering the room, he saw that Myrna's eyes were open. The eyes seemed to relax when he entered. Captain Rolle sat in a chair to one side of her. He had not left the house to go wrecking since Myrna had her seizure. Captain Rolle's eyes showed red and tired. He had obviously been crying. Samuel moved a chair to the other side of her pillow and sat down. He put a few drops of the medicine on Myrna's tongue. She swallowed. He told her the news about Mr. Lincoln freeing the slaves. "When we go to the United States, we won't have to be afraid of nothing."

Myrna smiled. She took a ragged breath. "Your daddy will be free. I ain't seen him since that night beneath them awful crying mahogany trees. Have I told you that story?"

Samuel squeezed her hand. "Yes, Mama. But you can tell me again."

"I will, but first I need to rest." Myrna closed her eyes. Samuel listened to her slow and struggling breaths. He offered a prayer for his mother's soul.

18

April 10th

Clarence was sitting at the small table in the RV when the text message made his phone buzz. Tripod lay beside him on the bench seat. Clarence picked at the frets on the Stratocaster and ignored the cup of coffee cooling on the table. His book lay facedown. Clarence had gotten up early, intending to read about plant life in the Everglades. Instead, he'd spent the early morning thinking about choices he hadn't made. Clarence set down the guitar and picked up his phone. Nance called a meeting for 6:30 a.m. in her office.

Clarence carried a fresh cup into Nance's office. In the other arm, he held Tripod. Clarence didn't know what the surprise meeting was about and felt he needed a wingman. If Nance was surprised that he'd brought reinforcements, she didn't show it. She waved him to the lone chair and resumed reading a report.

A dry-erase board stood in the corner of the small office. Nance had Hezekiah's picture at the top. A series of questions flowed down from the victim. Clarence studied the notes and wondered how much sleep Nance had gotten. "Do we need a plan before we go to the bar?"

Nance shook her head without looking up. "Tom will be here momentarily." She paused and glanced over at her phone, checking her texts. "He says he has the photos."

"That was quick."

She nodded. "Some parts of the government get better funding."

Tom LaFleur arrived a few minutes later. He had a manila envelope under his arm and a laptop in his hand. He must be feeling better, Clarence thought; LaFleur was back to wearing form-fitting shirts that showed off his pectorals and biceps.

The DEA agent opened the envelope. He dropped a stack of eight-by-ten-inch photographs onto Nance's desk. "Brought the laptop in case we want to zoom in on anything. I think you'll find the most interesting pictures near the back."

Nance, Clarence noted, did not race to the bottom of the pile. She took her time, studying the photographs in the order they'd been shot. After she finished with one, she passed it to Clarence. Most of the photographs showed the Everglades landscape. Heka had a series capturing the sawgrass at various times of the day. Clarence especially liked those that pictured the grass at sunrise. He turned one toward Nance. "What do you think? Look like a bruise?"

She didn't respond. LaFleur leaned in to examine the picture.

Other pictures focused on the cattails. Heka had pictures of the long, tapering blades while others concentrated on the brown head of the plant. They look a little like a hotdog on a stick, Clarence thought.

Another set of scenery photographs included pictures of a hammock, taken from a distance. Heka had zoomed closer and taken a series of a lone mahogany tree. A red flower sprouted from its twisted branches.

Nance tapped the picture. "Picture is probably useless to us, but it's pretty."

"The plant is a cardinal air plant," Clarence said. "It grows on the trunk of a tree. Not a parasite. Gets its nutrients from the air."

The other two looked at him.

"Clarence Johnson, Renaissance man. Note the humble shrug of my shoulders."

"The pictures near the end are the ones I think you'll find interesting," LaFleur repeated.

Nance moved through the stack. Other pictures showed trees on the ground and the junglelike vegetation of a hammock. She stopped near the back of the stack, frowned, and studied a photograph. She passed it to Clarence.

The picture showed a rusted-out Ford pickup parked on a barely visible trail near a cypress dome.

"I know that place. It's not too far from here," Clarence said.

"Within the boundaries of the national park?"

Clarence nodded. He noticed that she had not looked up; she focused on the following photograph. "Yes."

She passed him a picture showing a man standing in knee-deep water surrounded by cypress trees. His hand snaked through the wispy roots and gray-green leaves of a wild orchid hanging from the tree.

Nance passed him three more pictures showing the man. In each picture, he smiled triumphantly as he leaned in to pry the flower loose.

The next series depicted the same man stooped over a saw palmetto, picking the green olive-like berries. Nance flipped through the photos before handing them across the table.

"What's with the berries?" LaFleur asked.

"Cure for urinary tract problems, hair-loss remedy, sexual dysfunction. Pharm companies and natural food companies pay serious money," Nance said.

The final pictures showed a purple gallinule walking across the spatter-dock. Clarence remembered standing alongside the man when those photos were taken.

Nance tapped the picture of the man poaching the orchid. She looked at LaFleur. "I don't suppose you had a chance to run this guy through facial recognition software?"

"I know who he is," Clarence said.

The other two looked at him.

"His name is Joe Bob Jefferson. He runs Southern Nursery. I met him at the blues club Heka took me to."

Nance turned away from LaFleur and focused solely on Clarence. "What do you remember about him?"

Clarence took a deep breath. He closed his eyes, scratched Tripod gently between the ears, and replayed the evening in his mind. "Bit of a blowhard. Said they flew the rebel flag at the nursery."

"Charming."

"Argued with Hezekiah. Not angry. Just bickering. The pair clearly had some history."

"Remember anything specific?" Nance asked.

"Heka called him a racist."

"The man with the Confederate flag. Who'd have thought," LaFleur said.

"And he did say he was at the bar spending his poaching money," Clarence added. He stood up quickly. "Be right back." Clarence left Tripod on the chair and hurried out the door before either could speak. He grabbed his laptop from his Suburban and returned. As the computer booted up, he explained. "The camera at Heka's. The odd-looking one we found the original night. That camera takes infrared photos. Art historians sometimes use IR photography to look below the top layer of a painting, to see what's underneath. Enables them to see the *pentimento*, the changes an artist makes in the creative process." He looked at Nance. "When I went to Heka's house after our Miami road trip—"

"Over my explicit instructions not to go alone?"

"Yeah, that time."

Nance frowned. Clarence could see she was thinking about how to handle his insubordination.

"I promised I wouldn't dream of going." Clarence shook his head. "And I didn't. Completely dreamless."

"Thoughtless, more like it. What did you learn?"

"I took a picture of that unfinished painting. Remember the one with the yellow rectangle at the bottom? Like a Rothko."

Nance nodded.

Clarence scrolled through the computer's files until he found the picture. Clarence turned the laptop to face them. Nance studied the picture on the screen. Then she plucked one of the eight-by-tens and held it alongside the computer screen. The three of them compared the two images. Beneath the painting, a man bent over a flower, his pose identical to Heka's photograph of Jefferson. Clarence wasn't surprised that Hezekiah had not painted in the details of Joe Bob Jefferson's face.

"Whoa," LaFleur said.

Clarence said nothing, thinking about Mae and what she might say.

"You got something you want to share with the group?" Nance's eyes studied him. She'd caught his faraway look.

Clarence didn't want to share, at least not with them. He looked to LaFleur. "I need an expert on international affairs."

LaFleur sat up straighter in his chair.

"The anarchy symbol, the *A* with a circle around it. Everyone around the world uses it. An internationally agreed-upon symbol for anarchy, doesn't that seem ironic?"

LaFleur frowned.

Clarence may need to explain the hard words.

"I think we should concentrate on the case in front of us," Nance said. She smiled. "Looks like I'm gonna clear my poaching case at least."

"You might do more than that," LaFleur said. Reaching into the manila envelope, he slowly brought out another sheet of paper. He paused, keeping the paper pressed against his chest.

"So who won Best Picture?" Clarence asked.

LaFleur ignored the comment. "I got blood test results back. Heka had only minimal alcohol and cocaine in his system." He pushed the report to Nance.

Clarence read the document upside down. "No evidence of cocaine metabolite reported."

She sat back in her chair. "What does it mean?"

Clarence shook his head. He'd read his share of toxicology reports. "The cocaine hadn't been in his system very long. His body hadn't processed any of it yet. It's hard to predict how drugs are going to hit any particular individual. But, given that Heka had some history, I think the idea that this level would have him unconscious and facedown in a pond strains credibility."

Nance shifted her gaze to LaFleur, who nodded. "Got to agree with the man. And now you've identified someone with a motive."

She nodded. "Hezekiah caught him poaching. Had the pictures. Maybe blackmail, maybe planning to turn him in to the law. Man doesn't want to go to jail. He especially doesn't want to go because of a black guy. The two argued." Nance nodded again. "I can see that."

"I don't know," Clarence said. "Something doesn't feel right."

"Dude," LaFleur said. "You're the one who argued that the artist was murdered. You pushed us to buy into the idea." LaFleur wagged his index finger at himself and Nance. "We finally come around to your way of thinking and you want to change your mind?"

"I think he was murdered. I'm just not so quick to put it on Jefferson. I told you what the man said. But...it feels wrong." He looked at Nance. "Have you ever seen two people bicker when they were really expressing something else?"

If she caught a secondary message in his words, Nance's face didn't reflect it. She slowly shook her head. "I'm not a psychologist or a mind reader. We've got Jefferson's words. We're going to go with that." She tapped her pen on the desktop. "I'll write up an arrest warrant for poaching, for stealing the protected plants in the national park. I'm also preparing a search warrant for the Southern Nursery. If you're stealing plants, that's a logical place to put them."

LaFleur smiled and nodded. "Get inside and poke around. You have no idea how many times I've found stuff once I started looking. Then sit him in the interview room and get the man talking about poaching. Who knows what he might accidentally give up about the murder."

"That's the general idea," Nance said. "I need a couple of hours to prepare the warrant and find an assistant US attorney and a judge. I've also got to update the chief and get his sign-off. I'll be ready to roll this afternoon."

"Love to join the party, but I'm out," LaFleur said. "I've got day job responsibilities all afternoon. And I'm light duty. I can't run raids. Can't do it for DEA, and I sure can't be running around for some other agency."

"Take your name off the plaque?" Clarence said.

"Something like that."

Nance looked at LaFleur and smiled. "You've helped a ton. I can't thank you enough."

"I'm all about interagency cooperation, Alison." LaFleur flashed his smile at her and stood.

"Think about anarchy. I swear there's something there," Clarence said.

Nance walked LaFleur out. When she returned, she sat down and looked at Clarence. "You were right," she said, her voice soft.

He shrugged. "I got lucky."

Nance shook her head. "You saw things. You pushed your point. You knew you were right, and you fought for your side."

Clarence nodded. "And you didn't fold when the higher-ups pressured you to quickly resolve this case as an accident. You've let the investigation take its course, pulling at threads. Not always easy to do."

"Johnson, you're infuriating sometimes, but you're a damn good cop. I'm glad you're working with me." She paused. "Most of the time."

"I bet that hurt a lot."

"Only the nice parts." She smiled. "Look, I know you got a connection to the players. The warrants will be ready by the time you finish your seminar. But if you want to sit this out, I understand."

"If Jefferson murdered the man, I want him to go down. You type till I'm done talking and I'm with you all the way."

Her smile broadened. "I'm glad you'll be a part of it."

Clarence doubted that Mae would feel the same way.

"In tribute to Hezekiah Freeman, we would like to close the seminar by looking more closely at his art," Clarence said in the final session. Most of the audience remained despite the news of the murder. Kathryne Carroll had returned to her customary seat in the front row. Alongside her sat Matt and John Sucrito. Matt, Clarence noticed, had taken his mother's hand. She interlaced her fingers with his.

Clarence put up a slide of the sawgrass field dotted with cattails. "At the first session, Mae asked you to think about what emotion this painting elicited. Many of you agreed with me that it saddened us." He saw most of the audience nod. "But why does a waving field of sawgrass at sunrise disturb us?" Clarence paused. "That was the unanswered question." He flashed up another slide. Clarence heard a few gasps. "Photographed with infrared, we see that Hezekiah had an elaborate underdrawing. The roots of the cattails strangle the wildlife and the natives. An ugly scene occurs below the idyllic surface. Art historians often used the term *pentimento* to describe the alterations an artist makes to a painting. The changes we see when we X-ray, or IR scan, a work of art. Mae and I have taken to calling this a qualified *pentimento*. Hezekiah wanted this to lie below the surface." His eyes surveyed the group. "It registers. You feel it rather than see it."

Clarence felt a collective exhale from the crowd as they all saw for the first time that which had previously been hidden.

"Why did Hezekiah hate cattails?"

A hand shot up. "I know," a woman said.

Clarence pointed to her. "Let's crowdsource the answer."

"Phosphorus. Big sugar producers dump fertilizer on the crops. The runoff carries phosphorus to the Everglades. It completely changes the ecology. Cattails grow, they like the inflow of phosphorus. Sawgrass doesn't, and it gets pushed out of the way. Everything in the Everglades changes."

"We clean every drop of water that comes off our farms," Sucrito shouted. "This is environmental nonsense."

"It's science," the woman shouted back, "and yelling doesn't change that."

Many in the audience applauded. Kathryne Carroll grabbed Sucrito's arm and pulled him back to his seat.

Clarence held up his hands in surrender. He didn't want the meeting to get out of hand. "This session is about art. What matters is what Hezekiah Freeman believed and what he sought to express in his painting. The IR photo shows us what he wanted us to feel rather than see." Clarence looked around the room. "And I think we've seen proof that Hezekiah Freeman was capable of making people feel a great deal." He passed the lecture over to Mae, who offered her thoughts about the techniques for creating the image. "A radical departure from Heka's previous work. But as our Native

American brothers and sisters say, we are nature on two legs. He has a radical technique for exploring our relationship to our earth mother."

After the session finished, the Carrolls quickly departed, Matt escorting John Sucrito out of the theater. Clarence and Mae stood onstage, answering questions. Clarence monitored his phone. He read the message.

Warrants signed. Briefing the chief. Ready soon.

"You look like a man with plans," Mae said.

He pushed the phone into his pocket. "You know what they say about rangers."

"No."

He was stumped for a clever answer. "No rest for the weary."

Mae frowned; the lower lip pushed out in an attractive pout. "I was hoping we could go to the club. Get the band together for a reunion tour. Have a drink to celebrate the seminar's completion."

"I'd like that. But I got to work."

"Pity," she said. Mae grabbed her bag, turned, and walked out of the theater. Clarence watched the exaggerated sashay of her hips. Mae stopped and turned. "I knew you were looking."

"I got to work." He felt his pocket buzz. Clarence pulled his phone. When he looked up, Mae had disappeared. He checked the message.

I'm in the parking lot. Let's go.

19

April 10th

Nance held up two warrants while Clarence slid into the passenger seat, "Chief, US attorney, judge, everybody has blessed our actions. House or nursery?"

"Let's decide on the way." Clarence pointed toward the main road leading out of the park.

She nodded and stepped on the gas. "I uploaded Tom's pictures to the file."

"Pull in there," Clarence said, pointing at a convenience store. He borrowed the clerk's phone and dialed the number for Southern Nursery. A deep-voiced man answered.

"Is Joe Bob there? At the club, he promised to show me some fantastic silver palms. Said he'd make me a helluva deal." Clarence's standard, slight Southern accent became pronounced.

The deep voice grunted. "If you met Joe Bob, you should know you can't believe nothing he says when he drinks. He ain't here. But we got silver palms if you want to come by."

"I'll be heading that way," Clarence said.

Nance made a sour face after Clarence had disconnected the telephone.

"That accent is what happens when bad actors breed with Southern belles."

"I'm from Texas, that's the South. I just put it a bit on steroids, little lady. Let's start at the house."

They parked down the street and moved quickly. Clarence ran to the back of the property and scanned the yard. Decent landscaping, he thought, not surprising for a guy who runs a nursery. He saw no evidence of sudden flight. Clarence noticed a dead palm near the back fence. Too skinny for anyone to hide behind. He moved to the house. Clarence heard Nance pounding on the front door, announcing they were federal investigators. No one answered. Clarence peeked through the window. The room at the back was a mud room. He saw boots, rain gear, and shelves with boxes but no sign of a person inside. No vehicles filled the driveway. They entered and searched but found no one.

The house had only one bedroom that showed signs of regular use. The other had been converted into an oversized closet. Clarence led her into the kitchen. A few dirty dishes filled the sink. The coffee in the cup felt cold; the egg yolk had dried hard on the plate. He felt the stovetop. It gave off no heat. Hours had gone by since the kitchen had been used. "Nothing to suggest he ran out of here."

She nodded. "Look around. Let's see what we find."

Clarence headed to the bedroom. Nance looked elsewhere.

While he was opening drawers and feeling the contents, she returned. "Found these in the back room." She held a pry bar and a roll of silver duct tape.

"Not exactly a smoking gun."

"He's also got a rifle in a case stashed in the water heater closet. It's old and a bit rusty." Nance looked around the room. "What did you find?"

Clarence shook his head.

"Then I'm keeping the bar and tape." Again, she disappeared.

The search turned up nothing else. While Nance wrote up a brief inventory of what they'd seized, Clarence perused a bookcase in the living room. He saw a few gardening books and a small picture of Joe Bob standing next to Mae at her high school graduation. Nance finished the inventory and left it on the kitchen table along with a copy of the warrant.

They climbed into the SUV. "Next stop, Southern Nursery?"

She nodded.

"Could you tell a poached orchid, illegally seized from a national park, from an orchid lawfully grown in a commercial nursery?" Clarence asked.

She took a breath. "I know orchids. I went to my high school prom."

"So we're looking for an orchid not in a plastic box and without a rhinestone wristband."

Nance nodded. "Got any other advice?"

"I went to Hawaii once. Got an orchid lei upon arrival. Pretty sure they were legit. Don't confiscate any flowers hanging on a necklace."

"No jewelry seizures. Got it," she said. "Seriously, got any ideas?"

"Hopefully, you arrest Joe Bob. Maybe an employee blabs. Otherwise, we take a bunch of pictures of anything we find suspicious and show a local expert."

Nance nodded again and put the SUV in gear.

They hit Southern Nursery late in the afternoon. Clarence didn't see the Confederate flag. He also didn't see Joe Bob or anything resembling a stolen orchid. The place carried rows of palm varieties, an assortment of flowering trees, and enough different bushes to construct an exotic maze. The inventory, although diverse, was sparse. It didn't take long to walk through it. Neither of them saw anything that looked out of the ordinary to an untrained eye. The buildings on the property needed repair.

The deep-voiced man Clarence had spoken with on the phone stood by the cash register. He wore a short-sleeved shirt with the Southern Nursery logo on the left side. Both the man's arms had been tattooed with vines. Nance tried to hand him the search warrant when they entered. He'd refused to touch it, so she laid it on the counter before him. It hadn't moved.

Clarence smiled at the deep-voiced man. Before this charm onslaught, he'd wilt like a flower in the South Florida sun. "What's your name?"

The man said nothing.

Clarence showed him a picture. "Recognize that?"

The man nodded. "Yes, sir. That there is Joe Bob Jefferson, sir."

"How about the plant?"

The man squinted. "I'd say it's a cypress tree, sir."

"How about the flower?"

"*Cyrtopodium punctatum*, sir."

"What's that?"

"It's Latin, sir."

"Latin for what?"

"Folks around here call it a Cowhorn orchid, sir."

"Show me where you keep them."

The man shook his head. "I can't do that, sir."

"Show me where you keep them, please," Clarence said.

"The Cowhorn orchid is a state-protected species. They can't be harvested or sold without a permit, sir."

Clarence brought the picture closer to the man's nose. "And what does it look like Joe Bob is doing in this picture?"

The deep voice trembled slightly. "I'd say he was enjoying the natural artistry of one of God's most beautiful creations, sir."

"You wouldn't lie to me? I'd hate to see you get into trouble because of Joe Bob Jefferson."

The deep-voiced man slowly shook his head. "I did two years in Raiford. They said the car I was driving had marijuana in the trunk." His eyes had a look that Clarence could only describe as fatalistic. "A man with a record has trouble finding a job. Joe Bob Jefferson didn't care. He asked if I could look after plants. I told him that I wouldn't have gotten locked up if I couldn't. Mr. Jefferson laughed and hired me on the spot. He said that the nursery business was full of uncertainty. A hurricane can blow through here and put our entire inventory in Florida Bay. But if a man can laugh at his troubles, he can find a way through them." The man shook his head again. "You just go on and do what you need to do. If I have to take a hit for someone, it might as well be Joe Bob."

Clarence studied the man's face. "Hand me one of your flyers." Clarence wrote his cell number across the top. "If you should happen to see Joe Bob Jefferson, kindly ask him to call me."

The man nodded. "That I will do. Just as soon as I see him."

Nance slammed the door of the SUV. "I guess we wait for him to run a stop sign in Orlando or wherever."

"I got a place we need to look."

"The blues club?"

Clarence nodded. "But you got to let me go in alone."

Nance waited.

"Mae, my partner in the lecture series, is his daughter and Heka's goddaughter."

Nance glanced at her photo of Joe Bob. "Didn't see that one coming."

"I know. Mom must have been a supermodel to offset those genes. She said she might go to the club after the final session of the seminar. I think she knows her father is no angel, but I don't want to make a public scene if we can avoid it."

She shook her head. "He's got friends there. I don't want you having them at your back."

"I don't either. But I think the bar crowd liked Heka better than they like Jefferson."

"I don't like it."

"You don't know where the club is," Clarence reminded her.

"And you don't want a charge for interference with a police officer."

Clarence felt pretty sure she was bluffing. "Just cover the door."

She put the car in gear. "Where to?"

They pulled up outside the blues club. Clarence pointed out the features of the ramshackle building. "The entrance is at the back. Cover that. You can see the front is covered in a screened porch. The man isn't diving through a window and jumping through screens. I just need a few minutes. Joe Bob is a blowhard. If we back him in a corner, there'll be trouble. But he is a businessman. If we explain this, he'll see reason."

Nance surveyed the two sides of the building. "We walk around the other two sides so I can get a feel for the place. If I'm satisfied, we try it your way. You got ten minutes. Anybody drops a beer glass or has too loud a break at the pool table, I'm coming fast and hard."

"I'll tell them to shoot softly."

They got out and walked to the opposite side of the building. Straggly bushes and overgrown weeds entangled the ground. Nance looked at what she'd have to crawl through to complete the circle and stepped back. "Ten minutes."

Clarence strode through the doorway and pressed himself against the wall. His eyes adjusted to the dim light. He strolled across the floor, studying the room. Clarence didn't see Mae.

Joe Bob sat at the end of the bar, against the far wall. At the back of the club, a man circled the pool table, lining up a shot. Fortunately, he did so quietly. Clarence took a seat alongside Joe Bob. A half-empty beer glass marked the line of demarcation separating them.

Kemo, the bartender, appeared in front of him. "Back to kick it again?"

"Not tonight, I'm afraid. Can I get water?"

"You know this is a business, right?"

Clarence put a dollar in front of Kemo. "Drop a lime in it. Keep the change."

The bartender pocketed the bill. He found the yellowest, most sickly slice of lemon, dropped it into a mug, and then filled it with water.

"Thought you might turn up here," Joe Bob said quietly after Kemo had moved to the other end of the bar. "I didn't kill Heka."

"That's not what I'm here for," Clarence said. "There's a federal investigator outside with a warrant for stealing protected plants."

Joe Bob emphatically shook his head. "I didn't steal no plants. Heka asked me to pose by some orchids and saw palmettos so he could get some pictures. Needed a model for a painting. Paid me money." He turned to Clarence and pointed to his chin. "You know how often this face has been paid to be a model?" Joe Bob held up a calloused index finger, dirt permanently embedded into the ridges of his skin. "One time."

"You'll have a chance to tell that to the investigator. She's good, but more importantly, she's fair. She'll listen."

"How come you're here and she ain't?"

"I asked to come," Clarence said. "If I came in, I thought the two of us might walk out of here. I didn't want Mae to see her daddy getting arrested."

"Mae," Joe Bob said. He looked down at the bar. "She left a little bit ago. Talked a lot about you. Talked about how smart you were, figuring things out about Heka's paintings." He sat quietly. "I appreciate you doing me a solid."

"C'mon. Pay your tab, and let's leave here without trouble."

"I didn't kill Heka," Joe Bob repeated. "Hezekiah Freeman was my baby's godfather." The man blew out a long, slow breath.

Clarence recognized the look he saw on Joe Bob's face. He had made up his mind. Clarence needed to decide what he was going to do.

Joe Bob reached into his back pocket. He pulled out a cracked leather wallet. He laid the lone five-dollar bill on the polished wood bar top. Joe Bob angled his head and saw Clarence studying the wallet. "You could hear an echo in my billfold."

"Sounds like a man who could use some money."

Joe Bob closed his eyes, pushing forward bushy and untamed eyebrows.

He even has ugly eyelids, Clarence thought.

"You know," Joe Bob said, "there's family legend tells of an ancient bucket in the swamp full of silver. Riches for the man who finds it. If I wanted to get money from the 'glades, I'd be looking for that and not poaching plants."

"Tell her, she'll listen," Clarence said.

"If'n I tell her about some old pot, she'll assume I'm talking about smuggling weed."

"She'll listen," Clarence repeated.

"Let me go to the john. Jails and police stations have crappy toilets. I'll be right back."

"I can't let you go alone."

Joe Bob reached beside the beer and picked up a set of keys. He laid them alongside the five-dollar bill. "If I run, I can't go nowhere." He pushed the keyring closer to Clarence. "You don't want me wetting the back seat of the investigator's car."

Clarence looked again into the man's eyes. He knew what was about to happen. "You won't make trouble?"

"Pinkie swear," Joe Bob said. He raised another finger. This one, too, had dirt that would never come clean.

"Don't forget to wash your hands."

Joe Bob smiled. "Be right back." He stood and weaved his way through the bar. At the short hall leading to the restrooms, he turned and looked back at the bar.

Clarence raised his glass of water and took a drink. He'd been bold. He knew there'd be hell to pay.

As if on cue, Nance appeared at his side. "Your ten minutes are up. Where is he?"

"He went to the men's room."

Her eyes widened. "You let our suspect go alone?"

"I've got his keys." He pointed to the ring near the half-full beer.

Just then, the man from the pool table stepped to the bar and drained the glass.

"Those your keys?" Nance stabbed a finger.

The man's eyes dropped to her waist, seeing the badge and gun. He nodded. "But this is my only beer, I swear. One's my limit when I'm driving."

She didn't stick around to hear him. Nance raced to the back. Clarence heard her kick open the restroom door. She reappeared moments later. "Empty. And the window is open."

"We checked that side of the building," Clarence said. "You saw the scrabble."

"There's a path leading from outside the window. Plenty of beer cans and cigarette butts." She looked at Kemo. "Joe Bob isn't the first who needed to beat it out of here." She raced out of the bar, Clarence trailing behind. Along the street, several pairs of distant taillights showed. Nance unclipped her radio and called out a description of Joe Bob. She pulled the photo from the file in her SUV and read off the license plate.

She clipped the radio and turned on Clarence. Her eyes were livid. "You let him get away."

"I let him go to the john. You know what toilets are like in jail."

"Bullshit. You let him get away."

"He didn't kill the man," Clarence said.

"How do you know that? Because he's got a nice daughter?"

"Sometimes you've got to trust your instincts."

"My instincts said we needed to talk to him. Not put a fugitive on the loose. I got a warrant. And on top of everything, the chief thinks we're bringing him in." Nance grabbed the door handle. "Get in," she said when Clarence opened his mouth to speak.

They drove back to Everglades National Park. Night had fallen while they traveled. The two of them sat silently in the dark.

"I'm sorry," Clarence said. "We should have talked more."

"Remember when I told you about my high school trip to Florida for the catalog shoot? I got my picture on four pages. Years later, I started at the police academy. Someone in my rookie class papered the classroom wall with those four pictures. You know what I learned? You can be a cop and still be an asshole."

20

April 11th

Chief Ranger Zamora still didn't look jolly.

His red face glowered at them from behind his desk. Pictures of the chief in scuba gear, on the pistol range, and atop an airboat lined the wall behind. Farther down the wall, a young Zamora posed with fellow soldiers around the charred wreckage of a tank. "Last night, you told me you had a warrant and were about to arrest the guy for poaching and possible involvement in Hezekiah Freeman's murder. I went to bed happy. Cases cleared. Operations around the park returning to normal. Your reputation fully resurrected. Want to tell me how in the hell I've got nobody in custody and a murder suspect on the run?"

Nance stood at attention. Clarence saw that she made a point of looking directly at the chief, refusing to blink. She may be in trouble, but she wasn't backing down. "He wasn't at his home or place of business, sir."

"And this other location?"

Clarence had worn his crisp uniform to the meeting. If he was going to get his ass chewed, he wanted the boss to taste starch. "Losing him at the bar, that's on me. I thought I had a relationship with the guy. Hoped to get him to surrender without a scene at a bar. I overestimated our bond. He got away from me. Investigator Nance covered the most likely point of ingress and egress. She couldn't be everywhere."

"I appreciate your willingness to take one for your partner," the chief said. If the uniform impressed him, the chief failed to mention it. He shifted his stare back to Nance. "It never occurred to you that an experienced outdoorsman, a man you suspected of skillfully navigating the Everglades to poach exotic plants, might be able to blaze a trail through some Homestead bushes?"

Clarence thought it would be the wrong time to mention that the trail had been blazed with Budweiser empties.

"Sir, I covered the primary exit." She glanced over to Clarence. "And it was my responsibility to bring him in."

"First intelligent thing you've said all morning." The chief glanced down at his desk. He blew out a breath, fluttering the reports on his desk. "I'm not your chain of command. You're a problem for the Washington Support Office. But I am responsible for security in this park. Stop fucking it up. Hopefully, the locals will do the job you two couldn't. Dismissed."

Nance marched out the door and straight outside, stomping across the grounds. Clarence chased after her.

"Hold up," he said.

She turned in front of a saw palmetto displayed by the visitor's center, her face a picture of barely controlled rage. "What?"

"In 1699, Jonathan Dickinson wrote that palmetto berries taste like rotten cheese steeped in tobacco juice," Clarence read the information sign in front of the small tree. "From the look on your face, I'd say you had a couple."

"I'm not in the mood this morning."

"Some bosses are ladder climbers. Zamora looks like a guy who has spent time in the trenches. He's got to chew us out. But he understands exercising discretion."

"You didn't give the lead investigator the chance to use her discretion."

"I'm sorry." Clarence paused. "What are we going to do?"

"I don't know what you plan to do. I'm going to the office. Send an email to Montana Fish and Wildlife. Then, figure out how to catch the guy we let go last night."

"I told the chief that was on me."

"My case, my screwups, doesn't matter who made them. Talk later." She turned to walk away.

A car screeched to a stop in the parking lot. Mae Jefferson jumped out of the vehicle with the motor still running. She came straight at Clarence. "My daddy didn't kill nobody." She waved her arm at him.

He angled his body and struck a defensive position, ready in case she threw a punch at him.

"Oh, you gonna hit me now? Not happy unless you torture my whole family?"

Clarence kept his voice calm. He squared himself to face her, raising his hands in surrender. "Mae, let's just talk."

"You got no business accusing him." Her breath came in short gulps. Mae looked like she hadn't slept.

"Nobody is charging him with murder. We want to talk to him about stealing plants. Do you know where he is?" Clarence reached for her hand.

Mae pulled back. "No. Even if I did, do you think I'd tell you?"

"I want to help him. I wanted to help him last night."

"I heard about what happened. At the club, they say my daddy outsmarted you."

"Just help me talk to him. You know me. I'm not out to railroad anybody. But I need his help to clear this up."

"You're never going to find my daddy. Not if he doesn't want to be found." Mae shook her head. "And to think I was working hard to sleep with you." She shook her head again and turned back to her car.

"Mae, wait. Help me find him before someone gets hurt."

She slammed the car door and drove away.

He watched her go. Then he turned toward Nance.

She, too, turned her back to him and marched across the grass.

Clarence sat in the RV. Tripod, at least, hadn't scorned him. She lay curled on the bench beside him, snoring softly. He fingered a few blues chords on his guitar. It was a bluesy morning. His laptop lay open on the table. He didn't need coffee to wake up. Scotch, maybe, but definitely not coffee.

He thought about what Joe Bob had said. He opened the file and studied the pictures from Heka's camera. Clarence typed a subpoena request for Joe Bob's bank records and emailed it to Nance.

Financials might help us track a fugitive, he typed. Email seemed better than a phone call. He hit send. Almost immediately, his phone rang. "That was quick."

Silence followed. "Is this Johnson? This is Kemo from the club. I'm told you looking for Mae's daddy."

"You know I am."

"Not trying too hard last night to catch him, I saw that."

"Just want to talk to him. I'm not convinced he had anything to do with Heka's death. I want to find him before he gets hurt."

"An anonymous source says he's got a cypress dome in the 'glade he likes to go to when he wants to be alone."

"This source got a deep voice?" Clarence asked.

"My source paid good money to remain anonymous. But if you're asking if it was a man or a woman, I can tell you it was a guy."

"Deep-voiced guy?"

"He wouldn't be anonymous if I said too much, would he?" Kemo disconnected.

Almost immediately, his phone rang again. This time, he checked the number. The ID showed John Sucrito. Clarence answered.

"Heard you lost a suspect," Sucrito said.

The man must be driving with the top down, Clarence thought. He could hear wind noise in the background. "The investigation is ongoing."

"I just wanted to offer to help in any way I could."

"What do you think you could do?" Clarence asked.

The man paused. "I don't know, but if you need help, National Sugar wants to assist."

"We're currently pursuing leads. But if you have any information about the whereabouts of this or any fugitive, your assistance would be valuable." Clarence recited the lines.

"The Carroll family owns a helicopter. I can arrange access and a pilot. If you want an aerial search, just say the word."

"We are pursuing all available leads. If we form a public-private task force, I will keep your generous offer in mind."

"Don't be an ass, Johnson," Sucrito said. "We've had our differences, but I'm just trying to help."

"Then give me something helpful."

"You probably figured that Mae and I have some history from when we were kids. Her old man was the kind of guy who would always clean his guns when a guy would come to pick her up. He must have had the shiniest rifle collection in South Florida. The man also has a foul temper. Be careful."

"How many guns did he have?"

"At least three. That third date is the one I remember." Sucrito's laugh came straight out of the gutter.

"Thank you," Clarence said, because telling Sucrito to shut up and quit pumping for information would only prolong the conversation.

"Okay then. And if you decide that you want to try an aerial search, don't forget about the helicopter. I'm tight with the Carroll family. One phone call."

"Drive safely, John." This time, Clarence disconnected. He called Nance.

"I've expedited the financial subpoena, but I can't get the details this quickly," she said. Her voice suggested Nance had calmed down.

"I just got an anonymous tip that Jefferson might be hiding out in a cypress dome. I think the tipster meant the one where he went with Heka. Want to go for a wet walk?"

"Wade through a swamp with alligators and snakes?"

"We'll be noisy enough that I doubt we'll see any reptiles."

"Aren't you coming?"

"Ouch." Clarence breathed a sigh of relief. They seemed to be getting back to normal. "I'll pick you up," Clarence said. He hung up and went to change out of the crisp uniform. He needed clothes that would dry quickly.

They rolled along the Ingraham Highway. Nance stared out the passenger window. At the turn for Royal Palm, Clarence checked the odometer. He needed to go nine miles. Clarence told her about his conversation with Sucrito. He wasn't sure she listened. "So we've got a coupon for a free helicopter ride anytime we want."

"Flown a few times for rescue work in the Rockies," she said. "Don't miss the turbulence."

"Something on your mind?" he asked.

"Why don't you think Joe Bob's good for this?"

"When you look at the pictures, they're all centered. Middle of the frame. If you surprised someone in the act of poaching, I'd expect some to be off-center, out of focus. These look staged."

"You forget they were taken by a professional artist."

Clarence nodded. "My point. Covert op wouldn't be his wheelhouse. I'd expect the pictures to look like they were taken by a nervous guy. These don't."

Nance slowly nodded as she considered the idea.

"Another thing. The painting at the bungalow. Heka painted in the poacher. He didn't paint Joe Bob's face. He's not afraid of being sued, so why not use it? What better face to put on a man stealing from the national park than the ugliest human on the planet?"

"You might be right."

"Something else on your mind?" he asked.

She looked at him and shook her head. "No," she said before turning back to the window.

He steered into a slow bend in the road and slowed, looking for a small turnout.

"She said she tried to sleep with you."

"Football legend," he said. "I get so tired of women throwing themselves at me. Sex, sex, sex, sex, sex. Sometimes, getting a night of peace and quiet makes the best use of the bed."

Nance turned her head slightly further away.

Clarence took a deep breath. "Different time, different place, who knows. But coworker. That complicates things. It didn't feel right."

She nodded. She looked out the window. "I sent it."

"Sent what?" Clarence looked at her.

Nance faced forward, refusing to completely turn in his direction. "The application to Montana F and W. I hit send."

Clarence nodded. "If that's what you want, good luck."

Wordlessly, Clarence drove until they came to a small dirt trail. Ahead of them, the cypress trees mounded like a small hill. He followed an old road, barely more than a pair of ruts leading off the park's main route. The dirt trail sat two feet above the surface of the Everglades. Still, the slight rise in elevation kept the vegetation out of the water. Pine trees crowded them on both sides. They had to push to get the Suburban's doors open.

Up close, they could see what they already knew. Although looking like a hill, a cypress dome was, in reality, a water-filled low spot, a bucket out of which trees grew. The deepest water lay at the center. The trees grew tallest there. Smaller trees grew in the shallow water around the edges, giving the formation its bulbed shape.

Bald cypress dropped their needlelike leaves in the fall. They'd yet to grow back. Generations of decomposing foliage had stained the water brown. It looked as if they stood at the edge of a sink of dishwater.

"You really believe he's hiding in there."

Clarence shrugged. "I don't know. But we've got to look." He handed her a walking stick and waded into the dome.

With every step, the tea-colored water deepened. The pair moved slowly, feeling ahead with the walking sticks. The porous limestone rose and fell. Some steps brought them onto a rise. With others, they dropped down into pockets. Clarence felt his boot being nearly sucked off by the clutch of the accumulated cypress peat. He looked back at Nance. Her teeth chewed on her lower lip. Being shorter, each of the holes presented a greater challenge for her.

"Huh," she said and splashed.

Clarence turned. Nance had stepped wrong and fallen.

"I'm okay," she said, struggling back to her feet. She snapped her hand to flick off the excess water. "We might have just brought a bullhorn and yelled. We're not sneaking up on Joe Bob if he's in here."

Clarence nodded. "Let's take a minute." He took a breath. The cypress peat gave the enclosed dome an earthy smell. Clarence looked around. On the surface of the water, shiny black whirligig beetles spun circles.

Despite the difficulties, he saw that Nance also took in the landscape. Knobby cypress knees rose from the water like stalagmites. Above them, flowers bloomed. The bright red cardinal epiphytes seemed to be everywhere. Somewhere, a concealed woodpecker drummed at a tree trunk.

"I've never seen anything like it," Nance said. She turned slowly, studying the slough around her. "It's nothing like the Rockies. It's like a movie set."

Clarence pointed to a plant with small yellow flowers floating on the water. "That's bladderwort. It's a carnivore. Eats small bugs. See the little black dots?" He pointed along the stems to a line of small pea-like growths. "They're sacs. If a tiny bug floats by, the pea springs open, and the prey gets sucked inside."

"Really not the time to be talking about a trap for prey." Nance pointed to a long-stemmed plant topped with a bright purple flower. "What's that?"

Clarence closed his eyes. When reading the book about Everglades plants, he mainly concentrated on cattails. "I'm sorry…"

"Look over there." Her attention had already focused on something else. Nance pointed. "That looks like a Cowhorn orchid."

Clarence followed her finger and nodded.

"Shh, listen."

He focused, attuned to any sound of danger.

"Can you hear the breeze?" she said. "Hear it in the tops of the cypress trees. The limbs make an eerie creaking noise."

Clarence relaxed and listened to the gentle rasping sound. "It's a bit like a rusty hinge."

"Got your phone? We could use the sound at Halloween to spice up a haunted house."

The water exploded ten feet from where they stood. From somewhere, a rifle echoed.

Both dropped low into the water, scrambling for cover.

Another report, the water erupted as a bullet struck the surface. This shot hit closer.

Nance struggled to draw her gun. She held it level with her shoulder, water dripping from the barrel.

"Are you hit?" Clarence yelled.

She shook her head. She scanned the trees. "Where is it coming from?"

Clarence snapped his head in all directions.

Water rained down on him as a third shot hit the slough.

"We can't move, not in this muck," Nance said. "We'll be slow and exposed."

"Right now we're stopped and exposed. If he changes positions, we're dead." Clarence looked around, planted his walking stick, and pushed himself forward. He could not allow someone else to protect him. Clarence trudged as fast as he could. He passed Nance, slipping on the irregular ground and tearing his pants on the coarse rock and bark. He prayed his leg did not give out in this desperate rush.

A shot tore through the branches of the cypress over their heads. Clarence instinctively ducked. He heard something fall from the tree.

"Ugh," Nance grunted and splashed into the water. "I'm okay. Just fell." She shook the water from her firearm and looked around. "Damn it." She looked at her leg.

Clarence saw that the fall had gashed her pants and cut her. Blood oozed into the water. He grabbed a large handful of the moss floating on the surface, squeezed out the water, and pressed it against her thigh.

"Shit, that hurts," she said and placed her hand atop the mossy covering.

He tore a band of cloth from his shirt and bound the wound. Clarence looked at her.

Nance nodded. "I'm all right."

"We got to move."

She nodded again.

"You hear anything?"

Nance shook her head and peered into the trees. "You think he's gone?"

"Or lining us up."

Clarence slowed his pace and moved through the water cautiously, trying to keep the cypress trees between himself and his unseen enemy. He pressed forward, hoping that, with each step, he'd chosen the right side of the tree for concealment.

Clarence crouched low, sheltering himself behind a skinny cypress. The adjoining one partially covered Nance. He looked at her. "We're at the edge of the knob. The road is two steps above us. When we step foot beyond these trees, we will be totally exposed. Give me the gun. I'll go first."

"Because you're the guy?" Nance breathed heavily. The stress and exertion had them both breathless.

"Because you're hurt. Because I can't let someone else get shot protecting me. Because I couldn't live if something happened—"

"Tell it to your therapist," she said as she pushed up and out of the water. She bounded onto the road and quickly sought cover behind the Suburban.

Clarence followed behind. His eyes scanned the horizon, and his mouth scowled.

Nance pointed at the truck. The rear passenger tire lay flat with a gash in the sidewall. Clarence walked around the Suburban. "Whoever did this didn't care to trap us here. He just wanted to slow us down by forcing us to change a tire."

He looked at her. Nance's wet clothes hung from her. Her right calf oozed blood from a long scratch visible through her torn pant leg. A strand of hair hung across her face. He pushed the damp lock back behind her ear. Nance smiled. Then he walked to the truck and retrieved his first aid kit from behind the seat. He handed it to her. "Call it in. Then, tend to your leg. I'll handle the jack. Unless you want to prove something with it."

Nance untied the shirt bandage and began wrapping gauze around the moss. She grimaced. "You go ahead. I'll tell your therapist you were comfortable sharing. You don't suffer from macho hangups."

"Stick around," Clarence said as he assembled the jack. "When we find who did this, I'll show you a macho hangup."

21

April 11th

An ambulance awaited them at the visitor's center along with the superintendent, the chief ranger, and a horde of park personnel. Nance had called in a report as they sped back from the cypress dome. When she failed to mention her wound, Clarence snatched the radio away and added the missing details. The relayed report of "shots fired, officer wounded" had brought out every available ranger.

Chief Ranger Zamora, the superintendent, and Clarence stood at the back of the ambulance. Clarence's shirt had the bottom half torn off, exposing his abs. Water dripped from the remaining fabric. The chief handed him a replacement. "Got it from the gift shop." The pink T-shirt had a snapping alligator on the front below the logo for Everglades National Park. "Not many choices in your size."

Grabbing the old shirt by the collar, Clarence tore it from his body and dropped it onto the parking lot. He slipped on the new one. "It's perfect."

"Never seen periphyton used like that." The paramedic pointed at the moss as he cleaned and rebandaged the wound. "Super absorbent."

The command staff's eyes flicked to the ambulance. Then, they returned to Clarence.

His report was succinct. "Had an anonymous tip that Joe Bob was hiding in the dome. We went in. Somebody opened fire."

"Got a description?" the chief asked.

Clarence shook his head. "Never got a glimpse. Hard to pinpoint where the shots were coming from. Sound comes from everywhere in there."

The chief and superintendent nodded. They understood the acoustics of the cypress domes.

"We should take you to the hospital for X-rays," the paramedic said.

"It's a scratch," Nance said and began climbing out of the ambulance. "I'll sign whatever form you want. I'm good."

The paramedic looked at her before shifting his eyes to the chief ranger.

"Investigator Nance says she doesn't need to go to the hospital; take her word for it," the man said.

The paramedic nodded. "My work here is done." He began closing the ambulance.

The chief blew out a breath. "It's about to rain FBI."

"Can you wave them off?" Nance asked. "I'm fine."

The chief glanced at the superintendent and said what they all knew. "Standard procedure for an officer-involved shooting."

"I'm fine," she repeated.

"We never discharged our firearms," Clarence said. "Technically, this may not qualify as an OIS."

The chief raised an eyebrow and looked at Nance.

"It won't be a good look if the Bureau arrives and finds that we have an officer-involved scratch from a cypress stick."

The chief frowned.

"We'll be wasting time getting interviewed. Time that should be spent on a murder investigation," Nance added.

The chief closed his eyes and blew out another breath. After a moment, he opened them and nodded. The chief faced the superintendent. "I'll make some calls. I've got someone checking the video from the main entrance. We'll search for Jefferson's pickup. Unfortunately, we monitor inbound better than outbound."

Clarence checked his phone. He'd spoken to Kemo and John Sucrito just before leaving for the dome. He jotted the time down on his flip pad, tore off the page, and handed it to the chief. "Ask whoever is reviewing the tape to print photos of every vehicle arriving for the hours prior to this time."

The chief looked. "I thought the tip said that Jefferson was already hiding out there."

"That is what they said."

The superintendent pointed at them. "Get some rest. We'll let the locals catch Jefferson. Nance, stay off that leg." He turned and walked back to the office. The chief followed.

"You planning to stay off the leg?" Clarence asked.

"Hell, no," Nance said. "But I do want to shower and grab some clean clothes."

Clarence stood under the shower until he ran out of hot water. Tension had knotted his shoulders. The remains of his swamp-water-soaked clothes lay in a pile on the bathroom floor. Tripod walked around the pants, savoring the array of smells.

They met at Nance's house an hour later. She limped slightly as she walked away from the door.

Clarence wore his pink T-shirt. "I like the alligator. Fits my mood."

Shortly after he arrived, someone pounded on her door. Clarence opened it. Tom LaFleur looked at him, his face fell. Then the man smiled. "Glad to see you're okay." LaFleur stepped by him and hurried to Nance.

"Tom," she said, smiling.

LaFleur wrapped her in his arms. At first contact, she stiffened. Then Nance relaxed and hugged him back. "I needed to see that you were safe," he said.

"Just a few scratches. We're both fine," Nance said.

"I had to know." He reached into his pocket. LaFleur formed a fist and held his hand out to her. "I brought you something."

Nance looked at it, seemingly reluctant to open the fingers.

His hand unfolded. "It's your records, Alison. The bank expedited subpoena processing when they heard an officer had been shot."

She looked into his eyes and smiled. "You're a dear." Before he could say anything, she snatched the memory stick from his hand. Nance booted up her computer and inserted the drive. She waved Clarence over to her side. Then she turned back to LaFleur. "That's so rude. I'm sorry. It's just right now, I'm hyper-focused on catching the guy who shot at us. I forget my manners."

LaFleur nodded. "Totally get it." He took a step back. "You need anything?"

She patted her laptop. "You've given what I really want right now. Talk later?"

LaFleur nodded again. "See you, Johnson. Glad you're all right."

Nance stood in the doorframe and watched him leave. She waved. When LaFleur's Porsche disappeared from view, she came back to the kitchen island and opened the bank record files. The results disappointed them. Neither Jefferson's personal nor Southern Nursery accounts showed any recent withdrawals. Clarence noted that both accounts had low balances. Jefferson's personal account showed recent overdraft fees. The balances explained the limited inventory at the nursery.

"Nothing to give us a clue to his whereabouts," Nance said. "Could he be getting money from Mae?"

Clarence couldn't rule out the possibility. "Looks like the man is broke."

"Gives us a motive for poaching."

Clarence's phone rang. He answered.

"I swear I had nothing to do with any shooting," Joe Bob Jefferson said.

Clarence heard the panic in his voice. He pushed the speaker button on his phone. "This hole is getting deeper. Tell me where you're at."

Nance stood next to him, bringing her ear near the phone. The smell of her hair sat beneath his nose.

"I only went into the cypress trees so Heka could take his pictures. I didn't steal any orchids."

"Where are you now?" Clarence asked.

"I damn sure ain't hiding in the slough. Too damn hard to walk. A man can't even sit down."

"You own a rifle, Joe Bob?"

"It's South Florida."

"Bring it to me. Let me check the ballistics."

"You recover many bullets from that black water?"

"I'd still like to see your gun."

"You searched my place. The gun sits in the closet. Go get it yourself."

"What about the others? I heard you owned an arsenal."

"Had to sell a few. My daddy's gun is the only one I have left."

"I'd really like to talk to you," Clarence said. "I'm looking at some bank records. They show a man who needs money."

"Of course I'm broke. That's why I took Heka's money to let him snap my picture. But I didn't poach no orchids. I could lose my business." Joe Bob paused. "I don't need much money, just enough to make my payroll and buy a cold beer."

"Let's get together and talk about it," Clarence said. "Tell me where you are, and I'll come meet you."

"I'll have to call you back." Joe Bob Jefferson disconnected.

"Still think he's innocent?" Nance asked.

"I wish he'd surrender. This makes him look bad. But my gut says he's not our man."

Nance nodded. "Whoever was shooting wasn't trying to hit us. We were trapped out there. The shots ranged clearly wide of us and way over our heads. We weren't that hard to hit."

Clarence glanced at her leg. "I thought the same thing."

"He could've gotten away just by stabbing the tire. The gunfire was a show to distract us."

"Somebody wants us convinced that Joe Bob is the killer."

Nance nodded again. "But he's not. You know how I know?"

Clarence waited.

"Because the orchid in the picture is still there. Jefferson didn't steal it." Nance paused, her eyes distant, lost in thought. "How are we going to figure out who really did the shooting?"

Clarence stood and rolled his shoulders. The snapping alligator rose upward. "I'm going to ask a man who might know." He anticipated her question. "I'll ask him nicely."

They drove separately into Homestead. Clarence dropped his truck off to get a new tire and then rode with Nance. "Go to the club."

"A little early, don't you think?" she asked as she drove.

Clarence didn't answer.

The sparse crowd didn't look up when they entered. Kemo wiped the top of the bar with a towel. Clarence smiled and walked to the bar. Kemo nodded a greeting. Clarence grabbed him by his shirt collar and yanked him forward. Although Kemo was big, he hadn't expected the move. The wet bar top offered little resistance. The bartender slid over the top and crashed to the floor. Clarence wanted to get him subdued before Kemo could grab the baseball bat. Clarence stepped on his hand and put a knee on his chest.

"You said you were going to ask nicely," Nance said. She stood at an angle to the two men, allowing her to watch the rest of the bar.

"Kemo, tell me who the anonymous tipster was, please," Clarence said.

"Get off me," the bartender said.

"Nothing to see here," Nance said to the crowd. "Just enjoy your game and your drinks."

Clarence leaned forward, bringing more weight down on his leg. "When we followed your tip, someone in the slough started shooting at us. My partner over there got herself injured. Right now, you're about waist-deep in a conspiracy to kill a federal agent. So let me ask you again, nicely, tell me who your tipster was, please."

Kemo grimaced and shook his head. "I don't know. I swear I'd tell you. This Hispanic kid comes in and hands me an envelope. He says a guy approached him outside and asked if he wanted a sweet deal. Gave him fifty bucks to deliver the letter, he said. I opened the envelope. Inside were two one-hundred-dollar bills and some typed instructions giving me your number and telling me to say what I said."

"You get a description of the guy handing out money?"

Kemo shook his head. "The kid didn't say. I didn't ask."

"And you didn't think that sounded suspicious?"

"If the guy wanted me to know who he was, I figured he'd have carried the letter himself."

"You don't even know if it was a guy?"

"The Hispanic kid said a guy paid him. That's all I know."

"Where's the kid?"

"How the hell should I know? He just walked in off the street."

Clarence leaned into his leg. "And this didn't feel like a setup?"

"Of course. But two hundred dollars is two hundred dollars."

"You still got the note?"

"It's in the trash. I ain't emptied it yet."

Clarence looked at Kemo's face. "If I let you up, will we have a problem?"

Kemo shook his head.

"I need you to find the note, you understand?"

Kemo nodded.

Clarence quickly stood. He had his hands poised, ready to respond if Kemo charged.

The bartender lay on the ground for a moment. He took a deep breath and rubbed the spot on his chest where Clarence had knelt. Then, he slowly crawled to his feet and slapped his backside to dust himself clean.

Kemo turned to Nance. "Ma'am, I want to apologize for you getting hurt. I had no idea that something like that was about to happen."

She flashed a look at the crowd. Nobody had moved. She turned to Kemo. "I believe you. Please find the note that Ranger Johnson asked for."

"Yes, ma'am." Kemo went behind the bar and pulled out a tall plastic bin. He dug down inside, spilling trash over the edge. He pulled out a single sheet of wrinkled paper and held it up. "Got wet. Some of the typing is smeared."

"Don't forget the envelope."

Kemo pulled a stained business envelope from the bin.

"What about the two hundreds? Where are they?"

Kemo shook his head. "Already spent them."

"You have a clean, empty trash bag?"

"Got my dinner in a plastic grocery sack," Kemo said.

"That'll do."

Kemo set the letter and envelope on the bar and bent down. Clarence quickly stepped to the side to see what his hands reached for. They opened a small refrigerator beneath the bar. Kemo emptied the bag. He closed the fridge and put the letter inside the bag. He gave the bag to Clarence. The bartender's eyes went to Nance again. "I'm sorry somebody hurt you."

"Thank you, Kemo."

Clarence and Nance backed out of the club.

They sat in the parking lot, waiting to see if anyone emerged. Clarence held up the sack. "Send the letter to the lab for analysis?"

"The guy typed the letter and hired some unknown kid to deliver it. No way he left his fingerprints or DNA. But we have to check."

"Yes, we do." Clarence looked at her. "You noticed that I said 'please' unbidden."

"Unbidden?"

"Clarence Johnson, Renaissance man."

On the drive back to the Everglades, Clarence's phone rang. The screen showed a DC number. He answered.

"Ranger Johnson, please hold for Congressman Carroll."

"Clarence, this is Mike Carroll. I just heard from my brother that the same thug who killed the artist shot at you and wounded your partner."

"We don't know that it's the same guy. The investigation is continuing."

"How about your partner?"

"Fortunately, no one was seriously injured."

"Tough as old boots, you rangers. Thoughts and prayers, Johnson. Sit tight." The congressman's voice became muffled. "Tell them to push that back," he told someone in the room. "Johnson, I'm flying down to Florida tonight. Want to get you two together for a picture. That kind of press does us all some good."

Nance emphatically shook her head, signaling her displeasure.

"I'll have my aide call the superintendent. You've got this number. If you need anything, call me. I'll be in the air in a couple of hours. You need it this afternoon, call Mother. Kathryne Carroll will get the FAA to find me. Mother has her ways. Good talking to you. Got to go." The line went silent.

Nance frowned. "Now we have to be campaign ads too?"

"Never let a crisis go to waste."

"Ugh."

"Ask the congressman if he'll be a reference on your fishing license application."

She made a face. "Only if you promise me that you'll wear the pink shirt."

They pulled into the repair shop. The new black tire stood in sharp contrast to the rest of Clarence's dust-shrouded Suburban. "What do we do now?" he asked. Clarence's phone rang before Nance could answer.

"This is Johnson."

"Hey, it's John Sucrito." The man sounded friendly. "Heard you guys got into trouble. Calling to check if everyone is okay."

"My partner got wounded. Things are a little dicey here. We're thinking she'll pull through."

Nance made another face. She drew back her fist.

"Shit, that's awful." Sucrito sounded genuinely worried. "Anything I can do?"

"Pray," Clarence said.

"Look, I want to apologize for the other night. Beer. I'm sorry."

"Forget it. Our dick-measuring contest is the least of my problems. I've got to go, John."

"Wait."

Johnson held the phone.

"I had a thought," Sucrito said. "When Florida was a wilder place, if you had trouble and wanted to disappear, a guy would run to Chokoloskee in the Ten Thousand Islands region. I got to thinking. Jefferson is an old-time Florida guy. His family has been here as long as the Carrolls and old man

Freeman. I'm guessing that's where he might run. Escaping there is part of old Florida DNA, you know."

"Good idea. I'll ask someone to check it. The doc is taking her to surgery. I got to go." Clarence hung up the phone.

"Pray," Nance said. "You better pray I don't kick your ass for making the world think I'm lying in intensive care somewhere."

"You heard the man. Pumping me for information. Till we figure out who we can trust, I don't want to level the playing field."

"That's the second time he's tried that. You remember the first time?"

"Just before we went to the cypress dome." Clarence frowned, considering her point. "Kemo said that the guy who spoke to the kid offered him a sweet deal. Does that sound like language a sugar guy might use?"

Nance frowned. "That's a stretch. And checking to see if you're alive doesn't prove anything. But we might want to ask a few more questions about your new best friend."

"Mike said I should call Kathryne if I had any questions."

"Maybe later. First, I was thinking about something else. Follow me." She started the SUV.

"Where we going?"

"It's time for a little girl talk."

22

April 11th

Mae threw her arms around Clarence. She hugged him hard. "I heard about the shooting. I was so worried. Thank God you're all right." Then she dropped her arms and stepped back. "But I hope you don't think you can just show up here like you're all entitled to a little something just because you're some kind of hero."

"It doesn't make you a hero because the other guy missed," Clarence said.

"Now you're acting all modest," Mae said. She dipped her chin, and a slight grin appeared.

"Actually, today I'm just the escort."

Mae's face registered confusion.

Nance pulled the front door open wide. "Ms. Jefferson. My name is Special Agent Alison Nance of the NPS Investigative Services Branch. I wondered if I might talk to you for a few minutes. I have some questions."

Mae's grin disappeared. She stepped back; her eyes flicked from Clarence to Nance. "I don't have anything to say about my daddy."

Nance shook her head. "I don't want to talk to you about Joe Bob Jefferson. I have a few questions about John Sucrito."

Mae chewed on her lower lip. Her eyes again went from Nance to Clarence. He nodded. "She's for real. Wants to talk about things other than your daddy."

Mae stepped back from the door and turned. "Come on in. Y'all want something to drink?"

The living room of Mae's townhouse had a single chair and a sofa. A coffee table cluttered with art magazines separated the pieces. Clarence took the chair. Nance sat on the couch next to Mae. She rested her hands on her knees, palms facing upward. Everything about Nance's body language broadcast that she did not represent a threat. Her eyes roamed the room, taking in the art hanging from the walls. Art climbed the stairs leading to the bedrooms on the second level. "Are all these yours?"

A small smile cracked Mae's mouth. "I painted these. My style is different from Heka's."

Nance studied the artwork. Clarence followed her eyes. Like her godfather, Mae painted landscapes focusing on the watery wilds of South Florida. Unlike Heka, she relied on short brushstrokes and an array of colors to give her paintings energy. The paint was thick in many places, laid on with a palette knife, lending depth to her art. Her style displayed more abstraction than Heka's. In many of her landscapes, a folkloric animal appeared. Nance smiled. "They shimmer, the boundaries of land, water, and sky merge. Your art looks like this place."

"Thank you," Mae said, and her smile broadened.

"Of course, I'm not the art critic." Nance nodded her head toward Clarence.

"He'll just blather on about how they are reminiscent of some medieval Flemish painter he read about in some Art History for Jocks class." Mae turned to Clarence and waggled her shoulders.

"I was going to say that they reminded me of what might happen if Hieronymus Bosch got into a paint fight with Claude Monet. But I thought that would be unkind," he said.

"You just keep mentioning my name in the same sentence as Monet. I don't care what you say, baby." Mae turned back to Nance. "You want art, I'll sell you some."

"It would be hard to let some of them go, I imagine," Nance said, studying the walls.

"I'm selling all of them. I can't afford to stay in the business."

Clarence leaned forward in his chair.

Nance frowned. "That's terrible."

Mae shook her head. "Got a lead on becoming a graphic designer in Miami." She shrugged. "You can still call it art if it's a website, right?" Mae looked at her paintings and blinked. Then she turned back to Nance. When she spoke, her voice had an edge to it. "You didn't get him to lead you over here to talk about my art. What do you really want?"

"What can you tell me about John Sucrito?"

"You think he killed Heka?"

Nance brushed away the suggestion. "I'm so sorry if I gave you that impression. But I'm working on a couple of cases. Heka's murder is the top priority, of course. But law enforcement never has just one thing going on at once."

Mae leaned back, distancing herself from both investigators. "That sounds like you don't want to say he's involved in the murder, so you just keep talking around it."

Nance bent forward, her forehead nearly touching her knees. "Uhhh. God, this is so awkward. Okay, here's the deal." She paused and took a deep breath. She glanced over at Clarence. Nance looked red in the face. She babbled. "John has been texting me. It started out as legit work stuff. The last few have been more suggestive, like he's hitting on me. And I don't know, he's kinda cute. And I was thinking about hitting him back. But then, Johnson mentioned that you and Sucrito knew one another. And I thought maybe..." Nance broke off and bent down again. "God, I shouldn't." She sat up and looked at Mae. "But you know how it is. I travel all the time for the job. And I really don't get a chance to meet anybody. And the guys at work"—she glanced at Clarence—"I mean, they're nice and all, but we just end up talking about business, and there are so many rules about fraternization with coworkers." Nance sat back. She looked exhausted by the confessional.

Clarence stood. "This is weird." He turned to Mae. "I'm sorry, I thought we were doing something related to the case."

"Sit down, Nasty Man. It's cool." Mae gave Nance a half smile. "So you want to know what kind of man John Sucrito is?"

Nance shook her head. "Forget it. This is stupid. Bad idea. Terrible idea." She paused. "I mean, unless you think you know something."

Mae quickly glanced at Clarence. She shifted her gaze back to Nance. "I thought you two might be...maybe explain why he wouldn't take me up on my invitation."

Nance made a quick shake of her head. "My work husband."

Mae smiled and leaned closer to Nance. "I'm going to be real with you. Sucrito is not a long-term proposition. He is not your guy if that's what you're looking for. I have to tell you that it's been a long time since we went out, but people don't change. Not in some ways."

Nance nodded.

Mae paused. Clarence saw her eyes appraised Nance from a new perspective. "Not surprised that he might hit on some eye candy like you. John's got big ambitions. He's got style. Likes people to know about his money. Always likes to keep himself in name brands, you know. He'll treat you right. You'll get name-brand presents too. He wouldn't want any woman of his to be walking around in something that didn't have a label."

Nance nodded. She looked like she was taking mental notes.

"When we were in high school, he arranged a trip to Mexico to buy some fake Rolex watches. He wanted to look like he ran with the Carroll boys. Of course, now his watch is real."

Nance frowned. "He sounds a little, I don't know, statusy. I mean, I don't want a guy always checking himself in the mirror. I don't need deep, but I definitely don't want shallow. I want to do some talking." She gave Mae a suggestive smile. "You know, like afterward."

Mae laughed and pointed to Clarence. "We got to ditch this lump and find us some margaritas. Sucrito has ambition, always has. Hustled in high school and still out there working it. But you got to admire a guy who knows how to be bold, you know? He'll just lay it all out there and go for it. The Carrolls treat him like dirt. They knock him down. He just gets right back up, dusts himself off, and says, try again. He's got a plan. Jeffersons, Sucritos, we all been living down here taking scraps from the Carrolls for generations. John is one of those guys who's working hard to get to that next level." She raised her hand and gestured to an imaginary plane above her eyeline. "If you're a woman who likes a bold man who sees what he wants and goes for it, not taking no for an answer, you might have some fun with John Sucrito."

"Girlfriend, thank you." Nance frowned. "You won't tell him we had this talk, will you? I mean, I want the guy to think he will have to work a little for it."

"Girls don't snitch. You don't worry about me, sister." Mae dipped her head toward Clarence. "He's the one who might get all gossipy."

"I can't wait to tell him the next time Sucrito and I go to the bathroom together," Clarence said.

The two women burst into laughter. They hugged, excluding Clarence from the trust circle.

Nance didn't speak until the SUV had driven around the corner, safely out of sight of Mae's house. She stopped. "We'll probably need a different strategy when we get to the Carrolls' estate. Congressman won't be back yet. And when he is, I doubt you two can boy talk."

"We'd probably just go lift weights."

Nance chewed on her lip. "Why would somebody steal his computer? What did he have on it that they needed?"

"And didn't want anyone to know he had?" Clarence added. "If you just wanted the contents, you snatch the computer. You don't replace it."

"Real surveillance? Do you think he was snooping into poaching?"

"Heka said he was thinking about writing a memoir. *Three Times a Slave*, he called it. He might have written something that scared somebody."

"Or at least made them think they needed to be scared," Nance said.

"Maybe plans for the unfinished painting? You should have seen your boyfriend's reaction when an audience member suggested that the sugar industry was responsible for pollution in the Everglades."

Nance rolled her eyes. "You've never lied as part of questioning a witness?"

"Of course. And sometimes I tell the truth."

"It was a tactic. It worked. Would she have been forthcoming if we just threw questions at her? Mae would have been too afraid we were trying to locate her daddy."

As they traveled, the sky darkened. Rain began falling as they arrived at the Carrolls' estate.

A hint of the season to follow. Nance parked under the portico to remain mostly dry.

Matt Carroll opened the door as they cleared the final stairs. He ushered them inside and quickly closed the door. "Once it starts, it won't quit until Halloween." He wore khakis and an untucked button-down shirt.

Kathryne appeared in the hall. "Who was at the door, Matthew?" She stopped. Kathryne looked down at his feet. Matt wasn't wearing shoes. She looked at Clarence and Nance. "Ranger Johnson, Special Agent Nance, I apologize for my son's appearance. We didn't expect you until tomorrow."

Clarence couldn't tell which of the observed facts disappointed her more. "We're not here for the picture." He pinched the pink T-shirt. "I plan to change. But I had just a couple of quick questions for Matt."

"Matthew, why don't you take them to the dining room. I'll arrange coffee." Kathryne turned and disappeared.

"You heard Mother," Matthew said as he led them down the hall, pausing only long enough to slip on a pair of loafers.

They had all heard Kathryne. They knew she would join them. In the dining room, the conversation lagged as they awaited her arrival.

Clarence pointed his thumb over his shoulder. "May I show her the Audubons while we wait?"

Matt nodded and led them into the small sitting area where he and Clarence had talked the last time they were together.

Nance looked at the lithographs.

"And he calls these pictures the family tree," Clarence said, pointing to the family grouping.

Nance studied those, feigning interest. "I hear that your family, the Jeffersons, and the Sucritos were all among the first families down here?"

Matt looked at the family wall and nodded. "It would be cool if we had a photograph of the three families together. Have some local historical significance. But there weren't many photographers down in these parts back then. Photos were expensive. They didn't shoot candids or selfies."

The quiet woosh of the dining room door swinging open announced that Kathryne had arrived. They returned to the dining room. She stood at the head of the table. A maid poured and distributed coffee cups before disappearing.

Clarence tasted the coffee. He raised an approving eyebrow.

Kathryne's cup sat before her, untouched. "And what did you wish to ask Matthew?"

"I was hoping you could tell me a little about John Sucrito," Clarence told Matt.

"Mr. Sucrito manages one of our properties. He looks after our interests," Kathryne said.

"Is he paid well?"

"I believe money to be a private matter."

"He just seems to spend more than I'd expect a farm manager could."

Kathryne Carroll looked down at her cup. "As you've observed, Ranger Johnson, to Mr. Sucrito, status is important. I assume he is frugal in some matters, so he might be a bit ostentatious in others."

Clarence looked across the table. "Matt, what do you think?"

"John is a good guy. Great guy to have at your back if you're going into a bar. He likes nice things. I'm actually thinking about a business idea. I'd like to let him buy a fraction."

"What's the business?" Nance asked.

"It's land development for a tech incubator. I'm thinking about calling it Sunshine State Silicon." He paused. "Sucrito says that sounds like a plastic surgery center." Matt Carroll laughed.

"The whole concept sounds a bit speculative." Kathryne frowned as she spoke.

"What about the campaign? Does Sucrito do anything to help your son get elected?" Clarence asked.

"Mr. Sucrito's role is limited to helping the Carroll family on the business side," Kathryne said.

"Any particular reason he gets sidelined?"

"Ranger Johnson, the family's business interests are not a sideline. We have been a business family since the Civil War."

Clarence nodded. "Let me rephrase the question, ma'am. Is there any particular reason why you keep Mr. Sucrito away from the public eye?"

Kathryne inhaled a full breath. She repositioned the coffee cup. "Again, as you've undoubtedly observed, Mr. Sucrito can be a bit enthusiastic. Sometimes, overenthusiastic." She looked around the room. "Now, if you will excuse me. Michael returns late tonight, and we have a hectic day tomorrow. Please do be on time."

They all stood. Kathryne glided out of the dining room.

"Let me walk you to the door," Matt said. The three of them stepped outside. The shower had passed, clouds slowly blew away, and a few stars began to appear in the patches. "Sorry, but Mother gets worked up. The truth is that Sucrito's family has worked for us for more than a century. John, for all his bluster, is bright. He has a chance to get out from under the Carrolls' fiefdom. Old Florida, New Ideas." Matt grunted. "We like the Old Florida part. I want John to succeed. That's why I'm trying to bring him in on the tech start-up. And he wants it. He works hard and does extra work to squirrel away money. He's going to be a junior partner."

"Good luck with your business," Clarence said.

"And thank your mother for allowing us to disturb your evening," Nance said.

"Be on time tomorrow," Matt said. "She was serious. She has Mike scheduled for a busy day of appearances. The heroic picture of the two of you needs to happen quickly."

"Will do," Nance said.

"And Johnson. Wear the shirt tomorrow. Tell Mother you wanted to demonstrate the candidate's commitment to environmental issues. If you do, I'll buy drinks just to see the look on her face."

"You really want to see me killed by an elderly woman? What did I do to you?" Clarence asked.

They heard Matt laughing as he walked back inside the house.

"Sounds like we've got motive," Nance said as she drove back to the national park. "We've got a guy with ambition and a deep need for money. A man who is willing to be bold."

"If Matt's bar comment is true, not afraid of trouble," Clarence added. In the darkness, he saw the silhouette of Nance's head nod in agreement.

"A man who has been poor has a business opportunity dangling in front of him. This may be a once-in-a-lifetime. He needs to raise some capital to buy in." Nance slowed to make the turn onto the park road.

"I'll give you motive," Clarence said. "But lots of people need money. We don't have anything linking Sucrito to poaching, the murder, or our shooting. Joe Bob makes a better suspect. He needs money, and we've got a poaching photo."

"I thought you wanted him cut loose as a suspect."

"I don't think he's guilty either. I just mean, we have better evidence on him than Sucrito."

"But you know those feelings you keep talking about. That gut instinct that seems to drive most of your actions," Nance said.

"That's my stomach. It says we haven't eaten."

"I'm hungry too. But my gut says that I like this guy as a suspect. I got a box of frozen egg rolls and four beers in the fridge. You want dinner?"

"May I bring Tripod?"

"She gets one of your eggrolls. I'm starved."

Clarence's phone rang. "Johnson."

"My girl tells me you decided Sucrito put this case on me."

"Joe Bob, we didn't discuss Sucrito's involvement in the case with Mae. My partner had some questions about an unrelated matter."

"Yeah, Mae told me that they had girl talk. A story like that works with Mae. I know better."

"Come in. We'll talk about why you might not be guilty. I promise we're prepared to believe you."

"I got things to do. I'll talk to you later, Johnson."

"Joe Bob, wait—" Clarence stopped. He only heard himself on the line. He turned to Nance. "Joe Bob Jefferson doesn't believe you are interested in John Sucrito."

"Smart man. Smart enough to plan a murder." Nance pulled in front of the RV and stopped.

A few minutes later, he arrived at Nance's door with Tripod tucked under his arm.

She smiled. "Most guys bring flowers."

"I'm not most guys." He followed her inside. Clarence could hear the oven fan. He set his dog down. She began mapping the interior of the house, following her nose. Tripod circled the heavy punching bag Nance had erected in her small living room.

"Nice tackling dummy."

"You're not always around when I want to hit something." As she spoke, Nance had laid out two placemats with plates and forks, one on either side of the island. She handed Clarence a beer; her eyes watched the dog. "Remarkable animal."

"Tripod is an agile beast on three legs."

"I meant that she can live with you and remain so normal."

Clarence popped the top and deliberately blew the foam across the kitchen.

Nance slid her hand into an oven mitt and retrieved the egg rolls. "I cooked them in the microwave and put them in the oven to crisp."

Clarence took a baggie from his shirt and poured a serving of dog food onto a paper plate. He set it down. "And I decided I was too hungry to share."

Clarence took a bite of an egg roll, chewed deliberately, nodded, and then chased it with beer.

Nance finished her first roll and licked her fingertips. Clarence found the small action incredibly sexy.

"What are you looking at?" Nance asked.

Clarence blinked. "Trying to picture you as a model. What was that like?"

Nance's cheeks reddened. "Summer fantasy. Dreams of St. Tropez and the runways of Milan crashed against the reality of chain-smoking as an appetite suppressant." She ran a hand awkwardly along the side of her head. "And when my hair was long, it tended to get frizzy."

"Your hair looks great short."

Nance smiled and looked down at her plate.

"Is that why you quit? Bad hair day?"

Nance turned to the refrigerator. She handed him a second beer. "What should our game plan for tomorrow be?"

Clarence popped the top and looked down at the froth bubble. "Hopefully, the ranger reviewing the footage cracks our case. Then we go get our picture taken."

"I'm not holding my breath."

Clarence crunched through the crispy wrapper of the second egg roll. "Don't know if we don't look."

Nance nodded. "We waste a lot of time chasing leads that don't pan out in this business. The job would be so much easier if they'd only tell us the plan."

"Amen, sister. But then this job wouldn't be nearly as much fun."

Tripod chased the paper across the tile floor, pursuing the last morsel. Clarence noticed that Nance had fallen quiet. "Thinking about the case?"

She shook her head. "Montana F and W offered me a job."

Clarence swallowed and waited a moment to speak. "That was fast."

"The email said that in light of my exceptional résumé, they wanted to forego the usual procedures and offer me a position."

He forced a smile. "Congratulations. What are you going to do?"

"Nothing until we find this guy."

"That could take a while."

She shook her head. "I need to decide before the ice goes out on the northern lakes."

After a silence, Clarence polished off the second egg roll. Nance had, too. The beer cans stood empty. He stooped and collected his dog. "Thank you for a lovely dinner."

Nance didn't answer.

Clarence stepped toward the door. "I need to get my beauty rest. Some of us don't have experience with photo shoots."

He turned.

"Johnson."

Clarence turned back. "Yes, Special Agent Nance."

Nance rounded the island. She walked up to him, placed a hand behind his neck, and pulled his face to her. She kissed him hard on the mouth. The arm holding Tripod reached around to her back. The dog began to squirm, breaking the spell.

Alison stepped away. She wiped her mouth with her sleeve.

Clarence felt a little breathless. "What was that about?"

She looked him in the eye. "I've been curious. Somebody needed to be bold."

23

April 12th
(Before dawn)

The sliding door to Heka's house opened. Clarence walked inside without turning on a light. He couldn't sleep. Clarence had lain in bed, his mind churning. His restless energy had unnerved Tripod. His dog paced the RV, her toenails clacking up and down its length.

Clarence had walked to Hezekiah's. He searched for answers to myriad questions. At least here, he might channel all his pent-up energy into something useful. Clarence followed the path Heka's killer likely chose. Patiently, he walked into the house, his eyes searching for anything he might have missed.

What did it mean? he wondered. Clarence stopped and sat on the bed. Was he thinking about the case or Alison?

He surveyed the room from where he sat. The bookcase drew his eye. They usually did in any house he visited. What someone read or chose to keep said something about them. Clarence grabbed a chair, sat before the low-slung bookcase, and reviewed the titles. The books were a jumble with no order. Art books intermingled with novels by Ralph Ellison and Ta-Nehisi Coates. He pulled out a slim three-ring binder. Sheet protectors held pictures of Heka's paintings, beginning in the early days and moving forward. Clarence thought he saw an unwritten biography emerge as he flipped the pages. Critics and buyers recognized Heka's potential as a young man. Heady success followed. Clarence flipped back to the early ones. Mae displayed the same gift, Clarence thought. He wondered if he should talk to her and try to get her to change her mind about abandoning her dream.

Clarence shook his head to clear it. Maybe he needed to manage his own life before wading deeper into hers.

The next group of paintings disappointed Clarence. They lacked something, soul perhaps. They had likely been produced in mass across a series of sleepless nights while on a cocaine bender. Heka had been hot and could sell anything he signed his name to. He created art on an assembly line to feed his addiction. The paintings became increasingly erratic. Heka seemed to splash paint more than apply it. The colors skewed darker.

The last pages contained his recent work. The CARE gallery displayed some of these pieces. As he discovered, the photos didn't hint at the power of the original works. Photographs couldn't reveal the underdrawings, the qualified *pentimento*. Much of the power of the art got lost in a picture.

Behind the pictures, Heka had scrawled pages of text. Clarence tried to read them. The old man's handwriting was atrocious. Fortunately, he'd chosen painting over calligraphy as his vocation. The bookcase lamp proved inadequate to decipher the squiggles. Clarence carried his chair to the table and switched on the light.

Nothing happened. Clarence checked the closet in the kitchen for a replacement bulb. He found one in a box containing a pair of small LED lamps. He replaced the bulb and began struggling through Heka's handwriting.

The man wrote about his art, outlining the meaning behind the paintings. The middle section was brief: *Shit I did while high.* He read a brief scribble complaining that NFTs hadn't been around when Heka really needed easy dope money. Clarence flipped to the end. He hoped the artist might say who he intended to portray with the underpainted figures. Disappointingly, he found few details. Clarence read scattered notes about phosphorus and sugar runoff. Heka had a paragraph on poaching and insatiable greed. Clarence sat back in the chair. Perhaps the man hadn't had the time to write up his thoughts about many of his current works.

Was art, and its hold on Heka, the third enslavement? Clarence wondered. He stood and walked back to the bookcase. He collected another three-ring binder. Clarence sat down and opened it. Heka outlined his family's history, stories handed down for generations about his slave ancestors.

Heka's grandfather had related the tale. His family had escaped from an Edgefield, South Carolina, plantation. They had fled south, seeking freedom in the uncharted Everglades, with dreams of getting to the Bahamas. The fugitive slaves possessed only the things they could carry. Heka's grandfather told the story of the pot of dreams.

The dreams had been crushed when two evil slave hunters had captured the family beneath the crying trees. Hate and greed so consumed these men that one hunter killed the other. The crying trees represented death and sadness. Clarence looked up at the painting. It hung slightly crooked on the wall. The trees also represented freedom. A mother and her young son had been ransomed and allowed to leave. *That boy was pa-paw's great-grandfather*, Heka had written.

Clarence leafed through the pages. His eyes had grown accustomed to Heka's scrawl. He looked for anything that might point to the killer. Although the story continued in a mostly linear progression, detailing civil rights struggles and stories of his grandfather's service during World War Two, it included nothing about the present. At the back was an envelope addressed to Mae. He closed the binder.

Either the mystery dated back generations, or the memoir draft offered nothing of value to the investigation. Clarence put the binders back on the bookshelf.

If Clarence wrote his memoir, he wondered, what would it say about his life? Did he risk missing out on a significant chapter in his story? He remembered the security guard lying on the sidewalk in Fort Worth and a blood-soaked trail in Yellowstone. Clarence shook his head again. He needed to keep his attention focused. His hand slapped the table, rattling the desk lamp.

Clarence walked back to the kitchen and retrieved the box. Why does a man in an efficiency bungalow have so many lamps? He took one out. They were IR lamps, part of Heka's art supplies. Clarence collected them both and set them up facing the unfinished painting. He re-photographed the art and popped the disk into his laptop.

The results surprised him. Perhaps the cool night offered less heat to clutter the imagery. The added infrared light may have sharpened the underpainting. Clarence could only guess the reasons behind his success. What he knew without question, more details revealed themselves.

Little had changed with the man in the foreground. The sketch still had Joe Bob Jefferson's build. The shape of the head fit, but no facial details emerged, even in the enhanced light. To the side of the poacher, another man showed. He reached out to receive the poacher's bounty. While the poacher had the rough look of a man from the wild, the recipient appeared neat and corporate. The unfinished piece echoed the themes Clarence had found in the waving sawgrass's underpainting. The responsibility for plundering the Everglades went deeper than just the actual perpetrator who performed the act. Clarence wondered if the suited recipient was Sucrito, the well-dressed opportunist.

In the background of the painting, another man stood. Clarence leaned forward to study him. He had not been visible in the original IR photograph. This figure stood behind the well-dressed man. He handed something bulbous forward, another plant, or a bag of money. Like the Joe Bob model, Heka had painted a gray swatch across the man's face, obscuring his features. Another anonymous person committed crimes against the environment.

Clarence's phone rang.

"You awake?" Nance asked.

"Down at Heka's. Trying to figure things out."

"You can't go there alone."

"Couldn't sleep. Didn't want to wake you to ask permission."

Nance exhaled. "I was reading. Zamora called. The chief wants to see us in his office right away."

Clarence checked the time. "Are we in trouble?"

"He didn't say."

"I'd think taking fire would buy us a grace period."

"Unless he heard about you throwing a man over a bar."

"There is that. I better put on a clean shirt. It's always best to look good for an ass-chewing."

"Things I didn't need to know before we met," Nance said. "Hurry, he's waiting on us."

"On my way." Clarence hung up, dropped the phone into his pocket, scooped up his computer, and turned off the light. He paused before the picture of the crying trees and straightened it. Then, changing his mind, he took the painting from the wall and carried it out the door.

A quarter of an hour later, the pair again were in front of the chief's desk. Nance stood at attention. Clarence wondered how many times this might happen. He was running out of clean uniforms. He needed this one to remain crisp until after the photo shoot.

If Zamora found it odd that Johnson had entered the office carrying a framed painting, he didn't mention it. Clarence felt he detected less hostility in the chief's manner. The man still displayed his gruff demeanor. Clarence figured crusty was a job requirement. But the chief's gruffness seemed less...gruffy this morning.

"At ease, Nance. You're looking well. Feel okay?"

"The leg is fine, sir."

The chief nodded. "I had the men review the activity at the main entrance. They ran back through the tape and printed stills of every vehicle passing through." He handed a thick folder to her. "Here you go, Special Agent. Each picture has a time stamp."

"Thank you, sir."

"Just figure out who did this." The chief shuffled the papers on his desk. "And Nance. I'm glad you're not hurt."

"Thank you, sir," she repeated.

"Chief, may I ask a question?" Clarence turned the picture to face the man on the other side of the desk. "You've been here for years. Any guess as to this place?"

The chief ranger studied the picture. He frowned. "This is the picture from Hezekiah's house."

Clarence nodded. "When Special Agent Nance accompanied me to the crime scene, she directed me to collect it."

Zamora's eyes briefly flicked to Nance. "He asked me about it a few months back. I'll tell you what I told him. The shape resembles every hammock in the Everglades." His eyes ranged over the picture. "We've got the Mahogany Hammock just off the main road about twenty miles from here. It's got one of the oldest living mahogany trees, but just one. Nothing like this pair." The chief shook his head.

Clarence laid out the photos of the woods recovered from Heka's camera.

"Now these are of the old-growth Mahogany Hammock." The chief turned a picture around and pointed. "See the difference?"

Clarence and Nance both nodded.

"The Everglades are remarkably geologically stable below the surface. But, like any place, landscape changes around here. Hurricane Andrew reshaped the park. Fires sweep across the sawgrass. The hammocks are usually protected. They're built to resist a burn." The chief mused. "Is it important?"

"The place was important to our victim. We need to consider whether it means anything."

"Well, if you find anything significant," the chief said, "don't tell anyone that you got assistance from me. I wouldn't want people to think that a career law enforcement guy would rather be doing casework when he has a budget request and human resources paperwork to fill out."

Clarence touched his index finger to his lips. "Not a word, sir."

"Don't forget to smile for the camera. The publicity will do the park good." Zamora picked up the top page from his neat pile of paperwork. "If you need to see the entrance video, I'll get one of the visitor use assistants to walk you through it."

They hurried down to Nance's small office. She carried the folder with the stills. Clarence held the painting.

"What was it?" Clarence asked.

Nance paused with her hand on the door to her office. "What?"

"You said you were reading? What kept you up?"

"Montana travel guide. It's my porn." Nance pushed the door open.

"Seriously?" Clarence followed her inside.

Nance moved behind the desk. "No, not seriously. I pulled up some internet articles on the Saltwater Railroad. You seem to think Heka's slave past has some bearing on his art and maybe the case. Well, I decided the research was worth a few minutes."

"Learn anything?"

Nance nodded. "My lighthouse on Key Biscayne Beach made it harder to come down the coast. Some runaways resorted to slogging through the Everglades."

Clarence glanced at the dry-erase board. Nance had written *Saltwater* in a corner. He smiled. "I'm flattered."

She slapped a pile of pages into his hand. "Flatter yourself with half the entrance photos."

Clarence quickly thumbed through his stack. "No Porsche in or out."

Nance's shoulders slumped slightly. "I got nothing." They switched stacks.

"Blue truck, here." Clarence held up one of the pictures. "The Carrolls bought a fleet of blue F-350s. The farm staff uses them."

"Staff like Sucrito?"

"He had one in his driveway the night I went to his house."

Nance looked at him. "You never said you went over there."

"Personal call. Nothing official."

She shrugged and grabbed a magnifying glass. Nance bent over the picture. "It's a Ford. License plate obscured."

"Pretty common truck brand," Clarence said.

"It's South Florida, they're everywhere here."

"Including at Sucrito's house."

She nodded. "Let's go pull at some threads."

"And see if anything unravels."

On the drive, Nance kept her eyes on the road. She didn't speak. Clarence assumed she was considering the approach she might try with John Sucrito. Would she be flirtatious or businesslike, he wondered. Clarence would watch and see, then try to play a complementary role in the interview. Clarence hoped he'd get to play bad cop. He didn't like the guy enough to flirt.

Nance pulled the SUV over on the shoulder.

"Which way are we—"

"Wait," Nance interrupted. She took a breath. "I want to apologize for my behavior last night. It was unprofessional. I am your superior and should not have allowed it to happen. I hope that you will not find it necessary to report the sexual harassment to HR, but if you do, I understand." When she finished the rehearsed speech, Nance looked across at him.

"Alison, you're kidding, right?"

"No." Nance turned and faced the steering wheel. She spun back to face Clarence. "This is awkward. Yesterday, the stress. I was tired. I shouldn't have drunk beer. I used bad judgment. I'm sorry."

"It's okay."

Nance shook her head. "No, it's not okay. You don't force yourself on someone, regardless of the reasons." The words tumbled out fast and high-pitched. "Never, ever, ever. Nothing like that will ever happen again. I promise."

Clarence thought about making a joke. He knew this was the wrong time and swallowed the idea. "Let's finish the case."

Nance turned and looked through the windshield. "Sitting alone by a lake where the ice has just gone out. Listening to an elk bugle in the trees. Something uncomplicated like a license check seems pretty sweet right now."

"Catching a murderer sounds pretty sweet, too."

She stared into the distance for another moment, and then Nance nodded. "Yes, it does." She put the SUV back in gear and drove.

When they got to Sucrito's, the Corvette sat in the carport. Clarence didn't see the blue truck. He pointed to the personalized plate.

"Nice," she mouthed.

They approached the house. Clarence suddenly stopped. He felt Nance tense to full alert.

"What is it?" she asked.

Clarence pointed to the cameras at the eaves. "He's got a full security system. I've seen it. Either he's not here, or—"

"Johnson, the front door isn't latched." Nance quickly moved forward. "You cover the back."

Clarence raced to the back of the house. As he ran, he heard Nance's feet hit the step. Clarence hoped her injured leg could take a pounding. He knew the feeling of vulnerability when your wheel gave out at a critical moment. And it only occurred at critical moments.

He surveyed the back room. Nothing looked disturbed.

"Clarence, now," Nance screamed from the front of the house.

He kicked the door hard, and it crashed inward. Pain shot through his leg. Clarence limped inside. The mud room led to a short hallway. He had a narrow view of the living area.

Broad enough to see John Sucrito hanging from a ceiling beam, a rope around his neck.

Nance stood beside the limp body. She wrapped her arms around his legs and lifted, taking pressure off the neck.

Clarence ran to her and lifted the man higher. "I got him. Cut him down."

The rope had been thrown over a ceiling beam and tied to the kitchen island. A chair lay kicked over just below Sucrito's feet. Nance released her grip. She ran to the island. Her knife appeared in her hand, seemingly from nowhere. She grabbed the rope and sawed through it.

Clarence felt the man's total weight in his arms. He guided Sucrito's body to the floor. He worked the tight noose free from Sucrito's neck with his fingers. Clarence felt for a pulse. He tried again and then sat back. Clarence had seen enough bodies to recognize death.

Nance knelt on the floor next to Clarence. She looked at Sucrito's florid face. Pinpoint spots of blood dotted his eyes. An ugly welt marked his neck. Nance breathed heavily. Clarence stood and offered his hand to help her to her feet.

He pointed to a laptop computer open on the breakfast table. On the screen, Sucrito had typed.

I'm sorry for everything. It's all my fault. I did it all.

24

June 1st, 1886

Samuel Freeman walked to Boston Harbor, pulling a small trolley holding his brushes, easel, canvas, and paints. His circumstances no longer required him to transport his own supplies. He could easily have directed his assistant to handle the carry and setup. Still, when he went to the docks to paint the wharfmen conducting their business, it seemed only fitting that he, too, hauled his sled of freight. His assistant remained at the studio, preparing the canvas for his next commissioned portrait.

Samuel routinely set up his easel and painted the citizens of Boston as they plied their crafts around the harbor. Most of the men who unloaded the great ships recognized him. Some waved and called. More ignored him, but at least they gave him no trouble. The women who offered comfort to seamen no longer propositioned. They'd learned with experience that he would return home to his wife and son at the end of the day.

He had watched the harbor change over the years he had painted here. Great-masted sailing ships rarely arrived anymore. The masts had been taken down and replaced by the smokestacks of steam engines. He sometimes missed the sounds of the breeze snapping the sails and the squeaks of the ropes as they tightened. The belching smoke floating into the sky offered new colors and shapes for his paintings. They contrasted with the white clouds floating overhead. He supposed it was the way of the world, something added as something was taken away.

The *Fair Winds*, a worn and tired clipper, had carried Samuel to Boston in 1866. Captain Rolle knew the ship's master. He had arranged a passage for Samuel. Captain Rolle had accompanied Samuel to the harbor and pointed out the ship. "Dis boat is old, but she is sturdy. She will safely get you to your new home."

The words "new home" rang in Samuel's ears.

When Samuel's skills grew beyond Father Fredrich's abilities, the priest arranged for a new teacher. William Chatsworth had come to Nassau from London; the reasons for his sudden departure from England were never explained. Chatsworth thoroughly embraced the philosophy of John Constable. The new teacher pressed upon Samuel the importance of painting landscapes as he saw them and not idealized visions. He also showed his student the practical side of a working artist. Paint landscapes for love and portraits for money, Chatsworth repeatedly told his pupil. It seemed that Chatsworth and Father Fredrich conspired to teach the young man how to make a living as an artist.

When Samuel had absorbed all the knowledge Chatsworth could pass, they all knew it was time for the young man to leave.

Father Fredrich knew a priest in Boston. He provided Samuel with a letter of introduction. With his mother's death and the Civil War over, Samuel returned to his native country. He bid farewell to Captain Rolle, the man who had never been anything but kind. Still, Samuel felt himself an alien in the Bahamas. There, he was always the boy Rolle had rescued. Rolle understood Samuel's need to make his own way. He was, after all, a man who shipped off regularly to go wrecking. Captain Rolle had handed Samuel a leather wallet stuffed with banknotes. "Go to no port empty-handed. Dey offer nothing for free. But be wise, Samuel. Everyone in dis or any port town will want to separate you from your money." Samuel had lived around the Nassau harbor long enough to have seen firsthand the wisdom of the captain's advice.

As the *Fair Winds* sailed out of Nassau, Samuel stood at the back of the boat and watched. His strongest memory was of a boat carrying him away from a different island. He gazed into the distance, imagining the plot of Myrna's burial. Samuel thought about his mother's oft-repeated story. Nassau shrunk in the distance. He watched it become a pinpoint and then disappear. Again, he sailed away from a spot of land surrounded by water, a place of succor and death.

When he walked down the gangplank of the *Fair Winds*, Samuel heard the women calling to him. The sour smell of stale drink from the taverns crowding the wharf assaulted his nose, but Samuel ignored all the distractions. He kept his head high, observing everything, watching for anyone who might want to steal from a new arrival.

With his letter of introduction and Captain Rolle's money, Samuel had established his Studio for Portraiture in a small building not far from the harbor. More renowned studios located themselves in the center of Boston. Samuel had not been able to afford the expensive real estate. He slept on a small divan at the back of the studio to save money. He built his reputation slowly. The priest recommended his services to parishioners of lesser means. More business arrived when their portraits were judged superior to those of their wealthier neighbors. He completed a painting of Robert Gould Shaw, the Boston aristocrat who had been martyred in the Civil War, leading his black soldiers in the Second Battle of Fort Wagner. The portrait, based on a daguerreotype Samuel had seen, won praise from Shaw's friends and admirers. More Boston elites began arriving at Samuel Freeman's studio. He took their money and painted their pictures. A few of the patrons took home his naturalistic paintings of Boston Harbor.

On days when business was slow, Samuel and his brushes roamed the land around Boston. He painted the salt marshes and the estuaries where seawater met the river. He painted men and women stooped to dig for clams. The thin places where water and land merged fascinated him as a subject for painting. He never tired of chronicling them. Wherever he looked, Samuel saw subjects for painting.

A young woman and her family sold fruits and vegetables at a market near the water. She had skin the luminous caramel color of a sunset over the water. Her almond eyes seemed to know every thought in his head when she looked at him. Samuel tried to quickly look away, but her smile told him that she had caught him. He had no choice but to smile back.

Then, he bought apples he could not afford. When she handed him the basket, their fingers momentarily intertwined.

"You have sensitive hands," she said.

Samuel pondered the remark later. Delicate hands were the luxury of someone who didn't have to pick cotton. He pictured his father. Mostly, however, he thought about her.

Samuel and Willa were married a year later. In the following years, Willa bore Samuel two sons and a daughter.

In 1876, the American Revolutionary Exhibition called for paintings to celebrate the centennial anniversary of the Declaration of Independence. The paintings were to be displayed in New York City. Samuel submitted a rustic landscape picture. He poured everything he had learned about capturing that place where water and land merge.

The art he created showed a small island. He painted the water surrounding the land ambiguously. It was a marsh, water comingled with tall grass, a wild and forbidding environment. Samuel painted the island, like the water, full of contradictions. The vegetation on the land grew lush, green, and full of life. Two trees dominated the landscape. From each one, a crimson flower bloomed. The space between the trees he painted black. Some said the trees looked as if they wept blood. Some who viewed the painting saw Eden portrayed. Others described the painting as reminding them of Christ in Gethsemane. Still, others saw Satan's intervening hand in the landscape. Samuel's years of study observing the water around Boston shaped his image. The actual source, he knew, was a nightmare that wrenched him awake. The painting was part real and part imagined. It captured everything that haunted him.

He also knew the painting was inappropriate for an exhibition themed to celebrate American independence. Samuel feared that the inevitable negative criticism would damage his portrait business. He signed the work S.F. to maintain his anonymity when he submitted it.

Samuel correctly forecasted that the painting would become a lightning rod at the exhibition. Everyone had differing opinions about the meaning of the island painting. Some compared it to *Paradise Lost*, in which Lucifer's presence spoiled the Garden of Eden. Others saw America's entangled complexity and the Civil War's darkness. Critics disagreed. Was the painter sailing toward or away from the island? Was trouble looming or fading? Some marveled at the work's deliberate ambiguity. All could agree, however, that the artwork was masterfully executed. The jurors at the Centennial Exhibition awarded S.F. the gold medal for the finest painting submitted to the showing. They heralded his ability to pose profound questions through such a simple and uncomplicated work of art. They labeled it a masterwork.

Then, the judges discovered that S.F. was Samuel Freeman, a black artist.

The exhibition's organizers hastily tried to withdraw the award when they learned that S.F. was not a white artist. His fellow painters rallied around Samuel. The other recognized painters refused to accept their awards unless Samuel Freeman was given the honor that he was due. Faced with a unified artistic community and the glowing announcement about the work that the Centennial Exhibition had already published, the judges capitulated. Samuel received his gold medal at a very brief ceremony.

Samuel returned to Boston, carrying the medal and the painting with him. The medallion he displayed in his studio. Stories of his triumph filled the Boston newspapers. More local elites flocked to have their portraits painted by the accomplished artist. The painting, however, hung in the small office he kept in his home. It was never publicly displayed. From the end of the exhibition, it remained for Samuel's eyes only.

He would look at it at night. When the nightmares came and sleep proved impossible, Samuel would slip quietly from bed so as not to awaken his wife. He would walk down the hall past the bedrooms of his children. Samuel stared at the painting in the office and remembered the story his mother so often repeated. He would recount in his mind the man who claimed to have fought alligators and carried the tooth to measure gunpowder. He would remember how that man murdered his fellow slave catcher and then how his father had traded his life so that Samuel might be free. Samuel remembered the last horrible glimpse of William and of the trees.

Since the children were small, Samuel had told them the story of their grandparents. They had grown up, as he had, hearing about the island. Samuel had them repeat the story to ensure that they always remembered. When his family gathered at Samuel and Willa's house, he would take a grandchild, one at a time. Leading them by the hand, he would climb the stairs to his office. He would settle into a chair and plop the child onto his knee. There, he would tell the next generation the story. He would point to the trees with his index finger, bent with age, and explain what had happened beneath those forbidding eyes. Sometimes, the young children cried. Samuel never abandoned the practice. He needed them to know the price their forebearers had paid so they could live free.

Until the end of his life, Samuel wished he had been able to paint the pot his mother described into the picture. Myrna had described the glaze as mossy green. William had tried several times to add the vessel. It had been important to his mother. She had carried it from South Carolina. It held her scant possessions and had been her cooking pot. Besides her family, it represented everything she had in life. Despite his efforts, the olive dab of paint constantly distracted him. It pulled the eye away from the power of the twin crimson flowers, the eyes of the devil. Ultimately, Samuel had painted over the pot for the sake of the art.

Myrna had told him that the murderous man had taken from his family the silver that they had scraped together to pay for passage. The man had hidden the silver in his mother's pot and buried it in a hole on the small island. Samuel had satisfied himself with his art by painting a dark spot behind the two great trees. A dark maw that swallowed the future.

25

April 12th

Nance called the Homestead police and reported the death. Then they looked around the house, carefully avoiding touching anything while waiting for the locals to arrive. Clarence and Nance stopped when they heard the distant wail of the approaching siren. The pair sat at the opposite end of the living room, far from the body. The first patrol officer to arrive acted jittery when he saw a corpse and Nance's gun. He calmed down when she displayed her badge.

"Call a homicide detective and start your log," Clarence said. "This guy isn't getting better."

The detective arrived a half hour later. He wore jeans and a button-down shirt. He had sharp features and shoulder-length black hair flecked with gray and braided. The man's belly obscured the top of his belt. Clarence thought they looked to be about the same age. The man, however, had old eyes. Clarence knew the look.

"I'm Detective Tiger. It's tribal." Clearly, he'd been asked about the name before and wanted to get the preliminaries out of the way. "Tell me what happened."

Nance picked up that the detective wanted to avoid small talk. "I'm

Special Agent Nance of the ISB. We're investigating a homicide on park property."

Tiger nodded. "We heard. You the two who got shot at?"

She told him that they were.

The detective's eyes flicked between the two. He seemed to be reassessing them in light of the new information. "What got you out here?"

"We wanted to talk to Sucrito."

"You suspect this guy?"

"Not officially. When we got here, the truck was gone, and the door ajar. I came through the front. My partner," she gestured to Clarence, "he entered through the back. Found Sucrito hanging. Brought him down. Checked for a pulse but found no reason to proceed any further."

"The forced entry at the back is mine. I kicked the door. Sorry about your scene," Clarence said.

Detective Tiger waved away the apology. "And what have you found?"

"Once it was clear he was dead, we tried to avoid your crime scene," Nance said.

Tiger nodded.

"We looked at the laptop but didn't touch it."

Detective Tiger's eyes shifted to the table. He moved to the laptop, bent closer, and donned a pair of reading glasses. "I'm sorry. My fault." He read aloud and straightened. "Reads like a suicide note."

"Typed by someone," Clarence said. He opened his phone and scrolled until he found a particular picture. He showed the detective. "We got the same font on a different note. That message was used to call in the anonymous tip that led us out to the dome where we got shot at."

The detective studied it.

"That's not a default font," Nance pointed out to the detective.

"We do have computers at the Homestead PD."

"Don't mind her," Clarence said. "She's always woman-splaining."

The detective grunted a laugh. "Since I got all this investigative experience in the room, show me what else you found. The sooner we get this processed, the sooner we all get to leave."

"We didn't look—" Nance began. Detective Tiger's look cut her off before she could finish the thought. She directed his attention to the open scotch bottle, a tumbler with a splash of amber liquor puddled at the bottom, and loose pills on the bookcase.

Tiger looked at the scotch. "Eighteen-year-old single malt. Expensive. I might need to take this home for forensic testing." His eyes studied the scene. "Consistent with suicide."

"Or meant to look like it," Clarence said.

The detective nodded. He pointed to the gun case. "You already check the rifles?"

"We got fired upon in cypress dome. No projectiles recovered."

"Still should look," Detective Tiger said.

"We didn't want patrol to come through the door and find us with a rifle in hand. We waited," Clarence said.

"You have my blessing," Tiger said. "Let's get this finished."

Nance opened the case. "No dust on this one." She pulled a bolt-action rifle from the rack, opened it, and looked down the barrel. "It's spotless inside." She held it to her nose. "Smells like gun oil."

"Put it aside," Tiger told her. "I'll have my guy collect it." He stood at the security monitors, his gloved finger on the rewind button. "Looks like this thing picked tonight to malfunction. Nothing but blank screens."

"That's unfortunate," Nance said.

"Suspiciously inconvenient."

"Can you find a ladder?" Clarence asked.

Nance and Tiger both looked at him.

Clarence pointed to the beam. "Start up there. Work your way down."

"We can call the fire department and wait on them. Or since it's a farm, we can look in the barn."

"Y'all continue your search. I'll be right back," Clarence said. He returned a few minutes later with an aluminum ladder. Clarence set it up against the ceiling beam. He turned to Detective Tiger and made a sweeping motion with his arm.

The detective shook his head. "Have at it." He lifted his right leg off the ground and bent his knee. "Tore my meniscus. I don't do ladders."

Clarence offered the job to Nance. She tapped her leg just above where she'd been cut the day before. "Injured in the line of duty."

Clarence pointed at his own leg. "Want to see my scar?"

Nance looked to Detective Tiger, who quickly shook his head. She turned back to Clarence. "Not on a bet."

"It's hell to be the intern," Clarence said as he ascended the ladder. When he reached the beam, his eyes studied the top. Holding onto the ladder with one hand, Clarence got his phone and snapped some pictures. He scanned the length of it and took more photographs. Then, Clarence crawled back down. Back on the floor, he studied his text messages. He looked up to find Nance's and the detective's eyes staring at him. "Oh, that?" He pointed at the beam. "Sucrito really needed to dust."

"Asshole," Tiger said.

Nance looked at the Homestead detective. "And this is what I deal with twenty-four-seven."

"Seriously," Clarence said. "I think we can rule out suicide." He showed them the pictures on his phone. "This is what the beam looks like. Note the saw marks." Clarence saw their uncomprehending faces. "Imagine you decided to hang yourself. What would you do?"

Nance pointed at the beam. "Find a rope. Toss it over that. Tie off one end. Make up a loop and jump off the chair."

Clarence curled his index finger over the top of his bladed hand. "And the rope would sit on top of the beam. It might move side to side when your body starts to fight the inevitable death and you begin to kick your legs." He paused for a moment and let them picture the beam. "Let's assume instead that you wanted to stage a suicide. You'd throw the rope over the beam, make a loop, and hoist the dead guy off the ground. Then, you'd tie it up. You'd pull the rope. It would saw into the beam. Maybe it would slip back a bit when you changed your grip. You'd pull again, and it would saw some more." He showed them the pictures on the phone. "It would look like this."

Nance and Tiger crowded around the cell phone.

Clarence advanced to the following pictures. "The rest of the beam is smooth. No saw marks anywhere else." The other two nodded. Clarence knelt next to Sucrito and studied his neck. He stood, stepped away from the body, and wiped his hands. Clarence put on a single latex glove and walked to the bar. He picked up a glass with his gloved hand and touched the bottom with the other. Clarence set down the first and repeated the process.

"The noose cut into his neck in the front and upward along the sides. You'll have to wait for the medical examiner to confirm it, but I think you'll find a ligature mark straight along his neck at the back. It's obscured in the front by the damage from the rope."

Detective Tiger knelt, looked, and nodded. "What do you think? Maybe a belt? Faint bruising may show evidence of holes in the strap."

Clarence nodded. He held up one of the tumblers. "You need to get this processed. It's been washed, so you're not likely to find anything, but you still have to try. The others are dry. This one is slightly damp."

"So the killer comes over and tempts Sucrito with an expensive bottle of scotch," Detective Tiger said.

"He'd jump at the bait," Nance added. "Labels were his thing."

Tiger continued the narrative. "You pour two drinks and spike one with the barbiturates. When he is woozy, you strangle him."

Clarence nodded. "Stoned men struggle less."

"Wouldn't you taste the drugs and get suspicious?" Nance asked.

Clarence performed a quick internet search. "This label runs three hundred bucks a bottle. Would you know what a three-hundred-dollar scotch tastes like?"

"I'll stick to beer," she said.

Detective Tiger looked at her and smiled. "Then you pull him up, type the message, and wash your glass to hide any prints." As he spoke, Detective Tiger pointed around the room.

"I'd wash both glasses," Clarence said, "to remove the barb residue. Then, I'd pour a splash of whiskey into that one and degauss the hard drive."

"I'd want to hear what the ME has to say," Nance said.

Detective Tiger offered to let them accompany him.

"The ME will need to do tox," Nance said.

"Unless you know a guy," Clarence offered.

Detective Tiger looked at him.

"Inside joke."

"If this is true, you're looking for someone able to afford some expensive liquor." She ignored the LaFleur reference.

Clarence saw where she was going and interrupted the thought. "Before

I got a warrant for anyone in the Carroll clan, I'd remember that everyone who met Sucrito would know he'd jump at a pretty label. Three hundred dollars is a small investment."

"Wait a minute," Detective Tiger said. "You suspect Congressman Carroll?"

"No," Nance said. "They're just the rich folks for whom Sucrito worked."

Tiger folded his arms and rested them on his hint of a paunch. "Good. Because if you want me to go after the Carroll clan, I'm dragging this body over to the national park and making it your problem."

Clarence looked at Tiger. "You ever tried to manhandle a dead body?"

"Miami-Dade pays other people to do that."

"Hard for a lone man to hoist him up off the ground after he's dead."

Detective Tiger looked at Sucrito. "You think we might be looking for two?"

Clarence shrugged. "You're the detective. But if it's one man, he'd almost certainly have left trace evidence all over the body."

"You got somebody who can call liquor stores? Not every day they sell high-end scotch," Nance added.

Tiger's world-weary eyes dipped to the body. "Have you driven around Homestead? Have you seen how many liquor stores we got here?"

"Just thinking out loud," Nance said as she pulled out her phone.

Detective Tiger made a slow, acknowledging nod. "Keep thinking. It's good."

"I need to call this in," Nance said. She put the call on speakerphone.

The chief answered on the first ring. "Special Agent, can you go a whole day without screwing up?"

"What?" Nance asked.

"Kathryne Carroll just took a major piece of my ass. You two apparently decided you had better things to do than attend their photo shoot."

Nance's face glowed red. "We did, sir. We got distracted when we found John Sucrito's dead body."

"Shit," the chief said. Then the phone went quiet.

Tiger interrupted the silence. "This is Homicide Detective Tiger of the Homestead Police Department. Who is this?"

"Chief Ranger Zamora of the National Park Service."

"Chief, I've got a lot to do, so let me keep this short. These two arrived on the scene first. Their efforts to save the deceased were heroic. They are material witnesses to my investigation. They will be released when I decide. I apologize if this murder investigation interferes with picture-taking." Tiger's voice allowed for no disagreement.

"I understand," the chief said quietly.

"I sincerely appreciate this display of local cooperation by the federal government," Tiger said.

"Nance, Johnson. I'll call the Carrolls and tell them—"

"Do not say anything about Sucrito's murder," Tiger said.

"I have done this before," the chief said.

"Sometimes desk jockeys forget about the details of a real field investigation."

In the silence that followed, Clarence could feel the chief simmer. "I'll tell her they'll be along as soon as possible," he said finally.

"Be sure to allow them time to change their clothes. They got Sucrito smeared all over their starched uniforms." Tiger hung up the phone. He looked at Nance and Johnson and smiled. "You're off the hook. Your boss is officially far madder at me than he is at either one of you two."

26

April 12th

Nance's phone rang as she and Clarence walked back to her SUV. She looked. The screen said that the chief was calling. She put him on speaker.

"Are you alone?" he asked.

"Johnson is with me."

"Close enough. I've talked with Kathryne Carroll. I told her about the crisis at the park. Some woman tried taking a selfie with an alligator on the Anhinga Trail. She lost track of her child. The gator got between her and the trailhead. It was all hands to the rescue. You two got called into action. We needed to find the lost little boy. Mrs. Carroll knows you two will be along just as soon as you get the family reunited."

"All in a day's work for the National Park Service," Nance said. "How old is the child?"

"Hell, I don't care."

"In case the congressman asks, I want to be on the same page," Nance said.

"Five. He colored pictures of alligators in kindergarten. The kid begged his mom to see one. So they came to Anhinga. Disney World was the next stop."

Nance looked at Johnson. "I just so happen to have a lost five-year-old boy with me now. Detective Tiger has released us. He told us not to leave the country."

"Well, don't leave the driveway. I've got a volunteer bringing you some clean uniforms. As soon as she arrives, find a place to change and haul it to the Carrolls' house."

"Yes, sir. And thank you," Nance said.

"Detective Tiger around?"

"He is still in Sucrito's house. We're outside."

"Did he give you a hard time?" the chief asked.

"Nothing we couldn't handle, sir."

"Good to hear. I made a couple of phone calls. Detective Tiger has a reputation as a pretty tough customer. He's Miccosukee, you know. They're proud of the fact that the tribe has never surrendered to the federal government. Arresting a couple of federal officers might make his day. You know, be true to the tribal tradition. I'm glad we didn't have to bail you out of county." The chief paused. "Shot at, threatened by the locals. We're not doing much to make you feel welcome here in South Florida, are we, Nance?"

"I don't blame South Florida, sir. I blame the one guy who kills people."

Clarence heard Zamora's attempts to apologize. He felt relieved that Nance was making it easy for him.

"Chief, let me let you go. I can see the volunteer's car. We'll get changed and get to the Carrolls'."

"Call and let them know you're coming. And Nance."

"Yes, Chief?"

"Don't make any stops along the way. Not even for gas. We can only lose so many children in the Everglades."

"Yes, Chief," Nance said and disconnected.

Clarence looked but did not see anyone arriving.

"I had to tell him something to get off the phone. I thought he might get a little weepy if I didn't act quickly."

"You're becoming a real pro at office politics."

Nance slowly shook her head. "Shit."

The congressman's aide had the door to the SUV open before Nance had the car in park. "Come along," the aide said, tugging Clarence's arm. "We are so ridiculously behind schedule." She pulled them into a room at the side of the house. On one side of the room sat a large oak desk, cleared of paperwork, the desktop dotted with Florida-related mementos. Behind the desk, photos lined a credenza. Kathryne Carroll's photograph framed in silver held center stage. French doors looked out upon a sculpted lawn. Alongside the door, the congressman displayed a collection of Seminole coiled sweetgrass baskets. Across the room, a pair of flags, Florida and the United States, framed the fireplace. Above the mantel was an oil painting of the pristine Everglades. Congressman Carroll couldn't legally display his campaign slogan on an official government photograph. Still, Clarence couldn't think of anything better to broadcast "Old Florida, New Ideas" than this backdrop.

The photographer mirrored the aide's anxiety. He herded Clarence and Nance into place. Clarence had been shoved and bumped by far bigger men in his lifetime. He thought about shedding this guy with a quick arm swipe. Clarence held back. They were late, after all, very late. Nothing would be gained by flattening a photographer.

The man pushed them into position. He adjusted his lights. He tweaked Clarence's position, moving his arms forward and then back. Clarence had his hair feathered and his uniform smoothed. The photographer turned his attention to Nance. He glanced at her and angled his head. She had stepped automatically into position. "Perfect," he said. "You two look natural."

Clarence's arms felt awkward and his head locked in place. "I feel natural." He tried to speak without moving his lips for fear that he'd upset the delicate equilibrium of his pose.

The photographer spoke into a small walkie-talkie. "We're ready for the congressman."

Within moments, Mike Carroll appeared between the two of them. He dropped a hand on Clarence's shoulder and effortlessly beamed at the camera. Maybe he'd once posed for a catalog at Key Biscayne, too.

Clarence would have asked if he'd been allowed to turn his head. He heard a series of rapid clicks. The photographer lowered the camera from his eye. He gestured toward the congressman and Nance. "You two look perfect. But this one." He pointed at Clarence. "He looks like he's at a funeral."

"Find a picture where he looks businesslike and not sad. We'll use that one," the congressman said, dropping his arms. The words had a tone of finality. Mike Carroll looked at his aide.

She nodded. "We'll make it work."

Kathryne Carroll walked in and quickly glanced at her Cartier Tank watch.

"Good to see you again," the congressman said to Clarence. He turned to Nance and gave her a full-wattage smile. "And Special Agent, you could be a pro at this."

She threw an equally luminescent smile back at him. Nobody would be able to guess she'd been cutting down a dead guy a couple of hours ago. "I want to apologize for being late, Congressman."

"Call me Mike," he said. "And no apologies are necessary. I heard about the rescue of the lost child. Two acts of heroism in one week."

"Kids getting separated from their parents in the national parks occurs pretty frequently. We just needed to scramble to find him before we had a tragedy."

"Thank you for your service," Mike said.

"Would you mind if I ask you a question," Clarence said.

The aide cleared her throat.

Mike smiled. "How about while we head to the car? Neither one of us wants to get in trouble with the principal." He paused for a moment and kissed his mother on the cheek. Then he set off at a brisk pace.

They walked on either side of him through the house. "You'll need to get used to a security detail like this once you get elected," Clarence said.

Mike smiled. "If I get elected, you looking for a job?"

"I was looking for a job when I found this one."

Congressman Carroll gave a practiced laughed. "Good ambiguous answer. Says nothing, commits to nothing. I'm glad you're not my opponent." He stopped at the front door. The car stood outside with the motor running. "What did you want to ask, Ranger Johnson?"

"Chief Ranger Zamora said some nice things about us after today's rescue. Followed them up with an email that looks pretty good in a guy's personnel file."

Mike nodded. The aide checked the time on her phone.

"Special Agent Nance and I wanted to get him something. We were thinking about a nice bottle of scotch. You got any recommendations about where we might go?"

The congressman's eyes narrowed. He frowned. "Scotch. I'm not a drinker, so I really couldn't tell you. You might ask Matt, but he's almost exclusively a vodka guy, so I'm not sure he'd be any help either." He looked at his aide.

She shook her head and stabbed her hand toward the front door.

The congressman shrugged. "Try a liquor store."

"I thought of that." As he spoke, Clarence shifted his weight. His new position effectively blocked the front door. "But liquor stores will recommend the one with the greatest markup. I was hoping to get him some quality scotch. You have a liquor store you trust?"

Mike Carroll studied Clarence's face. The assessment didn't take long, but Clarence could feel himself being searched. "Let me think about it," the congressman said. "Swing back by tomorrow at—" He turned to the aide and snapped his fingers.

She scanned the calendar. "We can make some time at eleven."

Carroll nodded. "Swing by at eleven. I'll call my buddies on the Foreign Relations Committee. Scotland is foreign. Right up their alley." He took a quick sidestep and got around Clarence. The congressman shook Nance's hand again. "Make sure the chief ranger gets the scotch and it doesn't all end up in this guy. He sounds like he's up to something."

The three of them laughed with equal insincerity. Then the congressman disappeared out the door with his aide hurrying behind.

"I'm lost. Which way out?" Nance asked.

Clarence pointed down the hall. They set off in that direction.

"Senate security?"

"Sounds better than checking to see if you've exceeded your fishing limit."

"I'm not so sure. Slimy eels and sharks."

Clarence smiled. "Maybe not that different from game warden." He paused. Across the room, he recognized the maid. He walked to her. "Hi."

She looked at him, bobbed her head in a bow, and continued her work.

"You brought coffee the last time I was here."

She nodded.

"I drink gallons of the stuff, and I know an artist. Tell me your secret. How do you brew such a fantastic cup of coffee?"

The maid appeared confused. She chewed briefly on her lower lip. "Water, coffee, and switch on." The maid pantomimed with her hands.

Nance snorted.

"Thanks, I'll write the directions down. I've gotten a little turned around. I need to ask Matt a question. Which way do I go to find him?" Clarence pointed a shaky finger in the direction they'd been traveling.

"Mr. Matthew not here. He's gone out."

"Do you know where Mr. Matthew went?" Clarence asked.

The maid chewed on her lip and shook her head. "I'm sorry, no."

"No problem. Any idea when he'll be back?"

"Is there anything I can help you with?" Kathryne Carroll appeared at the other end of the room. She fluttered the back of her hand toward the maid, who promptly disappeared.

"Got turned around. Which way back to our ride home?"

Kathryne Carroll gave him a plastic smile. "I'll show you the way. Was there anything else you wanted?"

"I was hoping to say hello to Matt."

"Matthew is out of the house at the moment. I'll tell him that you asked after him." She stopped at the front door and opened it. Her arm guided the pair outside. "Ranger Johnson, Special Agent Nance, it is always a pleasure to see you. Please do come again."

27

April 12th

"Scotch for Chief Zamora?"

"Did you have a better idea?"

"Playing at politics yourself."

"And now you see why I've never run for office," Clarence said as they arrived at the SUV.

"Where to?" she asked.

"Do you mind driving into the park? I'm not ready to see other people just yet. I need a few minutes to think."

Nance put the car in gear. Neither of them spoke. She followed the gentle bends of the Ingraham Highway through the Everglades, sawgrass on both sides of the vehicle.

"Drive to the Mahogany Hammock," Clarence said before she could ask. "I want to look around."

Nance nodded. The silence continued through the drive. Nance parked. Clarence got out of the SUV. The pair followed the boardwalk across the shallow water and onto the slightly elevated bit of limestone.

"You can't go this long without talking," Nance said. "You're starting to scare me."

Clarence looked down. "That slight bump changes everything. A few feet. This high side is always out of water. Has been for a millennium. That small decline marks a spot that is always underwater." He read the small information sign tacked to the boardwalk. "A single step marks the difference between the Mahogany Hammock and the marsh. This mahogany tree has been here for centuries. It's been standing out of the water, looking down on this place."

Nance nodded. "I get the same sense in the Rockies. The granite has been there for millions of years." She paused. "What are we really doing here?"

Clarence leaned against the railing of the boardwalk. On the board, someone had carved, *God is the Creator*. Clarence read it aloud and frowned.

"A graffiti ministry," Nance said, pointing at the railing.

Clarence smiled. His finger directed her attention to the other side. Another person had scratched, *Charlie loves Susie*. "Because nothing shows true feelings like vandalism."

"Love expressed through crime," Nance said. "What are we doing here, Clarence?"

He shook his head, then turned and rested his elbows on the vandalized railing. He looked out over the hammock. "I don't know. This place was important to Heka. Maybe a stop for his ancestors in their run for freedom. It seemed to be relevant in his last hours. I wanted to see it." He turned to face Nance. "Sometimes I think that if I just look long enough, I'll see something I hadn't seen before."

"Or convince yourself you see something that isn't there."

Clarence shrugged. "Nobody's perfect."

"Hezekiah didn't know they were his last hours. Who knows what he'd have focused on if he had."

"Writing down the name of the person who killed him, I hope," Clarence said.

They walked back to the SUV. Nance opened the driver's door. Then she paused and looked across the boardwalk. Her eyes traced the slight land dip from the hammock across the marsh. She climbed inside, looked at Clarence, and smiled. "It's amazing when you think about it."

"What?"

"This place. I'm used to seeing changes in nature. In the mountains, aspens may be bare sticks at one elevation." She raised her hand near the headliner. "And leafed-out lower down." She put her hand near the dash. "But that's hundreds of feet of elevation change. Here, it's inches." She looked back out the window. "People should come here for an hour or a week."

"What do you mean?"

She nodded her head to the horizon. "A tourist can pop in here for an hour. Spot an alligator, buy a T-shirt, and check the Everglades off their list. Then drive to Miami and do whatever on South Beach." She paused and looked out again. "Or they should come here for a week. The place is subtle. You need to take some time to look at the place before you get the ecosystems. There is real beauty in the nuances of this place. It takes time to see it."

"A bit like a homicide investigation."

Nance smiled. "There's the slogan. Everglades: Like a Crime Scene."

"They'll probably prefer yours," Clarence laughed. "'Stay for a week and see if you can figure us out.'"

"Don't forget the other half," Nance said. "Everglades: Buy a T-shirt and Get the Hell Out." She laughed, too.

"Maybe we better stick to crime fighting," Clarence said. Nance's phone rang. While she took the call, he turned back and stared into the hammock. He saw a lone cardinal-colored bromeliad in the limb of the old mahogany.

Something clicked. Did Clarence see it, or did he just convince himself that something was there? He turned back to Nance.

She hung up. "Sorry to break up all this philosophical meditation. That was Detective Tiger. He asked to meet us."

"Always good to make nice with the locals."

At the RV, Clarence climbed into the Suburban and followed her to a coffee shop in Homestead near the police station.

Tiger looked up and waved them to his table. A ceramic mug and a half-eaten slice of pecan pie sat alongside his flip pad. "The ME has scheduled the autopsy for this afternoon. Want to see a part of Miami most tourists miss?"

Nance nodded.

"Do you mind if I sit this one out?" Clarence asked.

She looked surprised at his reluctance. "Sure, I guess."

"You don't look the squeamish type," Tiger said.

"I need to run some errands." He could see the vague explanation proved unsatisfactory. Clarence chose not to explore his latest theory with her until he'd had the chance to think it through. "I want to go see Mae. I think the decision to leave her art is ill-advised. I want to talk to her before she gets so far along that she can't back out. And I already know what the ME will tell us."

"Pretty confident in yourself."

"Only because I'm right."

Nance stirred her coffee. "May I ask a question?"

Tiger took a bite of pie and nodded.

"What do you know about poaching in the Everglades?"

"You think because I'm Miccosukee and all animals are sacred, maybe my spirit brothers tell me about stuff like poaching?"

"I was thinking you were local and I'm not getting any help from the Park Service."

Tiger's fork split off another bite. He chewed without speaking.

Nance leaned across the table. "Put me in the Rockies. I can tell you the difference between a valley scraped by a glacier and one cut by a river. But here, I'm a fish out of water. Help me out, please."

Tiger took a sip of coffee. He shook his head. "Little worth poaching. Can't eat the fish. The mercury levels from industry have poisoned the gar. People imported exotic snakes as pets. When the bastards grew out of their punk phase, they dumped their pythons and bought minivans. The damn reptiles have wiped out the deer and panthers. Phosphorous runoff has altered the plant life." He waved his hand at the city outside the café window. "All this progress has stolen our hidden shining river."

"So why do you stay?" she asked.

The corners of Detective Tiger's mouth curled in a grim smile. "If somebody doesn't adopt the white ways, how will my people ever learn about diabetes and hypertension?" He dropped some bills on the table. "C'mon, let's get our two lost souls to Miami."

Back at the RV, Clarence let Tripod roam about outside. While watching his dog patrol, he called Mae. They agreed Clarence would come by in two hours. He spent some time leafing through his books about Everglades plants and reading about nurse logs. Clarence and Tripod walked down to Heka's. There, he retrieved the envelope he'd found at the back of the three-ring binder.

Mae smiled when she opened the door. She led him inside. Clarence took the chair while Mae sat on the sofa.

He looked at her hands. "No fresh paint."

Mae shook her head. "I'm not painting. I'm boxing things up."

"That's what I've come to talk about. I really think you should reconsider."

Mae frowned.

"You got talent," Clarence continued before she could object. "And with what we've learned about the techniques Heka had begun to explore, I think you've got more places you could go. More ways to express what you're trying to say."

Mae's frown deepened. "And why are you so interested in what I do?"

"I played football."

"I know. I looked you up," Mae said.

"I loved playing. I took my game as far as I could. I've got a ton of regrets in my life, weights I carry around. But one thing I don't have is the feeling that I quit on my passion. I'm afraid you'll live with a burning question of what-if."

"You ever tried making a meal of sliced what-ifs and a side of 'maybe'? It don't fill you up."

"I know it would be tough. But I don't think Heka would want you to give up."

Mae crossed her arms. "Oh, that's low."

Clarence pulled the envelope from his pocket. "He wrote you a letter."

Mae shook her head; her eyes glistened. "I never seen no letter."

He handed her the envelope. Mae's hand shook slightly as she opened it. She blinked and tried to read. Then she sniffled and rubbed her eyes. Finally, she handed the letter to Clarence. "Can you tell me what this says?"

Clarence read the document silently. "It's a holographic will."

"A what?"

"The lawyer's way to say a handwritten will. Heka has named you his artistic executor."

Mae paused and closed her eyes. After a moment she spoke. "Tell me exactly what that means."

"You'll have to ask a lawyer. But I think Heka wanted you to decide what happens to his art. You control sales and licensing. Approve shows. It looks like he's made you the beneficiary of his estate."

"That old man didn't have no fortune. Part of why he was living in the CARE house."

"You could refuse the job. No one can make you take it." Clarence looked down at the letter. "He saw your potential. Heka knew you were his legacy."

Tears streamed down Mae's face. She sniffled. Clarence got up and retrieved a tissue box. She pulled four and promptly crumpled the tissues in her hand. Mae stared at the letter. Clarence reached out to hand it to her. She refused to take it.

"I'll just smear it." Mae dabbed at her eyes. She took an erratic breath of short inhales. More tears flowed.

Clarence went to the kitchen and filled a glass with water.

She took a small drink. Water dribbled from the corner of her mouth. She wiped it away with the tissue. "That old man. That bastard. Legacy. I got no money. Daddy has got no money. We never had money. Daddy always says if things had been different, we'd be rich like the Carrolls, but we ain't. Legacy." Her hands started shaking. Water splashed over the rim.

Clarence took the glass and set it on the coffee table. He wanted her to keep talking. It would settle her breathing and help Mae to regain control. "If what things were different?"

"Daddy says that way back when, all our ancestors was poor. Then our great-great-granddad or some relative died, and we had to sell our land so his wife could feed the family. We stayed poor ever since."

"You'd know more about the art market, but with Heka's death, the price of his pieces will likely spike."

She pointed at the wall. "I've got one. Daddy has one."

"There are several at the bungalow. Does Heka still have a dealer in Miami?"

Mae nodded. Her eyes cleared. She began to calculate the possibilities. "I don't want to sell everything. I want to hold onto...but, maybe, we could make enough..."

"Don't give up. Heka thought you were his legacy."

Mae smiled. "Still a bastard. A lovely, sneaky old bastard."

Clarence stood. He left the letter on the coffee table. "I'll leave. It looks like you've got some unpacking to do."

Mae wrapped her arms around him and hugged him. "I can't thank you enough."

"You could tell me where Joe Bob is hiding."

She dropped her arms, pulled her head back, and sniffled again. "Nasty Man, I'll do anything but that."

"I just want to ask him some questions."

Mae made a slow shake of her head. "Parents protect their babies. Children protect their parents. It's the way of the world."

Clarence frowned and opened the door.

"You know, she could do a lot worse."

Clarence stepped outside. "What do you mean?"

"If you can't figure that out, no wonder you haven't found Heka's killer."

Clarence followed a pair of taillights into Everglades National Park. When the lights turned into the employee housing area, he recognized Nance's SUV. He followed her to her bungalow. She got out, squinting as she looked into his headlights. Her hand rested on her waist, near her handgun. Her eyes showed wariness.

Clarence felt his pocket buzz. He ignored the phone call. He didn't want

Nance to see a silhouette plunge a hand into a pocket. That would be an easy way to get shot. Instead, Clarence turned off the headlights and called to her. He watched her relax slightly, although her muscles still seemed taut.

"The ME said exactly what we suspected," she reported. "Dr. Hsu said someone tried to mask a homicide by feigning suicide. Clear-cut. No question."

Clarence nodded.

"What about you? Talk Mae out of leaving the artistic world?"

"I didn't do much. Hezekiah made her his artistic executor. Asked her to be his legacy."

"How do you argue with a historical responsibility?" As Nance spoke, she tilted her head forward until her chin touched her chest. Then she rotated her head in a circle, stretching out her neck.

"Traffic?"

"Not bad. Just cities." She stretched her neck to one side and then to the other. "Miami has got me all knotted up. Don't know why anybody with a choice lives there."

"Want me to do anything?"

Nance turned toward her tiny bungalow. "I've got to brief the chief in the morning. We'll catch up later."

Clarence nodded and drove home. He sat at the table and picked at his guitar. Tripod stretched out beside him. On his laptop, Clarence sought the address for Sunshine State Silicon. He thought he might learn about the family if he could catch Matt away from his mother. The guy seemed to have something to say, but Kathryne always intervened. The internet offered the address of a strip mall on the edge of Homestead. Clarence jotted it down.

He texted LaFleur. *Can we meet tomorrow?*

Riding bike in the AM. I'll stop by about 9:00.

Thx, Clarence sent back. The screen reminded him that he'd missed a phone call earlier. He checked. Mae had left a voicemail. She thanked him for bringing Heka's letter. Then she said, "I've been thinking about my family and remembered some more things. Call me."

He dialed. The call went straight to voicemail. Mae had turned her phone off and likely gone to bed. Clarence had handed Mae a lot to consider. He left a message.

Thoughts niggled in his brain. He felt like the answers lay in there somewhere, just beyond his reach. Clarence set down the guitar and picked up Tripod. The dog sniffed Clarence's face. "We've got a lot to think about, too. Busy day starts tomorrow morning."

When Clarence placed Tripod on the floor, the three-legged dog scampered toward her bed. Clarence followed behind.

Tomorrow, he hoped, would provide more answers than questions.

28

April 12th

Clarence returned to the Mahogany Hammock at sunrise. He carried along copies of the photographs Heka had taken. He also had a picture of Samuel Freeman's oil painting on his phone. Clarence stood in front of the old-growth mahogany and studied the photos. Then he climbed over the barrier. Clarence wore his park ranger shirt. If anyone found him there, he wanted to look like he was on official business. In a sense, Clarence was.

He soon found the nurse log. That was what he thought he'd spied yesterday. The thick trunk lay on the ground, a victim of Andrew or some other hurricane that swept across this sawgrass prairie in the centuries this tree stood. Clarence looked at the massive fallen tree. He compared it to the great mahogany still standing. Judging the nurse log's thickness presented a challenge. Ferns and other vegetation sprouted along it; pink lichens colored the side. Bits of rotten wood crumbled in heaps as the earth slowly reclaimed the great trunk.

Clarence walked along the downed tree's length, picking his feet over the rough ground. He avoided the poisonwood and tried to keep his feet free from the strangler vines. He found what had once been the root ball. The trees, even great ones, could only grow so deep in the shallow soil atop the limestone base of the hammock. He opened his phone and oriented the oil painting's imagery to the great mahogany and the downed nurse log. Clarence picked his way around the trees, moving and then stopping to compare. He came to a plot of ground, overgrown but flat. Although the surrounding vegetation was thick, the growth was young. Ferns, vines, and young sabal palms. This could be quickly cleared away to create a space for a campsite. Ahead of him, he saw the open Everglades. The distance to the water, he knew, would be a fraction further than it had been two centuries earlier. That was how hammocks grew. The slow-moving river of the Everglades brought along leaves and twigs. When the flotsam's journey to Florida Bay was interrupted by a hammock, the material began to decompose, adding an incremental amount of soil to the hammock.

He turned. Clarence felt a chill. He could easily imagine the pair of trees before him looking like columns holding up the sky. An air plant clung to the crook of the standing tree. Its color, arrestingly brilliant red, captured his eye. Clarence's eyes returned to the oil painting's depiction. He visualized the second tree alongside the first, both crying tears of blood.

He had found the spot. What value did it hold for Heka?

Clarence walked back and forth, making at least as much of a grid as possible over uneven ground clogged with entangling vegetation. He stepped lightly, feeling for mounds or holes. When his foot encountered something, Clarence knelt and examined it. Each time he plunged his hand into the dense undergrowth, he thought about snakes.

Clarence discovered a great deal of limestone and a few knots of logs. He located neither snakes nor anything he considered of value to this search. His search located only an antique whiskey bottle.

He waved away bugs and pressed forward. Clarence checked the time. He would need to abandon the quest to meet LaFleur. He could not fight the feeling of disappointment. In his mind, this had been easy. His experience helped him push back against the sense of defeat. Clarence had combed through pages of cell phone records over the years, confronting failure after failure, only to find that one call record that tied his suspect to the victim. Patience and persistence were the keys to any successful search.

He worked his way through the trees. The laps back and forth became shorter. The nurse log blocked his path. He felt the ground dip. He knelt and touched a limestone ledge marking a slight depression. Clarence stepped forward and felt his foot sink. He quickly pulled back. Clarence had found an old solution hole. He moved around it and continued forward. Clarence stopped and returned. "Patience and persistence," he said out loud.

His knees protested as he pressed them against the gnarled stone for what felt like the hundredth time this morning. Bugs swarmed around him, feasting on his exposed flesh. Clarence's hands explored the outer edges, tracing a rough outline. The fissure of the porous rock had a rough outer edge and an interior lip, worn smooth by eons of flowing water. He dug through generations of accumulated humus. He knew these cracks in the rock were essential to the ecosystem. The water seeped through into the water table. His hands excavated water and decomposing vegetation. His heart beat faster. He could feel the solution hole tapering inward. Clarence dug down deeper almost to his elbow, pulling out loose soil. He neared the limestone bottom. Then he stopped. He leaned forward, nearly pressing his head against the musky-smelling earth. Nothing. Clarence's fingers touched only rocks.

He struggled to his feet. His legs ached, and his back hurt. Clarence stretched and pressed forward. He checked the time. Clarence could only stay a bit longer. Soon, he'd have to quit and plan to return another day. Clarence pushed down the thought of stopping. He knew if he rationalized quitting, he might never convince himself that a return trip was worthwhile. Clarence looked at the mound of cell records in front of him. Just find one number, he told himself and stepped forward.

And felt his foot sink.

Clarence nearly laughed at the comedy of it all. Just when he'd convinced himself the answer lay ahead, another obstacle to progress. Grunting, Clarence lowered himself and began probing this hole in the limestone. It felt identical to all the others he had explored.

Clarence stopped. It felt identical to all the others, except for the last one. That had been the only hole with the smooth interior rim. He pushed himself upward and hurried back to the solution hole. Clarence ran his hand around the edge and traced a smooth edge. Instead of the boundary of a fissure, had he discovered the outer edge?

Opening his knife, Clarence scraped away more accumulated marl. He rubbed his hand. The side felt too smooth for natural rock. Clarence worked more quickly, hollowing out the interior and emptying it of the accumulated organic material. He reached the bottom and pulled out the rocks he'd felt earlier. He discovered one of the stones had been another whiskey bottle, which was caked with encrusted dirt.

He buffed the side, wiping away the filth. Clarence shined his flashlight. He saw a brown glaze streaked with gray and olive. Clarence should stop and allow a professional conservator to finish the job. Clarence didn't need the pot for his job. It was enough for him to know he'd found it in the spot Heka had located.

Clarence also knew he wouldn't turn this job over to anyone else.

He returned to the exterior. When he had cleared as far down as his knife blade would penetrate, Clarence searched for an alternative. He broke a weathered piece from the boardwalk, promising to pay back the Park Service. Clarence pushed the organic matter to the surface with his improvised shovel and swiped it away with his hand. Decaying plant debris spattered him. Sweat ran down his face. He blinked it away. Clarence grabbed the edge of the pot. Freed from the earth, the vessel wobbled. He dug and swiped with renewed vigor.

Clarence laid aside the board, grasped the pot, and lifted. He felt movement upward. His mind noted where Clarence felt resistance. He eased the pot down and resumed digging.

When the pot came free, he laid it in the accumulated pile of soft humus. He sat quietly and looked at it. Nothing on his body hurt.

The pot looked dirty and water-stained but intact.

Clarence saw that the pot had two flared handles near the top rim. One of the handles had cracked. He wrapped his arms around the bulbous middle and carried the vessel to the water's edge. Clarence bathed it in the clear water of the Everglades. Dirt washed away, exposing more of the olive color. Clarence stripped off his shirt and wiped the pot, staining his uniform but freeing more of the clay's original glaze.

Clarence carried the pot to his Suburban. Placing it on the seat beside him, he seat-belted it into place. He covered the pot using his shirt and a tarp, protecting it as best he could. Clarence hurried back to his excavation site. He photographed the spot and then refilled the hole with the decaying leaves. Clarence dropped his improvised shovel near where he'd broken off the board. Clarence hopped back over the handrail.

Clarence drove carefully back to the RV. He didn't know how fragile rare, recently unearthed pottery might be.

Back home, Clarence looked in all directions. He saw no one outside. For the first time, he wondered whether his neighbors had security cameras. Clarence went to the passenger side of the truck. He put his arm beneath the pot and walked nonchalantly toward his door. Clarence hoped that, if he was observed, the brown thing in his arm would look like a brown paper sack. He tried to appear as if he'd just returned from the grocery store. A dirty, sweat-covered guy coming back from a quick trip to the market.

He carried the pot to the RV's shower. Tripod weaved between Clarence's legs, sensing the excitement of the moment. Quickly stripping off his clothes, Clarence jumped in alongside the vessel. Dirt streamed off both. Brown water swirled around the drain. Clarence jumped out and hurried to the small kitchen. He poured some vinegar into a salad bowl and dashed back to the shower. Mixing it with water, he used a washcloth to wipe away more of the two centuries of grime. The luster of the potter's glaze slowly emerged in spots. The shower ran cold when the hot water heater emptied. Clarence stayed beneath the stream. The excitement of the work kept him warm.

Clarence turned off the water and stepped back. Much of the muck had been cleaned away. He could see faint bits of writing etched near the rim. Clarence studied the words carved into the clay. He made out "pots of gold." The rest remained obscured. The glaze still held engrained dirt. The surface looked patchy, luminous in spots, and dull in others. Clarence didn't dare use anything harsher than mild vinegar as a cleaning agent. Those calls would be left to professionals.

Clarence checked the time. He had only a few minutes until LaFleur arrived. What could he do with a large antique pot? LaFleur was naturally inquisitive. The characteristic was a necessary job requirement. Clarence couldn't leave it in the shower stall with the curtain drawn and trust LaFleur not to snoop. The thing wouldn't fit under the bed.

He poured out the water that had collected in the bottom and wiped it dry. Clarence quickly slipped into a pair of jeans. The pink Everglades shirt sat on top of his T-shirt drawer. He pulled it over his head and carried the pot into the kitchen. The RV's kitchen cabinets proved too small. Clarence stood the pot in the corner and emptied a bag of Tripod's dog food into it.

The dog paced the kitchen floor, toenails clicking on the linoleum at the sight of the kibble. Clarence grabbed a handful and dropped it into Tripod's bowl. "Don't get used to second breakfast," he told the excited dog. "Today is a celebration." Clarence set the bowl in front of the pot and watched Tripod bury her face. Clarence dropped a dish towel over the rim to conceal the writing.

He studied his still life with a dish towel, dog, and historical art treasure worth a fortune. Clarence thought it looked natural enough in his kitchen to avoid notice.

Clarence brewed a cup of coffee. He paced the length of the RV. He grabbed a uniform shirt and hung it by the front door. Clarence did deep-breathing exercises. He wanted to return Mae's call but needed to calm himself. Clarence fought the temptation to tell her. He had seen her excitement when he'd shown her the underpaint on Heka's art. This artistic find might be next level.

When Clarence felt he'd regained control of his emotions, he punched in Mae's number. The phone went immediately to voicemail. He hung up, disappointed. He wanted to talk to someone even if he couldn't tell her. Clarence desperately wanted to share the excitement of the moment.

His door pounded. "Open up, it's me," LaFleur yelled outside the RV.

29

April 13th

LaFleur wore a half-zip cycling jersey adorned with pot leaves. The bands at the sleeves and collars showed the colors of the Jamaican flag. The black bicycle shorts hugged fit thighs. His hair, flattened by his helmet, lay matted with perspiration. On top of his head rested a pair of wraparound sunglasses.

LaFleur saw Clarence's eyes. He nodded. "Everybody thinks it's funny to give the DEA guy dope-print paraphernalia. Never buy a keychain. Call me. I got a hundred of them."

"I'll make a note."

LaFleur stepped inside the RV. His cycling shoes made him walk like he had duck feet. The bottom clips clicked more loudly on the linoleum than Tripod's toenails. "Dude, you smell like a pickle."

"My legs got cut up in the cypress dome and then soaked in marsh water, a potential bacteria incubator. The EMT recommended that I scrub them with disinfectant for a couple of days." Clarence grabbed at the tongue of his belt and undid it. "Want to see?"

"Keep your pants on, man. I'm good." He pointed down the hall. "Bathroom that way?"

"It's an RV. There is only one way," Clarence said as he refastened his belt. He got a bottle of water and brewed another cup of coffee. Clarence sat at the table.

When LaFleur emerged, Clarence held up both. LaFleur chose the water. His eyes swept the kitchen before he sat down. If he noticed the pot, he didn't say. LaFleur's eyes seemed drawn to the guitar.

"How goes the recovery?"

LaFleur flexed. "Feeling stronger every day."

"Good to hear."

"Did you really text me to stop by for a wellness checkup?"

Clarence sipped some coffee. He shook his head. "You DEA guys follow the money all the time. What can you teach me?"

"You asking for a favor?"

"Just a tutorial. I tried YouTube. They didn't have much on financial investigations. I was a homicide cop. We didn't delve into it too much in most of my cases."

LaFleur considered the question, turning the water bottle between his hands. "Publicly traded or private?"

"Sunshine State Silicon. It's private."

LaFleur frowned. "Publicly traded is easier." He punched numbers into his phone. "Hey, it's your favorite. Can you see what we have on a small business?" LaFleur paused and looked at Clarence.

Clarence quickly wrote the name down and passed him the paper.

"Sunshine State Silicon." He laid the phone on the counter and pressed the speaker button. Clarence heard fingers clicking on a keyboard.

"Can't give you much without a court order." The female voice on the other end paused. "From what I can see, the business looks newly minted and undercapitalized."

"Email me what you can," LaFleur said.

Clarence heard a single finger stab the keyboard.

"Sent. And when do I get this big payoff dinner?"

Apparently, Clarence thought, LaFleur always bartered for drinks and meals.

"Soon, I promise. Gotta run. Thanks." LaFleur disconnected. He checked his email and typed something into his phone. LaFleur's eyes shifted to Clarence. "I just forwarded you what we've got."

"I was hoping for a lesson."

LaFleur set down the phone. "We've got databases you could never access. I'm trusting that this is work related."

"The guy we think might have shot at us. We found him dead. He was a partner in Sunshine State Silicon."

"Don't sue for his half of the business," LaFleur said. "It doesn't look to be worth the litigation. Is that really all you wanted?"

Clarence nodded.

LaFleur began to stand, paused, and sat down. He pursed his lips.

"You all right?" Clarence asked.

"You and me," LaFleur said. "We've got an issue?"

"I'd say we have more than one. You took a bullet for me."

LaFleur rotated his shoulder, the one above where the bullet had struck. "Do you think I'd have charged down that trail if I'd known I was about to get shot?"

"From where I was lying, that's what I saw."

LaFleur grunted. "You give me too much credit." He rapped his knuckles lightly on the table. "I'm not sure I ever stopped to think about it. There was a situation, and I ran forward. If I'd paused, who knows what might have happened." He rapped again. "The point is, I didn't choose to take a bullet for you." LaFleur emphasized the word *for*. "So stop behaving like I did. You reacted at the scene. You killed the guy. And then you saved my life."

"Nance did," Clarence corrected.

"You two worked together. You finished the mission."

Clarence studied the table, saying nothing.

"Answer this. If Alison hadn't been there, would you have let me bleed out?"

Clarence kept his eyes down. "I didn't have to choose."

"Bullshit," LaFleur said. "We both know what you would have done." He rolled the shoulder again. "You don't owe me anything."

"That's not how I see it."

"I can't state my case any clearer," LaFleur said. "But don't let your overdeveloped sense of personal responsibility let you sit on the sidelines while I take the girl."

Clarence's head shot up.

LaFleur smiled. "I'll win. I just don't want you refusing to try. A little effort makes the choice more sincere."

"Act surprised when Nance tells you, but she is moving back to Montana to take a job with Fish and Wildlife."

LaFleur spun the water bottle between his two hands. "Montana. They got a real fentanyl problem up there. Someone needs to investigate it. I enjoyed my assignment there. That is, until you showed up." He winked at Clarence. "Johnson, don't let my injury keep you from taking your best shot. I'm not worried about the competition from a guy who smells like a dill pickle." This time, LaFleur stood and clacked toward the door. He turned and made an exaggerated rub of his stomach. "Do you mind loading my bike into the back of your Suburban and driving me to the Coe Visitor Center? My ride is there, and my six-pack abs…they hurt."

Clarence smiled. "Sure thing, asshole."

After dropping off LaFleur, he called Mae again, but there was still no answer. He tried again on the drive to Homestead. Clarence drove by her townhome. He didn't see Mae's car. Clarence rang the doorbell and pounded on the door. She didn't respond. He tried the door and found it locked.

Clarence pulled his truck closer to the house. He stood on the hood and pulled himself to the small upstairs balcony. Mae hadn't locked the glass door leading to the bedroom. Clarence's eyes swept the room. She did not appear to have slept at home last night. Clarence didn't see any sign that she had packed an overnight bag. He walked downstairs. Mae had left dishes in the sink. She had converted the townhome's dining room into her office/studio. Clarence ran his fingers along the brushes. The bristles felt dry. Nothing had been recently used. He didn't know her well enough to say for sure, but nothing at her house suggested that she intended to be gone overnight.

Clarence scrolled through his history and found the number for Joe Bob Jefferson. The man answered on the first ring.

"Let me guess. You want me to turn myself in."

"Yes," Clarence said, "but that's not why I'm calling. Have you heard from Mae?"

"No, but that ain't unusual. Mae gets to painting and forgets to eat, sleep, or call her dear daddy."

"I'm standing in her studio. She's not at home. I can't tell that she was here last night."

Joe Bob remained quiet for a moment. "She's an adult. Can't say where she might have stayed."

"I brought her a letter from Hezekiah. He asked her to be the executor of his estate. When I left her last night, she didn't seem like she'd intended to go out."

Joe Bob didn't say anything.

"If you hear from her, ask her to call me," Clarence said.

Joe Bob grunted.

"You know I could trace your phone and find you."

"But you won't," Joe Bob said. "If you really wanted to bring me in, we both know you'd have never let me go to the bathroom at the club."

"I never thought you'd jump out the window."

"Desperate men do desperate things."

"Joe Bob, don't make me regret that decision."

When Clarence went out the front door, he didn't find police cars lining the streets. Mae's neighbors hadn't noticed his entrance and exit or hadn't found it worth reporting. He checked the clock. If he hurried, he'd still have time to visit Matt before connecting with Congressman Carroll.

He punched in the address to Sunshine State Silicon. He found the business in the corner of a shopping center, a small, unremarkable office space. Vinyl blinds covered the windows. A small sign attached to the glass door identified the business. The sign showed a man in board shorts and a tank top in the shade of a palm tree, typing on a computer. A brilliantly yellow cartoon sun shone from the corner diagonal to the tree. Clarence noted that the happy sun cast a shadow on the wrong side of the palm. Maybe happy suns are that accommodating. "Sunshine State Silicon" was written out in script.

If Clarence was going to solve the case, he may need to know more about fonts.

He opened the door and went inside. A long table, divided into workspaces for three employees, lined one wall. The room had a chair grouping on the other side. A television on the wall had an attractive blonde in a bikini talking enthusiastically about the opportunities to grow a technology business in South Florida. Clarence saw an office at the back. He saw fluorescent light peeping out from beneath the closed door.

Clarence walked to the door and knocked.

"We're closed," Matt said through the door.

"Matt, it's Clarence Johnson."

"Come in."

Clarence opened the door. Matthew Carroll sat behind the desk. His eyes were red, and his unshaven face was pale. He looked like he hadn't slept. Or maybe he was hungover. Clarence saw a glass on the desk and an open bottle of vodka.

"What are you doing here?"

"I got tired of looking at alligators. Decided I'd search for something that looked really scary."

Matthew Carroll grunted. "Tough night. Business trouble. John Sucrito killed himself."

"Do you believe it?"

Matt's eyes narrowed. "Believe what?"

"That he killed himself."

Matt's gaze drifted to the ceiling. He looked like he was trying to find a thought through the fog of alcohol or fatigue. "That's what I was told. I don't know. The guy had a big football fantasy that ended suddenly. He had plans that never quite worked out. He dreamed of becoming rich, but I think he found that achieving his goal was more challenging than he imagined. My brother talked to him the other night. I think things got heated. If a guy has enough plans that don't work out, do you just get tired and quit trying?"

"How'd you hear?"

"My brother sits on the subcommittee that gives appropriations to the Everglades. Not too much happens around here that doesn't get reported. And little escapes Kathryne Carroll's notice."

Clarence pointed to a chair.

Matt nodded.

Clarence sat. "I don't see any mention of Congressman Carroll or the Carroll family around the office. Seems like that might help draw business to a start-up."

"John's family has served the Carrolls for generations. He wanted to get out from under the thumb." Matt belched a humorless laugh. "You've met my mother. She can be a bit controlling. We wanted the business to be apart from the Carrolls. John wanted to really be a boss."

Clarence looked around. "The name might help with financing."

"Maybe. But you let them in, and John knew he'd lose control. He knew my mother. Like I said, she can be a bit controlling."

"About your mother," Clarence said. "The other night, when I visited, you looked like you wanted to tell me something. She intervened, and you never got the chance. What was it?"

Matt's eyes returned to the ceiling. After a moment, he shook his head. "Sorry."

Clarence stood. "If you think of it or anything else, call me."

"Sure."

Clarence watched Matthew Carroll's blurry eyes. "You haven't, by chance, talked to Mae, have you?"

"No, something wrong?" Matt looked genuinely caught off guard by the question.

"No, I tried to call on the way over here. Didn't get an answer. Probably painting."

Matt nodded.

Clarence turned to leave.

"Johnson," Matt said. "Don't get the wrong impression." He raised his hands and pointed around the small office. "The place doesn't look like much. But we've got a good business plan. We've got the money to make this work. Did you know that the Homestead climate isn't very different than northern India? And people around the world are drawn to Miami Beach. We can draw some serious international computer programming talent to Sunshine State Silicon. The office is crap, but physical space isn't critical. It's an online operation. Check out the video we cut. This wasn't some charity case to make John feel better about his station in life. We are… were going to make a ton of money together."

"I'll be sure to watch the video on my way out."

30

April 13th

If the Carrolls had security cameras trained on him, they could watch Clarence change clothes outside their home. He didn't think an official visit to the congressman's home should be conducted in an alligator T-shirt. He swapped it for his uniform blouse and went to the door.

The maid led him to the small sitting area off the dining room. He checked on Audubon's birds and the family tree. The ancestors still glowered at him while the birds continued to exude life and remarkable color. Something picked at Clarence, a thought at the back of his mind. He turned to the drawing of the roseate spoonbill.

"I never get tired of looking at them," a voice behind him said.

Clarence turned. Mike Carroll smiled at him. The congressman dressed casually in jeans and an open shirt. "Ride with me," he said. Clarence followed him through the house and out the back door. A pair of identical blue pickup trucks had been parked outside the garage. Their noses pointed up the driveway. "Get in," the congressman said, pointing to the nearest one. Clarence climbed into the passenger seat. Mike Carroll shifted into gear.

"Where are we going?" Clarence asked.

"It's important I get out once in a while. Need to stay in touch with my community. We're just going for a little ride."

Clarence shrugged. Mike Carroll was a professional at noncommittal speech. There was no point in pressing. Clarence would find out when the man was ready to tell. "Did you learn anything about my scotch?"

Mike held up his hand and said nothing.

The pair traveled north from Homestead. Out his window, Clarence saw a series of plant nurseries. Signs announced bargains on all kinds of plants. He thought about Joe Bob Jefferson. No wonder the man had trouble competing. Besides the danger of the weather, the competition looked cutthroat.

"Cutthroat," he muttered to himself. What must someone be prepared to do to stay afloat in this business?

Mike Carroll looked at him. "Did you say something?"

"Talking to myself. Have you seen Mae Jefferson since yesterday?"

Mike shook his head but said nothing. He signaled and turned left. The pickup accelerated.

Clarence saw a sign for the Miccosukee Hotel and Casino out his window. Behind the sign, a building loomed. In his short time in South Florida, he'd never been to this area north of Homestead.

"You're on the Tamiami Trail." Mike seemed to hear Clarence's thoughts. "Visitors think it's a Native American name. In truth it means the road runs from Tampa to Miami. Officially, the road is US Highway 41, but nobody calls it that."

He paid little attention to the road. To be fair, Clarence thought, Mike didn't need to. The highway was a ribbon of concrete, straight and flat.

"Tampa and Miami mashed together. What's that called, a portmanteau?"

Clarence nodded. "Sounds right." He assumed that they'd get around to something besides local history and vocabulary at some point.

"Hard to believe, but this road used to be even flatter than it is today," Mike said. "We've elevated some of it and built bridges. This entire length of road used to be a dam, stopping water flow from Lake Okeechobee down through the Everglades. We're working hard to get the water flowing again the way nature intended. I'm proud to be a part of that effort."

Local history, vocabulary, and political speeches, Clarence mentally corrected himself.

Mike Carroll made a left turn into a parking lot. "We're here." He got out of the truck and waited at the front for Clarence. He pointed back to the highway. "The land on that side of the highway is Miccosukee property. This side of the Tamiami is Everglades National Park." Mike set off at a brisk pace. Clarence followed. The congressman led him toward the edge of the grassy water. A small dock had been built extending out into the Everglades. A muscular man wearing jeans and a T-shirt studied his phone at the foot of the dock. At the far end, an aluminum roofed stall stood.

At the sound of approaching footsteps, the muscular man looked up and pocketed his phone. "She's ready to go, Congressman."

"Thank you," Mike said. He paused beside the man. "Ranger Johnson, I'd like you to meet Miguel."

The two men exchanged nods.

The congressman stood next to the muscular man and flexed. "Mike and Miguel. We sometimes wonder if we switched jobs, would anyone in DC notice?"

Clarence saw that Miguel laughed on cue. He also noted that the congressman had better biceps than he'd noticed previously. Carroll looked strong enough to pick up Miguel or someone else.

"Want me to come along?" Miguel asked.

The congressman shook his head. "I'll be the captain today." He walked out onto the dock. His feet made hollow sounds on the boards.

Miguel handed Clarence a pair of ear guards and nodded toward the congressman.

Clarence followed. An airboat floated inside the stall.

Mike Carroll climbed up onto the driver's seat. He patted the chair alongside. While Clarence made his way, the congressman adjusted his ear guards and started the engine. The giant propeller behind them roared to life. Miguel pushed the nose of the shallow-bottomed aluminum craft away from the dock. Carroll pointed the boat out into the Everglades and gunned the motor.

They skimmed across the surface of the Everglades. Mike Carroll steered the boat, finding the irregular course through the water and around the vegetation. When that proved impossible, the flat bottom slid over the mounds of sawgrass. Mike kept his left hand on the stick, controlling the direction of the airflow shooting out from the great propeller. Clarence held his head down, his eyes nearly closed. The wind buffeted his face. He glanced over and saw that Mike had put on a pair of sunglasses.

The man looked down at Clarence and smiled.

Clarence lifted one side of the ear guards away from his head. It sounded loud, like standing on stage playing the guitar with the amp turned up. He dropped the ear guard back into place.

Mike Carroll made a 180-degree turn and stopped. The boat idled in the water. He pulled off his ear protection. Clarence did the same.

"What do you think?"

Clarence looked around. In all directions, he saw the unbroken grassy waters of the Everglades. Sunlight reflected off the water. Great wading birds stalked the shallow water. He nodded in appreciation. "I thought private airboats were illegal in the park."

"They are," the congressman said. "As the federal government's steward for the park, I'm allowed to maintain one. It's not really private, you see. The boat allows me to keep an eye on my constituents." He gestured toward one of the great white birds fishing in the distance.

"I think you've got his vote," Clarence said.

The congressman smiled. "Do you know the other thing the airboat does? It lets me get away from the constant interruptions of my office. Look around you, Ranger Johnson. Do you see any cell towers? There's no reception. No wireless internet. No interruptions. It's nice. Check your phone."

Clarence pulled his phone from his pocket and looked. He had zero bars.

"Are you wearing a wire, Ranger Johnson?" the congressman asked.

"You invited me, remember?" Clarence looked at him. This conversation was definitely different from what he expected.

"Deliberate avoidance once again. Are you wearing a wire, Ranger Johnson?"

Clarence began unbuttoning his shirt. "I'll strip, but if the paparazzi come along, it may be hard to explain what you were doing in the middle of the Everglades with a naked man."

Mike Carroll laughed. "You're good. Keep your clothes on, Ranger Johnson. You don't broadcast out here, even if you have a microphone. And the pitch of an idling airboat..." He waved his hands. "They've explained the acoustics to me. Anyway, it doesn't matter."

Clarence rebuttoned his shirt.

"I keep an airboat because I can. My job gives me access. It allows me to know things. Like medical details, for instance. Do you know the recovery time for someone who has had a gunshot wound to the vastus lateralis?"

"How did you...?"

The congressman waved away any comment. "Of course you do. But did you know that Chief Zamora doesn't drink alcohol, that he's a teetotaler? No, you probably didn't. You assumed that as a cop, he drank. I need to know things about people. Especially their vices. Why would you want to buy an expensive bottle of scotch for a man who doesn't drink alcohol, I wondered."

"Glad I didn't waste the money," Clarence said.

"I made a couple of calls. The Homestead chief of police told me that John Sucrito died yesterday. An apparent suicide, although the investigation is continuing. I'm told he hung himself after swallowing barbiturates and expensive scotch."

"I'm sorry for your loss. I know Sucrito was a valuable employee."

"Then I began to wonder why you were suddenly curious about my knowledge of scotch sales. I also became curious about why a national park employee might be involved in a local case of suicide. The chief told me that you and your partner found John's body. That helped me understand your tardiness yesterday and your interest in the case. But I'm still curious. Why do you want to know about my scotch purchases?" The congressman stared at Clarence. "Am I a suspect, Ranger Johnson?"

"The investigation is continuing. Reliable witnesses report that you and John Sucrito argued recently. Care to tell me what that was about?"

Mike Carroll showed Clarence his politician's smile. "The Sucrito family has worked with us for generations. We occasionally disagree. Nothing important."

"They haven't worked with," Clarence corrected, "they work for."

"We prefer to see it as a partnership." Carroll paused. He picked up a pair of binoculars and handed them to Clarence. "I want to show you something quite remarkable. Can you see out there in the distance?" Carroll pointed.

Clarence scanned the horizon.

"Do you see it?"

Clarence focused and strained to see.

Suddenly, the boat jumped forward and lurched to the left. Clarence felt himself falling. He grabbed at the railing, his hand slipping on the smooth wet metal. His leg banged into the side of the boat and went numb. Clarence lost his balance and fell into the water.

Although shallow, Clarence couldn't stand. The muck bottom swallowed his feet. He floundered in the water, scratching himself on the sharp edges of the sawgrass.

Mike Carroll circled him in the airboat. He idled the boat out of Clarence's reach. Ripples of water washed over Clarence.

"Did you know that Everglades National Park is bigger than the state of Rhode Island?" Carroll asked. "Imagine being alone in an entire state."

Clarence tried to push himself upright. His leg buckled, and he struggled to regain his balance.

"Think about the early settlers. Picture our ancestors struggling through this landscape. Or those runaway slaves splashing south, hoping to be free. Imagine the effort. They had to be willing to do what it took to survive."

He circled the boat around Clarence.

"People fear the alligators out here. They're not going to bother an adult unless you threaten them. The real dangers are the distance and fatigue and that sun. Every step becomes a test."

The boat circled again. Clarence blew the water out of his face. He felt his legs beneath him. He could lunge at the boat if he could find a solid piece of limestone to plant a foot.

"That hardscrabble existence bred tough people, Ranger Johnson. You've seen my mother. She is a direct descendant of those people who refused to quit. I am, too. That's why I'm going to win this race for Senate. And I don't need some washed-up cop trying to rebuild his reputation by slinging wild accusations. Do I make myself clear?" Mike Carroll stared at Clarence with cold, remorseless eyes.

Then the congressman laughed. "Washed-up cop. The phrase sounds funny, given the way you look right now. Washed-up, get it?"

Clarence didn't laugh. He felt something solid beneath his leg, the bad one. He hoped it would perform when he made his move.

Mike Carroll's expression changed again. His chameleon-like face broke into a smile. "Why don't you get back into the boat? I'm going to bring the nose to you. I'd appreciate it very much if you'd remain in the front of the craft during our trip back. Do you understand?"

Clarence nodded. The boat edged forward. Clarence grabbed the bow.

Mike Carroll made a quick pull of the steering lever. Clarence lost his grip on the boat.

"I just wanted to remind you, Ranger Johnson. The chairs in the front don't have seat belts. Please remain seated during the return trip. If you stand, you could easily end up back in the water. And if I didn't notice you'd fallen, you'd have a long slog back to dry land. It would be like crossing an entire state. Do we have an understanding?"

Clarence nodded.

The bow of the airboat slowly turned in Clarence's direction. He grabbed the front and pulled himself into the boat. He lay on the deck for a moment, catching his breath. Mud and water ran from his uniform and puddled in the bottom of the craft.

"You should find a towel. Please dry yourself off. We get quite a breeze blowing in our faces when we're zipping along in one of these airboats. In your wet clothes, I'm afraid you might catch your death."

Clarence found a souvenir towel. It showed the US Capitol surrounded by flowering cherry blossoms. He dried his face and hands, obscuring the image with mud.

Mike Carroll gunned the engine. The boat, again, leaped forward. He yelled to be heard over the noise. "The power of this thing. It really is quite exhilarating."

31

April 13th

Mike Carroll chatted the entire way back to the house. He pointed out new developments and described buildings that used to be located on the route. Carroll held forth on bits of historical interest.

Clarence wasn't interested.

The congressman pulled to a stop in front of Clarence's Suburban. He unleashed a smile. "I hope you found our conversation informative."

Clarence slammed the door on the congressman's blue F-350. He stripped off his shirt. Clarence wadded the stiff fabric into a ball and threw it onto his passenger floorboard. He pulled the pink T-shirt over his head and drove back to the Everglades.

Nance's SUV was parked at his RV. She had Tripod outside. The dog sniffed at the tires, performing her usual patrol. Nance looked up and smiled. "Where were you? I was beginning—" The smile faded. "What the hell happened to you?"

"Long story. Let me clean up. I'll tell you." Clarence walked to the RV and stopped, remembering the recovered pottery inside the door. "Damn, my hot water is busted. Could I ask a huge favor?"

"You've got to shower if you're going to sit in my car. Put your dog up." Nance hopped in her SUV and drove down to her house.

Clarence went inside the RV and grabbed a change of clothes. He checked the pot. Nothing seemed different. He briefed Tripod on her responsibilities and walked down to Nance's bungalow.

He had nearly washed the Everglades off when Nance pounded on the bathroom door. "Get dressed fast. There's someone outside."

He rinsed off the remainder of the soap, hurriedly dried, and threw his clothes on as quickly as possible. It wouldn't be a good idea for a coworker to catch him at Nance's house in a towel. Of course, if it was LaFleur, maybe Clarence would dash back into the bathroom and strip.

Clarence came out of the bathroom, finger-combing his hair. Nance gestured at him to sit. He took a chair where he could monitor the entrance. Nance looked at Clarence and then opened her door. Her face showed surprise.

The door blocked Clarence's view. He moved. When he did, Clarence recognized the man standing outside. He made formal introductions. "Special Agent Nance, I'd like you to meet Joe Bob Jefferson."

Nance took a step back and frowned. Clearly, she did not like the idea of a suspected murderer knowing where she lived.

Too late to worry about that, Clarence thought. He invited the man inside and pointed to the small table. Joe Bob and Clarence sat. Nance made a lame excuse and walked into the other room. Clarence knew she intended to collect her firearm and handcuffs.

"Come to surrender, Joe Bob?"

The man slowly shook his head. "If that's what I need to do. You got to help me find my baby girl."

"I've been trying, Joe Bob, I swear. We should notify the Homestead police."

"Fat lotta good that will do. The cops think her daddy's a murderer. When they hear that Heka named her his guardian, they'll decide she's gone off to get revenge. They'll likely blame Sucrito's murder on her."

"Revenge for what?"

Joe Bob pressed his lips together.

Nance entered the room and leaned against the wall. She looked casual, but she could easily block any escape out the door.

"You want help, you got to give me something."

"Johnny was a good boy. He wanted things. Things he couldn't afford. He doesn't make enough money overseeing that sugarcane farm to pay for the things he buys." Joe Bob's lips whitened.

Clarence circled his fingers. "Don't stop now, Joe Bob. Tell us why these things matter."

"He was the poacher, not me. Heka wanted to paint a series about environmental destruction in South Florida. Some serious political shit. Take things back for generations. He'd never get Johnny to pose, so he hired me. But Sucrito did the stealing—the flowers, the berries, the turtles. Anything there was a market for, he treated the Everglades like his personal store."

"And the money?"

"Blew it on jewelry and the things he thought would impress women like my Mae." The man's eyes clouded. He began to sniffle. "You got to help me find my baby girl." Joe Bob buried his head in his hands and began to cry.

Clarence looked at Nance. She read his eyes. She closed her own eyes for a moment and then made an incremental nod of her head. Then she walked across the room and laid a hand on the man's arm. "Joe Bob, here's what we're going to do. I'm going to look for Mae. I've got access to resources that Johnson doesn't have. You and he are going to ride over to your house. He's got to investigate the murder—"

Joe Bob's head shot up. "But I didn't kill no one."

"We've got to investigate. He's going to look at your house. While he's there, Johnson is also going to look for anything that might help us find Mae. Understand?"

Joe Bob sniffled and nodded.

"And know this. You're in his custody. If you run off while Johnson is looking, the federal government will label you an escaped fugitive. Both he and I will have to stop searching for Mae. We will be required to conduct a fugitive manhunt. You understand?"

"I won't give you no trouble. Just help me find my baby girl."

Nance frowned but nodded.

"Let's get started." Clarence stood from the table but hung back as Joe Bob walked out the door. "You do remember I'm not commissioned," he said quietly to Nance.

"We've got more jobs than manpower. Can't even call LaFleur. DEA sent him off to teach a seminar this afternoon." She shook her head. "I guess cowboys don't only ride in Wyoming and Montana."

He could see her face looked grim. "Saddle up."

The men drove to Joe Bob's house. Inside, the air felt stale. Clarence knew that no one had opened the doors since he and Nance had been there. "Where have you been hiding out?"

"I took the Presidential Suite at the Ritz Carlton. Don't get the stone crabs from room service."

"So you're not going to tell me?"

"At least not until we find Mae."

"Does she own a gun?" Clarence asked.

Joe Bob shook his head. "Never told me so."

"Could she have gotten one from here?"

Joe Bob went to the water heater closet. He dug in the back and came out with an antique rifle. Again, he shook his head. "This is the only gun I own. No ammo."

"Tell me the truth, Joe Bob."

The man covered his heart with his hand. "I swear. I used to own some rifles and a Smith and Wesson semiautomatic. But..."

"But what, Joe Bob?"

"I had to pawn some things to make payroll. The business ain't exactly booming." He reached into a drawer and opened an envelope. He showed Clarence half a dozen pawn tickets. His eyes scanned the house. "If I have to pay a ransom, I don't know where it'll come from."

"If Mae's been kidnapped, it has nothing to do with ransom."

Joe Bob's face lost color. "What do you think has happened to her?"

"I don't know, Joe Bob. You see anything out of place?"

The man walked around the tiny house. He broke down in Mae's old bedroom. Clarence pulled him outside. "Take a breath," Clarence ordered.

The man stood by the Suburban's door. He pulled deep, ragged breaths of air. He closed his eyes. After a moment, he opened them, looked at Clarence, and nodded. "I didn't see nothing out of the ordinary."

"We're going to Mae's and doing the same thing. Tell me if you see anything that doesn't look right."

Joe Bob Jefferson looked in the passenger-side mirror as his house disappeared in the distance. "I'm going to miss that place."

"What do you mean?"

"I'm going to have to sell my house or my business. I can't afford both. I can sleep at my business. Can't sell any plants here. Haven't gotten around to filling that hole in the backyard." The man's eyes went back to the passenger-side mirror. "Carrolls will likely buy it up. History does have a damned old way of repeating itself."

"Mae told me about your great-great-grandmother selling off a farm."

Joe Bob nodded. "We weren't alone, just first. Men came back from the Civil War with debts. The Carrolls were the only ones with hard money, not Confederate script."

"Maybe if your family hadn't fought for the rebels."

"My ancestors loved their state. Their country went to war. Were all the German soldiers in World War Two Nazis? My people never owned a single slave. Couldn't afford to. Don't know what they'd have done if they had the Carrolls' money." He paused. When he spoke, he lowered his voice. "Now, to be honest with you, my old family did make some money hunting runaway slaves. But that was legal."

Clarence grunted.

"Let me ask you this. If you lost your job and you had a family to feed, would you consider being a bounty hunter, catching criminals who skipped court?"

"That's different."

"Back in the day, they was running down criminals. That's all they was doing. On one of those catching trips, my great-great-granddad got himself killed. I'm told he was trying to drag a slave back to a plantation and the slave didn't want to go. He got killed. Don't like it, but can't say it wasn't fair."

Clarence didn't argue.

"But it did leave my great-great-grandmama in a tough place."

"With children to feed."

Joe Bob nodded. "But we did our duty. We kept our promises. It ain't popular thinking, and I'm not saying we should go back. If those rules existed today, I know a few people who would be enslaved. They are all better humans than I am. It wouldn't be right for that to happen. But I won't apologize for something that happened way back when. We stayed true to our word. Not like some."

Clarence assumed he meant the Carroll family but didn't care to pursue the issue. He wasn't here to argue history with Joe Bob. He'd let the man have his rationalizations. Clarence wanted to find a killer and a kidnapped victim. He'd save the history lessons for another day. He glanced over at his passenger. Joe Bob's face showed a man in anguish.

"We'll find her," Clarence said. When they got to Mae's, he again looked across the seat. "You got a key?"

"No. I'm not that kind of daddy. Want to break the door down?"

"The upstairs door is unlocked. I'll go up and let you inside. I can trust you, Joe Bob?"

"I told you I wouldn't run."

Clarence grabbed the rail and pulled himself up to the balcony. As before, he slid open the glass door and let himself inside. This time, Clarence didn't listen for the alarms of approaching squad cars. He learned about the neighbors during the last visit. And Clarence had the owner's father in tow. He unlocked the front door. Joe Bob hurried inside.

"I poked around earlier but don't know Mae like you. Search the place and tell me if you see anything out of the ordinary, anything at all."

Joe Bob nodded and disappeared.

Clarence called Nance. She answered on the first ring. "Any news?"

"Nothing. We've been fighting the Civil War."

"Turn out any different?"

"Nope. Joe Bob is checking Mae's house to see if anything is out of place. He showed me pawn tickets to prove the only firearm he owns is that antique. You got anything?"

"She's gone silent on social media. No posts in the last day. I've given her license plate to Sun Pass admin office. They're checking to see if her car has been on the toll roads in the last twenty-four hours. They'll let me know."

"Let me know if you hear anything." Clarence hung up the phone.

Joe Bob reappeared in the front hall. His red eyes told Clarence the trip through his daughter's townhouse had refueled his grief. The man shook his head. "I can't find her computer anywhere. But her clothes, her sketch pad, everything else is here. Baby girl doesn't go anywhere without her sketch pad."

"She got any friends who she might stay with?"

"I already tried all of them. Nobody's seen her."

"Call the club. See if Mae has been by there," Clarence said.

"You think my calling is a good idea? I caused them some trouble when I ran out of there, I expect," Joe Bob said.

"You did. And when trouble came, I brought it. Between us, you're the better choice."

Joe Bob dialed. Clarence heard Kemo yelling on the other end of the line. Joe Bob shouted back, attempting to get his attention. Neither man stopped yelling long enough to listen. Clarence wrenched the phone away from Joe Bob. When Kemo paused to take a breath, he broke in.

"Kemo, this is Ranger Johnson."

The bartender sounded momentarily confused when he heard a different voice on the line. Then, the name registered. Kemo's volume began climbing again.

"Kemo, if you don't answer my question, you're impeding a federal investigation. The next time you see me, I'm hooking your ass up."

Not true, but the ploy worked. The man sounded sullen but calmed down. His tone turned to concern when he learned that Mae had disappeared.

"Tell Mr. Jefferson I'm sorry, but I've not seen or heard from her," Kemo said.

Clarence gave the bartender his phone number. "Call me if you learn anything."

The man apologized again and hung up the phone.

"I think you got your saloon privileges back," Clarence said.

Joe Bob's eyes welled. "Can't go without my baby girl."

Clarence's phone showed Nance calling.

"I heard back from the toll authority. They gave me the information. Looks like Mae was driving to the Carrolls' house."

32

April 13th

Clarence had Nance on speaker as he and Joe Bob drove to the Carroll estate.

"How do you want to play this?" she asked.

"Special Agent Alison Nance of the Investigative Services Branch will ask nicely when we get there. You'll bring the full weight and authority of the federal government to your request," Clarence said.

"A sitting congressman might not be impressed by a federal agency employee. What if that doesn't work?"

"Then I ask, and I bring my fist's full weight and authority. Antique furniture may get broken," Clarence said.

"You'll have to tell me what happened this morning," Nance said.

"As soon as this is over."

In the other seat, Joe Bob growled.

Clarence looked at Joe Bob. "Remember, you sit in the car. If you step one foot outside this vehicle, you're a fugitive. Nance and I stop whatever we're doing to pursue you."

Joe Bob growled again but nodded.

"I talked to the Everglades' public information officer. She has some after-hours contact numbers to Mike Carroll's staff. Works closely with them on park-related matters. She was reluctant to do anything that might endanger the relationship with the congressional field office. But I convinced her that it was urgent," Nance said.

Clarence steered onto the exit ramp. "Learn anything?"

"PIO called. Told the staffer that she needed a quote from the congressman on short notice. The Park Service had decided to publish a memorial to Hezekiah. The staffer told her that Congressman Carroll had canceled his appointments for tomorrow. She didn't expect to have contact with him until the next day at the earliest. The staffer assumed he had gotten sick. According to the PIO, she reported that he didn't sound quite right."

"He was healthy enough earlier," Clarence said. "How he'll be later depends on him."

"You let me go first."

Clarence didn't respond.

"Agreed?"

This time, Clarence grunted approval. "We're right outside. Where are you at?"

"Be there in five."

"We'll stage by the front and await your chariot's arrival."

Clarence parked and looked at Joe Bob.

"I'll stay. I'll stay."

Clarence held up his hand. "Pinkie swear."

Joe Bob's face mirrored his confusion.

"My truck, my rules. Pinkie swear."

Joe Bob shrugged, lifted his hand, and interlocked pinkies.

"Now, repeat after me. I, Joe Bob Jefferson, do solemnly swear."

"I, Joe Bob Jefferson—"

Clarence slapped a handcuff on his wrist and fastened him to the steering wheel.

Joe Bob pulled back, but his arm remained clamped. "What the hell?"

"I couldn't remember the rest of the sacred oath." Clarence spoke softly. "I borrowed the cuffs from Nance. Joe Bob, I believe you intend to keep your promise. But when you get it in your head that Mae is in trouble, you'd come running. You'd charge in. I can't allow that. Some duties take priority."

Joe Bob's eyes flared with anger. He pulled at the handcuff. He did not disagree.

Nance's SUV pulled alongside. Clarence exited the truck, walked over, and entered the passenger side. She looked at him.

Clarence saw the question. "Joe Bob will stay. I made him pinkie swear."

She didn't look convinced.

"And I handcuffed him to the steering wheel."

Nance put the vehicle in gear. "Do you know if the gates are open?"

"Too dark to see."

"We don't have enough to get a warrant."

"Let's hope they're open and welcoming."

The heavy wrought iron gates framed by brick gateposts were closed.

"Ring the bell, and you can start asking nicely," Clarence said.

Nance pressed the button and introduced herself. After a moment, the gates swung open. She looked at Clarence. "You ready, cowboy?"

He nodded. "Let's ride."

Nance drove forward. The Spanish moss cast eerie shapes on the approach. The fountain in front had been illuminated. The lights alternated among red, white, and blue.

Matthew Carroll opened the door and stood atop the portico. "Government working kinda late this evening. Makes me proud to be a taxpayer."

"Hey, Matt," Clarence said. "We're here to see the congressman. I think he's expecting us."

"If he wasn't, he knew you were coming when the security cameras picked you up." When he spoke, Matt's breath smelled slightly of alcohol. He pointed into the house. "His office."

The pair strode inside. Matthew followed them for a few steps before branching off and walking upstairs.

"Hold on." Clarence paused outside the sitting area just off the dining room.

"Don't bring the fireplace poker," Nance said.

"Won't need to. There's one in Mike's office." Clarence studied the small room.

Nance's expression said that she was trying to judge whether he was serious.

"Besides, the fireplace tools in the office are heavier." Clarence winked at her.

Mike Carroll sat behind the desk and looked up when they entered. His face appeared haggard, Clarence thought. Carroll's shoulders slumped, and his brow furrowed. His glazed expression cleared when he recognized who entered. Carroll assumed his politician's mantle. He threw them the practiced smile. "Ranger Johnson, you're sure we didn't hire you? You've become quite the regular. I'm surprised to see you again so soon."

"Congressman," Nance said, "what do you know about the whereabouts of Mae Jefferson?"

Carroll shifted his focus and looked at her. "Nothing, Special Agent."

"The records of the toll authority show her coming here. She has not been seen since. Where is she?"

"I have no idea," Mike Carroll said. "You'd be surprised to learn that the Carroll family does not have our own freeway exit. She may have gone anywhere in this area."

Clarence's hand flew across the desk. He grabbed Mike Carroll by the shirt collar. Clarence pulled forward, and the man slid across the top of the desk, scattering Florida knickknacks. Mike Carroll landed with a thud on the thick-piled rug surrounding the desk. "Let's try again," Clarence said. "Where is Mae?"

"Johnson!" Nance said.

"I let nice go first. Now it's my turn." Clarence squeezed on Carroll's shirt collar.

The congressman stared at Clarence. His eyes blazed with anger. "I am not going to have you fired. I'll have the Park Service transfer your ass to the biggest homeless camp in Washington, DC. You'll spend your day sweeping up addicts' syringes. I'll drive by every morning just so I can see the most miserable human being on the planet."

"I guess I won't be interviewing for your security detail?" Clarence sighed and drew back his fist. "I might be miserable later, but for the next few minutes, you'll do the suffering."

"Johnson, no!" Nance said.

"Wait." Mike Carroll's eyes looked wild with panic. He threw up a hand to shield his face.

Clarence stood over him with his fist cocked.

Carroll took a deep breath. He lowered his hand. "She came by here last night. She left."

"Don't believe you." Clarence squeezed the shirt collar more tightly.

The congressman's eyes widened.

"Let him up, Clarence," Nance said.

"Check the drawers."

She circled the desk, searching. "No weapons."

Clarence looked at her. Then he pushed and released his grip. Carroll coughed and slowly crawled to his feet. He had his hands out in a sign of surrender. Holding the desk for support, Mike Carroll stumbled over the scattered mementos until he reached the chair, then dropped heavily into it. The congressman took a deep breath.

"You were saying, Mike?"

Mike Carroll's eyes had lost their fire. He looked first at Clarence before locking his eyes on Nance. "She came by here last night. She showed me a copy of a letter. That artist, Hezekiah Freeman, had made her his executor. She was excited. Wanted to talk about some kind of permanent exhibit at the Coe Visitor Center. She wanted me to help her get some funding. We talked." He circled his finger. "I didn't promise anything. Said I'd think about it. I think she heard my full support. Then, she left. I swear."

"Where'd she go?" Nance asked.

He shook his head. "I don't know. If I had to guess, she drove to Miami. I think she wanted to talk to Freeman's art dealer. She was pretty hot to get this display established."

Nance shook her head. "He's lying."

"How can you tell?"

"His lips are moving."

Clarence nodded. "Good enough for me." He drew back his fist. In the distance, he heard a car horn. Clarence nodded. "It'll muffle the sound of this."

"I'm not lying." Mike Carroll's voice cracked. His eyes flickered with panic.

Nance nodded. "I called the toll authority. If she'd driven to Miami, they'd have notified us. We'd be there and not here."

"And your face would look better." Clarence reached down and grabbed at Mike's shirt.

The congressman's desk chair skittered backward until it collided with the wall and stopped.

Clarence stepped closer and pulled him back to the floor.

Mike Carroll's hands grabbed Clarence's wrist. "I'm telling the truth. I told you that I guessed she went to Miami. She talked about Hezekiah's art. I assumed she was off to see his dealer."

Clarence released the congressman's shirt. His head landed on the carpet. Mike Carroll lay on the floor, breathing heavily. After a moment, he sat up on the rug. He held his arms open. "She's not here. I swear. Search the house."

The man's body language told Clarence that Carroll spoke truthfully. He looked at Nance. "You stay here. I shouldn't be alone with him. I'll look around." Clarence walked to the fireplace. He reached behind the Florida flag and picked up the poker. Clarence handed it to Nance. "If he makes a move, even budges an inch, take out a knee with this." Clarence looked at Mike Carroll. It was his turn to smile. "After the election, you might sit in the United States Senate. But you'll need some assistance to walk there."

Mike Carroll shivered. His head shifted to Nance, who held the poker in her right hand and bounced the shaft against her left palm. "Ranger Johnson."

Clarence turned in the doorway.

Carroll spoke with a high and quivering voice. "Please stay out of Mother's room. It's the first one at the top of the stairs. She is resting. She was genuinely fond of Hezekiah and John. The last few days have been very trying for her."

"She's not the only one." Clarence left to begin his search of the house. Off the plush rug, his steps echoed on the hardwood floors of the quiet home.

33

April 13th

Clarence set off at a brisk pace. The house had many rooms, and he intended to examine them all. To hell with anyone Clarence might awaken.

His steps slowed. Clarence stopped near the sitting room. He did not need to look there. The space was too small to conceal a person. There were no closets. The only door connected to the dining room. Yet, for some reason, he felt drawn to it.

And then he saw it. He could almost hear an audible click as a piece fell into place.

He entered the room and took a picture off the wall. Clarence crossed back to the office. He saw Nance had allowed Congressman Carroll to crawl back into his chair. Mike had regained some of his earlier composure. Maybe the power flowed from the leather upholstery. Clarence might park himself in the chair after he dragged Mike Carroll out of it. Clarence looked at Nance. "You want to hit him, or should I?"

"I told you the truth," Congressman Carroll said. His voice had more authority than it had moments earlier.

"No, you didn't. It took my brain a moment to catch up," Clarence said. "No dear friend called him Hezekiah. He wanted his friends to call him Heka. I'd known him for less than a day, and he instructed me to call him that name. His granddaughter gave him the name, and he was proud of it. Your mother didn't have a friendship. She had a business relationship."

Mike Carroll began to sputter an explanation.

"I'm still talking," Clarence said. "If he interrupts me again, Nance, use the poker."

Nance bounced the poker against her palm. She looked like a villain in a Hollywood movie. Clarence wasn't sure she knew he was bluffing.

Mike Carroll didn't know either. He fell silent, eyes darting between the two of them.

"I told Mae about Heka naming her artistic executor. I recommended that she talk to their agent. I told her about her control over sales. I'm sure those ideas got talked about with you, but they weren't her priority. Mae wanted to talk about Heka's family and her family. She was thinking about her ancestors who got left behind while the Carroll family established its fortune. That was where her head was."

Mike Carroll opened his mouth. Then, he looked at Nance and closed it again.

Clarence nodded and smiled. "Good call. I think she made a connection last night and came over here to confirm it." Clarence laid the sitting room picture on the desk. It showed the Carroll family patriarch. The man sat in his chair and stared straight into the camera.

Nance bent over the desk. While the two studied the sepia photograph, Clarence scrolled through his phone. He resumed talking when he found the image he'd been searching for. "Look at your patriarch's photograph. What do you see on his cheek, a blemish or perhaps a scar?" Clarence laid the phone down on the desk alongside. "This is the painting Heka was working on at his death. Notice the man in the back. He is handing the Everglades to the suited man in the foreground. The man in the back has the same blemish on his face. That's the Carroll family patriarch. What do you suppose it means?"

"You're the art expert," Mike Carroll said.

"Special Agent Nance, care to take a guess?"

She squinted at the picture. Nance sat in the leather guest chair; her level gaze locked onto the congressman. "The man in the back looks to have a man down on all fours with a rope around his neck."

"Very good. You get an A." Clarence turned back to Mike. "Your patriarch was a fugitive slave hunter. He captured humans and returned them to plantations for money. Unless, of course, they could bribe him."

"This is nonsense." Carroll waved his hand over the display. "The man in the painting doesn't resemble the man in our family picture. Your story has no proof to back it up, just some wild accusations." He stopped talking. His eyes shot to see if Nance would advance with the poker.

Clarence nodded. "I don't know if it's true. But Heka believed it. And Mae put it together. I'd be willing to bet that she considered it true. At the end of the day, it doesn't matter what I believe. But when a man running for the United States Senate gets tagged as being the scion of a family whose fortune was built upon the slave trade." Clarence snapped a string of tsk noises with his tongue and teeth. "And when a prominent artist of South Florida amplifies that theory." Clarence looked at Nance. "When you hear the phrase, 'Old Florida, New Ideas,' do you think that encompasses slavery and land profiteering?"

She glanced at the pictures. "I do now. And I think it would affect the way I vote."

"I agree," Clarence said. "I think that in a close election, being labeled as the pro-slavery candidate might be a stain that won't wash off." Clarence felt another piece click into place. "And an employee of yours engaged in rampant poaching in one of the jewels of America's national parks. That wouldn't sound good at a candidate forum. That poacher ends up getting murdered." Clarence looked again at Nance. "Even if you're not pro-life, I'd be willing to bet that you're not pro-murder."

"It's a shame," Nance said. "I mean, I never studied statistics and don't have any polling data, but I think these allegations could sink a promising campaign."

Clarence rested his big hands on the desk and leaned in, closing the distance between himself and Congressman Mike Carroll. "And I think a serious candidate would do anything to keep that information from coming to light. Let me ask you again, nicely. Where is Mae Jefferson?"

"You're making dangerous guesses." Mike jabbed his head toward the fireplace. "See those ashes? They're the charred remains of your once-promising careers. You'll be lucky to get out of this without an indictment."

Nance turned the poker over in her hand; the ash left a fishhook pattern on her palm. She looked at Clarence. "If we're already screwed, I don't see any point in moderation."

He nodded and took a step toward the congressman.

Mike Carroll's hands shook. "I swear to you I don't know where she went. You're right. She came to see me. Mae sat in the chair directly across from the desk, just like you're doing. We talked. She laid out the same farfetched theory about my family and Heka's more than a century ago. And you're correct. I saw the damage even an unproven accusation would have. I tried to reason with her. Offered her some opportunities. I said we could make her art big. I could secure her a federal grant. She accused me of trying to buy her off and stormed out of the room. That's the last time I saw her. I swear it."

Clarence looked at Nance. He wanted to see how she would like to act next.

She opened her mouth to speak.

Before Nance could utter a word, a crash interrupted. Joe Bob Jefferson kicked open the French doors, shattering glass panes. He charged across the room and wrapped his hands around Mike Carroll's neck.

34

April 13th

Nance took a step forward to grab Joe Bob.

Clarence caught her arm. "What's your rush? The man has gotten off easy to this point. I only threatened to hit him."

"You did drag him over the desk."

"True. But feel the thick pile of this rug. It's like a two-foot fall onto a pillow."

Gasping interrupted their conversation.

Clarence studied the situation. Strictly speaking, Joe Bob had not wrapped his hands around Mike Carroll's throat. Joe Bob's right hand ran down one side of the congressman's neck. Joe Bob held the steering wheel in his left hand and pulled. The small piece of handcuff connecting the steering wheel to Joe Bob's wrist lay across Mike Carroll's throat.

Carroll's face had turned red. His eyes bulged. He pawed at the air, trying to grab Joe Bob. Clarence could see that the arm movements were becoming weaker. "Joe Bob, stop!" The man ignored Clarence, or, in his rage, his muted senses failed to register the command. Clarence snapped a kick to Joe Bob's left elbow, breaking his hold on the steering wheel. The wheel whipped around Mike Carroll's chest. Nance quickly grabbed it and stepped behind Joe Bob, bringing his right arm behind his back. She lifted, forcing the arm upward, until he cried in pain.

Mike Carroll tumbled to his side. He lay on the floor, making a rasping gasp. Saliva trickled from the side of his mouth, dampening the thick rug. Carroll had a thick red welt beneath his chin. His pants were soiled in the front. The room smelled of urine and fear.

"You might have killed him, Joe Bob," Clarence said.

Jefferson shook with rage. "I would if you hadn't stopped me. He's got my baby girl. Y'all both heard him. He's lying."

"He might well be," Clarence said. "But he won't tell us anything if you kill him."

"I'll wring the truth. He'll tell if it's the last thing on earth." Joe Bob's eyes were hard slits when he looked at Mike Carroll.

The congressman's eyes flickered before looking away. He could not meet Joe Bob's murderous gaze.

"If my Mae weren't reason enough, I heard you say he killed John. John wasn't perfect, but he weren't no bad boy. Just wanted the money he couldn't inherit. Didn't warrant getting killed for."

Mike Carroll groaned.

Clarence looked around the room. He saw that Mike Carroll's eyes were open. Blood spots marked his eyes where blood vessels had broken, but he seemed otherwise intact. His natural color slowly seeped back into his face. Joe Bob's rage had dissipated. He appeared capable of careful listening and reflection.

"Joe Bob," he said. "I thought you promised not to leave my truck."

"Sorry." His head dropped, and his tone sheepish. "I know I promised, but I couldn't just sit there. It's my baby girl."

"Special Agent Nance."

Nance looked at him. "Technically, he brought a piece of the truck with him."

Her words surprised Clarence. He hadn't expected her to take Joe Bob's side. Clarence recovered. "Why don't you and I complete a search of the house and grounds. If we separate, we can meet back here in thirty minutes."

Nance nodded. "Thirty minutes, check."

"Joe Bob, just like you promised me you'd stay in my truck, will you promise me you'll leave this man alone? I do not want to return and find that he's been harmed."

Joe Bob smiled, showing a cracked line of stained brown teeth. "I promise. I won't harm one hair on his head."

"Good enough for you, Special Agent Nance?" Clarence asked.

"I'm satisfied. I see no reason not to trust Joe Bob."

"No," Mike Carroll gasped. His eyes danced with fear. "He'll kill me."

"Didn't you hear him promise?" Clarence asked.

Tears ran from the congressman's face, further moistening the rug. "No, please. He'll kill. You heard. That man will kill me the moment you turn your back." His raspy voice wavered.

"Mr. Jefferson will do no such thing," Kathryne Carroll said as she marched into Michael's office. "And you two." She wheeled and pointed at Nance and Clarence. "Shame on you for scaring Michael."

35

April 13th

Clarence noticed that Kathryne spoke of the congressman as if he were a child.

"Mother, help me," Mike Carroll said in his raspy whisper.

She stood over him and looked down. Her eyes held sadness. "There, there, son. Just breathe. You'll be all right." She strode across the room to a small bar. Kathryne poured water into a glass and carried it back. She knelt and handed it to him. "Sit up and drink this," she said.

Mike Carroll's hand shook. The water sloshed inside the glass. When he had a firm hold, Kathryne Carroll released her grip. She stood upright and, again, her eyes surveyed Nance and Clarence. "How dare you. He is a good boy. A bit spineless at times but trainable."

"We need him to tell us where Mae is, ma'am," Nance said.

Kathryne's face pinched. "He doesn't have a clue where she is."

"He knows, and I aim—" Joe Bob yelled.

"Hush, Mr. Jefferson."

Joe Bob fell silent. Such was the power of the woman's presence.

Kathryne Carroll's eyes moved from Nance, to Clarence, and finally to Joe Bob. They revealed nothing about what she might be thinking.

"Michael doesn't know where Mae is," Kathryne repeated. "Because I put her upstairs without his knowledge."

"You bitch," Joe Bob yelled.

"Mr. Jefferson, you will not speak that way in this house." Her icy tone would not allow for any disagreement. "It's really quite simple." Kathryne turned to Joe Bob. "Your daughter arrived here last night to see Michael. Although it was quite late, he indulged her. She is, after all, a constituent who had lost a godfather and mentor. Mae began making several ill-considered and hurtful allegations." Kathryne gestured to Michael, who had pulled himself off the floor and crawled back into his chair. "Although everything she said was without merit, my son made very generous suggestions to appease her. Mae demonstrated the implacability of youth, dear child. I, of course, heard all of this."

"Because you were listening," Clarence said.

"Because it is my job as a mother to see to the welfare of my family, past and present."

"And when Mae and the congressman had finished their conversation?"

Kathryne Carroll's face reflected pure innocence. "Her father was accused of a host of most terrible crimes; the poor dear seemed quite distressed. I could hardly allow her to leave in her condition. I didn't want some terrible mishap to occur while she drove home. We've all read about the dangers of distracted driving."

Joe Bob took an angry step toward her. "What did you do with my Mae?" Clarence threw out his arm, blocking the man's path.

"Mr. Jefferson, there really is no call for such behavior. Please, sit down so that I may continue."

Joe Bob perched on the arm of the chair.

Kathryne Carroll looked at him without speaking. Joe Bob slid off the arm until he rested on the chair's seat. Kathryne nodded. "Manners, Mr. Jefferson. Our deportment is what separates us from the beasts." Her eyes passed over the gathering. "As I was saying, I could not in good conscience unleash Mae upon the streets of Homestead in her condition. It would have been irresponsible."

"So what happened?" Clarence hoped to get a calm question asked before Joe Bob's next eruption.

"What do you suppose happened? Do you honestly believe that I murdered that poor girl? No, I invited her to join me for a nightcap. The two of us made our way to the sitting room." Kathryne pointed at the picture on the desk. "I do so like that room. Quite cozy and intimate. These larger rooms can sometimes feel cold. And the art, the room reminds me of who we are." Kathryne gazed into the distance for a moment before returning to the present. "I poured us each a brandy. Mae needed something to steady her nerves before she drove. The poor dear remained quite upset. She repeated everything to me that she had already burdened Michael with. I tried so very hard to explain stewardship. How we had acquired a great responsibility to look after things. Jeopardizing everything good that we have built," Kathryne paused and looked at Michael, "and everything that we would continue to build. To threaten all that simply because of some historical legend and something a drug addict painted beneath a rather pedestrian landscape...well, that was reckless and foolish."

Her eyes swept the group. Clarence saw that she sought approval. He wanted to keep her talking. Clarence nodded.

She saw the nod and smiled. "I'm pleased that you understand, Ranger Johnson. I had difficulty getting Mae to appreciate the nuances of our family's path. She remained quite upset. A second brandy did not help to settle her. After a time, it became quite clear that with the alcohol, she was in no condition to drive. Perhaps it's something in the artistic temperament. I put the poor dear upstairs. I asked one of the workers to move her car."

"This all happened last night?" Clarence asked.

Kathryne Carroll nodded.

"And she is still unconscious?"

"Yes. As I said, artistic temperament leads to a delicate constitution."

"What else did you give her?"

Kathryne Carroll rolled her eyes at the ridiculousness of the question. "Hardly anything. But I thought it advisable that she have a little medication. A fragile and unstable girl who consumed two glasses of brandy would suffer a terrible headache if she woke the next morning. Sleeping a bit longer will help her to feel better. A bit of rest would allay her anxiety."

"You gave her drugs and alcohol?"

"I did not force alcohol. As I said, Mae joined me voluntarily. We are not some mischievous fraternity house, Ranger Johnson. We are the Carrolls."

"And just how long were you intending to keep her sedated?" Nance asked.

"I was quite certain that with some rest, Mae would return to being the reasonable young lady our family has known, and supported, for years."

Clarence looked at Michael. He saw the man's genuine horror at what was unfolding. "You didn't know."

"Michael can't be bothered with every detail. It's a mother's duty to help her child succeed," Kathryne answered.

Joe Bob stood. "I'm going to get my girl."

"She is not up there, Mr. Jefferson. I've asked one of the workers to take her someplace more restful."

Joe Bob's face paled, his jaw sagged. He looked as if he had been punched in the stomach. "Where is she?"

"In due time, Mr. Jefferson. When Mae has calmed down."

"Mother, no," Michael's ragged voice cried.

"Dear boy, you know how much commotion we can have around this house during the campaign. I did not think that hustle and bustle was conducive to a proper rest." She paused. "And these constant interruptions disrupt all of our hard work."

"Not Mae. Mother, no," Michael said.

"You will be elected senator, son. Think of where we can go. There is no limit to what we might achieve." She glanced down at the picture on the desk. "They are all watching us, Michael. We can't have someone like Mae hold you down."

Joe Bob's color returned with force. His face flared red. "Someone like Mae? My baby girl is twice the person your slave-napping, stick-up-your-ass bastard family could ever hope to be."

"Mind your language, Mr. Jefferson. Control yourself. Your family has always been coarse, Mr. Jefferson." Kathryne's eyes again swept the room, searching for allies. She saw none. "You are all fools. You don't have the slightest idea about what you're doing. What you are imperiling by rash actions. Everyone, especially you and that girl, Mr. Jefferson, must pause and consider the long-term consequences." Kathryne paused. She turned and looked out through the French doors to the lawn, her eyes skipping over the broken glass on the floor.

Clarence followed her gaze. In the darkness, he saw only Kathryne's reflection. Yesterday, Clarence would have described her image as stately. Tonight, he saw only ugliness.

"These grounds, the weather has been most unkind. We could use some significant landscaping work, including a number of new trees and bushes. And, of course, the follow-up maintenance. Good work would likely lead to some prestigious referrals. Many in this area look to the Carrolls for guidance. Mr. Jefferson, I would be pleased to offer you that contract."

Joe Bob's mouth snarled. "You can take that contract, roll it up, and shove it right up next to that stick."

Kathryne tsked. "Pity. I think you demonstrate my point, Mr. Jefferson. Your station in life has nothing to do with some historical anecdote. Rather, it derives from your family's lack of self-control. Would you have ended up with a daughter like Mae if you could manage your animal impulses?"

Clarence lunged for Joe Bob. Clarence caught a piece of shirt, slowing the man slightly, as Joe Bob grabbed at Kathryne Carroll.

"I'll rip your damn head off," Joe Bob yelled.

"Stop," Matthew Carroll said. He entered the office, a handgun pointed at Joe Bob.

36

April 13th

Nance reached for her sidearm. Her fingers wrapped around the butt of the gun.

Matt quickly turned, his weapon pointing at her. "Don't."

Nance stopped.

Clarence felt a twinge of rising panic. When he'd been on this end of a gun barrel, things hadn't gone well. He set his jaw. He didn't want to display fear to the guy holding the gun.

Matthew gestured with the tip of the firearm, pushing it closer to Nance.

The panic surged. Clarence hated seeing the weapon threatening Nance.

"First, drop the poker."

The fireplace tool thudded onto the rug.

"Take your right hand away and then pull the gun out slowly with your left hand."

Nance did as he directed. She stood with the barrel pointing down.

Tension welled within him as Clarence stood by helplessly. He needed to say or do something.

"Put it on the floor and kick it over here."

With her eyes locked on Matt, Nance stooped and laid down her firearm. She kicked it with her boot. The gun barely moved through the thick rug.

Matt frowned. At that moment, he looked a great deal like his mother. "Pick it up and drop the clip."

She removed the magazine.

"Throw it into the fireplace."

Nance did as Matt directed. Then, in response to his order, she cleared the chamber. The ejected bullet arced through the air and buried itself in the rug.

"Now toss the gun in the other direction." Matt pointed his pistol away from the fireplace.

Nance tossed the gun.

"That's going to leave a mark. Sure glad I don't have to sand that one out," Clarence said, hoping to draw Matt's attention and his firearm away from Nance. He realized he'd been accusing the wrong Carroll.

"Matthew, I'm proud of you," Kathryne said.

Matt Carroll smiled.

"You have regained control of this situation. Now we can resolve this affair," Kathryne said.

Clarence looked at Matt. "You know you're not coming out of this well." He needed to drive a wedge between Matt Carroll and his mother.

"Don't be silly, Matthew. We will act, as we've always acted, in the family's best interest."

"Family," Nance said. "You hear that, Matt? That's code for helping your little brother get elected to the Senate."

"How much have they been doing to help with that Sunshine State Silicon start-up?" Clarence asked.

"Pfft, Matthew knew very well that idea had issues," Kathryne said.

"Did you, Matt?" Nance asked. "Is that how you see it?"

Matt Carroll's eyes looked at her before flicking to his mother.

"You knew that idea had challenges, Matthew. We discussed it," Kathryne said.

"No, Mother. We didn't discuss it. You told me that you wouldn't support my business idea."

"And that's why you got Sucrito involved, isn't it, Matt?" Clarence said. "Without the family name, you couldn't get a bank loan. Your mother wouldn't support your dreams. She chose to focus on your little brother, Michael."

At the mention of Michael, Matt turned the gun toward his brother. Mike Carroll had his head in his hands and didn't seem to notice.

"Matthew, give me the gun," Kathryne said. "This is ridiculous. These people want us feuding among ourselves. They want to destroy what we have worked to create."

"Your family has created your brother's career," Nance said. She kept her voice soft, like she was talking to a child. "Your brother has gone off to Washington. You're left here to manage the family business. But how much managing do you really get to do?"

"Matthew, don't listen to her. You know perfectly well that you run things here in Florida. Now give me that gun this instant." Kathryne reached out her hand.

"Who got to carry the ball, and who had to block and absorb the hits?" Clarence asked.

Matt frowned.

"John Sucrito had to poach in the Everglades to raise start-up capital for your company. No one here is helping you. He was wading through the slough picking berries and flowers for the dream you two had," Clarence said.

"Matthew." Kathryne's head sagged slightly. "We will find some money for this Sunshine Syllable. You and I will talk about your little plan as soon as we get this current matter resolved."

"Do you hear what she called Sunshine Silicon? And how does your family take care of this, Matthew? There are two murder charges. They won't go away," Nance said.

Kathryne shook her head. "My Matthew has made some mistakes. He regrets those decisions, but he hasn't killed anyone."

Clarence caught the look in Matthew's eyes. "Your mother doesn't know, does she?"

"I didn't kill anyone," Matthew said softly.

Clarence thought the tone lacked conviction. He pressed forward. "You and Sucrito were poaching in the Everglades. Didn't have a choice when no one in your family would support your dreams."

Matt's expression showed bitterness.

Clarence didn't want Kathryne to speak. "Hezekiah learned about it. You thought he would paint you two into his art and expose you to the world. The pair of you went into his home to stop him."

"This is absurd," Kathryne said.

From Matt's eyes, Clarence knew he'd hit pay dirt. "You two switched the laptops to get Hezekiah's memoir, hoping to find out who he might name. That was smart. Must have been your idea."

Matt smiled.

"Matthew, don't say anything," Kathryne commanded.

"But Sucrito was dumb. He forgot that Hezekiah was a brush-in-hand old guy. Heka thought of journals as books and not blogs."

Matt frowned.

"But you two got lucky when we found that Hezekiah had used Joe Bob as a model for his painting."

"We got on the wrong trail, and you thought you were home free, didn't you, Matthew?" Nance added calmly.

Matt made a nearly imperceptible nod of his head.

"But then word got out that we were having second thoughts. Sucrito overreacted. John didn't trust your plan. He lured us into the cypress dome and then fired some shots at us. Sucrito hoped to convince us that Joe Bob Jefferson was an armed felon. It was a crazy and ill-advised scheme. Impulsive, not thought out," Clarence said.

"You didn't have anything to do with him shooting at us, did you, Matt?" Nance asked.

Again, Matt made a slow head shake.

"We knew you weren't involved. You, me, and Clarence, there has never been a problem among us."

Another headshake, bigger this time.

"Can't you see what they are trying to do, Matthew?" Kathryne took a step in his direction.

Matthew pointed the gun at her. "Don't move, Mother."

Shock registered on Kathryne's face.

Matthew saw the reaction and smiled. "Who gives the orders now?"

"We all know you're in charge, Matt. That's why you couldn't have John Sucrito running loose. He brought undue attention to the Everglades and what you were trying to accomplish. Sucrito got the local cops interested. That's what happens when an officer gets shot at. He was a loose cannon, dangerous to your operations."

Matt's head didn't budge.

"And that's why he had to go away," Nance said.

"Took a clever man to make it look like suicide," Clarence added. "How did you get him up there by yourself?"

Matt made a small smile. "Wasn't easy."

"Don't say a word, Matthew," Kathryne said. "That's an order."

Matt Carroll looked at her. He seemed to see something for the first time. "They know, Mother. Can't you see that?"

"They may think things, but the police must prove. They won't be able to prove anything if you don't talk."

"Matt, listen to me, please," Nance said. "You are smart. You know someone has to go to jail for everything that's happened." She held up her index finger. "Will it be your brother, the congressman?" Nance shook her head and then extended her second finger. "Will it be your mother? Do you believe Kathryne Carroll will go to jail?" Nance shook her head again and held up a third finger. "So, who is left, Matt? Who is the only person left to take the fall for all the trouble unfolding? Someone must go to jail to save your brother's Senate campaign. Who will it be? I think we all know. But why don't you ask your mother? See what she says."

Matt looked at his mother.

Kathryne pursed her lips. She stood straight and assumed her full bearing as the family matriarch. "Matthew, give me the gun. There is a place and a time to discuss these matters, and we will, but we do not need to involve these sorts of people in our private matters."

"Did you hear an answer, Matt? Because I didn't," Nance said.

"We have the best lawyers in Florida," Kathryne said. "We can arrange so that nothing serious comes of any of this."

Michael Carroll turned and looked at his brother. "You know that I know people, big brother. I can fix this for you. We will be able to wipe almost all of this away."

"Somebody has to get thrown away to save the campaign," Clarence said. "You're smart. You can figure this one out."

"And when you finish with whatever has to happen, we'll put all our family energy into ensuring your Southern Silicon is a huge success. And we will all live happily." Kathryne's tone made it sound like she was reading a fairy tale.

"What do you say, bro?" Michael asked. He gave his brother his politician smile.

The smile disappeared when Matt pointed the gun at his brother's chest.

"Here's what I say, bro," Matt said.

Mike's eyes widened.

Then Matt pivoted slightly and shot his mother in the chest. The noise exploded in the office. Clarence's ears rang. "No!" Michael shouted. He collapsed on the floor and cradled his fallen mother. Clarence and Nance both lunged for Matt. The gun barrel turned in their direction. Everything seemed to take place in slow motion. Before either of them could reach Matt, Joe Bob lunged. A second shot rang out in the office. Clarence heard glass shatter. Joe Bob swung the steering wheel like a club. The first blow struck Matthew Carroll solidly on the head. He dropped the gun. It landed soundlessly on the thick carpet. Matt took a step, staggered, and collapsed to the floor. He lay alongside his mother, her blood soaking through her silk blouse and staining the carpet pile.

The blow rendered him unconscious. Matthew Carroll never heard his mother's final words.

"I love you, Michael."

37

April 13th

Chaos reigned.

Clarence looked at Nance. Without speaking, they divided up the tasks necessary to gain control of the scene. She moved quickly to Matt Carroll and put a knee down on top of his handgun to secure it. Nance handcuffed the unconscious man and checked his pulse. "He's steady."

Clarence, meanwhile, raced to where Kathryne Carroll lay. He shouldered Mike out of the way and put his fingers to her neck. He moved his hand and felt again. Clarence looked at Nance. Her eyes watched him. Clarence shook his head. He didn't want to say the words in Mike's presence.

He needn't have worried. Mike Carroll apparently saw the movement. He rocked backward, sat on the floor, and cried. His hands cupped his face, elbows balanced on his knees. The blood on his hands formed a row of parallel lines on his cheeks. Tears streamed, the drops making lighter pink streaks as they ran across the blood. His glassy-eyed stare looked transfixed at his mother's face. "Can you close her eyes?"

Clarence ignored the request. He looked over to Joe Bob. He sat on the floor, wide-eyed, seemingly overwhelmed by the scene he beheld. Joe Bob had his right hand pressed against his shoulder. Matt Carroll's second round had grazed him. Clarence's steering wheel dangled like a clock's pendulum.

Clarence moved in front of Joe Bob, filling his field of vision and commanding his attention. "Are you hurt?"

Joe Bob frowned. He hadn't seemed to have considered the question. He pulled his hand away and studied his arm. The bullet had done little more than tear the shirt. Joe Bob shook his head.

Michael Carroll pushed back from his dead mother. He climbed back into his chair and stared at the blood on his hands, his face ashen.

Clarence crawled to Nance's side. She had Matt's gun in her hand. Beside her, their prisoner began to moan. Clarence's eyes swept over her, looking for signs of injury.

"I'm okay," Nance said, breathing hard. The stress of the encounter had begun to wane, and the surge of adrenaline had left her gasping. "You?"

Clarence nodded.

Joe Bob whispered something. Clarence crawled back to where the man sat.

"Baby girl," Joe Bob repeated.

"We'll find her." Clarence stood and walked to Michael. The man had leaned forward and had his elbows on the desk. His eyes were glassy.

"He's in shock," Nance said. "Be gentle."

That approach hadn't been Clarence's first instinct. He studied the man and realized that she was right. Clarence sat beside him on the desk. He kept his voice low. "Mike, it's Clarence. Will you look at me?"

The man stared straight ahead.

Clarence put a hand on his shoulder and gently shook it. After a moment, Mike Carroll turned. "Mike, we need to find Mae."

The man looked at him, uncomprehending. Clarence could easily be speaking Portuguese.

"We need to find Mae," he repeated. "Where would your mother put Mae?"

The man stood. He walked robotically to a framed map of Florida hanging on the wall. His feet shuffled across the floor. Mike stopped at the map, staring at it. The blank expression remained.

"Where would your mother have put Mae?" Clarence repeated.

"Fish camp," Mike whispered. His shoulders slumped. Clarence put an arm under his elbow to support him. Mike Carroll looked as if he were about to collapse.

After a moment, Clarence felt the man stiffen. Mike seemed steadier on his feet. Clarence released his grip and crossed the room to Nance.

"They've got a fishing place in Chokoloskee. West side of the Everglades. Ten Thousand Islands. Old-time Florida fugitives hid there," Joe Bob said.

Clarence nodded. "Makes sense."

"Gulf Coast Ranger Station in Everglades City. They might send—" She stopped mid-sentence. "Detective Tiger might have a local contact."

"He's got to hear about this anyway." Clarence's eyes swept the room. That was when he saw Mike approaching with a gun in his hand.

Mike Carroll stood over his brother. In the confusion, he had recovered Nance's tossed firearm. "You killed Mother." He pulled the trigger. Nothing happened. He hadn't picked up the magazine. He held the gun stiffly with his hands shaking. Clarence stood and pried the firearm from Mike's fingers. He passed it behind his back to Nance.

"You've protected your mother," Clarence said, his voice calm. "Go sit down, Mike. Let's wait for the police."

Congressman Carroll nodded and collapsed into his chair.

Clarence had the handcuff and steering wheel off Joe Bob before they heard the sirens announcing the arrival of the uniformed officers. Detective Tiger arrived shortly afterward. Nance had called him directly. His eyes surveyed the scene. He had a dead matriarch, a handcuffed businessman prone on the floor, moaning, and a blood-streaked congressman. His shoulders slumped.

Tiger took a deep breath and slowly shook his head. "I already called Collier County Sheriff's Department. They've got a patrol in route to the Carrolls' fishing place." He paused. "They knew which one without me having to tell them." His phone rang. Tiger answered and listened. "They've recovered Mae. Whoever was with her took off as the black-and-white arrived. A paramedic has checked her. She's drugged but stable. They're taking her to the hospital at Marco Island."

Joe Bob brushed off the paramedic who examined his arm and stood. He strode to the door.

"Where do you think you're going?" Detective Tiger blocked the door.

"Marco Island." Joe Bob dipped his shoulder. He growled and looked ready to charge.

"You're free to go," the detective said. "But it's a long walk."

The angry expression marking Joe Bob's face disappeared. Confusion replaced it. He looked at Clarence.

Clarence turned to the detective, who nodded. Clarence handed Joe Bob the steering wheel. "If you can put this back, you can take my truck."

Joe Bob grabbed the steering wheel. "A working man has got to know how to do things. I might set the horn blaring again." He rushed out the door.

Nance and Clarence talked Detective Tiger through the crime scene. Around them, crime techs photographed and collected evidence. Tiger asked a few questions. Mostly, he nodded as he took in their report. "Political shitstorm," he said when they had finished, "but nothing complicated about what happened here." He shook his head again as he looked around the room. "My lieutenant will want to hear it firsthand. I need at least one of you to come with me."

"Will you go?" Clarence asked Nance. "I've got something I need to do."

Nance looked at him, her eyes asking the question that Clarence didn't answer. She exhaled and nodded. "Talking to Homestead higher-ups will be good practice for briefing the chief." She exhaled again. "I don't know about you, Tiger. But the bureaucracy of this job is my absolute favorite part."

Detective Tiger gave her a wan smile. "I'll buy you a burrito on the way and tell you about the lieutenant."

Nance smiled at Clarence. "This is how you charm people. Take notes." She turned to the door. "Lead on, Detective."

"One more thing," Clarence said.

Nance paused and looked back.

"May I borrow your ride? When you're finished, call me. I'll come pick you up."

Despite everything that had happened, Clarence's mind felt clear. He knew what he needed to do. He detoured off the road leading back to Everglades National Park and stopped at Southern Nursery. They remained open. Desperate businesses kept odd hours. He had the only car in the lot. Clarence bought a small palm tree. The employee with the vine-tattooed arms remained behind the counter. Clarence explained that he was purchasing the tree for Joe Bob. The man let him borrow a shovel but didn't help him load the palm.

He also didn't discount the price.

Next, Clarence returned to the national park. Tripod scratched at the door as he approached. She raced outside. The dog patrolled the yard while Clarence finished his business. He picked Tripod up and offered his apologies. Clarence settled her on the dog bed. Tripod whimpered, and her eyes looked forlorn. He relented and carried her to the SUV.

The pair of them drove to Joe Bob's house. Together, they walked to the backyard. While the dog inventoried the smells, Clarence enlarged the hole where the former tree had been. He finished after midnight. Clarence left the silver palm alongside, its root ball wrapped in burlap. The planting should be left to landscape professionals.

Nance called as Clarence washed the soil from his hands. He drove to the police station to pick her up. "You've got burrito grease on your shirt," he said.

"And you've got dirt under your fingernails. We both need to clean up. We're meeting with the supe in a couple of hours." Nance sat in the passenger seat with Tripod on her lap. She scratched the dog's ears. If she wondered what he'd been doing, she didn't ask. Nance yawned. "I'm exhausted."

He nodded and said what they both knew because talking would help him stay sharp. "It's the adrenaline. First, you can run through walls. When it ebbs, you can barely keep your eyes open. But I can't go to sleep yet. I've got to do laundry. Need a clean uniform for an ass-chewing. When we're done, we'll likely be burning weeds in Tuzigoot."

"I thought your hot water heater was broken."

He thought for a moment, trying to remember. Then, Clarence nodded. "So I'll wash in cold. Likely won't notice. I expect our reception tomorrow will be a little chilly."

38

April 14th

"Nice shirt," Nance said as they waited for the supe's door to open and admit them.

"Fresh from the dryer," Clarence said. "Want to feel my fabric?"

"Not right after breakfast."

Despite the casual attitude she affected, Clarence wondered whether Nance had eaten anything. Superintendent Ramirez's text had been brief and to the point. They had been summoned to be in his office at 7:00 a.m. The terse message had not been accompanied by either heart or smiley emojis.

The door opened. Chief Zamora ushered them inside. The supe sat behind his desk. His eyes focused on the paperwork lying in front of him. Clarence looked at Zamora. His face conveyed nothing.

"The chief and I have both read your reports," the superintendent said as he thumbed the pages he had printed. "Homestead PD has also forwarded copies of their incident and arrest reports. Do you have anything else to add?" He raised his head and looked at them.

Clarence reconfirmed that the supe had a pretty good stare. He must have gotten an A in Hard Looks 101.

Nance didn't wilt. She kept her eyes on the boss, refusing to break. "No, sir. I believe my report is truthful and complete. I am sure that the Homestead officers accurately captured the information."

The supe's eyes shifted to Clarence, who said, "I agree with Special Agent Nance."

"The Homestead reports have been supplemented by an email from Detective Tiger." The superintendent fanned the pages across his desk and pulled one. He read over it silently. "The local detective seems pretty impressed with you. What did you pay him?"

"Sir?"

"That was a joke, Nance," the superintendent said. "Management is allowed a sense of humor, too."

Couldn't tell from that joke, Clarence thought.

The superintendent turned his head. "Chief."

Chief Ranger Zamora took over the meeting. "The way it appears, we have solved the park's murder of Hezekiah Freeman and assisted the Homestead police in clearing up two homicide cases for them—John Sucrito and Kathryne Carroll. The principal suspect is in custody."

"That's accurate, sir," Nance said.

The chief frowned. "Relax, Special Agent, you're not in trouble."

"I'm fine, sir."

Clarence noticed that no one advised him to relax.

"The evidence shows that Sucrito fired the shots at you two in the cypress dome."

Clarence and Nance both nodded.

"With his death, we can close the two cases of assault on a federal officer," the chief said. "We can also report that we've smashed a major poaching operation within the Everglades. The PIO is excited to post that news later today."

"That story will help us at appropriation time," the supe added.

Clarence hated killing the room's happy vibe but felt compelled. "We didn't endear ourselves to the local congressman."

"We've heard unofficially that Congressman Carroll will be suspending his Senate campaign to deal with matters of a deeply personal nature," the superintendent reported.

"His likely replacement in the House says at every campaign stop that he supports the Everglades," Chief Zamora added.

Superintendent Ramirez shrugged. "We've endured fires, drought, phosphorous, and Burmese pythons. We'll survive an angry congressman, at least for a few months."

The chief laughed. Clarence and Nance both smiled.

"The pair of you have done some amazing work in a short time," the supe said. "Everglades will be sorry to lose you."

"What do you mean, sir?" Nance asked.

"I've been on the phone with the higher-ups. The Washington Support Office wants you to get yourselves up there."

Nance stiffened.

"Apparently, there is a problem out in Yosemite. DC thinks your particular skill set would be right to deal with the problem."

Clarence jerked his head toward Nance.

The superintendent's eyes caught Clarence's flinch. "Is there a problem, Ranger Johnson?"

Before Clarence could answer, Nance spoke. "I think Johnson might be concerned. There's a rumor going around that I've taken a job with Montana Fish and Wildlife."

Chief Ranger Zamora's eyes narrowed.

"Montana F and W offered to make me a game warden, but I declined. ISB is where I want to make my career."

The supe smiled. "Good to hear. You're a valuable part of the team. The Park Service would be sad to lose you."

"And I didn't want to spend my day checking fishing licenses."

The chief nodded. "Glad you've decided to stay, but you know game wardens do more than that."

Nance smiled. "Not as much as three murders and a poaching ring."

The chief nodded again. "Not many jobs do."

"I can leave the day after tomorrow," Clarence said.

"You know Washington Support is our boss, right? It's an order framed as a request. You've been voluntold to be there," the supe said.

"I have to get my truck to the mechanic for some work before it hits the road."

"We heard about that little problem with the steering wheel." He paused. "We decided to leave that part out of our report to Washington." The chief glanced at his paperwork. "Be sure the mechanic rotates the tires. You might be on the road for a while."

39

April 14th

Clarence climbed down off the stage. He and Mae had ground through another blues set. He'd let the jukebox provide the entertainment. Clarence dripped with sweat. He collapsed into a chair at a small table near the stage. Kemo came over and brought him a beer. He set down a mug filled with cola and topped with a maraschino cherry beside Mae.

"A Heka Special for you, babe," Kemo said before turning to Clarence. "I put both drinks on your tab."

He supposed it was Kemo's way of evening things out after being thrown over his own bar.

"Don't worry, Nasty Man. Daddy and I are buying. This is our party."

Clarence looked at Mae.

She held up the glass. "Doctor ordered no alcohol. It's only soda. You want to see somebody drinking, you'll have to look at Daddy."

Clarence's eyes turned to the dance floor. Joe Bob held a beer in one hand and Nance in the other. He twirled her around, navigating through the other dancers on the floor. When you've accused an innocent man of murder, maybe the least you can do to make amends is dance. Or perhaps she was just having fun. Her T-shirt looked nearly as soaked as Clarence's.

At the end of the song, the pair parted. Joe Bob shimmied to the table where Clarence and Mae sat. He wore a broad smile.

"Daddy, you be careful. I don't want you to end up in the hospital."

"Baby, I feel like celebrating. It's been a good day. I got you home. And I found that." He pointed behind the bar. Kemo had turned one of the spotlights to illuminate a clay pot. In the spotlight, the brown glaze streaked with green dazzled. He turned to Clarence. "We put it back there. I wanted everyone to be able to see it but no one to accidentally break it. My baby girl says it was made by someone called Dave Drake, a famous artist, and it might be worth a hundred grand."

"Daddy, I said it might be a Dave the Potter piece. We won't know for sure until it gets authenticated."

"And you also said it might be worth more if its province showed it had been carried here by escaped slaves."

"Provenance," Mae corrected.

"Baby girl, you showed me where he'd carved that little poem in the clay. That's how you know." Joe Bob grabbed Clarence's arm. "Can you believe the University of South Carolina has a historian of ceramics? This doctor lady specializes in Dave Drake pots. She's gonna come down here to look at it. With that money, we can save the house and the business."

"I'm happy for you, Joe Bob," Clarence said.

Joe Bob's face turned serious. "Damndest thing. I had some nervous energy after the last few days. They've been a little stressful. I brought Mae home and got her to bed. That's when I noticed a new silver palm tree in my backyard. I don't know how it got there, but I figured that planting it would be just the sort of relaxation I needed. It was sitting in the yard where the old one used to be. I start widening the hole, and that's when I find the pot. An antique clay pot buried right in Homestead. You know anything about it, Ranger Johnson?"

Clarence pinched his face and appeared to be thinking hard. Then, he tipped his mug and swallowed some beer before shaking his head. "No, Joe Bob, can't say that I do."

"Because my employee Lucius says you came by the nursery and bought a silver palm yesterday."

Clarence took another drink. "Pure coincidence."

"The dirt was damn soft and loose."

"Lucky you."

Joe Bob's hand squeezed against his glass. "In shallow dirt, you'd think that a pot would've gotten broken in the last two centuries. Seems like it would be just shards unless it were protected by stone casing."

Clarence watched a moisture bead trace a path down the side of the mug. He shrugged.

Joe Bob eyed him, then shook his head and smiled. "Well, you being an investigator and all, if you ever find the man who gave me the palm tree, tell him how deeply grateful I am. He helped me hold on to everything I love." Joe Bob's eyes misted.

"I'll make sure to remember, Joe Bob."

Joe Bob walked around him and hugged Mae. She slithered to her feet through his embrace and returned the hug, patting him on the back. After a long final squeeze, he released her and danced off toward the bar.

Mae watched him. "I've never seen Daddy so happy." She turned to Clarence. "Since we won't be crazy desperate for money, as Heka's artistic executor, I'm giving his sawgrass picture and Samuel Freeman's hammock painting to the CARE gallery on a permanent loan."

Clarence nodded. "That's an extraordinary thing to do."

Mae looked down into her drink. "I want people who come to the visitor's center to always know about Hezekiah Freeman and his ancestors. I want them to know about the troubles the Everglades had in the past and the troubles it is still having. I want people to know about the Saltwater Railroad and fertilizer pollution. Maybe these pictures can help do that."

While Clarence struggled for the right words, his phone buzzed. He recognized the number that texted him.

Meet me outside

He excused himself and went out to the parking lot. A blue pickup truck idled near the door. Clarence opened the door and climbed into the passenger seat.

"Didn't know if I'd be welcome if I came inside," Mike Carroll said.

Clarence nodded. "Probably right to stay out here. Not everyone is a fan. I hear you've suspended your campaign."

Mike looked out through the windshield. "But only temporarily. My polling says I've gained three points since everything happened. A little tragedy, it seems, is good for a campaign. It humanizes a candidate." He turned to Clarence. "To lose your mother and have the world learn that your brother has a mental illness…" Mike took a deep breath and exhaled. "It makes a guy into someone who has to deal with problems, just like the good people of Tampa, Tallahassee, and Miami." He turned and looked back through the windshield. "I'd almost be suspicious that Mother didn't somehow arrange it."

For the second time in the last few minutes, Clarence was at a loss for words.

"After a few days to grieve, we'll resume the campaign. I'll carry on as a tribute to Mother and her desire to serve Florida. What do you think?"

"I think she'd be touched by your cynicism."

"Mother would call it playing the hand you're dealt." Mike Carroll turned back toward Clarence. "Of course, it helps that a rare pre–Civil War pot was recovered in the middle of Homestead. The find was astounding. It's drawing attention away from my family's story and pushing it out of the public eye." Mike Carroll shook his head. "Again, it's almost like Mother arranged it."

At this instant, Clarence wished that it had been Kathryne Carroll who had arranged it.

"You're an interesting man, Ranger Johnson. I just came by to tell you that I'll remember you after I'm elected to the Senate." Mike Carroll flashed Clarence the smile that revealed nothing. "See you around, Johnson."

Clarence got out and watched the taillights disappear. He wondered if he'd see them again while he pushed a broom through Lafayette Square.

"Everything all right?"

Clarence turned to see Nance walking his way. "Just needed to get some air."

"Well, don't stay outside and hide too long. The crowd is getting anxious to get their guitar player back."

"Little-known secret of the music business, give the audience what they want." Clarence took a step toward the door.

Nance caught his arm. "Speaking of secrets—"

Clarence stopped and looked at her.

"You know it's illegal to remove artifacts from a national park. It's a serious criminal offense."

"Of course I know. I'm a seasonal Park Service employee, remember?"

"I'm asking because that rare pot in the bar looks remarkably like Tripod's dog food container."

"It does?" Clarence pulled his head back in surprise. "I got that pot at the Garden and Home Supply in Homestead."

"When I'm at the RV, I'll look for the label."

Clarence shook his head. "I had to get rid of the pot. It didn't fit with my décor."

"I hope you're telling the truth, Johnson. I'd hate to find out that you committed a crime."

"If I committed a crime and you harassed your junior coworker, we'd just have to keep one another's secrets. That's what partners do."

"You stole a historical art treasure—"

"Allegedly."

Alison drew an exasperated breath. "You allegedly stole a historic art treasure. That's way more serious than a kiss."

"If it would make you feel better, we could do something more serious than kiss. You know, just to even things out."

"Nice try," Alison said. She turned away and looked across the parking lot. "I've got some things I need to sort out."

She's got someone to sort out, was the message Clarence heard. He nodded and began walking back into the bar. It was definitely the time to play some blues.

Alison grabbed his shirt and pulled him to her. After a long, wet kiss, she stepped back. "I'm not saying no. I'm saying not right now."

The Firefall: A Murder in Yosemite
Book #3 in the Johnson and Nance Mysteries

A vandal's final act in Yosemite National Park uncovers a hidden message—and a deadly legacy.

When a graffiti artist defaces part of Yosemite National Park, Special Agents Clarence Johnson and Alison Nance expect a straightforward case. But when the suspect falls to her death from Glacier Point—just as another member of her synagogue did years earlier—the investigation takes on a far more ominous meaning.

The eerie coincidence hints at a deeper, darker truth behind the artist's final work. As Johnson and Nance unravel the layers, their search points to a historical puzzle stretching back to 1938, when a Jewish violinist, fleeing the shadows of Nazi Germany, disappeared into the park's vast wilderness, carrying a secret that could alter the course of history.

Decades later, the past refuses to remain hidden. The agents begin to link the contemporary murder to the long-unsolved disappearance and a mysterious legacy hidden in Yosemite's rugged terrain. But as they close in on the truth, they realize they are not the only ones searching. A relentless adversary is also on the trail, willing to kill to claim the secret and reignite a dark chapter of history. Now, Johnson and Nance must outwit a ruthless enemy before history's darkest forces rise again.

Get your copy today at
severnriverbooks.com

30% Off your next paperback.

Thank you for reading. For exclusive offers on your next paperback:

- **Visit SevernRiverBooks.com** and enter code **PRINTBOOKS30** at checkout.
- Or scan the QR code.

Offer valid for future paperback purchases only. The discount applies solely to the book price (excluding shipping, taxes, and fees) and is limited to one use per customer. Offer available to US customers only. Additional terms and conditions apply.

ACKNOWLEDGMENTS

First, I'd like to thank Betty, the love of my life, for your support. Thirty-five years ago, you never imagined that "I do" would mean wading through a cypress dome looking for an alligator hole. I am forever grateful that you joined me on this and all the other adventures.

I sincerely appreciate the many people who have helped tell the Johnson and Nance stories. Thank you to the team at Severn River Publishing, particularly Andrew Watts, Amber Hudock, and Cate Streissguth. Kate Schomaker has continued to edit my stories patiently. I am grateful for your efforts.

Thanks again to Paula Munier, my agent at Talcott Notch.

I want to recognize the Everglades National Park Institute for helping with the technical details of the story. Your guides taught me about the incredible Everglades. Thanks again to Steve Yu, retired National Park Service, Investigative Services Branch, for technical assistance. Thanks also to Charissa Terranova, professor of art at the University of Dallas.

Thank you to the friends and family who have encouraged and inspired me, specifically Brad Kiley, Blair Mastal, Kathy McDorman, and Barbara Adkins. Your kindness helped us make our research in Florida memorable. To Tamla Ray, I appreciate your thoughtful comments on my draft.

The danger in expressing gratitude is that I will omit deserving names. As with the technical errors and geographic liberties, the fault lies with me.

ABOUT THE AUTHOR

Award-winning author Mark Thielman has published short stories and novellas in *Alfred Hitchcock's Mystery Magazine, Black Cat Weekly, and Mystery Magazine*, as well as numerous anthologies. He draws upon his career as both a criminal magistrate judge and as a prosecutor in his writings.

Sign up for the reader list at
severnriverbooks.com